FC

Underland

Underland

MICK FARREN

A Tom Doherty Associates Book
New York

UNDERLAND

Copyright © 2002 by Mick Farren

A Tor Book
Published by Tom Doherty Associates, LLC
175 Fifth Avenue
New York, NY 10010

www.tor.com

Tor® is a registered trademark of Tom Doherty Associates, LLC.

Library of Congress Cataloging-in-Publication Data

Farren, Mick.
        Underland / Mick Farren.—1st US ed.
            p.   cm.
        "A Tom Doherty Associates Book"
        ISBN 0-765-30321-3 (alk. paper)
        1. Nazis—Fiction. 2. Reptiles—Fiction. 3. Vampires—Fiction. 4.
    Antarctica—Fiction. 5. Intelligence officers—Fiction. I. Title.

PS3556.A7727 U93   2002
813'.54—dc21

                                                    2002002109

First Edition: October 2002

Printed in the United States of America

0 9 8 7 6 5 4 3 2 1

For Laura, Craig, and Berry Pfeifer

chapter One

Victor Renquist had rarely encountered a human whose mind had been so drastically reorganized. The word *brainwashing*, as far as Renquist was aware, had fallen from favor, but in his considered opinion, the young man's brain had not only been washed, but also fluffed and folded. It was neat, malleable, and it followed orders without reflection or question. The young man was conditioned to be the perfect implementer. Original thought had been all but eliminated, and so had all but a permitted modicum of individuality. In another century he might have been called a vassal, a minion, or a bondsman. These days, Renquist supposed, he'd be a midlevel bureaucrat, and doomed in the bargain to make never more than a nominal advancement in the power structure. It didn't matter that the power structure he served, or the bureaucratic subdivision in which he performed that service, was one of the most disturbingly sinister human institutions Renquist had encountered since the KGB under Stalin. The young man no longer possessed, if indeed he ever had, enough imagination to postulate ethical questions or entertain doubts as to the morality or even the effectiveness of what he was doing. He had taken the concept of "his not to reason why" to the extreme of a perverted, near-unthinking pleasure in his own, almost canine obedience. This one would do just about anything his masters suggested, no qualms, no reservations, and with a willing eagerness and a probing attention to detail that Renquist found unhealthy in the extreme.

Victor Renquist, from his unique perspective, had seen this insensitive corporate amorality steadily growing, especially in the United States, since at least the 1970s, and suspected it was a fresh, and probably malignant phase of capitalism. Greed had been declared good, corruption was seen as a virtue of power and practiced with a vindictive glee. Admittedly the young man was an employee of the federal government, but that hardly negated Renquist's basic premise. Wasn't the federal government of the United States nothing more than the biggest, most labyrinthine, and certainly the most inefficient, greedy, and corrupt, capitalist corporation on the surface of the Earth? Normally capitalism and its convolutions were of little concern to Renquist, unless they pressed overly close to where he lived. With his almost infinitely extended life span, he had seen belief systems flourish, flower, then wilt and die, or mutate to the point that they became unrecognizable. He had seen nations change flags like dirty underwear. He'd watched regimes and dynasties rise and fall, and even empires totter and collapse. All the way from those long-ago days when

Crusaders had fought their way through Turkey to Jerusalem, and when the threat of the Great Khan and his Golden Horde of Mongols had been massing in the East, he followed humanity's murderous folly as the Mamelukes rose to power in Egypt, at the very end of the thirteenth century, and, later, in the eighteenth, Abd al-Wahhab converted the belligerent Saudi tribes to his grimly intractable sect and sowed the theocratic seeds for the deadly flourish of the Al Qa'ida in the twenty-first. Renquist had ridden the waves of human history and survived, and found it little more than a bubble-stream of circular patterns repeated over. He had long ago come to the conclusion that, in deep reality, the only objective difference in competing social designs was in the color of their flags and the degree of misery they were able to perpetrate.

Not being human, Renquist normally distanced himself as far as possible from the machinations of those who sought to control the mass of humanity. If one human structure became too onerous or out of control, Renquist had always exercised the option to move on. Just at this moment, however, Renquist couldn't move, and he needed to give this young man's mental state some serious consideration. Detachment was impossible since the young man was not only Renquist's face-to-face interrogator and the immediate representative of his captors, but he also controlled the powerful laser that was aimed squarely at Victor Renquist's right eye.

"In my time I have met torturers with more grit and sinew."

The young man was surprised. "You see me as a torturer?"

"From where I'm sitting."

"Have you been harmed in any way?"

Renquist was unable to move his head to look at the young man directly, so he spoke to the dark and unblinking lens of the laser. "No, not so far."

"Then what makes you think I am your torturer?"

"You have the look."

"The look?"

"I've met a lot of torturers and seen a lot of torture."

"Indeed?"

"In my time."

The young man raised a sparse eyebrow. "In your time?"

Renquist would have gestured to the thick binder the young man held in his hand, except the nylon-and-steel-mesh restraints held him immobile. "You have the dossier."

"This dossier makes the claim you have lived over nine hundred years."

Renquist was unable even to nod. "Nearer to a thousand."

The young man paused and placed a hand lightly to the earpiece of his lightweight headset. He listened with rapt concentration, indicating to Renquist he was hearing more than a communication, and the entire interrogation drama was being choreographed from elsewhere. As far as Renquist could penetrate the conditioned firewalls in the human's mind, he had been told that Renquist was a dangerously psychotic serial murderer under consideration as the fall guy for a termination/suicide mission. The young man had further been instructed that he should maintain and, if need be, cling to that belief in the face of any or all evidence that might contradict the hypothesis. The young man's dossier was a blue loose-leaf binder, with red EYES ONLY stickers and the combined NSA-FEMA logos. It contained the sum total of the data on Renquist that had so far been amassed by the two agencies, but the young man was under the all-enveloping impression that its contents were the collected ravings of a deadly psychotic, the imaginary parameters of a watertight fantasy world created by an advanced and dangerous paranoid schizophrenic. Nothing could force him so much as to entertain the idea that the information contained therein might actually be the truth or some approximation of it. After about thirty seconds of silent attention to the headset, he turned back to Renquist. "What makes you think I'm a torturer?"

"The goal is to elicit my cooperation or confession isn't it?"

"We'd like the truth."

"You have the truth. Your problem lies in accepting it."

The room in which Renquist and the young man faced each other was a near-perfect cube with scarlet walls, floor, and ceiling. Without question, its design was the product of some half-witted, but probably very expensive, psychological study. He doubted the hellfire shade of red, or the vaguely disturbing spatial relationships, really had very much effect on humans beyond an intimidating first impression, and on a creature like himself they had no effect at all. If his situation had not been quite so desperately perilous, he might have held the whole process in utter contempt. Only the laser precluded too much hubris. It was no mere pointer or gunsight. This was an industrial-strength instrument that would burn and penetrate, and probably cauterize as it burned. At the touch of the young man's remote, Renquist's right eye would be destroyed beyond all reclamation, a nanosecond before the gemstone beam speared the soft tissue of his brain. Victor Renquist's brain did have some chance of recovery. Tissue would regenerate with nosferatu cellular alacrity, and complex paths of function would be rerouted according to freshly devised synaptic mapping, but recovery from such massive trauma would take time; time in which he would be effectively helpless, and his human captors could do what they liked with him. They could follow any whim of their choosing from driving an iron stake through his heart if they were in the mood for re-creating the crudely medieval, or cutting him up in some state-of-the-art operating room like a frog in a biology class.

Confident the odds were effectively stacked against Renquist, the young man permitted himself an ironic smile at the nosferatu's last remark. "Our problem? You think we have a problem?"

The young man wore loudly striped suspenders over a pale blue shirt, a lighter shade of the same blue as his immaculate pin-striped suit. He had taken off his jacket in a gauche display of getting down to business. The young man had the kind of cool but still angry determination almost unique to African-American Ivy Leaguers. He had not loosened his tie, which was of a loud and jagged, black-and-yellow pattern. Renquist assumed that the tie, the braces, and the man's smoothly shaved head were cultural nods to his ethnicity. His job, as it was defined, was very simple. Questions, asked elsewhere, were relayed over the headset, and all the young man needed to do was to repeat them and wait for Renquist's reply or reaction.

"You think we have a problem?"

"You do not know how to handle me."

The young man walked slowly round Renquist. "We seemed to have handled you fairly efficiently up to now."

The statement would bring no argument from Renquist. He was seated in a somewhat more upright version of a dentist's chair, secured at the wrists, ankles, and waist by straps of reinforced nylon from which not even he could tear loose. Two more straps were crossed over his chest, while his skull was clamped in a vise of stainless steel and rubber that held him at the very precise mercy of the laser. He was also the focal point of a great deal of electronic attention. A high-tech mass of medical paraphernalia had been attached to his body—the sensors, electrodes, and blood pressure cuffs that, had he been human, would have monitored his vital signs. His speech and image were also being relayed elsewhere, and, he supposed, recorded for posterity. Three video cameras were aimed at him. A studio-quality microphone was supported on a boom about fourteen inches in front of his face, and black cable snaked away behind him to a point that he was unable to turn his head or body to see.

Renquist could, of course, have scrambled all the data about himself by nothing more than a strenuous but un-complicated effort of will. He was quite capable of con-verting the video images into abstractly menacing fractal patterns, the audio to a voice from the abyss, and his vital signs well off any conceivable scale. To do so, however, while flamboyant theater, would have been tactically asi-nine, and he hadn't walked the Earth for nearly a millen-nium by dint of his stupidity. Such a display might put the fear in his human captors, but it would also, at the same time, reveal the extent of his undead capabilities in one comprehensive package. The information the humans al-ready had on him was unquestionably a mass of miscon-ceptions, myths, and inconsistencies, and Renquist very much wanted to keep it that way. He didn't mind their being afraid, but he didn't want them very afraid. Extremes of fear caused humans to spook, to lash out, to kill the monster, and, as the monster in question, he had a su-premely vested interest in not being killed.

Even as the orderlies were strapping him into the chair, he had formulated maybe not a plan but a set of guidelines as to how much he was prepared to reveal to the humans. He could easily keep his vital signs flatlined at some inexplicable and neutral level that should confuse and frustrate whoever was recording them. He also decided that he would allow them to run their cameras and microphones without any interference from him. The individuals monitoring the remotes would only see what they already knew—the unimpressive spectacle of him strapped helplessly in the chair in the red room—and they'd only hear what the young man with the tie, braces, and shaved head would hear. Again, very little would be revealed of his true nature.

The young man halted in front of Renquist, positioning himself between the laser and a fixed video camera. "You must agree we took you very easily."

Renquist would have been foolish to claim otherwise. They had come at him at high noon at the Watergate, while he slept in his sealed, tenth-floor suite, and was at his most vulnerable. He had been under the illusion that hardly anyone was aware of his presence in Washington, except those who were supposed to know; and he could only conclude that one of them had decided to take the escape route of betrayal and had dropped a dime on him somewhere in the security/intelligence community. He hadn't been slow in recognizing the grim humor in that he should be taken by federal agents in a hotel that had, for over thirty years, lent the suffix "gate," to a score of federal government scandals.

Victor Renquist was making one of his infrequent visits to the nation's capital, performing renewal and maintenance work on his network of political influence peddlers, and also reminding a select few in the corridors of power that their shameful secrets only remained secret because he made sure they stayed that way. In addition to this overdue assessment of the state of his covert influence, he also wanted to observe firsthand how the power structure might have shifted and been modified under the new administration. He was also curious to see what might have changed since the president had seen fit to appoint Mervyn Talesian as his Special National Security Advisor. Renquist was one of the very few who shared the knowledge that Talesian and the ancient Merlin were one and the same, and he was only party to this knowledge because he had been one of the group who had woken the creature from its fifteen-hundred-year sleep.

It was far from being the first time that Renquist had been taken by humans. Many had tried, but none had held him for long. His survival was all he needed as proof that humans had never succeeded in imprisoning him on anything but the most temporary basis. If they had, his essential nosferatu limitations were such that he would simply not have survived. Through his long existence, the tsar's secret police had tried to make him their captive, as had the Gestapo. On no less than four occasions, the Inquisition had come very close, but, each time, he had managed to sidestep their vicious piety and equally vicious instruments. Orthodox vampire slayers and Lutheran witchfinders had all set their traps for him, but he had always eluded them. The Knights of Sevastopol had held him, then lost him. In more recent times the Clan Fenrior had made him their prisoner, at the time when Merlin had awakened, but the Clan Fenrior was, of course, hardly human. The unique factor in his current detention was that no mortal men had ever come at him with such an arsenal of technology as these twenty-first-century Americans.

The NSA-FEMA assault team had arrived fully loaded, with a SWAT-style battering ram and Mossberg pump shotguns. The federal ninja in gas masks and Kevlar were interagency heavies from the common XYY-chromosome pool of the dedicatedly violent; men and women whose tactics and training were based on both the positive and negative lessons taught by incidents like the ATF attack on the Branch Davidian compound at Waco. This fed A-team first tried to gas him down with CS or something similar, but that had done nothing except make him angry and prove that their data on nosferatu vulnerability were severely limited. They also soaked the suite with all kinds of microwave emissions that did manage to make Renquist feel a trifle queasy but would never have stopped him had he not decided to give up voluntarily. On the more elementary levels, these Feds knew their business. One had threatened to rip down the metal foil over the windows that protected Renquist from the sunlight, while the others trained their riot guns on him, at the same time informing him in professionally neutral tones that the weapons were loaded with stolid, chrome-steel slugs coated with liquid Teflon. The projectiles would not only pulverize his head, but quite easily go on to plough through a wall or floor.

Renquist was well aware how survival was the better part of the valor, and, as he raised his hands in the universal gesture of surrender, he had wondered what had happened to the people staying in the adjoining rooms and how they were reacting to the sudden appearance of this armed, armored, and highly determined miniforce. It was only later that he learned that two full floors of the Watergate had been cleared before they'd actually moved to lift him. The cover story was that terrorists had issued a bomb threat. In the new century, government agents only had to use the word *terrorists* and all those around them became blind to any flouting of the Constitution or any other illegality.

With both Renquist and the suite secured, the squad in the dark blue jumpsuits and helmets had called in the men in white coats, who brought the thick rubber body bag and the strap-down wheelchair. Renquist had offered no resistance when they'd spread out the body bag and ordered him to lie flat so he might be zipped into it. His only remark had been to the pair of fed ninja who were gathering up his personal belongings. He'd gestured to the ancient fur rug that covered the bed. "Please bring that with you. It's mine, and it's come a long way with me."

He'd watched until they had started to fold the rug, and then lay back and prepared himself for the darkness of the prison. In theory Renquist could have stopped the intruders in their tracks simply by freezing their minds, and, indeed, that had been his first instinct after being woken by the attack. In the next instant, however, he'd seen the futility of such a move. Outside was bright, brisk, Washington winter daylight, with temperatures fractionally below freezing. How far would he get without encountering a lethal beam of direct sunlight? Maybe, with an unnatural degree of luck, he could have made it to the dark bowels of the Watergate complex, to subbasements where he could lurk like a cinema alien, among vents, conduits, fuse boxes, and emergency generators until sunset, then make good his escape, but Renquist didn't allow his immortality to depend on unnatural degrees of luck. Far better to give in and go with the goon squad, to hold his not inconsiderable array of resources in reserve until they could be deployed under more advantageous conditions.

He had observed that the assault team's headsets were broadcasting a wide band of white noise as though that was supposed to protect them from attempts at mind control on his part. The use of such devices made clear that whoever had ordered and planned this abduction knew at least a little of the nosferatu's psychic capabilities. The thinking behind the devices was completely in error, and he could have mentally cut through the cushion of sound like a knife through butter, turning the brains of the intruders inside out; but that was another display of power he'd decided to hold back for later. He offered no resistance as they enclosed him in the rubber-smelling dark of the body bag and strapped him into the wheelchair, and he had continued in the same state of passivity all the way to the scarlet-walled psycho chamber, where he now found himself confronted by the young man with the shaved head, the loud tie and suspenders, and the laser pointed at his eye.

"What would you have done if I hadn't come quietly?"

"You would have been insane to do otherwise."

Renquist laughed. "Where in the dossier does it say I'm sane?"

The young man didn't answer, and no help seemed to be forthcoming from the headset. Renquist might have chosen the path of least resistance, but it didn't mean he had to be totally docile. This interview in the red room had to be some form of initial examination, and it was safe to assume that the young man was only a lightweight, sent in for the warm-up, while the heavy hitters waited until later. The young man was already slightly perplexed. What he thought of as the subject in the chair wasn't at all what he'd expected, and Renquist decided he would exploit this revealed weakness by adding a little induced disorientation. He let a psychic suggestion float free like an evil perfume on the air, then gave it time to take hold before he asked the casual-sounding question. "Are you afraid of me?"

The young man frowned. "What makes you say that?"

"You have me strapped down very securely. Isn't that indicative of a certain trepidation?"

"Routine measures after an arrest."

"So I'm under arrest, am I?"

"You could look on it as that."

"I don't recall being read my rights."

"We both know you're a long way from any Miranda warning, my friend. And besides, you have a consistent record of homicidal episodes."

The young man opened the binder as if he was about to quote from what he believed was Renquist the serial killer's file, but as he found the page he wanted, Renquist upped the psychic ante, and, in a small, imposed hallucination, caused the type on the page to dance with tiny flames. The young man quickly snapped the book shut as though he believed he could put out the illusion by depriving it of air, and, at the same time, Renquist lightly brain-slapped him into near dizziness. The young man didn't connect the sensation, though, with anything Renquist might have done. His thinking was too ordered and his imagination too dulled to forge that link. His first reaction was a heart-attack alarm and a burst of adrenaline. Renquist could read from his panic that heart disease ran in his family. His grandfather and uncle had both gone that way, and his father seemed on the same path. Renquist wondered. Should he push the cardiac button a little harder?

"Bauer is losing his equilibrium. His heart rate's up, and any minute he'll start to sweat."

"What's his problem?"

"He seems to be having some kind of anxiety attack, but I'm showing no external cause."

"How are the vitals on the vampire?"

"Unchanged, but weird as ever. It simply doesn't seem to have electrochemical reactions, or it's able to control them totally."

"How's that possible?"

Schultz and Lustig craned forward, staring at the bank of flat-screen color monitors with rapt attention. Coulson leaned back with the relaxed patience of one who has believed from the beginning that the entire exercise was an ill-conceived waste of time. Jack Coulson could afford a dispassionate and superior attitude. Schultz and Lustig were company men. He was the hired gun recruited from outside to solve their problem for them. Both his job and his pleasure were to be as irritatingly critical as he could be. He inclined his head so he could better see the display of Bauer's vital signs. "The kid looks like he's building up for a fucking heart attack."

The small, dimly lit room in which Schultz, Lustig, and Coulson watched the interaction between Bauer, the junior agent, and Renquist, the alleged vampire, was not unlike a small TV control room, and indeed, within the limitations that it served a small and very exclusive studio, that's exactly what it was. Of the twelve screens in front of the three men, seven showed Renquist strapped into the custom-designed chair from various angles, one showed the increasingly uncomfortable Bauer, while the remaining four blankly flickered. Bauer put a hand to his headset, the signal for one of the three to feed him the next answer. Schultz and Lustig turned and looked at Coulson. "So how should we respond?"

Coulson shrugged. "I'd pull him out of there right now."

"The Old Man ordered him in. We can't pull him out yet."

"It could be a life threatener."

The voice of Renquist came over the audio speakers. "Shall we talk about the irrationality of fear."

Lustig spoke into the mike of his own headset. "Get a grip, Bauer. This is no time to be going to pieces. Get him off the subject of fear. The role of the interrogator is to instigate, not respond."

Renquist kept up the pressure in Bauer. "Fear is a matter of the possible rather than the actual."

Bauer's vital signs became even more erratic. Schultz glanced at Coulson. "You think it's doing this to him?"

Coulson shrugged. "How the hell should I know? Despite all the paperwork, we don't understand squat about this thing."

"Still no doubts to its authenticity?"

Coulson shook his head. "None whatsoever. But that still makes this Renquist a totally unknown quantity, and we should get Bauer out of there right now."

Lustig muted the link with Bauer. "Bauer was selected for his formulaic thinking and lack of imagination. We thought it was the best defense against any possible influence Renquist might attempt to exert on him."

"His neckties should have been a warning he wasn't the one."

Schultz's eyes narrowed. "What's that supposed to mean?"

Coulson didn't answer. Renquist was speaking to Bauer. "I think, young man, it would be a very good idea if those who are feeding you your orders ended this and perhaps attempted to communicate in a more civilized manner."

Coulson laughed. "It seems the vampire agrees with me."

Lustig turned and stared at Coulson. "Is this a conspiracy?"

"We may have to face the fact that it may not only be stronger, but actually more intelligent than many of us."

Schultz's eyes narrowed. Company men never trusted hired guns. "But we have it. It doesn't have us."

Coulson smiled. "And I'd pray hard that situation is never reversed."

Lustig angrily reopened the link. "Turn it back on him. Ask him if he's afraid?"

Bauer complied. "Are you afraid?"

Renquist actually laughed. "Of course I'm afraid. What would you expect. I'm in extreme jeopardy, but don't imagine that will yield you any particular advantage."

Finally Coulson leaned down and picked up the headset he hadn't previously been wearing. "Ask him what he would consider to be a more civilized means of communication?"

As Bauer repeated the question, Lustig looked bleakly at Coulson. "You really think we can simply negotiate with that thing?"

"Its history would indicate so, and its present behavior certainly confirms it."

"We might attempt a simple conversation that dispensed with all this machinery."

Coulson's smile broadened. "I mean, it would appear it's negotiating already. As a matter of record, Renquist is nothing if not a pragmatist."

"But you can't trust that thing."

"Only as long as the trust is in its interest. I wouldn't turn my back on it, even for an instant."

"But we take Bauer out?"

Coulson gestured to the screens. "Is this getting us anywhere?"

Lustig made a gesture of resignation. "So we pull out Bauer. Who's going to tell the Old Man."

Coulson looked bleakly at Lustig. "Blame me. I don't have a career to protect."

Now Schultz turned on Coulson. "The vampire. We have to keep it alive. What about its . . ."

Coulson removed his headset. "You mean what euphemistically might be called its survival needs."

"Yes. That."

"We're going to have to provide for it. We knew that from the start."

Schultz shook his head. "The thing's a horror."

"Compared to the horrors we want to send it up against?"

Renquist knew something had changed a microsecond before the young man reacted. He pulled off his headset, glared once at Renquist, and walked past the imprisoning dentist's chair without a word. Renquist couldn't, of course, turn his head to watch the young man go, but he knew he'd made his exit by the faint waft of air and the sound of a door opening and closing. Now Renquist was alone, watched only by the cameras and the dead eye of the laser, with very little to do except wonder if he had won some kind of victory over his unknown captors or merely precipitated himself into worse unpleasantness. They could, of course, decide he was too dangerous to exist and fire up the laser, dispatching him into the oblivion of the true death. It would, at least, be fast. Better, he knew, than burning up in the sun or the traditional and hideously painful stake through the heart. He speculated, though, that if they were going to use the laser—whoever they might be—it would not only be fast but soon, and as time passed he felt it safer and safer to assume that a spear of amplified light was not going to be his immediate fate. This was confirmed when the door was opened again, more noisily than the young man had closed it. Men moved into his field of vision. They were dressed in the same navy blue coveralls and Kevlar body armor, and carried the same riot guns as the team that had stormed into Renquist's suite at the Watergate, and, for all he knew, behind the woolen face masks, they might have been the very same ones.

Three lined up in front of the chair to which he was secured with shotguns pointed at him in a way that left Renquist in no doubt that the weapons were loaded with the same Teflon-steel slugs as the ones used in his capture. He could also sense others behind him, and he deemed it best to remain still and not say a word. Humans with firearms were too easily spooked to be handled with anything but extreme care. A voice came from somewhere behind him. "Okay, secure."

A fourth Kevlar-clad figure entered Renquist's field of vision. He was attempting an attitude of threatening authority, but his voice and aura betrayed anxiety and tension. "You're being moved."

Renquist was tempted to ask where, but refrained. "Yes?"

More humans were coming into the red room. Orderlies in white lab coats surrounded his chair and, taking care not to position themselves between Renquist and the shotgun, worked with the precise speed of individuals who knew their business and wanted that business over as quickly as possible. They unfastened the straps and moved back, as though relieved not to have to stand close to him any longer than necessary. After the orderlies were through, Renquist decided to speak without having first been spoken to. He radiated all the calm he could under the circumstances. "Should I stand up?"

"Very slowly and without any sudden moves."

Renquist kicked his feet loose from the ankle straps and eased himself up. Once standing, he again kept very still. One of the troopers pointed with his gun, past the chair to the side of the room Renquist hadn't previously been able to see. A flush-fitting door stood open, the same color as the walls around it so it was all but concealed when closed. He also observed, from the thickness of the door, that the cubical red room was aggressively soundproofed. He had long made a practice, in times of danger or crisis, of making mental notes of even the most seemingly irrelevant details. He had learned from experience that one never knew when a detail might suddenly spring into relevancy or even become the missing piece that solved a critical puzzle.

"Okay, Mr. Renquist, through the door nice and easy."

He had to duck slightly to pass through the door. Renquist was six feet tall, but the door seemed to have been designed for people standing five feet six and under. He couldn't imagine any technical reason for the inconvenient height unless it was a psychological trick, forcing all who entered the chamber to bow. Renquist recalled how the Christian Church had tried a similar technique at various times in the Middle Ages. Fads had erupted for building church doorways so low that the congregation must all abase themselves entering the presence of their supposed god. The trick had been particularly prevalent along the routes of the various Crusades, when humiliation, oppression, and slaughter had reached their eleventh- and twelfth-century zenith at approximately the same time as Renquist had passed through the Change and come to nosferatu estate. Not that Renquist had ever entered churches except under the most exceptional circumstances, as in setting torch to them or seeking refuge in the heat of battle. The concept that the nosferatu were repulsed and terrified by religious artifacts and could not set foot on consecrated ground was, of course, a complete fabrication of human folklore, most certainly amplified and fostered by the priests who had always been prime among the archenemies of the undead. This is not to say that the nosferatu didn't avoid such places out of unadorned good taste.

On the other side of the low, narrow red door, Renquist found himself in a long, neon-lit corridor that could have been a part of any corporate office building anywhere in the world, except, for some reason that he couldn't quite consciously define, he had the impression of being some distance underground. This impression was strong enough to make him wonder if he had been brought to one of those legendary, but never publicly acknowledged strongholds like Iron Mountain, where dark and unaccountable government business was conducted in deep, sheltered sanctuaries allegedly safe from even an all-out, thermonuclear attack. The small American eagles incorporated into the weave of the dark blue carpeting confirmed that he was in federal custody. Bit by bit, the pieces of the picture were gathered.

Renquist again stood relaxed and still as the tall Kevlar troopers, stiff in their armor and utility belts, ducked through the door behind him. Now that they were on the move, he was even more careful to do nothing to trigger a sudden panic-flurry of uncontrolled gunfire that would unquestionably be directed at him. Once through the door, two troopers moved up beside him, and the rest deployed behind. "Just walk with us, sir."

Although doors occurred at regular intervals in the corridor, all were closed, and Renquist could detect no signs or sounds of life or activity. Indeed, to Renquist, even the sound of their footsteps, the nylon rustle of his guards' body armor, and their collective breathing was muffled. The sensation was sufficiently present to cause him to wonder if unseen humans were trying out another invisible technological trick on him, a heavy dosing of microwaves or high-frequency transmissions? If that was the case, the only result seemed to be to render him ever so slightly deaf. Thus far his captors seemed to be having little success with their attempts at covert control of their captured vampire, and the vampire himself hoped desperation or the need to save face wouldn't drive them to apply more overtly destructive force. In the meantime, he kept pace with his guards and asked no questions.

Jack Coulson walked quickly down the corridor leading to the conference room, moving with a sense of extreme urgency. It was imperative he arrive there before Renquist and the goon squad. He needed the psychological edge of being calmly seated before the vampire was ushered in. Instinct told him that if he was to get anywhere in his attempt at an unprotected, one-on-one negotiation with the creature and not lose his life or worse in the process, he must show absolutely no fear. The company men saw him as rashly arrogant, and this added an extra edge to the need to prove himself right. The more he thought about it, the more he was convinced that Renquist had somehow manipulated Bauer to the point of believing he was on the verge of a coronary. As far as Coulson was concerned, the only remaining question was whether the vampire had managed to conjure Bauer's anxiety from scratch, or did it need to work with an emotion that was already there? He did not, however, wish to learn the answer the hard way and was doing his best to plan accordingly. To be in the room first was the foundation of all that would follow. He must be seated—comfortable, composed, and outwardly calm. If even a tiny part of the collected data was accurate, the creature was possessed of extraordinary powers; but it was reportedly a reasoning, logical, highly educated, and very intelligent entity. He couldn't see that its first reaction would be to fall on him, tooth and claw, with only the taking of his blood on its mind. That was more an image from an antique B-movie than anything that related to the current situation. The long if incomplete record of Renquist's movements through the world, and the creature's alleged manipulation of politicians and princes, bankers, bureaucrats, and big-time criminals made any such initial savagery less than credible.

Coulson was well aware that if his theory didn't work out, and his appeal to the thing's rationality failed, he could look for little or no help from the company men. In opposing their absurd and bizarre brew of technology and witchcraft, Coulson had alienated almost all of those with whom he was supposed to work. Some of them, like Schultz and Lustig, would be positively delighted to see him fail. It would prove them right and him wrong, and there would be few repercussions. Hired guns were always expendable. It went with the unpredictable and mist-shrouded territory. In his case, a fatal error would actually be cost-effective. If he died, the company would be free of its obligation to make good on his exorbitant fee, since no one would be left to collect. Coulson had no spouse or family to receive a discreet government pension or lump sum payout from the company's black budget. Indeed, to Schultz and Lustig, his death would be an all-around career-enhancing advantage, at least in the short term, until they found themselves forced to deal directly with Renquist without Coulson to act as an intermediary and scapegoat.

He fished in the pocket of his suit coat for the hastily scrawled map. This was the third time that Jack Coulson had been inside the NSA-FEMA Paranormal Operations and Research Facility, but he still didn't really know his way around. The underground part of the complex was maze-like in its geometric construction and faceless in its uniformity. It was a labyrinth without landmarks, in which it was all too easy to make a fool of oneself by getting lost. He seemed to be okay though. According to his calculations, he needed to make one more right turn, and the conference room where he had his date with Renquist was the third door on the left.

"Jack! Jack Coulson!"

The voice was unmistakable. It was the rasp-from-the-tomb of Herbert Walker Grael, known to his underlings as the Old Man. To his face, they called him Mr. Director, since both in authority and title he was the Director of the Paranormal Warfare Facility, and perhaps much more besides. Herbert Walker Grael always struck Coulson as resembling a short and disgustingly ancient lizard, perhaps already partly mummified, in a dark three-piece suit, always with an idiosyncratic and signature red carnation in his button hole; the flower that Coulson had privately dubbed *la fleur de mal*. In something close to a departmental ritual, a fresh carnation was delivered each morning by special courier. In most sectors of the intelligence community, such idiosyncratic excesses had been abolished in the cold wave of reform ushered in by the new millennium. Somehow, in defiance of the shifting times, Grael managed to hold on to his.

Grael was about the last person Jack Coulson wanted to see just then, but he was also Coulson's employer, so he halted and turned. The Old Man was shadowed by his ever-present companion and bodyguard, the ubiquitous Vargas, a hulking Salvadoran with the features of an Olmec statue who had reputedly been selected, some fifteen years earlier, from a paramilitary death squad to exclusively protect and serve the Old Man.

Coulson turned and nodded in acknowledgment. "Director Grael."

The Old Man advanced on Coulson. His walk was a trifle unsteady, and Vargas tried to take his arm, but Grael shook him off. "I can manage on my own, damm it."

According to both protocol and good manners, Coulson should have walked back himself and saved the elderly director the effort, but Coulson remained exactly where he was. A certain level of insolence was permitted the hired gun. If the director didn't like it, he could go elsewhere to get his plausibly deniable dirty work done for him. The Old Man was breathing hard by the time he reached Coulson. Word was he suffered from advanced emphysema, although he never showed any signs of dying from it. Word was also that the Old Man was too mean to die. "So you pulled Bauer out, in direct contradiction of my original orders."

The Old Man didn't mess around with niceties or courtesy. Coulson stiffened and nodded. Time was wasting. "He was getting nowhere and seemed about either to go into cardiac arrest or at least make a total fool of himself."

"So you're going through with your own damn fool plan?"

"I am, and if you'll excuse me, I have to go. The operation is already under way."

To Coulson, the Old Man looked like an unholy amalgam of corpse and reptile that should not still be rightfully walking around, much less wielding—alone, unelected, and completely unaccountable—close to the same powers as did the President of the United States. It was openly admitted that Grael was in his eighties, but other, more subterranean estimates claimed he was, in reality, pushing one hundred. Grael was, by far, Coulson's best and most lucrative paymaster, but Jack Coulson loathed the Old Man and took some pleasure in collecting the better tidbits that circulated concerning the hidden horrors of his life and personality. Lustig, after a couple of tequilas, and confident he was away from all eavesdropping devices, liked to flex his imaginary independence by telling tales out of school. It was a drunken Lustig who'd claimed the director still had a sex life, stimulated by Viagra-like chemical complexities that would not be available to the public for many years to come, if ever. Seemingly, though, his partner had to be completely inert. How had Lustig put it? Grael "simulated necrophilia by inducing insulin coma, then bringing the bitch back with a sucrose shot." Close up the Old Man's skin was the color and texture of albino parchment, and Coulson swore he could smell formaldehyde. Grael looked Coulson up and down. "How do you know you won't end up with nothing more than your blood drained?"

"I don't."

"But you intend to prove your point anyway?"

Even before Lustig had shot his mouth off, earlier informants had sworn themselves blind that Grael was very close to being the human fountain of all evil in the power elite. He had more than once been credited as a core conspirator in the murders of both Kennedy brothers, Marilyn Monroe, Lee Oswald, Jack Ruby, and all the others who had died in the resultant cleanup. He was also reputed to have been as much the political power behind Sidney Gottlieb and the MKULTRA mind control experiments as CIA Director Richard Helms, and later actually controlled the unraveling mind of President Ronald Reagan in his latter days in the White House. Another source placed the Old Man as a shadow figure behind Charles White's mad dog LSD experiments in San Francisco in the early sixties, when North Beach hookers had been hired to dose their unsuspecting tricks with acid while Charlie White, and the agents under him, watched and filmed the unholy results from behind one-way mirrors. Coulson had also heard how Bill Clinton had done his Arkansas best to uproot Grael and banish him to a long-overdue retirement. Seemingly Grael had swung his blackmail and disinformation machine into play and, using Clinton's taste for women who were young and at least visibly alive, poisoned the air around the president. Clinton had been impeached and all but convicted, and then his statutory term had run out. Grael, on the other hand, remained bunkered in Deerpark with his carnations and apparent corpses.

In close proximity to Grael, these nasty tales became all to easy to believe. Coulson smiled grimly. "If I don't prove it, you'll have a perfect record of the vampire making its kill. That ought to be worth something to someone."

"You haven't forgotten that the investigation of this thing isn't our primary objective?"

"Of course not."

"That the recruitment of the vampire is only a preliminary to the real mission?"

Coulson was becoming impatient. Time was pressing. "No, I haven't forgotten anything. My priorities are as ordered and intact as always, but, in this totally unique situation, I believe it's advisable to concentrate on one phase at a time."

"I'm sure you'll do it your way, Jack. You always do." The director's eyes were a watery blue, with a frozen detachment that hinted he might have actually been born without the normal checks and balances of mortal morality, rather than merely discarding them as the course of his long and infamous career unfolded. Coulson could all too easily imagine those weird eyes watching the slack face of a simulated corpse as he indulged his supposed sexual preference. If Grael really was close to a hundred years old, it occurred to Coulson that he must have spent at least the previous thirty years warding off death, and the subject of dying had to be constantly on the Old Man's mind. It was all too possible that a subtext to this business with Victor Renquist was that Grael hoped a by-product of the operation might be his learning the secret of supposed vampire immortality. That worried Jack Coulson. The task at hand was hard enough and quite sufficiently fraught with unknowns and pitfalls. He didn't need Herbert Walker Grael attempting to run agendas within agendas. Also, Coulson's reading on the subject had taught him that the quest for eternal life was a dangerous game played with deadly fire. History clearly proved that searches for immortality usually ended badly; invariably in the deaths of many. Chin Shih Huang Ti, the builder of the Great Wall of China, was a perfect example. He had searched for immortality in the second century B.C., and finished up systematically slaughtering all his hundreds of shaman, priests, astrologers, and alchemists when they failed to produce a satisfactory antidote to death. Coulson could easily believe the Old Man capable of similar petulance when disappointed. The idea that Grael was tempted by the possibility of a personal world without end was reinforced by the Old Man's next statement. "Also remember that, when all this is complete, I want the thing back alive, warm and walking."

Coulson frowned. "That might be easier said than done."

"Then I need the body for dissection."

Coulson glanced at his watch. The director was screwing with his timing. "Whether the vampire is alive at all is surely debatable in the strictest sense?"

Grael's eyes were as hard as pack ice. "Don't split hairs with me, Jack."

"We also have yet to be certain what happens to one of them when they supposedly die."

"Didn't you say you were pressed for time?"

"I did."

"Then you'd better get on. Nothing is achieved by standing here talking."

The director turned and walked away, this time leaning on Vargas. Coulson stared at his bent departing back for a moment, using a long-practiced lack of expression to mask his disgust. *Did power really corrupt or did it merely attract the already corrupted?* Mercifully, the Old Man was, for the most part, only a theoretical problem, and someone else's to solve. Coulson turned on his heel and hurried to the nearest wall-mounted internal phone. He needed time. He keyed in the number of the room where Schultz and Lustig still waited.

It rang once, and Schultz answered. Coulson's tone

made it clear he was in no mood for argument. "I just had an encounter with the director. I need Renquist to stay where he is for a few minutes."

Schultz was less than helpful. "They've already started moving him."

"Damn. Where is he now?"

"They've got him in the corridor. Right now he's getting the alpha waves, but they'll be at Conference Room D in just a moment."

"That's the trouble. I'm not in Conference Room fucking D."

"What happened?"

"I already told you. The Old Man waylaid me in the corridor right after I left you."

"What are you going to do?"

"I want you to call the escort. Have the goons to walk him around the corridors for a while. I need about five minutes."

"I'll try."

"Don't try, okay? Just do it."

Renquist was puzzled. They had been moving along corridors for what seemed like an inordinate length of time. It might be that the same phenomenon was interfering with his hearing was also afflicting his sense of direction, but he was close to believing his escort had been doing nothing but walking him round in a variation on simple circles for the last three or four minutes. The corridors, with their blue, eagle-patterned carpets, white walls, and unflattering neon, might all look the same, but he'd had the foresight to count the left and right turns at the various junctions and intersections, and he was convinced they were deliberately meandering. He was at a loss to know why. One explanation was that somehow he was being deliberately stalled, as part of a calculated plan; but if that was the case, this plan of the humans had a definite *Alice In Wonderland* quality. On the other had, it was possible that some glitch had occurred in the preparations for whatever interrogation process awaited him. He could take a certain modest comfort in that option. A lapse in efficiency on the part of one's adversary was never a bad sign.

Renquist and his escort finally turned into a corridor that differed from all the rest in that yet another armed guard, again in dark blue coveralls, body armor, and baseball cap, stood in front of one of the anonymous doors. The sense of expectation in the new guard's aura strongly suggested to Renquist that this was their destination. No sooner had he entertained the thought than the guard came to a loose, law enforcement version of attention and opened the door. Renquist glanced at the trooper beside him who appeared to command the escort. "Inside?"

The man nodded, and Renquist turned into the doorway, curious at what he might find.

The red room had been weird, the corridors had been blank and austere, but the room beyond the door was spacious, with a government/corporate smug opulence. It's walls were paneled, a draped Stars and Stripes hung in one corner on a gold-topped flagstaff, and a large portrait of the current president took pride of place among the framed landscapes and military prints. The room's purpose was clearly to accommodate fairly large formal meetings. The carpet underfoot was still blue and patterned with eagles, but it felt richer and more dense. The highly polished walnut table was long enough to accommodate twelve or fourteen and leave enough room so no one was banging elbows with his or her neighbor, or invading their defensible space.

The row of lamps with green glass shades, which were suspended in a line down the middle of the table, lent a soft air of businesslike intimacy that suited the fact that, at the moment Renquist entered, just a single male was seated at the head of the table, in the traditional seat of power. Without looking up, he waved curtly to the lines of high-backed leather chairs. "Take a seat please."

"Anywhere?"

"Anywhere."

Renquist didn't immediately do as the human instructed. He remained standing, slowly looking around the room. He could tell from the auras of his escort that his action, or lack of it, made them nervous, and that, in itself, provided Renquist with a degree of satisfaction. Only after a leisurely inspection of the room and its decor did he finally follow the human's orders. He selected a chair about halfway down the table, close enough for conversation but with enough distance to preclude any sense of connection unless it was absolutely warranted. He pulled back the chair of his choice and turned it so he faced the human across a long diagonal. The human glanced up, but not at Renquist, simply to dismiss the guards with another curt wave. "You won't be needed any longer."

As the guards withdrew, Renquist decided he'd had quite enough of this. "And what about me?"

"I'll be with you in just a moment."

"Don't do that."

"Do what?"

"Play the paper shuffling, 'I'll be with you in a moment' game."

"Is that what I'm doing?"

"Of course."

The man pulled his paperwork together, gathering the

loose pages, tapping them once on the desk so their individual edges were aligned, and placing them in another blue folder with the NSA-FEMA combined logo. "And you don't like it?"

"It's not a matter of what I like or dislike. It's simply not credible."

Dressed in a darkly elegant and expensively tailored suit, the man had the look of education and intelligence, but, at the same time, he also appeared to have been through the mill. A fast and undetectable psychic scan showed that, unlike the young man in the red room, this human had a mind of his own and retained his own internal demons. No brainwashing or conditioning had ordered his thoughts or shaped his attitudes. He totally lacked the rigidity of one who had grown and prospered in the military, or as an agent of law enforcement. His face had the battered resignation of an individual who, although he didn't appear to relish violence, was painfully familiar with both it and its dirtier mechanics. His nose had been broken at some time in the past, and he had a scar on his upper lip as though he had ducked from a knife or broken bottle but had not been quite fast enough. The laugh lines around his eyes, however, spoke of a certain amused insolence, the knowing smile of the subversive or the rebel. Even his dark hair, although thinning slightly along a distinguished hairline, was worn longer than any federal agent's. The man at the head of the table might work for the government, but he was definitely not a part of any company hierarchy. Two hundred and fifty years ago, he might have been a gentleman buccaneer who had ultimately made good, received a pardon from the monarch and an appointment to the governorship of a colony. Since such characters no longer existed, Renquist could only assume that the adversary he faced was some kind of outside consultant, needed by those in power but far from wanted by them.

"My behavior isn't credible?"

"It's also unworthy."

"In what way?"

"I am fairly certain that I'm the first of my kind you have faced like this, but you pretend to be too busy with your pieces of paper even to look at me."

"I am being that obvious?"

"I know you'd like to avoid appearing excited or apprehensive, but that's hardly the way to do it."

"You say your *kind*? What do you mean by that?"

"You know very well what I am."

The human drew an abstract pattern with his forefinger on the folder in front of him. "So you admit you're a vampire?"

"We do not use that word. We consider it offensive?"

"What do you prefer?"

"I am nosferatu."

The man half smiled. "You state that like a declaration."

"You could take it that way. I'm in no way ashamed of what I am."

The man paused, as though considering his next question before asking it. As far as Renquist could tell without going too far and alarming him, the freelancer had a genuinely open mind and was seeking to learn all he could. "How would you define a nosferatu?"

"Are you trying to sound like a psychiatrist? You certainly don't look like one?"

"I wasn't aware I even sounded like one."

"You have a similar oblique approach."

The man stared down at the fingers of his right hand as though inspecting them for flaws. After a few moments silence, he looked up. "Are you able to read my mind?"

"To a degree."

"To what degree?"

"I'd be a fool to tell you that, now wouldn't I?"

"Would you agree to refrain from doing it for the duration of this interview?"

"This is an interview?"

"What else?"

"I don't know. So far I've been abducted and strapped in a chair with a laser pointed at my eye. I suppose this is the soft approach."

"You didn't answer me."

"No, I didn't."

"So will you do that?"

"Not read your mind?"

"I'd be grateful. And you might benefit from my gratitude."

Renquist turned and stared at the portrait of the president. Renquist's faith in the power and justice of democracy had never been overly strong. "I'd be giving up a considerable advantage."

"It would help me."

"Why should I help you?"

"By helping me, you'll find you'll be helping yourself."

"I have no reason to believe that. I have so far been abducted and confined. There's been little help forthcoming that I can see."

An impasse had been reached. Renquist leaned back and let the human devise the next move. The man took a deep breath. "Can we come at this another way?"

"By all means."

"If you stayed out of my mind, it would place us on a more even footing. That could be productive."

"I would still be doing you a favor."

"Perhaps."

"You have a lot of audacity, my human friend."

"I do."

"You begin by kidnapping me, then you require a favor?"

"I stand between you and some much worse people than I."

"Have you considered I might read your thoughts without your knowing it?"

"That's a chance I'm prepared to take. I believe I'd sense something."

"So we're using an honor system?"

"I suppose you could put it that way."

Renquist didn't respond for some moments. Instead he gently stroked the outer edges of the man's mind. As he expected, the human didn't react at all. So much for mortal vanity. He decided that, for the time being, he would go along with the man's presumptuous request and see where it took them. The human clearly didn't understand that Renquist, should he so desire, could reach into his brain, twist it inside out, rip loose any and all information that he needed, and reduce the man's remaining shell to blubbering idiocy. Renquist would play the game for the moment and keep the true extent of his powers a continuing secret. "Suppose we struck a bargain?"

"A bargain?"

"If I don't read your mind, will you answer my questions?"

Now it was the human's turn to fall silent. He stopped moving his hands and even took them off the folder. Finally, he made a decision. "I will if I can."

*   *   *

So this was the vampire in the flesh. If nothing else, it had a massive self-assurance. As far as any of those who had participated in its capture could tell, it was at their mercy, except it in no way acted like a captive. Instead, it was offering deals.

"Why don't you start by telling me your name?"

"Jack Coulson."

Renquist gave a formal nod. "And I am Victor Renquist."

Coulson gestured to Renquist's file. "I already know that."

"You're not a federal agent?"

"What makes you say that?"

"I have dealt with a number of so-called company men over the years. You're not like them."

"I'm an outside consultant."

"A hired gun?"

"That's one way of putting it."

Coulson knew that the deep and inherent danger in dealing with Renquist was the temptation to lapse into thinking the vampire was a man and treating him accordingly. To all outward appearances, the being facing him across the table was a dignified and cultured man in his early forties, a dandy almost, verging on the slightly eccentric, with dark curly hair almost as long as that of an old-time rock star, a single silver ring in his left ear, and a large onyx on the third finger of his right hand. Perhaps the skin was unnaturally pale, but that, on its own, was far from sufficient to reveal the creature as the undead monster it was in reality. To imagine this urbane if bohemian exterior transforming itself into the savage and ravening predator of legend was close to impossible. And yet, if all the reports were true, hundreds, indeed thousands, had seen Renquist as exactly that, and it had been their last vision of the living world. The only possible giveaway was the nosferatu's eyes. Where the depth of human eyes was always finite, Renquist's were windows into something unfathomable, everlasting, and potentially frightening. As Renquist asked his next question, Coulson made a mental note never, ever to lock eyes with the vampire.

"So why have you been selected to conduct this 'interview'?"

"They seem to think I have a certain expertise in the realm of the . . ." Coulson searched for the right word. ". . . unusual."

Renquist raised an eyebrow at the euphemism. "The unusual?"

"That's their stock-in-trade in this place."

"And what is this place?"

"Officially it doesn't exist."

"Are we dealing in official smoke and mirrors, Jack Coulson? I thought we were endeavoring to get past that kind of thing when I agreed not to read your mind. Don't forget that I also am not supposed to exist. Not by government order but by simple human rejection and disbelief."

Coulson focused on Renquist's mouth. It was a way of looking into the vampire's face while still avoiding the eyes. His lips were full if colorless, but there was no sign of any prominent or penetrating teeth. Were the teeth of the nosferatu retractable, or was there more to learn about their feeding habits than was suggested by the accepted texts on the subject?

"The estate is known as Deerpark."

Renquist slowly nodded. "I've heard of this place."

Despite his efforts not to react, he was surprised that Renquist even knew the name of Deerpark, and he was aware that his surprise registered. "You have?"

"It has long had a certain reputation of being a government center for research into the extreme and . . . what was the word you used . . . unusual?"

Coulson had not expected Renquist to be this well informed. "All governments need places to hide the darkside from their subjects."

"That is certainly true. Wasn't this the place where the very first lysergic acid experiments took place?"

"That's right."

"Mind control?"

Coulson sighed. "I guess. Back when. Legend has it they prepped Sirhan here before he whacked Bobby Kennedy."

"And research into improved interrogation techniques?"

Coulson shrugged. "Some torturers have been through this place, but, as far as I know, the School of the Americas at Fort Benning was the real sado-psychotics' Disneyland."

"And this was where they trained the children? The ones educated from infancy as bait for highly placed pedophiles in foreign governments?"

"So I understand."

Renquist laughed. "Don't look so uncomfortable, Jack Coulson. You Americans are no worse than many, and actually better than some. I am not one to make value judgments." Renquist paused and looked around. "I have the feeling we're some distance underground. Is that correct?"

"Deerpark was once just the mansion on the hill, but now the entire hill is honeycombed with corridors and tunnels. You're very perceptive."

"I think in some way my kind is closer to the wild than yours. We have a well-developed natural sense of direction."

"And you're also at the top of the food chain."

"Indeed we are."

Coulson laid a hand on the closed folder. He couldn't allow Renquist to run the encounter completely. "Do you mind if I take a turn and ask you some questions?"

"I need to know just one more thing."

"What's that?"

"My feeding requirements?"

Coulson had been wondering when the question would come up. When the plan to trap Renquist had been approved by Grael, Schultz, Lustig, Brauer, and a half dozen other company men had drunk themselves jubilantly stupid in a Washington bar later the same night. Netting the vampire was a much-needed justification of their work in very uncertain times. A chant had even broken out. "We're getting a vampire! We're getting a vampire!" Coulson, as drunk as any of the others but holding it better had, at that point, asked the same thing Renquist was now asking. "If you get a vampire, who's going to feed it?" By so doing, he had stopped the party in its inebriated tracks. Lustig had been the first to recover, offhandedly suggesting that Washington had enough junkies and crackheads to satisfy any vampire.

Coulson regarded Renquist with all the neutrality he could muster. "Mercifully that is not my direct problem or responsibility. Plans have, however, been made."

"An exclusive diet of drug addicts is not advisable. They make me sluggish and stupid, and eventually I sicken."

Coulson looked hard at Renquist. "I thought you agreed not to read my mind."

"I'm not reading your mind, I was just anticipating the obvious and pragmatic. Crackheads will make me ill."

"The nosferatu are that fragile?"

Renquist shook his head. "No, my friend. Humans are that toxic."

As far as he could hold in any esteem a creature he might later have to kill, Renquist was starting to like Coulson. The man was nimble-witted and seemed reasonably honorable for a human. In consequence, Renquist had been more or less true to his word. He had stayed out of the man's mind as much as was reasonably possible while still protecting his own very vital interests. He had, however, scanned to some depth when the matter of feeding had been broached, and had observed the memory of the night in the bar. Coulson still felt shame at the behavior of the idiots who employed him, and Renquist had used that shame as a cover to observe without Coulson becoming aware of the intrusion. Renquist could not resist slightly tweaking the human with the remark about a diet of drug addicts. Coulson needed to be kept insecure and guessing. The worst thing a nosferatu could do when confronted by a tough, smart human professional was to fall into the trap of underestimation. Humans might not have the same power as the nosferatu, but they were a species loaded with dangerous contradictions. The majority were dull, self-interested, and easily influenced, coerced, and overcome. But the weak and stupid were by no means the absolute rule. Every so often an alpha would appear among the epsilons, one who couldn't simply be bulldozed by superior physical and psychic strength. The alphas could conjure tricks of their own and prove worthy adversaries when it came down to a simple clash of intellect. Renquist had no doubts that Coulson more than qualified as an alpha.

"You have questions for me?"

"A great many, I'm afraid."

Renquist shrugged as though it was only to be expected. "Questions are the first burden of the detainee."

"You are not in the least what I expected."

"Do not relax too soon, Jack Coulson."

"Believe me, Victor Renquist, to relax is not my intention." He picked up the folder. "This is the dossier the organization has on you to date. Much of it strains human credulity, but . . ."

"But my very existence strains human credulity, so you're not sure where to start?"

"Perhaps we should start at the beginning?"

"The beginning?" A sudden wave of incalculable and unbidden sadness threatened to engulf Renquist. The beginning was now so very far down the passage of centuries, he could hardly relate to it. It had become like a story he had heard, told about another person. He fought down the cold and powerful emotion as Coulson opened the file to a page marked with a Post-it. "You're the supposed son of the Earl of Cambray."

Renquist qualified this with a wry smile. "The bastard son. My human mother was Gwendoline the Saxon, not Roger of Cambray's lady." Renquist paused for a moment, gauging Coulson's reaction without noticeably entering his mind. "Of course, the true parent of the being you see before you was the Great Lamia."

His human interrogator smiled. "The Great Lamia?"

"She made me what I am. Contemporary accounts credit her with great, if not unsurpassed, skill at the Changing."

Coulson turned ring-bound pages in the dossier as though seeking for a confirming reference. Renquist quickly stopped him. "You'll find nothing about the Great Lamia in there. Long ago I spent more than fifty years seeking any trace of her, but all was blank. I can only assume she vanished into one of the black holes in nosferatu history."

Coulson thought about this, again turning pages in the dossier. "There would appear to be a great many holes in your history."

"Would you expect otherwise? The history of my kind, as recorded by humans, is little more than a messy brew of lies and fables. Our own written history has been repeatedly destroyed, and that which remains is well hidden. The books of the nosferatu have been an anathema to religious leaders from Ikhnaton to Pope John Paul. They have been considered as deserving of burning as were we ourselves."

Coulson seemed to have no response to this, so, after a short pause, Renquist continued. "The human need to bring destruction upon us seems to have been something of a cyclical thing, usually a product of some mass hysteria. Not unlike the burning of witches. Indeed, the two often coincided."

Coulson frowned. "You make it sound as though it was a long time ago, but I thought I read in the research that there was a final extermination of . . . nosferatu . . . as late as the twentieth century. A Catholic bishop . . ."

Renquist nodded. "Bishop Rauch."

"This Rauch . . ."

Renquist made a dismissive gesture. "Why don't I just tell the basic story myself and save you reading some secondhand account. I was there, after all."

Coulson indicated the floor was Renquist's. "By all means."

"This Rauch instituted a purge of the undead in France and Germany, in the aftermath of the First World War. It became known as the Great Slaughter of 1919. Hundreds, if not thousands of us were staked, burned, or beheaded, and at least five important libraries destroyed. Rauch had the perfect recruits for his holy carnage. He offered whores and alcohol to the new veterans of four years in the trenches and on killing fields of the Western Front, the ones cheated of their youth by shot, shell, and gas, who had nothing to go home to except hunger and revolution in the streets. He enlisted the *Freikorps*, who would later cleave to Adolf Hitler. These hollow-eyed former cannon fodder, still in their stinking uniforms, needed something to hate. He found willing followers in the men to whom the industrialized meat grinder of barbed wire, artillery, and the machine gun had become the only normality."

"And you say that thousands of your kind were massacred?"

"Such were the estimates. They hunted us through the deadly bright murderous days, scouring the countryside for our hiding places to the point that some of us who survived actually took shelter in the very trench and bunker systems that had been so recently fought over."

"I find it hard to believe vampires . . . sorry . . . nosferatu could exist in such numbers without being generally noticed."

"We had foolishly proliferated during that war. Death on such a scale was the best natural cover we'd ever enjoyed. When fifty thousand humans could die in a day, we of the nosferatu saw no reason to place restraints on ourselves. Some even believed that humanity was going to butcher itself into functional extinction, and we would replace them as the dominant species."

Coulson thought for a few moments. "I have only the most perfunctory knowledge of this process you refer to as Changing, but wouldn't it have been very easy to restore your numbers in a comparatively short space of years."

Renquist almost laughed. This human was learning fast. "If nothing else, the Slaughter taught us circumspection. When the nosferatu become too visible, disaster inevitably follows."

"So you're not one of the ones who wanted to replace the human race?"

Renquist smiled and shook his head. "Why should I want to do that? I have enough responsibilities."

Coulson was discovering that his best course of action was, for the moment, to accept everything the vampire said at face value. By suspending disbelief he could carve out a reasonably flat playing field across which to face Renquist, an area of territory in which he could operate without having to immediately confront the hurdle of whether or not he truly believed that a whole other sentient species walked the Earth. He had even started thinking of the monster as "he" rather than "it." He also knew that whatever might be achieved with Renquist was going to have to be achieved slowly. He needed to study, observe, and avoid assumptions. To jump to erroneous conclusions and act on them might very well prove fatal. If Director Grael wanted a fast result, he could either accept his disappointment or pay off Coulson and assign some other asshole to deal with the vampire. In the meantime, this would be a slow chess game, not a mugging.

Coulson had decided, after the first exchange with Renquist over the matter of mind reading, initially to assume a passive role. Strict Sun Tsu. He would simply watch the creature as he ran through a set of highly routine, historical questions taken from the information in the dossier. Later, Schultz and Lustig could run over the audio- and videotapes of the conversation looking for possibly revealing inconsistencies and anomalies. Right there and then, he'd allow Renquist to talk freely and see where it took them.

"You saw action against the Turks?"

Renquist seemed hardly interested. "The Turks were a serial problem."

"But you resisted their advances into Europe. It states here you raised and commanded your own unit of cavalry."

"Only by night."

"But you fought side by side with humans."

"I had my boyars. They were content to do battle in the darkness. I think we were about equal in our levels of martial savagery."

"They didn't find you strange?"

Finally, Renquist permitted himself a faint and modest smile. "Perhaps, but they also worshiped me."

"Later you turn up in England under Elizabeth I, apparently working against the Spanish for her spymaster, Sir Francis Walsingham?"

"That's part of the record?"

"It's not true?"

"Oh yes, it's perfectly true. I worked for Walsingham."

"And how did you hide your true nature from him?"

"I didn't. Walsingham didn't care what you were as long as the mission was accomplished. You have to remember that Sir Francis had his back to the wall. England was in grave danger of becoming part of the empire of Philip II. If he didn't coin the phrase *by any means necessary*, he certainly lived by that maxim."

Coulson could not help but be awed. Even if the story were a total fabrication, he found it fascinating. "You actually met Walsingham?"

"At one point, just prior to the Armada, I met him very frequently."

"He's credited by many as being the inventor of modern counter espionage."

"He was." Renquist gestured round the room. "Don't you think he had a place like this?"

"What do you mean?"

"Sir Francis had his own 'Paranormal Division.' He had his own Deerpark with his necromancers, alchemists, mind readers, witches, and astrologers, not to mention his poisoners, and torturers. He didn't give a damn if one of his assassins was a monster, under the cloak and behind the dagger, as long as the target died. That's why it might be a good idea if you came out with the proposition right now."

This final statement took Coulson completely by surprise. Renquist had seemed so relaxed and uncaring, then suddenly, just as Coulson was relaxing his vigilance, the vampire struck. "The proposition?"

"If you're seeking to recruit me to your cause or conspiracy, it will not be the first time such a thing has been tried."

Renquist's stab in the dark was so close to the mark that Coulson was momentarily at a loss. The thing was reading his mind after all, or was it just phenomenally smart? "What makes you think anyone wants to recruit you?"

"Either that, or you want to dissect me. I would prefer, for my own peace of mind, to think it is the former."

Coulson took a moment to control his surprise. "Shall we just go on with the questions?"

"I would have thought better of you, Jack Coulson."

"You would?"

"Indeed I would. You don't seem the kind to follow an imposed and preordained structure."

"Unfortunately, the decisions are not always mine."

"Quite so. I understand. So let's continue with the catalogue of my adventures. We've covered the Turks and Walsingham. What would you like to know about next?"

"Wellington?"

"The Iron Duke?"

"We have a record of you being at Waterloo."

"I wasn't at Waterloo."

"No?"

"The Battle of Waterloo was fought by day. Mainly in the afternoon."

"Ah."

"It is often repeated that, at the height of the battle, when the British were hard-pressed by the French, Wellington exclaimed, 'Give me night or give me Blucher.' Blucher and his Prussians came before sunset. I followed with the night. My function on Wellington's staff was more complex than mere combat."

"I can imagine."

Renquist's expression turned bleak. "I doubt you can."

Coulson thought he was starting to see a pattern emerge in the way that Renquist played the game. Long lulls of indolent indifference were followed with short unexpected jabs to keep him off-balance. He knew it was little more than surface sparring and wondered when the vampire might decide to take the confrontation to a deeper level. Coulson could happily postpone that escalation indefinitely, so he went back to the file. "You were in St. Petersburg?"

"I was in St. Petersburg a number of times down the years."

"In 1917, at the time of the revolution, you worked for the Romanoffs."

Again Renquist smiled. "In 1917, at the time of the revolution, there were many who believed I was on their side, but trust me, Jack Coulson, my objectives were all my own."

"One story has you participating in the murder of Rasputin."

"I merely smoked a cigarette and watched. It was entirely Prince Usopoff's party, although I must confess I was happy to see the Mad Monk go. He suspected too much about me and would never have kept it to himself."

Coulson hadn't exactly gone down in Renquist's estimation, but he had hoped for a little more frankness from the man. He had offered him a chance to cut short the preliminaries and get down to the real reasons that so much trouble had been taken to bring him to Deerpark, but Coulson had sidestepped, erring on the side of caution and correctness. Renquist had expected better of him than just a return to a litany of questions that did little more than confirm what was already in the company's dossier. Coulson had reached the period during World War II when Renquist was once again in England, this time representing the Undead Cartel. His task had been to monitor the work of an occult warfare unit working out of Ravenkeep Priory under the command of the Duke de Richleau. Like Walsingham four hundred years earlier, Winston Churchill, the wartime prime minister, had entertained any idea, no matter how outlandish, if it could conceivably help defeat Hitler and the Nazis. Renquist, in common with most of the nosferatu community had thoroughly approved of the overthrow of Nazism, but some of the elders, including Dietrich, Renquist's ancient mentor, had feared that de Richleau and his people might stumble too close to crucial nosferatu secrets.

"Were others of you also monitoring the SS?"

"Of course. I had the easy brief. The SS were considered much more potentially dangerous. Remember, they had been born out of the *Freikorps*, who went on the rampage for Bishop Rauch. The upper echelons of the SS knew very well what we undead were all about."

Coulson was about to move on to another set of questions, but Renquist held up his hand, as though calling a halt. "How long do you intend to continue with this?"

"You're tired?"

"I'm a little fatigued. Your boys in blue woke me from my sleep, and this has been going on for some time now. Also I am growing hungry."

Renquist put sufficient menace on the phrase "growing hungry" to attract Coulson's undivided attention. "Hungry?"

"You told me plans had been made."

"Give me a moment to check."

Each position at the table came equipped with both a phone handset and a speaker for conference calls. Coulson picked up his handset and keyed in a four-digit number, obviously an internal call. He waited a few moments for someone to answer. "Yes, this is Jack Coulson. I need to know if the arrangements have been made for our guest." He paused while whoever was on the other end of the call attempted to check. "Fifteen minutes? I can count on that? Okay, fine."

He hung up and looked at Renquist. "It seems that everything is being organized to make you comfortable."

Renquist found himself wryly amused by the euphemisms. So he was their "guest," and a human victim was an "arrangement." Humanity really had taken the art of self-deception to unequaled levels.

"We have to wait fifteen minutes?"

"Something like that."

Renquist nodded, then folded his arms, saying nothing, making it clear that, as far as he was concerned, the question and answer session was at least temporarily over. Coulson had other ideas. "There is one more thing I'd like to know before we conclude this first session."

"What's that?"

"I'm curious about the DuMont Library."

The question came as such a surprise that Renquist came near to betraying himself. All he could do was lean forward, downplaying alarm to mere interest. "You know about the DuMont Library?"

"About two years ago you broke in there and removed some very old books?"

Renquist answered slowly and cautiously. "They were ancient books."

"Books of the nosferatu?"

"Yes."

"And you feared for their safety?"

Renquist treated Coulson to a long look, but exerted no psychic influence. "I feared humans would attempt to translate them."

Coulson's information was completely accurate. Word had come to Renquist that the books in question were in imminent danger. Previously they had been safe, part of a highly esoteric personal library belonging to a human who could be trusted in his isolated neurosis. After the man's exceedingly messy shotgun suicide, however, the collection, along with all of the rest of his personal effects, was slated to be sold at auction by the IRS to cover the eccentric's outstanding back taxes: and, if that happened, the hand-lettered volumes with their unique flamelike script, and the arcane and potentially dangerous information they contained, could fall into literally anyone's hands. The interconnected nosferatu community in North America, Europe, and Asia had looked to Renquist to dash to Savannah, Georgia, by a chartered night flight, commit burglary, and then hightail it back to California before he was caught by the sun. Renquist hardly believed that the Feds had hauled him in to answer for his discreet breaking and entering. That would be plainly absurd. What worried him was that any human at all should know about the incident. "Where did you get this information?"

Coulson turned pages in the folder. "I'm not sure. I didn't make up this dossier. It was handed to me when I hired on. There should be a source somewhere in one of the footnotes."

"You're willing to reveal the source?"

Coulson stopped turning pages. "If I didn't, I suspect you'd abandon our agreement and go into my mind and look for it."

"I would in this instance."

"So what would be the point of my trying to keep it from you?"

Renquist smiled. "None whatsoever." He liked the way Coulson was ever the realist.

"Wait a minute." Coulson read for a few moments. "Could the story have come from de Richleau's files?"

Renquist shook his head. "The de Richleau archive only goes up to 1945."

"Hold on." Coulson again turned pages. "I think I have it. Does the name Julia Aschenbach mean anything to you?"

This time Renquist hid his shock better. He managed merely to purse his lips. "I know that name."

It wasn't easy to keep his emotions so tamped down. A deep-seated rage threatened to boil over and destroy the enigmatic and guarded calm he'd sought to cultivate since his capture. The news fully merited an outburst of fury and indignation. He didn't just know the name Julia Aschenbach. She was one of his own, not only nosferatu, but a member of the very colony over which he ruled. The betrayal went deeper, however. Julia was Renquist's personal creation. He had been the one, in Berlin, back in the 1930s, who had brought her through the Change. That had been the root of many of the conflicts between them. The neophyte all too often initially resented the elder undead who brought them to their new nocturnal immortality, but with Julia the resentment had lasted longer than the first few weeks, or even months, of hard acceptance and adjustment. It hadn't helped that Renquist had almost immediately abandoned her to fend for herself in the full flow of Hitlerian madness.

Julia's relationship with Renquist was a temperamental pendulum that swung between intense hatred and a recurring desire to bond with him and become his consort. In both states of mind she proved herself dominating, duplicitous, and an intense liability. She connived and deceived, and even plotted against him and his accumulated power. Her manipulations of the already fraught inner tensions of the nosferatu colony had indirectly caused the destruction of at least four of her kindred undead, and she had been lucky not to pay an ultimate price for her destructive scheming. During her seventy years as nosferatu, in a flamboyant and frequently reckless career, Julia had numerous brushes with intelligence and counter-intelligence operations on both sides of the former Iron Curtain. This on its own would have been neither a surprise nor a concern to Renquist. He had his own history of such transactional encounters. When the undead offered their skills and services to humanity, espionage, blackmail, disinformation, and assassination were all leading items on their bill of fare.

"It would seem that this Julia Aschenbach has been having regular contact with this and other agencies."

Even Julia's connection with the underbelly of the federal government would not have bothered Renquist unduly. Certainly it was dangerous, but Julia was an habitual risk-taker who liked to play close to the edge. Shopping items of information about her fellow nosferatu and the colony that had been expressly devised for all their mutual safety and protection was something else entirely and quite beyond the bounds of decency. Although he did his best not to reveal it to Coulson, Renquist was murderously furious. The human, unfortunately, appeared to notice. "You seem concerned about this."

Renquist sighed. "Now you sound like the psychiatrist again."

"Just curious."

"I think I've been the subject of enough curiosity today. You said something about fifteen minutes?"

"I did." Coulson again picked up the phone. "Is everything prepared for our guest?"

Apparently it was, since Coulson hung up without any further questions. "I'll call the guards to escort you to your temporary quarters."

"I'm fascinated to see what's been devised."

Renquist pushed back his chair and rose to his feet. Coulson did the same. He came round the table, and, to Renquist's surprise, actually extended a hand. After a slight hesitation, Renquist grasped it and noted that, despite making the offer, Coulson repressed a slight shudder.

"There are some things I need if you intend to keep me here."

"Aside from the obvious?"

Renquist smiled. "Aside from the obvious."

"And they are?"

"I believe your people brought all my luggage from the Watergate?"

"That's correct."

"I could use some clean clothes, and the fur rug. It has long been my habit to sleep on that rug."

"Those things shouldn't present a problem."

Renquist was now happily giving orders. "I need a supply of drinking water."

"That should have already been provided."

"I will also need a small ornamental silver tube that should have been somewhere in the suite."

"The one that contained a hidden blade?"

"Exactly as you describe."

Coulson frowned. "I can't see that happening. The security here isn't about to let you have a weapon of any kind, no matter how small."

"It's hardly a weapon, the blade is little more than two inches long."

"Security tend to go by the book on these things."

Renquist began to grow impatient. "That could be a little shortsighted. It can be a problem to feed without it."

Coulson blinked. "But I thought . . ."

"You thought I had retractable fangs?"

Coulson became extremely uncomfortable. "Yes, I suppose I did."

Renquist laughed, enjoying the human's unease. "That

was the olden times, my friend. I had the fangs removed a long time ago."

"Do all of your kind have their fangs removed?"

Renquist dismissed the question as though it were a minor matter. "In Europe there are some who, how can I put it, are still . . . naturalistic . . . about these things, but here in the USA and in Japan, fangs find little favor. They are considered too obvious."

"I have a lot to learn."

"So do I get the object?"

Coulson shook his head. "I really don't know. I'll ask, but somehow I doubt it."

Renquist shrugged. "Then my feeding here could become a very messy business."

chapter Two

S o you're the vampire."

"And you?"

"I guess I'm lunch, or breakfast, or whatever you things call your meals."

Her eyes and cheekbones had preceded her into the room. The cheekbones were prominent in a skeletally thin face and the eyes enormous, staring, green-brown, and more vacant and devoid of interest than any human eyes Renquist had ever seen. Her voice matched her eyes, the sleepy, almost languid monotone of one who has lost all interest in anything and everything. The slow flippancy no longer masked fear. Slow flippancy was all the woman had left. As she entered, Renquist rose from the bunk over which he'd draped his fur rug. He hadn't been aware of her approach until the very last minute, just moments before she appeared on the other side of the Plexiglas wall and swiped a keycard to open the double doors of the air-lock. He stood still as she stepped through the outer door, and waited as the inner door sighed shut behind her. Renquist was so curious, he made no move to approach her.

"By letting the door close behind, you've effectively locked yourself in with me."

"I know that."

"You can't use the keycard on this side."

"My instructions are very clear. When you've finished with me, you simply summon the guard by pressing the call button." She indicated the button set at chest level be-side the inner door. When Coulson had assured Renquist that his physical needs would be met, Coulson had, at his own request, not been apprised of the details, and, even by quickly checking the man's thoughts, Renquist had gleaned little clue as to what to expect. The NSA-FEMA idea of care and maintenance of a nosferatu "guest" was impossible to predict. For all Renquist knew it might be a delivery of defrosted plastic packages of whole blood, but he doubted that. He didn't believe either their data or their imagina-tions were sufficiently sophisticated. His best guess was that some bottom feeder would be thrown in to him, a bum, a wino, a schizoid mental patient, or the inevitable z-grade prostitute. Nothing in his speculation, however, had even come close to the woman who now confronted him.

"Who gave you your instructions?"

"The Old Man, who else? He always gives me my in-structions personally. He owes me that much. Let's not forget that I've died the insulin death for him four times now."

She was something entirely different from the inevitable prostitute. That she came on her own was a phenomenon all by itself. He had certainly anticipated that whatever might have been brought to him would be dragged in by the goon squad, either kicking and screaming, or heavily drugged. He had never imagined the prey would arrive under her own steam. It also surprised him that he hadn't sensed her coming, but coupling that with the fact he still seemed to have the slight impairment of hearing, it added strength to the theory that he was being subjected to microwave bombardment or something similar. The female's feet were bare, and she was wrapped in an oversize, terry-towel bathrobe of the kind provided for guests at the better, big-city hotels. Her dark hair was cut short, cropped just below the ear, and appeared to be still wet, as though she had just come from a bath or shower. In many respects, she reminded him of that dark-haired, anorectic-looking TV actress. What was her name? Renquist had little memory for that kind of trivia. The robe was cinched tightly at the waist by a knotted fabric belt, and her waist seemed very slender, but the otherwise bulky garment tended to disguise the rest of her figure.

"Do you have a name?

"Does it matter?

"Yes. It adds an individuality to how I'll remember you.

"You'll remember me, vampire man?

"Of course."

"I've had a number of names. Rather a lot, actually. One of the most recent was Thyme Bridewell."

"Thyme Bridewell?"

"That's what I said. Will it be a sufficient hook for your memory?"

"It should serve."

"A common herb can be easy to forget."

Her speech continued to be a zombie monotone, and

Renquist felt he had to ask the obvious question. "Have you been taking drugs of some kind?"

For a single instant Thyme Bridewell managed to look wearily amused. "My undead dear, I am way past drugs."

Despite being tired and hungry, Renquist found he was intrigued. They had promised him sustenance, but brought him mystery like a side salad. Since leaving Coulson, however, nothing had been exactly what he'd expected. He had gone with his escort, out from the conference room, down three stretches of corridor until they reached an elevator. Inside the elevator, his escort bunched up along the walls of the car. The goons had plainly either been ordered not to make physical contact with him, or they simply hadn't wanted to. They had ridden down three floors, then the doors opened on yet another corridor. This one had no blue eagle carpeting—nothing more fancy than rubberized cement, and cinder-block walls, painted over in institutional beige. He sensed he was entering what passed for the brig, lockup, or holding cells of the Paranormal Operations and Research Facility. At first sight, he couldn't decide if his quarters were a cell or a tank. Later he would learn they were referred to as a pod; but mercifully, whatever the terminology, it was reasonably comfortable by the standards of a prison, and some essentials had been brought from his luggage at the Watergate, including his fur rug and some changes of clothes.

What he didn't find was the silver tube with the steel spike. Apparently Coulson had not made a persuasive enough case to Security. That was a pity. If he was to feed on live prey, the blood would be splattered everywhere. Renquist regretted that. Aside from the mess, the need to rip out the victim's throat with his bare hands or short teeth would cause the prey quite unjustified suffering. He knew human prisoners were not expected to kill their food and consume it with their bare hands. They were at least provided with plastic knives, forks, or spoons. Although the humans would have trouble accepting it, what they really had here was a gulf of both culture and etiquette, and really very little more, despite the implied repulsion of it all.

The pod in which they had placed Renquist was quite luxurious on any general scale of detention areas. It was a roomy twenty feet by twenty feet, airy beige again, but separated into two separate areas by a floor-to-ceiling divider of inch-thick and presumably bulletproof Plexiglas. On one side was Renquist's habitat, while on the other was a kind of corridor from which guards and visitors could look at him, safe from any physical contact. This had the slightly unfortunate effect of making his confinement resemble a zoo exhibit rather than any routinely imprisoned enemy or criminal. The single bunk was comfortable if narrow, with a pristine foam mattress and freshly laundered and folded sheets and blankets. With his fur rug spread out, it more than adequately met his needs. In many respects, the fur rug was more important than the bed itself. The rug had been with him for a very long time, and he could hardly imagine retiring without it. Humanity had its own weird ideas about the nosferatu; the folklore of men made absurd claims about how the undead slept in their own coffins, or needed to carry chests of their native soil around with them. It was all nonsense, except insofar as the undead did seem to have a requirement for permanence that caused a majority of them to have similar almost fetishistic attachment to some inanimate object that went everywhere with them.

A small refrigerator was built into the wall of the cell, next to the bunk, and when he first opened it, he found it contained a selection of bottled waters in plastic containers. The Deerpark Security clearly didn't trust their detainees with anything made of glass, but at least they had provided for the original basic need as he'd expressed it to Coulson. A fifteen-inch TV set was bolted to a bracket on the wall beyond the Plexiglas, but he could operate it himself with an infrared remote and choose his own programs. Before the arrival of Thyme Bridewell, he hadn't felt in the mood for this so very human entertainment, and then, with her in the picture, he had far more important considerations. He had, on the other hand, discovered that the remote also controlled the lights, and he could—to a degree—raise or dim them according to his mood or preference, but not black out his prison altogether. One Gestapo lamp always remained on, for basic security, and probably to provide a minimal operating light for the video camera also mounted on the wall beyond the Plexiglas divider, right above the TV. At regular intervals, the camera turned, like the head of a watchful bird, and panned across the width and breadth of his enclosure, reinforcing Renquist's sense of being a zoological exhibit.

The two things he didn't understand was the airlock-style double door construction, and why the pod needed the capability for being hermetically sealed. Renquist could only imagine that it came into full use if a prisoner had a contagious disease, or if gas of some kind was used to contain, pacify, or kill. That started him looking for vents through which the theoretical gas could be pumped, or even ones that might be a part of the normal climate control on the subterranean levels in the Deerpark complex: but he failed to find any, and that constituted another small mystery. That his cell should be airtight, but hardly lacking in air, set him wondering if perhaps someone at Deerpark subscribed to the totally erroneous human concept that the nosferatu were able to shape-shift; even reduce themselves to insubstantial vapors, and flow under doors or through the gaps in window casements. Nosferatu legend insisted the shape-shifters had once existed, but in his thousand years, Renquist had never encountered one, and basic reasoning tended to suggest they were the stuff of myth. Any primal germ of truth was more likely to have been born out of the nosferatu's talent for psychic confusion rather than some distant ancestor who was able to rearrange his or her own molecules.

It had been at around this point that further exploration of his new miniature world, and continued speculation on the purpose of the airlock, was interrupted by the arrival of Thyme Bridewell. After her less-than-conventional entry, introduction, and opening statements, she had looked around. "They've remodeled. They've converted to pods."

Renquist was becoming quite as intrigued with this woman as he had been with the design of his cage. "Remodeled?"

"It's certainly changed since the last time they tossed me in here."

"You've been a prisoner here?"

"When I started disintegrating, the Old Man decided I'd be better off confined. He claimed it was for my own good, although I didn't believe him. Mental health interventions are never for the benefit of the patient. They're always for the peace of mind, or the peace and quiet, of those who have to deal with them."

Is that what they'd sent him to feed on? A madwoman? Renquist decided he needed to investigate further. "What do you mean 'when you were disintegrating'?"

"I had the idea I was going to burn up and vanish . . ."

She made an airily expansive if equally vague hand gesture. ". . . like a flare of white phosphorous."

"And why did you think that was going to happen?"

"The wiring in my head is incorrectly routed."

That would seem to confirm it. They were going to feed him the insane. "The wiring in your head?"

"Maybe you can see for yourself. The Old Man told me you were probably able to look inside my mind."

Renquist did his best to sound as though he was humoring Thyme Bridewell. "That doesn't bother you? You don't care if I look in your head?"

"Not in the least. Feel free. Take a good look. Be my fucking guest. You wouldn't be the first. Since you're not human, you might just grasp the pointlessness of it all."

"It doesn't frighten you that I'm not human?"

"After what I've seen and been through? Give me a break. The evil that men do is hard to equal, Victor Renquist."

"You know my name?"

"I was briefed."

As she spoke, Renquist made a preliminary scan, but what he saw stopped him in his tracks. A golden spider of microcircuitry had been surgically implanted above her left eye. Renquist knew very little of human electronics and was unable to put a name to any of the thing's components, or so much as hazard a guess at what its capabilities or precise purpose might be. What he did know was that, in all his experience, such a thing was completely unique, although he had, of course, long heard the rumors that experiments in the use of brain implants were taking place deep in the secret bowels of psywar research.

"You saw?"

"I did."

"You ever see anything like that before?"

"Never."

"There aren't too many of us still walking around."

The body of the "spider" was a gold rectangle, the shape of a square-cut diamond, with what looked like tiny engravings on the surfaces of the flat facets. From this central point not just eight, but dozens of gossamer thin fibers like legs, also of spun gold, insinuated their way into the tissue of Thyme Bridewell's brain, ending in what Renquist assumed to be tiny electrodes.

"They did that to you here?"

"Here and at another of their concealed places. It took a fuck of a lot of open-head surgery before they had it like they wanted it. In fact, I've been through most of our national vaults of horror. They've done a lot to me over the years. The next time you see a crazy woman on a downtown street explaining to no one in particular that the CIA are beaming coded orders into the fillings in her back teeth, don't dismiss her out of hand. She might just be telling the truth. That's one way they dispose of the failed experiments. They just dump the lab rats on Skid Row to survive or not, any way they can." She looked around the pod one more time. "I suppose this qualifies as another means of disposal." She moved to the bunk and tentatively stroked the fur rug as though exploring the texture. "This must be yours, unless times have really changed."

Renquist watched her as she continued to fondle the fur. He had met many odd and outlandish humans down the centuries, but Ms. Bridewell, if only by dint of the hardware in her head and the software that was presumably running it had to occupy a prominent position on the list. "Yes, it's mine."

"It's so soft."

Renquist could suppress his amusement. "It's an irrational comfort."

"We all need those. The more irrational the better."

Renquist moved toward her for the first time. "The irrational can be an invaluable protection against the overly real."

Thyme Bridewell made no attempt to elude him. Quite the reverse. She delved into the pocket of her robe. "I have something else of yours." She produced Renquist's silver tube, found the recessed button, and pressed it so the sharp steel spike sprang out with a metallic snick. "I was told you were going to need this."

"Were you told why I needed it?"

"The Old Man said you were going to use it on me."

"That's my intention."

"Will there be pain involved?"

"It can be avoided."

"The question is do I want to avoid it, or even do I really care? My attitude toward pain is somewhat ambiguous. It can hurt, but it can also make life briefly more interesting."

"Hyperreality as a defense?"

"Fucking A." Bridewell had no difficulty understanding Renquist even when he was deliberately oblique. She might be damaged, but she was still very smart in her own way.

Renquist made a small bow. "I can also be of interest."

Thyme Bridewell looked Renquist squarely in the eye. "Yes. In that, I completely believe you."

"You don't have to believe me. Let me show you."

Renquist gently eased into her brain and fleetingly caressed a pleasure center near one of the gold electrodes. Her reaction took even him by surprise. She immediately convulsed, face contorted, head snapping back, spine arching. "Ooooooh! Oooooh, you *bastard!*"

For a moment, Renquist, didn't know whether Thyme was in agony or ecstasy. He had used but a feather-soft touch, and in no way anticipated such a highly dramatic response. He quickly withdrew and stepped back. "What happened?"

Thyme Bridewell was still trembling. She took a number of deep gulping breaths and abruptly sat down on the bunk. "Can you . . . do . . . that again?"

Renquist's voice was satin smooth. "If that's what you want."

Thyme breathed and swallowed hard. "Perhaps in . . . a little while. I think I need some time to recover."

"Did something happen there? I never intended so intense an effect."

"Random, unplanned amplification. Normally it's the bane of my life. Some of my wiring is less than perfect. Can you make me feel like that when you're feeding?"

Renquist nodded. "Of course. My purpose is always practical rather than cruel."

"And when you feed do you have to kill me?"

"No. Not if I maintain an elementary control."

Thyme thought about this. "It would certainly be a way to go out."

Renquist blinked. "You want to die?"

"If I did die, would I automatically change into a vampire? And become immortal and prowl the night? Or is that only in the movies?"

Renquist's expression was sad. "Only in the movies, I fear. The Change is a great deal more complicated. If every feed produced a new nosferatu, we would have overrun the Earth long ago."

Thyme handed Renquist the silver tube with the steel spike. "Then I think I'd rather live if it's all the same to you. Survival may only be a matter of academic interest, but I believe I'd like to continue a little while longer in this mortal coil."

She rose from the bunk. Her hands went to the belt of her robe, quickly loosening it. After a single shrug, the robe dropped from her shoulders. Her body was porcelain white and wisp-slender, her breasts small, and her legs long. She stepped close to Renquist and placed a hand on the flat of his chest. "Your flesh is cold."

"Such is the nature of my kind."

She seemed to consider this. "Yes." She looked up at him. "So feed on me, Victor Renquist. Do what you have to do, but God's sake take me to that place again."

Renquist placed an arm around her, and, with his other hand, he picked up the remote and dimmed the lights.

Jack Coulson had always considered the Wardroom an affected fucking name for the Deerpark agents' bar and commissary. A century earlier, back in the days of Teddy Roosevelt and the smokestack robber barons, the large room had either been a ballroom or formal dining room on the ground floor of the original country house. To Coulson, the place had an unacceptable smell of furniture polish and Ivy League bullshit. The dark wood paneling, the phony regimental crests, the trophy cases, the mounted antique weapons, and the oil paintings of historical military engagements were pathetic attempts at ersatz tradition, faux-regimental pretensions, built out of nothing. In reality, the joint served booze to some of the most deformed personalities on the entire planet. Hemple, the bartender who did the serving, was a close-mouthed old-timer with a missing eye concealed behind a piratical eye patch that was at complete odds with his immaculate mess jacket and neat bow tie. Hemple was maybe the only real institution in the whole place. Rumor maintained he was in his late sixties, with a history that went all the way back to the Bay of Pigs. It was even claimed he had driven a getaway car in Dealy Plaza back in November of '63, but Coulson tended to doubt it. Just about every mysterious old geezer was credited with a place on the JFK task force, and they couldn't all have been there. Coulson settled on a stool and caught the bartender's eye. Hemple acknowledged him. The closest Hemple ever came to a greeting. "The usual, Mr. Coulson?"

"I think so, Hemple. Why switch after so long?"

Whatever his other attributes, Hemple knew how to mix a near-perfect martini. He scooped ice into a shaker and threw in a measure of vermouth. He shook it once, then, using a mesh filter, dumped out the vermouth. He poured the double shot of gin over the vermouth-flavored ice, shook it one time, decanted the brilliantly clear liquid into a chilled conical glass, and added an olive. Outside, beyond the French windows at the end of the room, a Security helicopter clattered in the distance, amid low dark clouds, on a routine circuit of the Deerpark campus, making sure that all was as it should be on the extensive estate. Coulson sipped his first martini of the day and nodded. "You have the gift, Hemple."

"Thank you, Mr. Coulson."

With the ritual of obtaining a drink behind him, Coulson turned on his stool and glanced round the room. He had expected that Schultz, Lustig, Brauer, and Poulson would be in the Wardroom sharing a table, but he'd also hoped he might be wrong. Unfortunately, he wasn't. There they were in a far corner, bent forward over beer and burgers. They'd glanced at him as he'd walked in, and, now he was

settled at the bar, further looks cast in his direction were
enough to convince him he was the subject of their current
conversation. Schultz, Lustig, Brauer, and Poulson were
the original company crew on the Renquist project, and
the quartet deeply resented how the Old Man had not only
brought in an outsider but slotted that outsider above all
of them in both the pecking order and the chain of command. Since none of the four had the courage to voice even
the mildest complaints to Grael himself, they tended to do
their venting in Coulson's direction, and that mostly manifested itself as petty and ineffectual attempts to undermine
his status. Not that they could really do anything tangible
to or about Jack Coulson. At worst they impeded and ir-
ritated him, and attempted to cut him out of minor information loops to make him look bad in the eyes of the Old
Man. To do worse would be the same as openly stated
criticism, something of which these company sons of
bitches were rendered incapable by their on-the-job conditioning.

Coulson was amused that the four were unable to share
so much as a meal without looking like conspirators. The
way they leaned forward with their heads lowered was the
body language of deviousness, skullduggery, and dirty work
at the crossroads. The worst part was that, in the context
of the Deerpark Wardroom, their apparent plot-hatching
was not in the least out of place. Each table was its own
conspiracy. Even when just two sat together, a man and a
women in head-to-head conversation, they managed to give
what was merely a flirtation, or, at best, a seduction, the
appearance of scheming. Intrigue couldn't help but be the
overriding tone in any place where off-duty spooks gathered. Coulson had observed that intelligence work quickly
eroded any capacity for candor or openness, and the dirtier

the work, the faster the erosion. In Deerpark, the repository for some of the dirtiest work of all, the atmosphere could at times turn into a positive miasma of suspicion, distrust, and paranoia.

Not that there wasn't more than adequate reason for suspicion, distrust, and paranoia in the Wardroom. By far the majority of those gathered could count themselves lucky to be there at all. All branches of the intelligence service had been rigorously purged after their collective failure to anticipate the Al Qa'ida and other terrorist attacks: and still more heads had rolled when Mervyn Talesian had, out of nowhere, been appointed to the newly created post of Special National Security Advisor. Coulson would have assumed that a massively expensive boondoggle like the Paranormal Warfare Facility, indeed the Paranormal Division itself, should have been among the first to go under the axe. It did very little and cost multiple fortunes in tax dollars. The PWF's success with remote viewing, and the occasional coup like the capture of a Renquist did little to offset all of the intervening years of outlandish failure. And yet the Old Man still held Morlock court, assured in his subterranean power. Coulson had to assume that Grael had more dirt on the president and his henchmen than he had previously suspected, that maybe he also knew some secrets about Talesian, despite the general scuttlebutt that the Special National Security Advisor's past was a firmly closed and jealously guarded book.

Coulson picked up his drink, slid off his stool, and sauntered. He was the outsider in this place, and he might as well behave accordingly. He walked slowly to the end of the Wardroom, avoiding eye contact and the risk of casual conversation, to where the French windows opened on a paved terrace. In spring, summer, and autumn one could take one's drinks out there in the evening and enjoy the end of the day, but, in February, the French windows were firmly closed and misted from the outer cold. The area just inside them was devoid of drinkers and diners, and Coulson could, for the moment, have it to himself. He cleared the condensation from a section of one windowpane and looked out. Light snow had started falling on the Virginia countryside. He wondered if it would ground the Security helicopters. The snow seemed so pristine and innocent, it was hard to believe the dark and twisted labyrinth of Deerpark could exist in the same geography.

The illusion of innocence was quickly dispelled, however, by the approach of Schultz and Lustig. Coulson wondered if he could make a break for the bar, Hemple, and another martini, but he hesitated too long, and they were on him. He was forcibly reminded how much he loathed both them and those like them. They were always so clean-shaven, so neat, so certain. They'd never known the deep shit of reality themselves. They'd never had to live with the fear, and their idea of courage was to consign some other poor bastard to the night and fog. They smiled and played pocket politics while others did the killing and the dying. They were so uniform in their trim, clonelike standardization that Coulson wondered if they were actually created in some weird underground government-run Stepford. The current breed of company men had so few signs of anything approaching a human upbringing, he was hard-pressed to find any common ground with them. Maybe they were just *in vitro*-grown replacements for the Feds' anthill.

The old school of black ops, the classic players like Rodriguez, Messer, White, and, to some degree, the Old Man himself, were far easier for Coulson to understand. They were psychopaths, plain and simple. The old-timers, who had learned the game facing down Moscow, wanted to see a world that ran according to their own deranged sense of order and obedience. If the realization of their ambitions meant nuking a city, napalming a village, murdering a head of state, clipping electrodes to prisoners' genitals, or even impaling babies in spikes, so be it. They'd go at it with a will, gleefully up to their elbows in metaphoric blood and intestines, and enjoying every moment of it, only afterwards drinking and drugging away the nightmares. When the old guard had coined the phrase *psychocivilized society*, they had meant a society ruled and controlled by psychos. Schultz, Lustig, and their ilk used the same phrase but apparently imagined a hive world of blind compliance, as bland and unthinking as they were. The new generation seemed to enjoy very little. No regrets or horrors haunted them. They only functioned. They operated with a prosaic and unshakable denial and slept soundly every night.

"Coulson, could we perhaps have a moment of your time?"

"Isn't the weary day through by now?"

Schultz and Lustig exchanged a smug and knowing eye contact, making clear to Coulson that they were above such blue-collar concepts as quitting time. "We were just discussing a possible test that might be performed on your vampire."

"My vampire? Since when did it become my vampire?"

Again the knowing glance. "You seem to have been the one most concerned with its welfare."

Coulson was beginning to wish that he hadn't come to the Wardroom at all, but driven instead into the nearest town to drink in an anonymous neighborhood bar, where the words *paranormal*, *assassination*, or *vampire* would never be heard. He turned from the window, but instead of fac-

ing Schultz and Lustig, he headed back to the bar, forcing
them to follow.

"Hemple, please mix me another, just like the last."

"Of course, Mr. Coulson."

Only when the second of Hemple's martinis was set in
front of him did Coulson give Schultz and Lustig his full
attention. "What test? My intention was merely to go on
talking to him. I believe there's a rapport being established,
albeit a very strange one."

"You have no real idea if it's reading your mind,
though?"

"I believe we have made an agreement."

Schultz and Lustig all but smirked. "An agreement with
a vampire?"

"He's consented to stay out of my mind."

Lustig became sneeringly bold. "I'd say you were out of
your mind. How can you trust a nonhuman thing?"

Coulson refrained from observing that he found Renquist less of a nonhuman thing than Lustig. "I believe he's
interested in proving that negotiation's possible."

"I notice you're referring to Renquist as 'he' and not
'it.' "

Schultz joined the chorus of doubt. "Are you sure it's
not having an effect on you, Coulson?"

"He's not having an effect on me. I'm merely adjusting
to the interface." Coulson inwardly winced. He'd only been
back at Deerpark a couple of days, and already the facility's
mendacious vocabulary was taking him over.

"We talked to Norris in telepathy."

Coulson scowled. "Norris? What the hell did you talk to
him for? Norris is from Mars. He was a fuck-up when he
headed up remote viewing, and he's a worse fuck-up now.
You two haven't been around long enough to remember

the disaster his fire-starter program turned out to be."

Lustig all but bridled that Coulson should be impeaching his plan. "Norris has some nearly confirmed telepaths. We feel a team of them should be assembled to examine Renquist."

"Nearly confirmed telepaths?"

"Yes."

"Did you consider that we have a fully authenticated vampire down in the subbasements, and the odds are he can turn Norris's telepaths into oatmeal if he took a notion?"

A hint of the previous smugness crept back into Lustig's expression. "You seem to be very impressed with Renquist."

Coulson finished his second martini and set the glass on the bar. "Yes, I am. Not only impressed, but starting to take him very seriously. I don't think I want to be throwing him to any of Norris's mutations quite yet." He glanced back at Hemple. "Another, please, my friend."

"My pleasure, Mr. Coulson."

Lustig was stiffening to protest Coulson's rejection of his idea. "I think we need to discuss this, Coulson. We have a time factor to . . ."

He was interrupted by a phone ringing behind the bar. Hemple put down the vermouth bottle and answered it. He almost immediately gestured to Coulson. "It's for you, sir. The Old Man wants to see you right away."

At the mention of the Old Man, Lustig's protests faltered and died.

"You still want the martini, Mr. Coulson?"

"I may need it, Hemple."

Hemple nodded and resumed his mixing. Coulson grinned at Lustig. "I'll tell you what I'll do, boy. I'll run your telepath idea past the Old Man and see what he thinks of it."

She could hardly remember the name she was using. Her life had been in fragments for so long, she could riffle through her past identities like a tapped-out gambler's dirty and thumbed-over playing cards. The dealer needed to call for a new deck but, in her case, he never did. For who and what had Thyme Bridewell been designed? She could scarcely remember. The covert missions and seductions to blackmail, the dark places and black operations, the perverse and the atrocious had long ago taken on the blur of a dull and discolored, half-forgotten nightmare. Had the Thyme Bridewell character been invented to kill, or merely bait a trap with her body and proclivities, and did it really matter anyway? To be culpable was enough, and Thyme knew she was culpable forever and amen, and the real her, whatever and whoever that might be, was damned as a result. Right at that moment, though, her damnation didn't seemed to matter, and the dread of her tattered memories had retreated to irrelevance. The vampire Victor Renquist had pushed them away so easily. He had banished the past and isolated her in a delirious and ecstatic present as no human lover, man or woman, had ever been able to do, although many had so striven, and she had striven right along with them.

"Oh my God, Victor, what are you doing to me? This is perfection. This is better than oblivion."

"It's symbiosis, my dear Thyme."

The word *swoon* crossed her mind. She didn't think it had ever done that before. Her voice was a kitten-purr whisper. "Symbiosis?"

"I'm providing what you need while you do the same for me. Isn't that symbiosis?"

Renquist was an all-enfolding velvet presence. He was around her and within her, and yet a part of her knew he wasn't even touching her except with his mind. Some scattered relic of rationality wanted to tell the rest of her that the joyous euphoria and freedom from guilt were merely illusory, but she had no time for killjoy verity. Factual or imaginary, she was in a place from which she never wanted to return. She could hear her own sibilant gasps. "Symbiosis. Yes, symbiosis. Please, oh please."

For the duration, where she came from and where she was going were lost to her. Where she came from was all in her NSA-FEMA jacket, the file that would inform generations to come of who she'd been, and all that she'd done, until it was reduced to ash in some future, and, she hoped, all-consuming conflagration. Her jacket told how she was a foundling raised by nuns in a Catholic orphanage in Maryland. The nuns were members of a stringently conservative order whose fixation on sins venereal and medieval discipline bordered on the obsessive. She had been routinely whipped for the most minor infraction, and with enough heavy-handed, liturgical ritual to cause her to decide in retrospect it was, in reality, a degree course in high-ceremonial sadomasochism. The nuns' piety did not, however, stand in the way of their cutting a lucrative, long-term deal with some CIA black operations people to supply the agency with children, especially the older and unwanted females and the more androgynous little boys, for purposes that had to remain hidden beneath the dread blanket of national security.

Bridewell had been one of those selected for the heinous

exchange. She had never known the exact criteria that had decided her fate. Seemingly the nuns had decided, when she was little more than an infant, that her soul was lost, and she had been placed on the list. One dark night, she and two other girls from the orphanage had been heavily tranquilized and bundled into the back of a formidable Lincoln with tinted windows, and, after an hallucinatory ride, she had arrived at Deerpark. She had been just nine years old when she commenced her career as Class B Fem-Juv 8-79. The only mercy was that she was spared being one of their five-year-old baby whores in heels and makeup, all bent out of shape by steroids, estrogen, and psych-conditioning. Most of those had either died or killed themselves by the time they reached fifteen. Class B Fem-Juv 8-79 had survived to become Thyme Bridewell and face the vampire, and, right there and then, despite all that had befallen her, she regretted none of it. If she was to be terminated at the hands of a vampire, so be it. She was so totally past caring that she could only think of it as an apt end to her sorry, if not uneventful, life.

"Oh Victor . . ."

The pleasure centers in her brain were running at an intensity beyond anything she had ever known or even imagined. She palpitated beyond orgasm, perhaps beyond death. Electric jolts zigzagged through her nervous system like abstract thrills of passionate frenzy and colors that moved so fast she had no chance to name them. Her body undulated shamelessly. She cupped her own breasts, and her hips ground in involuntary response to the imaginary stimulation. Her head rolled from side to side, and sweat had broken out on her brow. Class B Fem-Juv 8-79 was being led through the houses of the holy and shown all the unearthly delights of the garden. A deceived endocrine system let go a flood of pheromones and endorphins. Some part of her knew that Renquist was watching, standing close but distanced, his steel spike in his hand, but the rest of her didn't care. If he could take pleasure in the total abandon of the spectacle, let that be his gift. Let him bring on his spike. Let him use it on her.

"Victor, Victor, please do it. Please make the penetration. I don't care."

She knew that he permitted her to experience the swift, small, icy stab so there would be no misunderstanding. His business at hand had nothing to do with her immodest diversion or salacious display, it was entirely about her blood. She felt his lips on her throat, cold, but soothing to skin that was damp and close to fevered. She could feel the power flowing out of her, and, at the same time, her desire, her languid lust, was to give it all to him until there was nothing left. Her angry screeching, and wrenching passion was being replaced by a glorious and golden lethargy, an amazing and wonderful weariness, in which she could sprawl, stretch out, and luxuriate. When she tried to speak, her voice was a weak kitten-whisper, muffled by a groaning rushing and a slow, slow pulse.

"Remember . . . Victor, you . . . promised not . . . to kill me."

"Victor . . . you promised . . ."

"It would appear you have a live one here, Coulson."

"I believe so, Director."

Grael was deep in a leather wing chair with a forty-inch video monitor in front of him. He was wrapped in a shogun's kimono, a flowing, oversize creation of gold calligraphy on black silk. While he watched the images on the screen intently, the palm of one hand cupped a brandy snifter and the other held a remote. A Cuban cigar jutted from one side of his mouth, causing him to talk out of the other. The pugnacious mannerism would have seemed incongruous in one so old and frail, except Coulson knew that the Old Man's career went back to World War II, where he'd served his apprenticeship under Wild Bill Donovan, in the shadow of men like George Patton and Omar Bradley, when warriors chomped cigars and barked orders like human Gatling guns. "Will you look at it? The thing's amazing."

The screen showed a high-angle shot of the pod in which Renquist was confined. The cell's single bunk was covered with the fur rug that Renquist had insisted be brought from the Watergate, and a woman's white body writhed on top of it as though in the throes of an atavistic, and uncontrolled passion although Renquist stood a good three feet from her with no physical contact. The colors of the video image were a little strange. Coulson realized that the vampire had probably dimmed the lights to the minimum to at least create an illusion of privacy when it fed, and digital enhancement had cut in.

"Isn't that Thyme Bridewell?"

"I believe that's the name she's going by now."

Coulson was appalled "You *gave* her to him."

"She was expendable. She's scarcely been functional over the past few months. She had one of the first implants, one of the early models, and the flaws are showing."

"But she's one of ours."

"It would be less morally reprehensible to bring in a stranger off the streets?"

"I've slept with Thyme, for chrissakes."

"Just watch the picture, Jack. An attack of sentimental guilt doesn't suit you."

On the screen, the vampire moved closer to the woman and leaned over her. Grael used the remote to go to close-up for an image of Renquist's right hand holding the ornamental silver tube down at his side. The steel spike was out and naked. The hand moved, and the Old Man followed with the remote but wasn't quite able to hold the focus. The lower half of Thyme Bridewell's face came into the shot, and Grael pulled back a little as Renquist placed his left hand on Bridewell's throat, fingers spread, almost like a billiard player forming a bridge.

"Fascinating."

The delicacy with which the vampire punctured the vein in Thyme's neck, allowing the spike to be guided between the first and second fingers, had both Coulson and the director unabashedly riveted. Then Renquist lowered his mouth to the wound on the throat and Grael took it into tight-focused close-up.

"Goddamn." Despite himself, Coulson was awed.

The Old Man spoke without taking his eyes from the screen. "He's promised not to kill her, and we are now observing if he's able to keep his word. I think that revelation should be worth the sacrifice."

Coulson was suddenly very aware of his own breathing. "It's her sacrifice, not ours."

"He's also told her that she won't automatically become a vampire if she should, in fact, die."

"Did he volunteer the information, or did she ask him?"

"She asked him. She was, I believe, quite disappointed with the answer. That one has always had a well-developed sense of adventure, ever since she was just Class B Fem-Juv 8-79."

Coulson was suddenly at a loss for words. The huge image on the screen, the pixel trail of blood down the woman's throat, the part profile of the vampire. Reality TV was swallowing him alive. The Old Man sensed what was happening to Coulson. "You'd better pour yourself a brandy, Jack."

Coulson forced his gaze from the screen, and stood up. Cognac on top of three martinis? Yes, that was exactly what he needed if he was expected to watch the feeding rituals of the undead, live and in color, and with no cutting from the explicit penetration or the gore. This was paranormal pornography as hard as it came, the kind that made you disgusted with yourself when you couldn't look away. Coulson only hoped more booze would help him shake the sick sense of the unnatural and take him to a colder place in his mind, where he could laugh at how it beat the shit out of the Discovery Channel. He made his way across the director's study to the sideboard where the liquor was kept. Aside from the monitor, the only other lights in the room came from a Tiffany shade suspended above the sideboard, the screen savers that unreeled on the two computers, and an aquarium that contained a large multicolored and hyperactive eel, that doubled back on itself, over and over, like an animated whip, and seemingly with no intention of ever stopping. Coulson found a second brandy glass, poured himself a healthy measure, drank some, and poured himself some more. A lesser man might have asked himself how he had come to this juncture; how he found himself looking for refuge in fine old cognac, because, on the other side of the room, one of the top ten most evil sons of bitches in the Western Hemisphere was watching a vampire feed. Coulson had no introspective questions, however, because he knew exactly how he came to be there.

Given the time, mood, and inclination, he could easily and accurately have cataloged all the star-crossed encounters on one side of the scale and the happy accidents on the other that had shaped his career and his fortune: but this was no time for reflection or retroactively charting the by-ways and detours of fate. The blood-drinking horror on the screen might represent a nightmare peak in the mountain of skulls that, in rare moments of self-doubt, Jack Coulson used as a metaphor for his highly unorthodox life and vocation, but his long familiarity with the unbelievable and the unthinkable should have left him prepared. It wasn't that he was unaware such creatures existed. Over a decade earlier, he had stumbled across his very own irrefutable evidence of the reality of the undead. He also knew it didn't pay to question or complain. To rail against a sequence of circumstances that had turned him into an acknowledged expert in the ways of the hideous and atrocious only wasted time. Just then time was at a premium. The Old Man was being energized by the closed-circuit vision of Renquist feeding and would very soon be demanding his undivided attention and professional analysis.

And yet Jack Coulson demanded time of his own, if only a couple of minutes, and a couple of stiff drinks, to prepare him for what was to come. He had talked with the nosfer-atu, this Renquist. Coulson had accepted it as an intellectual equal or more. It had seemed so civilized, and, with its impressive history, it had actually gained a certain uneasy respect from him. He knew dispassionately that Renquist, by his very nature, must regularly revert to the savage inner beast, but a huge gulf yawned between the idea and the huge videocam close-up. He could even tell himself how humans were little better. They did more to disguise the obvious origins of their nourishment, and organized others to do their slaughtering for them in anonymous stockyards, but he knew that was a rationalization. He still needed a short respite while he assimilated what he had just seen. To some degree, at least, he was still human. Respites, however, were not something Herbert Walker Grael handed out on any regular basis. Already he was calling to Coulson from in front of the screen.

"Our guest seems to have finished his repast."

Renquist lifted the woman who called herself Thyme Bridewell with one arm, and slide the fur rug out from under her with the other. She made no protest, in fact no sound at all, and her aura was at best a tentative flicker. Had he gone too far? Was the female dead? Renquist had to listen carefully to hear the faint pulse, but then, as he laid her back on the bunk, she took a shallow breath and murmured something from the depths of an uncertain aftermath dream. He had, after all, kept his promise, and not consumed her life force to the point of death. She was weak and insensible, but she had a pulse and respiration. She was alive, and, provided the NSA-FEMA Paranormal Division had no further potentially lethal plans for her, she would survive.

What Victor Renquist had neglected to tell his uncommonly willing prey was that survival might come with an unquiet and eventually overwhelming desire repeatedly to regain the primary rapture and sacrifice her blood over and over again until finally granted immortality. Not every spared victim succumbed to the condition known as darklost, but instinct told him Thyme was ripe for it; she was exactly the kind who might become a problem. He simply hoped she'd be taken away by the guards for debriefing and he'd never see her again. He hadn't warned her of this catch in the deal because he certainly had no desire to plant the suggestion where no darklost latency existed. He had never felt himself under any obligation to share the secrets of his species with such sundry humans who gave up their blood so his immortality might continue. The truth was that the darklost could be a damned nuisance — walking, wide-eyed guilt trips, whining and whimpering to be brought through the Change and given the gift of everlasting night and dark, unfettered savagery.

That he might have created a darklost was the least of Renquist's current considerations, however. His immediate and most pragmatic desire was that the humans would be good enough to leave him alone for a while. In quick succession he had been kidnapped, transported, interrogated, and now he had been fed. A nosferatu could not simply go on and on like the mechanical rabbit that once advertised flashlight batteries on television. Even more than a human, a nosferatu needed to sleep, digest, and reenergize. At a stretch, Renquist could perhaps make it without sleep for some forty hours, but after that he would find himself disoriented, and confused. If he still remained awake, he would rapidly lapse into delusion and hallucination, and ultimately collapse. Normally, the far more serious nosferatu problem with the lethal effects of sunlight caused their sleep patterns to conform easily to the cycle of day and night, but all this had been snarled for Renquist by the humans' desire to observe and learn all they could from him and their insistence on keeping him in this underground vault.

He was also noticing that his innate sense of day and night were starting to desert him, and he was hazy about how much time had elapsed since he had been taken from his suite at the Watergate. Was this an indication that he had already been awake too long, or was it, like the impairment of his hearing, an effect of some kind of radiation, alpha waves, or other externally imposed confusion? Although he knew to sleep there and then was to leave himself exposed in the hands of his enemies, he felt he had little choice. Allowing Thyme Bridewell to remain on the bunk, he spread out the fur rug on the floor; but, before settling on the rug, he looked up at the TV camera that had now resumed its birdlike side-to-side motion. Renquist had not been so overtaken by the delight of feeding that he wasn't aware of the camera following him, tracking his every move, its lens revolving and adjusting as some remote zoom capability was put to use. Now Coulson, and those to whom he reported, had a visual and auditory record of how a nosferatu dealt with a victim. That was unfortunate, but, for the moment, at least, he could do nothing about it. With a smooth, yogic motion, he sank to the fur and sat cross-legged for a few seconds, before easing back to lie prone, with his arms folded across his chest in the traditional attitude of slumber. Now, if the humans so desired, they could use their video link to watch a nosferatu sleep.

"He has done the equivalent of retiring to his coffin?"

"It would seem so."

"The monster sleeps with unbelievable ease. I envy him."

The rumor around Deerpark, and even at Langley and in Washington, was that the director now rarely slept more than two or three hours a night. Some stories attributed his sleep patterns to the intense cocktails of more than fifteen life-preserving drugs he took on a daily basis. Others attributed it to the rotting sickness of his soul and the weight of his past deeds bearing down on him. Coulson favored the chemical explanation. Nothing Herbert Walker Grael ever had done while Coulson had been around him so much as hinted that he owned a soul or seriously regretted anything in his past.

With the images of the sleeping vampire and his unconscious and naked victim still on the screen, Grael rose from his wing chair. "The question is: Do we leave him to sleep, or do we begin to apply a little stress?"

"We have no information as to what sleep deprivation might do to him."

"Then perhaps we should gather some." The director suddenly halted and grabbed for the back of the chair in which he'd just been sitting. As he stood swaying and struggling for breath, Coulson moved to help him, but Grael waved him back. "No, no, don't touch me. Just a spot of dizziness. I probably stood up too fast. You'll find a little dizziness is one of the lesser burdens when you get to my age."

"Is there something I can do?"

The director straightened up with a visible effort and moved slowly to the sideboard to pour himself a brandy, but even before he picked up the decanter, he had to lean heavily and again catch his breath. Coulson didn't approach but frowned uneasily. For the Old Man to croak on him at this juncture would be highly inconvenient. "Are you sure I can't do anything?"

Grael sniffed his brandy and sighed. "I suppose you'd better call Vargas."

Coulson moved to the desk. It was littered with papers, folders, scrawled notes, electronic gadgets, small irrelevant objects, and dozens of pens. "Do you mind if I turn a light on?"

"Just pick up the red phone and speak into it. Can you do that in the dark?"

Coulson nodded. "No problem."

"Then I'd rather the lights remain off. The room is bright enough already."

Coulson wasn't sure what this was all about. He'd never seen the director show a sensitivity to light before. He picked up the phone and spoke into an open line. "The director wants Vargas with him right now."

He hung up the phone and turned. The Old Man was laboriously making his way to a second wing chair, away from the monitor in a darkened corner of the room. "I have to thank you, Coulson."

Coulson simply nodded and continued to stand by the desk. Grael reached his objective and sank down gratefully. "Jack, did I ever tell you that you are one of my most trusted operatives?"

"No, Director, you've never told me that."

"There's none more reliable than one whose loyalty can be bought for hard cash."

"Your company boys might not like to hear you say that."

"They're conniving little flunkies. I'm under no illusions."

Before Grael could further disparage his underlings, Vargas entered the room. It seemed that when summoned on the red phone, the big bodyguard was not required to knock. He also knew why he'd been summoned. He carried a shrink-wrapped and presumably sterile med-pack. "It's past time, boss. Now you're sitting in the dark. You know it's bad when you can't stand the light."

"Yes, Vargas, give me the shot. I had hoped the excitement of the vampire's feasting would be enough to sustain me, but . . ."

Vargas placed the med-pack on the arm of the Old Man's

wing chair, moved to a nearby floor lamp, and turned it on. The director immediately protested. "No lights, god-damn it."

Vargas must have heard all this before. "I can't help it, boss. I have to see what I'm doing. It's hard enough to find a vein at the best of times."

Grael fumbled in his pocket and crammed a pair of dark glasses onto his face. "Very well. Leave it on. Let's get this over with."

With the extra light, Coulson could see that the med-pack was a plastic tray containing a disposable syringe and two pale blue ampoules. Coulson turned away as the Old Man rolled back the sleeve of his kimono, and Vargas tore the shrink-wrap off the med-pack. He felt he was intruding and did his best to be as inconspicuous as possible. While Vargas shot up the Old Man with whatever cocktail of dope was currently needed to keep him from disintegrating be-fore their eyes, Coulson took the chance to look around at the director's private quarters. Grael grew decidedly weirder each time Coulson came to Deerpark, and the place was progressively turning into the lair of some aristocratic al-chemist. What the study lacked in dried bats, retorts, and cauldrons, it made up for with gleaming technology—all the electronic regalia of the twenty-first century; black and racked monoliths with glowing LEDs and dancing displays. Coulson had no idea of which of the rack-mounted systems were related to the work of the facility and the paranormal, and which might be part of the Old Man's extensive life support. The number of books and file folders seemed to have doubled, if not trebled, since the last time Coulson had been there, and the growing collection of CD-ROMs was now competing for space whereas before it had hardly existed.

Aside from the main entrance by which Coulson and then Vargas had entered, two other doors opened into the director's study. They were the subject of more Deerpark legend. Two were painted a neutral blue, which went with the color scheme, while the third was a significant dark red. The two blue doors were supposed to lead to a private bedroom and bathroom. Nothing unusual there except for some minor speculation about Grael's sexual preferences and his supposed use of a hyperbaric chamber. The red door, on the other hand, was the focus of a wealth of conflicting gossip. Some claimed it was the entrance to the Old Man's inner sanctum, the unholy of unholies, the closet space in the heart of darkness, where all the records of the truly unthinkable were stored. A more imaginative suggestion was that the door gave access to Grael's own private maze of passages and tunnels. These in turn led to rooms where things were confined that no one but the director himself had ever seen. The most fanciful theory about the red door was that it was nothing less than the disguised portal to some nameless elsewhere where the great ancient horrors lurked. What was the point, supporters of the extreme theory argued, in running a paranormal research operation if one couldn't force an opening into some approximation of Hell?

The Old Man was weakly massaging his arm while Vargas dropped the spike, swab, and used ampoules into the disposal bag that came with the med-pack. "You can stop being self-effacing, Coulson. The deed is done. I will live to fight another day."

The Old Man's voice had changed. It had risen by two or three tones, and where once it had been an exhausted and grating sigh, the sound of an ancient turtle too long in the sun, it now had a sense of urgency, more the wrinkled komodo dragon on an old rampage. The director was still short of breath, but it was now the tense wheezing of one who forces himself on, come what might. "When I first took over the Paranormal Division some of my colleagues thought I was crazy. Did you know that, Jack?"

Coulson saw no reason to pull any punches because the Old Man was getting a rush from his meds and wanted to talk. "From what I hear, there's some who still think that."

"The ones who call me the 'crazy old fuck at Deerpark'?"

Coulson nodded. "The same ones."

The Old Man produced a fresh Cuban from a pocket in his kimono and lit it with a Dunhill. "Mercifully, they're too terrified to do anything more than whisper behind their hands." He gestured to Coulson. "Why don't you get me another brandy, Jack. You don't have to stand over there in the dark like you just witnessed an atrocity. My drug consumption is hardly a well-kept secret. Everyone in this wonderful establishment wants to see me live forever. I am their vested interest. They know they're finished if I shuffle off. If I die, the protection I afford them dies with me, and their skeletons will rise from their closets to strip and expose them." He waved urgently to Coulson. "Come over here, man. Step into the light. I want to see you."

The Old Man was as high as a kite so Coulson poured brandy for each of them. He didn't know if the liquor would mellow Grael or make him worse, but didn't really give a damn either way. As he approached, the director took the glass from him and gestured impatiently with his cigar. "Pull up a chair, Jack. We have a while before we run the next test. There are a few things I should fill you in on."

Coulson assumed there was plenty of time to indulge this desire by Grael to tell all. On the video monitor screen, both vampire and victim were inert. He wondered what this next proposed test might be, but decided it was not the time to ask.

"The twenty-first century will be the era of the paranormal, Jack."

"I thought it was to be the era of asymmetric conflict."

"The paranormal will be the key."

Coulson raised an eyebrow. "You really believe that?"

Grael nodded. "Indeed I do, my boy. In fact, I intend to do everything to see my prophecy comes to pass. The best way to predict the future is to control it."

"How much future do you imagine you have, Director? How much longer can you exercise this control?"

The rule at Deerpark was that you never mentioned the Old Man's mortality to his face. Coulson had half expected Grael to be furious at his flouting of the convention, but the director merely smiled and swirled his cognac. "You refuse to lie in the accepted box, don't you, Jack?"

"I thought that was why you trusted me."

"I will live, Jack. Have no fear. The riddle will be solved. You don't need to worry about that. And who knows? Maybe you'll be one of the lucky few with whom I'll share the secret."

"If I live that long, Director?"

"Exactly, Jack. If you live that long." The Old Man dragged hard on his cigar and let smoke trickle from his mouth into the glass before he sipped the brandy. "As they might be applied to social control, physics, chemistry, and biology are very close to having gone as far as they can go on their own. We have mapped the human genome, and we can incinerate large cities in a single atomic flash. We took religion out of the schools and substituted Ritalin. We have spy satellites that can read a newspaper from space.

To go further we will require the paranormal, the mystic, the occult if you like, to provide the fulcrum for our efforts. It will be that extra and crucial factor, the dimension in which true control of the masses will really begin to become effective."

Coulson looked sideways at Grael. What had been in that shot Vargas had given him? Some of the ingredients could only be distant, more sophisticated cousins of tried-and-true amphetamine. "I'm not sure I follow you, Director."

"You have to look at it this way, Jack. Physics has given us the capability to deliver a nuclear fusion weapon by means of an intercontinental ballistic missile. Islamic mysticism has given us individuals so devoted to the worship of Allah that they will deliver a nuclear fusion weapon in suitcases on a commercial airliner. For the price of a ticket and some primitive ingenuity, the entire Strategic Missile Defense Shield is rendered redundant. If nothing else, the paranormal is cost-effective."

Coulson glanced at the monitor screen. Renquist and Thyme Bridewell were both still motionless. "Cost-effectiveness isn't the goal, though, is it, Director?"

"Of course not. It's power from a long-hidden direction. What we're dealing with is an entire branch of science we know close to nothing about. Imagine for a moment the crew of an airborne Stealth system who were also an inter-linked telepath coven. We have barely scratched the surface, little more than played with the elementary toys—implants, psy-ops, nontechnological biofeedback, trance states, psy-chedelics, remote viewing, pre-cog, telekinesis, all that stuff from Sid Gottlieb and on. It's all kindergarten level, Jack. It's the equivalent of Lego. And while we play with Lego, there's a thousand of years of unexamined data locked up in the Vatican, but it's going to take nothing short of a tactical nuke to pry anything loose from those quasi-celibate fucks. What we have right now is hardly enough to enable us to so much as see the signs." Grael paused. "Is there something wrong with me, Jack?"

Coulson realized he'd been staring all but openmouthed at the Old Man as the director's frustrations began to run away with him. Later Coulson would reflect on his answer as little short of inspired—the absolute truth but wholly irrelevant. "I keep seeing my own reflection in your dark glasses, Director. I guess it's the booze and maybe the time of day, but it's getting a little unnerving."

The director made no attempt to remove the glasses, and, in a way, Coulson was relieved. Right there and then he believed he'd rather look into Renquist's eyes than those of the Old Man in the middle of his discourse on occult megalomania. "You've got to keep a lid on those kinds of thoughts, my boy. You're no use to me staring at your big toe. Maxwell is dosing that Renquist thing with a whole spectrum of nasty microwaves."

"And I'm getting the backwash?"

Grael shrugged. "It can't be helped."

"I'm expendable?"

"That shouldn't be news. You knew that the first time you hired on."

"That's why you pay me the big bucks?"

The Old Man smilingly corrected. "That's why a grateful nation pays you the big bucks. I'm just a public servant, remember."

Coulson sank down in his chair and inhaled his own brandy. "Right."

"The Ancient Ones are very close."

Coulson had quit smoking four years earlier, but at that

moment he wished he had a cigarette. The director saw his discomfort and laughed nastily. "You really hate it when I talk about the Ancient Ones, don't you, Jack? You still can't quite make the final transition, can you? You can't bring yourself to believe."

"I don't have to believe, Director. I'm just an operative. I'm not looking to inherit the Earth."

"My God, man, you were brought in as an analyst on the material we obtained after the Apogee collapse. You know what Marcus De Reske was trying to do. He all but opened a portal to another dimension. He nearly accessed R'lyeh and reached Cthulhu, for chrissakes. The speedup is happening, Jack, and you don't want to be left behind. Back in the eighties, we had to invent a Satanist conspiracy for Reagan's retards. Now the Satanists are on the Internet, and very soon they'll be lobbying for tax exemption as a legitimate religion."

Coulson wasn't buying that. "Satan worship is bullshit, Director. We both know that."

"But it's a symptom, Jack. Massive cult growth was only to be expected. It's the other side hitting back."

"You're losing me." What the fuck had the Old Man taken? It was a long time since Coulson had seen him so bad. He wondered if he ought to recall Vargas and check that someone hadn't screwed up the dosage, but he didn't see how he could as Grael rattled on with the impromptu lecture. The director didn't take kindly to being interrupted.

"Not only do we know little about the paranormal, but I firmly believe that, in our ignorance, we are doing incalculable damage. We have been hammering at the laws, principles, and basic mathematics of other dimensions for many decades now. We cannot do anything as fundamental as splitting the atom, we cannot touch off a piece of a star right here on Earth, and not cause a ripple effect down the curve of time and in all branches of science, both known and unknown, in this world and others. We find it so hard to accept the existence of unknown worlds that cannot even approach the idea that they might exist in violent motion, buffeted by resonances created right here, as we in our turn are buffeted by them."

The Old Man paused to sip his brandy, and Coulson moved quickly in an attempt to divert the monologue. "You said something about a test, Director."

The ploy worked better than Coulson could have hoped. He thought that he actually saw the Old Man's mania visibly change direction, like a freight train crossing a set of points, as the appeal of theorizing and the love of hearing himself talk gave way to the allure of real live action. "You should have stopped me sooner, Jack. I tend to have a great many ideas after my evening medication, and then I talk too much if I have company. The test, yes indeed. We should run the test. In fact, we have to run the test. We have to run the test before the Renquist creature wakes again."

The Old Man looked quickly round at the screen, but Coulson was there before him. "It's okay. I've been checking them. Neither has moved."

Grael stared at Coulson from behind his shades. "You really don't need to be a believer, do you? You sweat the details by nature."

Coulson nodded. "I'm worth more to you as a detached asset than a zealot."

The director gestured to the desk. "Get Vargas again. Tell him to wake up his boys. Tell him it's showtime."

Coulson remained seated. "Perhaps, before the show

starts, you should give me a brief synopsis of the script."

The Old Man puffed on his cigar. "I was hoping to surprise you."

"I work better when I'm not surprised."

"So you want me to explain the nature and objective of this test?"

"I'd be more comfortable knowing."

"Well, Jack, I wouldn't want it said I was insensitive to your comfort. Fortunately, it's all very simple. No complications at all. What we're going to do is attempt to kill the beast in the traditional and time-honored manner. I know you've been counseling caution to anyone who will listen, but I think we need a gauge of its strength before we proceed any further. Vargas has three strapping young *charros* who will attempt to drive a stake into Renquist's heart."

Thyme Bridewell drifted in a place of rose and amber, an afterglow that surpassed any mere animal satisfaction. A slow, rolling boom echoed from far in the distance, beyond the light of the rainbow horizon, single sonorous beats, long-spaced but sleepily rhythmic, and it took her some time to recognize that it was the sound of her own heart and that Victor hadn't killed her. Her nervous system had continued to vibrate with the last shocks and gasps of what he'd done to her even as she had been dreaming her way in and out of consciousness, but it hadn't been enough to convince her fully that she was still alive. The heartbeat was the glorious evidence that Victor had honored his promise and spared her, and she loved him for it. Indeed the word *love* didn't have the necessary power to describe what she felt. She didn't love Victor Renquist, she adored him, she worshiped him. She knew he was nearby, but she couldn't see him. She wanted to push herself up and look at him, but she hadn't recovered sufficiently to move. The best she could manage was to stretch herself slightly and let out a protracted sigh.

"Oh, Victor. I want you."

Thyme knew he wouldn't respond. He was no longer in the reality of Deerpark. He had departed to his dark and private dreams, to measureless places she couldn't follow unless he completed the Change in her. Even though she had yet to begin marshaling her emotions, she knew that she must accept that he would leave her on her own, but also that she had no choice but to resent his not being there. He had brought her through an experience of the kind that would never permit her to be the same again. Admittedly he hadn't chosen her to be the one. For him, she was merely a random selection, but she could only protect herself by holding him responsible. And yet how could she maintain anger in the face of what he'd done? The experience had hardly left her. The night-music was still ringing in her head and in her loins—deafening and overpowering, sensual and psychic.

"Oh, Victor. I want you."

Very, very slowly she began to curl her body on the prison bunk. She moved her knees, imperceptibly at first, up toward her chest. It was to keep out the cold of reality. She sought the warmth of a fetal position because she was unwilling to face the trauma of being reborn as a composite being, part of which she neither knew nor understood. Renquist had promised not to kill her, and he had kept his promise. He had told her if she died, she would not automatically become a vampire. In that, too, she supposed, he had also spoken the truth. What he hadn't told her was that, by his very actions, he had shown her what ecstatic power was possible and planted a hopeless craving in her for his touch to be once again on her mind, her brain, and its pleasure centers, and that, in itself, was a teasing fore-taste to vampirism. She was still alive and still human, but she had become deeply dissatisfied with that condition, and her whole being longed to be like Renquist. She knew a terrible conflict was to come, but she was mercifully still too weak to engage in it.

"Oh, Victor. I want you."

Unfortunately, she was recovering all too fast. No sooner had she uttered the whispered whimper than she despised herself for regressing to the infantile. Victor Renquist had a hold on her. She couldn't debate that with herself. He held the power of life and death over her: thus he was, by very definition, her superior. Superiority didn't mean, though, that she needed to mewl like a baby or grovel for his uncertain affections.

"Oh, Victor. I want you."

Her voice was stronger, deeper, more contemptuous of her naked need, but not so dizzy, drained, and foolish that she didn't recognize it as such. She had been trained in an uncompromising school, and that training would still be with her no matter what she might become. The human monsters who had been her substitute parents hadn't raised her to cry over what she could not have, but to go out and get it by any means she could conceive. Class B Fem-Juv 8-79 didn't mourn for an unfulfilled craving, she demanded satisfaction and didn't stop until she got it.

"Victor. *I* want you."

Thyme still whispered, but now a determination had crept in. She stressed the word *I*. "Victor, *I* want you," in a tone only separated by one degree from the next two logical statements.

"And *I* will have you, and *I* will have your secrets."

She knew her hands were in front of her face. She opened her eyes. It took a few moments for the floating, hallucinatory afterimages to clear, but, when she could see again, she gently flexed her fingers. She could move, and she wasn't blind. Her humanity was returning. Inch by inch she eased her way across the bunk until she could see the floor by just turning her head. And there was Victor, death-like on his fur, pale hands, a large onyx ring on one finger, crossed across the front of a midnight blue silk shirt, resting on a chest that neither rose nor fell. How beautifully he concealed the truth about himself. His face was in total repose, expressionless beyond any echo of cruel sensitivity. Nothing external revealed him for what he was, except perhaps features that were a fraction too chiseled, the lips a little too flawless, and the way his long hair drifted back from his brow implausibly perfect. Certainly nothing to suggest the reality beneath the human mask. But she had seen that other face, and, like the old rock & roll song said, it was the face she loved.

"*I* will have your secrets, Victor, and the power to take these things out of my head."

As she whispered, she saw the shadow's furtive move. They were in the detention block, and her first assumption was that it had to be a guard who approached, except everything was wrong. Prison guards didn't come furtively. They had no need. They strolled, they sauntered. Their lives and moves were all ordered routine. The movement in the shadow was stealthy, and guards didn't use stealth. This was something else. An attack? A rescue bid? Conditioning kicked in, and Thyme Bridewell tensed, her exhaustion pushed to one side. Something way out of the ordinary was about to go down, and Victor should not sleep through its descent. The question was, would she be able to wake him? How soundly did the predator sleep? Surely not so deeply to make him totally vulnerable to intruders? With one more effort, she leaned over the side of the bed.

"Wake up, Victor. Wake up right now."

"Watch carefully, Jack, as you will observe all three of the mission team are Salvadorans, recruited because they have the necessary levels of superstitious belief. Vargas still has his sources."

Coulson stood behind the director's wing chair, looking over his shoulder at the monitor screen. "I'd seriously advise calling this off while you still can."

The Old Man shook his head. "No, Jack. We don't want to do that. We don't want to do that at all."

Coulson was barely keeping his anger under control. So he was just hired help, and if the director, on some doped-up whim, decided to do away with his uniquely prized specimen, that was his choice. He had the right. Coulson really had no say in the matter. So he'd put in time with Renquist, and this ending might seem highly unsatisfactory, but he'd still be paid his fee. That was ensured by the contract. If nothing else, though, Jack Coulson hated waste. To destroy Renquist now was criminal waste, pure and simple.

"I know you're fuming, Jack, but why don't you just wait and see what happens."

Now and then, it almost seemed that the Old Man could read his mind. Coulson's face became set. "I've given my best advice. I've got nothing else to say."

"Just wait and see what happens, boy."

On the screen, the three figures moved cautiously down a corridor. The underground levels of Deerpark had so many thousands of yards of corridor that Coulson could not immediately recognize the particular section, but he knew he could safely assume it was somewhere close to the pod that held Renquist. The three men wore baseball caps and the standard, dark blue coveralls, but no body armor. They had sidearms, but no heavier weapons, and one carried a weighty club hammer and a pair of foot-long iron spikes. At first the trio were in shadow, but when they entered a patch of light Coulson saw that they all wore large silver crosses around their necks, prominently displayed over their uniforms. A reflection burn flashed from one of them, and the sight left him speechless. "Don't they know those crosses are of no use?"

The Old Man cut him off. "Recruited because they have the necessary levels of superstitious belief. Weren't you listening to me, Jack?"

"Jesus . . ."

"Just shut up and watch. You're starting to irritate me."

Thyme tried to pull herself off the bunk, but she didn't have the strength. "Victor!"

Three men were on the other side of the Plexiglas divide, but Renquist didn't move. She could see the crosses around their necks, and the spikes, and the hammer that one of them had in his hand. Beyond any reasonable doubt, they were coming to destroy Renquist, and she could not allow that to happen. The door to a new dimension of life might not as yet have been opened to her, but it had certainly been unlocked, and she had been allowed to peer through the keyhole. Without Victor, it all would never be, and she had lost enough of her life to might-have-beens and the conspiracies of killers.

"Victor, wake up. You have to wake up."

The three men were now at the double doors. One had

a keycard. The outer doors slid open, and still Renquist didn't move. With an almost superhuman effort, but with little idea of what she intended to do, Thyme swung her legs off the bunk, and attempted to stand. The three men were through the inner door. Under the uniform baseball caps, they were swarthy, maybe from some place in Central America, muscular and expressionless, with those blank shark eyes unique to death squad veterans. The Old Man kept a few around for when dispassionate, pre-Columbian sadism might be required. For a moment she was on her feet facing them, but then her legs gave out on her, and she dropped to her knees. One of the men took a couple of paces toward her, but, quickly realizing she posed no threat, turned and joined his companions as they closed silently in on Renquist.

Crouching on the floor, Thyme Bridewell cried out frantically one last time. "Victor, you have to save yourself!"

"Victor, you have to save yourself!"

"She seems to have fallen for him."

Now Coulson was quite as rivetted as the Old Man. Was this part of the vampire's strength that its surviving victims should fall in some unholy approximation of love with him? And did it always happen, or was it some special influence he had used on Bridewell to recruit her as an asset? Unfortunately, it was starting to appear that the questions would turn out to be wholly academic as the Old Man saw his experiment through to the end, over all of Coulson's protests. Despite how Renquist's feeding had disturbed and disgusted him, it seemed absurd in the extreme to capture the first living vampire in recent history, then throw away all chances of anything but postmortem study on an elderly lunatic's willful caprice.

On the monitor screen, the three Salvadorans moved fast, but with an attendant caution. One knelt beside Renquist and briskly took an iron stake from his companion. The third of the trio readied himself with the hammer as the point of the stake was positioned squarely in the center of Renquist's chest. They had obviously rehearsed the routine. The Old Man grunted. He seemed disappointed that the vampire was failing to put up any kind of a fight. "When they sleep, they're completely unconscious?"

"It would seem so."

Grael shook his head. "That would seem to be an unconscionable weakness for a nocturnal predator."

"Unless, of course, it's a deception."

"Are you suggesting the vampire is playing possum?"

Coulson shrugged. "I imagine we'll see in a matter of seconds."

The very act of opening his eyes froze his attackers just long enough for him to move. Later he would learn that the three Salvadorans had been selected for the experiment because of their supposedly high levels of superstition. The *vampira* still loomed large in their personal mythology, and that proved to be their undoing rather than their strength. Fear had immobilized them when they should have hammered home the iron spike with all urgency. Renquist's hand moved faster than a striking snake. It gripped the brown wrist that held the stake, and it didn't let go no matter how much its owner struggled. Bones audibly crunched, and the man let out a scream that must have taken every last cubic inch of his lung capacity and seemed to shake the Plexiglas wall like a sounding board. Furious at what he saw as a shameful assassination bid, Renquist rose to his feet in a single movement, still holding on to the human's arm. He only hurled the man from him when he'd drawn himself up to his full height. The attacker crashed into the wall beside the bunk, and flopped like a rag doll. The iron stake he had previously held in his locked fingers clattered to the floor. The one with the hammer swung at Renquist, but he slapped the implement easily aside. Simultaneously he let loose with a full-scale psychic counterattack.

In front of the subjective eyes of the two men and, collaterally, the crouching exhausted Thyme, he transformed himself into a demon straight from the burning pit of the men's own Catholicism. Hellfire red and stinking of sulfur, blackened horns, cloven hooves, and the face of a skull, he towered over them, drawing the images of horror almost entirely from the Salvadorans' own minds, with some added touches from Day of the Dead festivals, and the masked Mexican wrestlers he'd seen on TV in Los Angeles. Renquist had to admit the two humans didn't lack courage. Even though confronted with one of the worst nightmares from their devil-ridden ids, his remaining attackers managed to retreat in good order, slowly backing away, holding up their crosses, irrationally believing the Christian charms would keep him at bay.

He laughed and pointed out in Spanish that they were wasting their time. At the same moment they realized that, with the keycard to the pod only operating one way, they were effectively locked in with the monster. Now the true depths of horror gnawed with elemental rat teeth at the men's minds, but, once again, they demonstrated the sternness of their stuff. The one with the remaining steel spike lunged at Renquist, and the other fumbled for the fashionable 9mm Glock automatic holstered at his hip. Renquist doubted the one with the spike could do him much harm, but a bullet was another matter. A nine millimeter wouldn't kill him, but it could slow him down critically. The problem would be magnified if the gun was loaded with hollowpoints or vest cutters. The nosferatu had a phenomenal rate of recovery, but not fast enough that a gunshot wound to the body wouldn't give the two men the chance to be all over him.

"I don't believe it. Will you look at the speed of the thing?"

On the monitor screen, the vampire was just a blur, followed by a trail of distortion. One of the Salvadorans appeared to collide with the other, then fly through the air. The man had been in the process of drawing his pistol, but that, too, went flying. Coulson shook his head. "Look at the pure fury. I'm damn glad I'm not down there."

The Old Man stared at the screen. "We have to replay this in slow motion."

"It's much stronger than we ever imagined."

The Old Man slowly nodded. "All our previous estimates will have to be revised." He paused. "What the hell is it doing now?"

Renquist had picked up one of the Salvadorans, but almost immediately dropped him again. As the man fell, Coulson observed the odd angle of the head. "I think he just broke the man's neck."

"Now he's going for the last one."

In his rage, Renquist advanced on the single surviving Salvadoran, bent on taking the blood of his attacker. The man had come upon him to drive the stake and destroy, so to drain him was close to a matter of honor. The illusion of the walking demon fell away, but the small steel blade with the silver-tube handle that he used to feed on Bridewell was in Renquist's hand. Behind him an expression of pure horror spread over Thyme Bridewell's face. "Victor!"

Renquist turned. Thyme's aura was the purple of those who see themselves hideously betrayed. "You'd take his blood after mine?"

Renquist lied, but his mental caress allowed her to believe him completely. "No, of course not." To further convince her he slowed his approach. The man tried to crawl away from him. Renquist allowed this last attacker to go a couple of yards, but then moved quickly forward and dispatched him with a simple thumb and index finger to the windpipe, killing fast with a minimum of pain. To feed would have been a moment of ancient animal rapture, but he in no way wished to alienate Thyme Bridewell. A single glance told him that the longing of the darklost was in her eyes, and that was something too useful to be wasted. She might not have any direct power, and that she had been willingly sacrificed to feed him clearly indicated her lowly status in the hierarchy of Deerpark, but that didn't mean she couldn't be shaped to a purpose. Like a more conventional prisoner might secrete a paper clip or plastic pen to be used in some future, unrevealed eventuality, Bridewell could be squirreled away. She'd be walking among his jailers, but devoted to him, and ready to be utilized anytime he saw a way to deploy her effectively.

Renquist turned away from the dead attacker, went to the small fridge, and took out a plastic bottle of designer water. He drank half of it in one go and looked down at Thyme. "I imagine reinforcements will arrive at any moment."

Thyme sat up as best she could and gestured to the weapons the Salvadorans had dropped. "You have their guns."

Renquist's lip curled in contempt, "Firearms? A nosferatu doesn't fight his battles with firearms."

"Never?"

"Never."

"Isn't that a little shortsighted?"

"We have powers far beyond those of humans, and little need to copy their weak reliance on . . . devices."

"They'll be coming at you with guns."

"That still isn't reason enough to reach for one myself. If nothing else, the reliance on firearms makes one lazy. The brain itself should be the weapon, not merely the control behind it."

"I hope you know what you're doing."

Renquist drank some more water and glanced significantly at the bodies of the Salvadorans. "They came at me with weapons both old and new, and presented no major problem. I have survived a long time, my dear. Too long to perish in this twenty-first-century dungeon.

All through the flurry of violence the Old Man had seemed in a trance; but the moment when, on the video link, Renquist had finished the last Salvadoran, he had suddenly become brisk and businesslike. "So, now that the experiment is complete, let's go and confront our vampire."

Coulson was less than enthusiastic. "I think we have to assume the vampire is now as mad as hell. He seemed, to me, distinctly pissed off as he was killing those Salvadorans."

"I wonder why he didn't take their blood."

"Perhaps he had drunk his fill from Thyme."

Grael began to rise from his chair, but it took considerable effort, so much so that Coulson moved to help him. As he attempted to grasp his arm, the Old Man snarled,

"Get away from me, Jack. You know I can't stand being touched by anyone except Vargas."

Coulson backed off. The director was definitely crazier than the last time Coulson had worked for him. "Is there any point in offering the opinion that this is not a good idea?"

"None whatsoever, Jack."

"I wouldn't like to confront him only to discover he was confronting me."

"Where's your sense of adventure, Jack?"

"It's directly beneath my imperative for self-preservation, Director."

"You're acting like a man preempted, Jack."

"I thought I'd established a dialogue with Renquist. I believed we had a certain rapport."

"All you had was his pragmatic acquiescence. I have his attention. I know you meant well, but we needed to cut to the chase. It was in his interests to hear you out, but I'm his real jailer, and we have just transacted a little test of strength to define our positions."

"And what are those positions as you see them, Director?"

"It's very simple. I hold him, but he's just wasted three of mine, and proved that he's hard to hold. I feel a certain kind of honor has been satisfied, and now we have some parameters within which we can deal."

chapter **Three**

His very first look at the elderly human's aura was quite enough to show Renquist his abnormal hunger. This Herbert Walker Grael, this Director of the Paranormal Warfare Facility, was gripped by a hunger to rival that of a nosferatu. He clung to life with a baleful fury, and, aside from a long-practiced joy in the manipulation of his fellow humanity, all his remaining passion and energy were invested in an intense and personal crusade to cheat death. The same look also told him that it had been Grael, not the taller, younger, generally more stable Jack Coulson who had ordered the attack on him. The two humans stood side by side beyond the Plexiglas, with a guard of more faceless men in blue jumpsuits and baseball caps, carrying shotguns at high port behind them. Grael was personally attended by yet another Salvadoran. A quick scan of the man's mind revealed that his name was Vargas, and that he possessed a past that encompassed two long intervals of obscene political murder and torture. The relationship between Vargas and Grael was akin to master and dog. In Grael, Vargas had apparently found his match and bowed to his will as his lord and *jefe*. Vargas was the kind who was either at your feet or at your throat, and he needed a strong and patriarchal authority figure on whom to lavish this devotion. Certainly Vargas felt more loyalty to Grael than to the three countrymen he had personally selected to make the attack on Renquist. The fact that they now lay dead in the pod was a matter of complete indifference to him except in how it might affect the plans of his director.

When Grael and his escort appeared, they had found Renquist sitting calmly on the bed drinking from a fresh bottle of water. Thyme Bridewell, who had recovered slightly but was still as pale as a corpse, sat naked at his feet, leaning lightly on his right leg. Renquist believed he could detect a crude, impromptu ceremony in the way Grael and his escort made their entrance. The threatening pomp told him this was not another attempt on his life but the preliminary softening up to some kind of negotiation. In some respects, Renquist had done the same, having arranged the three dead Salvadorans, faceup on their backs, in a neat row just inside the door, like a three-man body count, or perhaps a domestic cat bringing gifts of mice. While Renquist had arranged the dead, Thyme had weakly gathered up their weapons and now had the three pistols placed beside her, intending to use them if any others tried to do harm to either of them. She accepted the possibility that, now that Victor hadn't killed her, the Old Man or one of his underlings might decide she was surplus to their requirements, but she was much more concerned with Renquist's safety. She seemed to feel obligated to protect him despite what she had seen him do to the previous would-be assassins. Such obsessed protectiveness was not uncommon among darklost. They became totally concerned with the well-being of the predator who had fed from them. At root it was really a matter of the victim's self-interest. The nosferatu they so slavishly worshiped was, after all, the one who could bring them through the Change and make them what they increasingly aspired to be. The predator held the keys to the kingdom of immortality and more, and must be preserved at all costs.

The group around Grael and Coulson stood for a moment staring at the tableau Renquist had arranged for them, and Renquist again felt like an exhibit in an exotic zoo. He was gratified, however, that the combination of himself, his newly created darklost, and his fresh kill made the humans decidedly ill at ease and reminded them they were not as all-powerful as they pretended they were. A technician handed Grael a microphone, and a moment later his voice boomed over a set of speakers concealed somewhere inside the pod.

"Victor Renquist."

"Director Grael."

Seemingly a concealed microphone went with the speakers because Grael and his party had no problem hearing Renquist through the Plexiglas. "You know my name?"

Renquist could feel Thyme Bridewell tremble each time the director's amplified voice grated from the hidden speakers. Renquist nodded. "Of course I know your name."

"And you have killed three of my men. What do you have to say about that, Victor Renquist?"

"I assumed it was my purpose to resist them as best I could."

Grael looked at the lined-up casualties of his experiment. "You seem to have done that."

"If you'd wanted to know my physical capabilities, you needed only to ask. Perhaps a demonstration could have been arranged that was less costly in lives." Even in the controlled light of the detention area, Renquist noted that the director concealed his eyes behind dark glasses. It was usually a sign that a human had things to hide.

"You put a value on human lives, Victor Renquist?"

"Renquist smiled and shook his head. "No, but I do observe the niceties."

"And where should the niceties take us now?"

"I don't know. We seem to have reached something of an impasse."

"An impasse?"

"You have me, but you don't know what to do with me. I also suspect that you want something from me, but don't know how to get it."

"What could we possibly want from you?"

"The traditional answer would be knowledge, information, data if you like, but I suspect your motives go deeper."

"Are you reading my mind?"

Renquist shook his head. "No, I made an undertaking with Coulson that I've more or less adhered to. For the moment, I've extended the same courtesy to you, as the director of this place."

"I believe I could block you even if you tried."

"Perhaps you could. Perhaps for a while, but, in the long run, I doubt it."

What Grael didn't know was that Renquist had already made a cursory examination of his mind and discovered that the outer layers were such a roiling mire of drugs, near hallucinations, and paranoid possibilities he was unwilling to wade through all the mental undergrowth. In a way the director actually was blocking him by having a psyche that was distasteful for Renquist to enter. He knew there had to be an inner area beyond the miasma and mania, where some jewel-in-the-skull controlled a pure and rational cunning. Grael could never have maintained his considerable and long-held power base on psychosis alone.

"You doubt it?"

"We are different species, Director. The concept of competition is totally absurd."

Renquist felt Thyme move beside him and glanced down. She was reaching for one the Salvadorans' discarded weapons. Her exact intention was unclear, even to herself, but it seemed that, as she recovered her strength, she also manifested a hatred for the director of a depth and intensity that Renquist had not previously observed. Her hand was on the pistol, but none of Grael's people seemed to have noticed. She pulled it toward her, and her fingers curled, closing around the grip. Renquist probably should have stopped her immediately, but a malicious curiosity wanted to see her act out what she had in her mind. She paused for a moment before trying to lift the pistol, but once started, she seemed to gain strength. Her powers of recovery were quite phenomenal. Even though Renquist had drained her almost to the point of fatality, he also seemed to have infused her with some kind of chemical stimulant.

It wasn't until her hand was about halfway to being level with her shoulder that Coulson and Vargas spotted what Thyme was doing. The Old Man's microphone picked up Coulson's warning shout. "Gun!"

Vargas was instantly in front of Grael. Coulson, who was unarmed, spun out of the way, while the escort in back of them raised their weapons. Thyme's voice was still fragile but also grimly determined. "Why don't you bastards all just go away and leave me alone with Victor?"

The 9mm Glock was Thyme Bridewell's only tangible reality—metal and plastic, hard and in focus—when all else was blurred and unreal, a whirlpool of fragments and a world turned wholly upside down. Her voice was still fragile but, at the same time, grimly determined. "Why don't you bastards all just go away and leave me alone with Victor?"

All of her concentration was required to aim the weapon at the Old Man, but Vargas was shielding him with his body. Had she expected otherwise? Vargas, the human rottweiler, would always take a bullet for his master. A part of the director's black-and-gold kimono still showed, though, and she drew a bead on that. She recognized the kimono. She had seen him wearing it before. Indeed, she had seen him slip the garment off his shoulders to reveal a body so deformed by age it looked hardly human, more like something out of a tank of formaldehyde or an alien autopsy. Fortunately, that one time the Old Man had revealed himself in decrepit undress, another woman, the one they called Lara, who had vanished soon afterwards, was the primary recipient of his erotic attentions. Thyme had only acted as one of the secondary companions whose roles were limited to looking pretty and pornographic and helping where they could while he acted out his gasping reptilian fantasies.

The act of aiming the weapon increased Thyme's area of focus. Now a precise line was drawn from her eye to the front sight of the pistol, and on to the portion of the Old Man's shoulder that was exposed behind Vargas. Within that linear projection, the hallucinatory haze was gone, and all was sharp, precise, simple, and real. With the target acquired, and without losing her aim, she reached around with her free hand, seeking a second of the three guns by touch alone. Again her fingers felt metal, and she grasped the piece. Thyme was aware that the idea of rising to her feet stark naked, and with a Glock in each hand, was, to say the least, overtheatrical, and probably well within the outer bounds of madness. Something inside her had definitely snapped. She had accepted a lifetime of abusive insanity from the Old Man and his kind, and it was time to take her stand, to make her play. She might be going to her own death, or an entire new world of pain, but she was determined to put fear, if not a serious hurt, on Grael and those around him. She had the second gun. Now if she could just get to her feet without swaying, losing her balance, or fainting, she would be in reach of achieving her goal.

As Thyme steeled herself to stand, Coulson took the microphone from the Old Man. "Renquist, do you have any control over that woman?"

That Jack Coulson should be talking to Renquist and not her, even though, during one of his previous visits to Deerpark, they had been lovers, plainly indicated to Thyme that he knew she was beyond any appeal to reason. If she hadn't irrationally loved Renquist already, she might have fallen for the cool nonchalance of his response. "None whatsoever, Jack. Surely she's one of yours. Perhaps she's angry that she was sent to me like a packed lunch."

Thyme knew she had to remind herself at regular intervals that Renquist was a nosferatu and not a man, that the allure was either an imposed illusion or the projection of her own willingness to do anything for him if he only would give her the gift of immortality. They had trained her as a whore, so why should she not act the part now that she was confronted by the greatest payoff imaginable? Whores, however, had to be circumspect and not fall in love.

Coulson spoke again, and Thyme was pleased to hear that he was treating her as a worthy threat. "You know we could be teetering on the edge of a burst of uncontrolled gunfire?"

Renquist actually laughed. "Why so alarmed, Coulson? The Plexiglas is surely bulletproof?"

"In theory she could keep shooting until it exploded or shattered."

And, indeed, that had been Thyme's original plan insofar as she'd had one at all. The NSA-FEMA issue Glock 9mm autos came with the now-illegal seventeen-round clip, and twenty-eight impacts surely should be enough to blow out the transparent wall. After an almost impossible effort, she was on her feet. She felt Renquist's glance as he looked at her for the first time. She could sense his approval, and, despite herself, she delighted in it. She felt thin and strong, a reed now reinforced, and she silently brandished her pistols, posing like a demented work by the sculptor Erte.

"How can we discuss anything when you have a naked woman with a gun in each hand beside you?"

Thyme had seen the scrawny hand of the Old Man gesture for the microphone, and she'd seen Coulson hand it to him. Nonetheless, when his voice came over the speakers, she all but lost her poise. One of the changes wrought by the night's experience was that her long-smoldering hatred for Director Grael had flared up into a potentially lethal rage, but that didn't mean she wasn't still fearful of him. Fortunately, Renquist's fast answer covered her tremor. "How can we discuss anything when I am sealed in a giant aquarium with this naked woman? I believe we have reached the impasse again, but now it's a standoff."

When Grael replied, Thyme was chilled by how advanced the madness in the Old Man's voice had become. "So what would you suggest, Renquist? Nothing can be done while she stands there like some art deco *Nude with Pistols*."

Three random vectors of destruction had Jack Coulson all but triangulated, causing him to reflect how suicide wasn't in his job description. The Old Man was artificially stimulated to somewhere far out of his already hyper gourd; Thyme Bridewell had clearly lapsed into total insanity after being handed to the vampire; and Renquist, of course, wasn't even human. The worst part was that he couldn't see any way to extricate himself. The director appeared hellbent on confronting Renquist, and Coulson was irrevocably locked into the terms of the confrontation. He could never understand why men like Grael hired men like him as advisors and facilitators, then completely ignored their advice. The whole party was now crouched low, and Coulson eased himself in beside the Old Man. "Can I try talking to Thyme?"

Surprisingly, Grael passed him the microphone without question or argument. "Do what you can."

Coulson took a deep breath to calm himself and spoke into the mike with the fake equanimity of a hostage negotiator. "Put the gun down please, Thyme."

"I can't do that, Jack."

"Why not?"

"Willingness to go out in a blaze of glory is the only asset I have left."

Behind Coulson, the Old Man muttered angrily. "At least have her put some fucking clothes on."

Coulson ignored him and switched his attention to Renquist. "Can't you do anything about this?"

Renquist seemed unperturbed. "Why should I, Coulson? You have, after all, just attempted to destroy me. I had an idea earlier that I could trust you, but now I see there's no possibility of that."

"Thyme, would you put down your guns if Renquist asked you to?"

If anything, Thyme Bridewell held her weapons more stiffly and with less compromise. "Let him ask. It's the only way you'll find out."

"Renquist?"

"I'm sorry, Coulson, but why would I want to do that?"

"Suppose I were to offer an inducement?"

Coulson had been present at a number of standoffs, including what he considered the big one, the FBI's Mt. Zion debacle at Waco, and he was well aware that those engaged in them were frequently pressed to extremes of attitude, resorting either to infantile demands or pedantic observations. He was somewhat heartened when Renquist went for the second choice. "That's really the nature of an inducement, isn't it? That it should be worthy of consideration?"

Coulson smiled. Renquist was playing the game, at least opening a window to the possibility of a negotiated resolution. "Why don't you save some time? Just tell me what you want."

"What does any prisoner want?"

"I don't know, Renquist, what does any prisoner want?"

"To cease to be a prisoner, Coulson, to cease to be a prisoner."

"Are you suggesting you simply be set free?"

Renquist laughed. "Yes, of course. That would be ideal. Just return me to the Watergate, and we'll forget the whole thing. But I doubt that's going to happen. On your side, institutional paranoia is going to rule it out, and, for my part, I'm not going to forget. My pride isn't going to allow me to rest comfortably until I know why you felt the need to take me in the first place."

If Renquist's history was even close to what was claimed in his NSA-FEMA jacket, he had been making deals with the hardest of men, in half the hot spots of Europe and the Middle East, along an unbelievable thousand-year time line. This walking nightmare had seen the Crusades, and the Thirty Years' War, and the Holocaust. Forget the vampire's repertoire of superhuman powers; he could hardly have lived for as long as was claimed, or been undead, or whatever the terminology was, if he wasn't a master manipulator and virtuoso horse trader. It was no disgrace for Coulson to bow to a reputed millennium of experience and let Renquist make the running. "So? What do you suggest?"

"Defuse this in easy stages."

"Easy stages to what?"

"To the point that you humans stop probing, testing, and observing, and accord me the respect of telling the truth about why and for what you've brought me here."

"And what would be the first stage?"

"For you to tell the men behind you to lower their weapons and move out."

"I can hardly do that. I have the safety of the director to consider."

"He can keep Vargas with him."

Before Coulson could reply, the Old Man was already

snapping his fingers impatiently. "Give me the damned microphone."

Coulson handed it over without a word. He was past arguing with Grael.

"Renquist, this is Grael. I'm ordering my men out."

"Thank you, Director, you won't regret this."

Grael gestured to Vargas, cupping the microphone with his hand so Renquist couldn't hear him. "Get them to lower their weapons and move out into the corridor, but make sure they don't go too far."

Vargas relayed the order. The men complied, but demonstrated they weren't total robots by exchanging baffled and uneasy glances. As they filed out, a part of Coulson wanted to leave with the guards. Screw his fee. He'd forfeit it. This farce had gone on long enough, and he wanted out. Unfortunately, a misplaced sense of duty insisted he remain beside the Old Man. The Old Man removed the muffling hand from the microphone. "Now tell Miss Bridewell to put down her pistols."

Coulson watched tensely as Renquist turned to Thyme. "Can you do that?"

"I'd still rather blow the bastard away."

"I fear that would be a short-lived gratification."

"How do I know I won't be taken down the moment I lower my guns?"

"You're going to have to trust me to handle this."

"Trust you? You're asking me to trust you?"

Coulson couldn't help his own half smile of respect, as Renquist laughed ruefully and shook his head. "No, I'm not asking you to trust me. I'm just asking you to put your guns down."

*   *   *

"What do you think I've being doing for close to a millennium, my friend? Stalking young women and bringing babies home to the damned castle in a burlap sack? Be real. I am an active and highly motivated creature, with resources, skills, and natural attributes absurdly distant from any point of human comprehension. If you are seeking to recruit me to your cause or conspiracy, it will not be the first time such a thing has been tried. I am hardly a blushing virgin in that respect. Your own dossier on me offers a catalogue of my more illustrious former employers. I believe it speaks for itself despite being highly incomplete."

Renquist closed on the verge of anger, and yet the humans seemed too slow-witted to realize it or contemplate how little they would enjoy that anger when it came. They had made a deal. The armed guards had been withdrawn. Thyme had put down her guns, and, waiting only for her to slip into her bathrobe again, Renquist had gone to the airlock of the pod. Coulson worked the keycard, and Renquist emerged, followed by the reluctant Thyme. The next phase was smooth and civilized. With the armed guards maintaining a discreet distance, they had been moved to the room they now occupied. It was a comfortable and well-appointed combination of conference room and small viewing cinema, in which rather luxurious swivel reclining chairs formed a loose semicircle around a 120-inch, high-definition screen. Subsequently, he would learn it was designated a briefing room.

As they entered, Grael took up a position in what had to be the command chair, so defined by the assortment of controls built into the armrests, and his first act as captain was to push a button to summon an aging servant to take orders for drinks. The man was a ramrod-stiff, pensioned-off mercenary with an eye patch, and an immaculate white mess jacket. The American secret government liked its comfort as it fought its invisible wars and managed its empire-with-no-name. Coulson ordered coffee and brandy, Grael one of his serial cognacs. Both looked at Renquist to see what he would do.

"I drink . . . vodka. Frozen, straight up, please."

That was indeed the truth. Although Renquist's metabolism was such that he could not experience anything approaching human intoxication, he could derive a certain pleasing shudder from the impact of the cold harsh liquor, and, of course, Renquist also knew the best way to disarm a human was to drink with him.

Thyme smiled at the servant as if she knew him well. "I'll have vodka, too, Hemple, but I want mine as part of a very spicy Bloody Mary, and put a large stick of celery in it." She rose to her feet and indicated she was still in her bathrobe. "If you gentlemen will excuse me, I think I'll get dressed while the drinks come."

Coulson glanced up. "There's really no need for you to come back. Go to your room and we'll speak with you later."

Renquist quickly intervened. "I would prefer it if Ms. Bridewell returned." He didn't want them separated just then. Fresh darklost could be unpredictable, and he preferred Thyme where he could watch her. Coulson was about to put up some kind of objection, but Grael merely beamed. "Hurry back, my dear. Look decorative. Victor Renquist seems to have taken a shine to you."

Thyme laughed with complete insincerity. "I'll be back with the drinks."

In that, she was not only as good as her word, but when she returned, directly in the wake of Hemple and his tray of drinks, she was totally transformed. Her dark hair was brushed out, and she was made up for dramatic effect — 1940s-style silk lounging pajamas clinging to her narrow body, as she swayed like a model on Lucite mules with matching feathers. A velvet choker was around her neck, hiding Renquist's bladework, and he was mystified at how she had achieved so much in so short a time. Nosferatu females could take forever on their looks, being forced as they were to employ various wiles and devices to overcome their lack of mirror reflections. She smiled brightly as, just inside the doorway, she moved around Hemple and lifted her glass from the tray. "My Bloody Mary, how wonderful." She then went to a couch in the back of the room, away from the screen and the discussions of the men, and draped herself dutifully. Only the brightness in her eyes gave away that she was focused and alert.

While Hemple handed round the rest of the drinks, Renquist made the mistake of looking into the man's mind and discovered a loyalty so intense that even he shouldn't have invaded its privacy. The servant would kill anything that threatened the director and, right at that moment, Renquist was right up there on the enemies list with the doddering Fidel Castro. Renquist was reminded how Grael hadn't always been ancient and unstable. There could well have been a time when he cut a dangerous dash. Such loyalty was only engendered by some shared semblance of combat, and Renquist withdrew from Hemple's mind before the intrusion was noticed. He saw that Grael and Coulson were once again watching him. Earlier they had waited to hear what he would order, now they were waiting to see him drink it. Renquist picked up the chilled glass, observed that it was a double, if not a treble, raised it in semitoast, and drank it down. He took a deep breath while savoring the effect,

then looked at the two humans with barely concealed
mockery. "So, gentleman, to business?"

A game pattern was starting to emerge in the way that
Grael and Coulson were dealing with him, but Renquist
theorized that it was more a product of familiarity with
each other and past habit than a rehearsed and preordained
plan. Coulson played his hand carefully and methodically,
not hurrying matters, and, at times, frustrating Renquist by
holding back information and generally delaying progress
toward any kind of conclusion. Grael, on the other hand,
maintained the forward momentum in his own peculiar
way. He would keep quiet for long periods of time, then
suddenly interpose a tangential leap, as when he'd resolved
the standoff with Thyme by capriciously acquiescing.

Renquist could only suppose it had been Grael who had
ordered the attack on him by the three Salvadorans, and
Coulson had probably opposed it. He could only hope that
Grael would save time by making a few of his unpredictable
course changes in quick succession. The briefing room
could only have been chosen because some form of show-
and-tell was intended, an eventual revelation of secrets complete with video visual aids, and Renquist wished the pair
would get to that stage without further delay. His sleep
had been interrupted twice, and he was beginning to feel
the resulting fatigue.

The great temptation was to rip into the minds of the
two of them and cut his way directly to the root of what
was behind his capture and imprisonment. Having looked
at the outer thoughts of both Grael and Coulson, he knew
that each, in his own individual way, would be able to block
all but the most devastating psychic violence. Furthermore,
he was far too vulnerable, confined as he was in Deerpark,
to attempt that kind of direct assault. Renquist might be

powerful, but he was neither invincible nor omnipotent. He wasn't going to be able to fight his way out of the facility single-handedly, past all the assembled operatives, agents, spooks, armed guards, and automated electronic security, without being finally and fatally taken down. He really had no choice but to go along with Coulson and the director and let them play out the game.

"Does the word *Pelucidar* mean anything to you?"

The question came out of nowhere. Grael had made another of his surprise jumps. Thyme had been chewing on the celery from her Bloody Mary, but now she looked at Renquist to see how he might react. He hid his surprise as well as he was able. "Yes. I haven't heard it used in quite a long time, but isn't it one of the names for the supposed Hollow Earth?"

"*Agharta?*"

"Another of the same?"

"*Nagaloka?*"

"I believe that's the Hindu name for it."

Now Coulson joined in. "You called it 'the supposed Hollow Earth.' Does that mean you don't believe in such a thing?"

Renquist shrugged. "When I think of such a thing, which is not often, I suppose I keep an open mind. I've never been in a situation where Hollow Earth theories had any practical import."

"Suppose you were in such a situation?"

"I guess I would search for a way to deal with it, at least learn the truth as best I could. Why? Am I in such a situation?"

Grael sipped his cognac. "I'd like you to look at something." He switched the glass to his left hand and tapped a command sequence into a keypad in the arm of his chair.

The lights dimmed, and the screen flickered into life. "I would advise you to watch this at least once through without comment."

A plain title appeared, white sans serif letters out of a black background that read—"NEUSCHWABENLAND, November 5, 1947." The image that followed was a grainy daylight snowscape, also in black and white, filmed by what appeared to be a handheld newsreel camera contemporary with the date in the title. It came without sound, which added an eerie archaic quality in a world accustomed to even their home videos coming with audio and living color. For some fifteen seconds the screen showed nothing but a pristine snowfield stretching to what looked to be smudgy, unfocused mountains or hills forming a distant horizon. Then the anonymous cameraman made an awkward turn and the cargo door of a World War II-vintage DC-3 came into medium close-up. A crew of ski troops, muffled against extreme cold, manhandled boxes and bales out of the plane with a sense of great urgency. The camera abruptly panned again. The cameraman must have heard the second DC-3 coming in to land. Its was rigged with giant skis for a snow landing. The sky was clear, visibility good, and another aircraft was on a descent path, some way behind, still high in the middle distance.

A sudden cut moved the filmed sequence up in time. A number of DC-3s were on the ground unloading men and cargo, but this was rapidly interrupted by confusion and camera shake, as if something sudden and violent had taken the cameraman completely by surprise. Images jumbled as he turned and searched, then he focused on one of the recently landed cargo planes, which was now skewed off its skis and burning, and the men who fled from it, some with their clothes on fire. Confusion and panic intruded on the foreground, and the camera was again jostled. The camera-man seemed to be searching for something in the air, but when he found it, it was nothing more than a dark, out-of-focus ovoid.

Another cut, and the thing in the sky was revealed, this time in considerably more detail. The size was hard to gauge without reference points, but it was a flying machine, circular, like an inverted soup plate, with an unidentifiable mechanism on the underside, and a domed superstructure of armored greenhouse glass. The thing was coming almost straight at the camera, and its Iron Cross markings were plainly visible. Flashes of some kind of projectile fire came from two points of the superstructure as though it was on a strafing run. As it passed over his head, the cameraman tried to pan with it, but lost the image. The picture went through a violent shaking and then spiraled, as though the camera had been dropped or thrown while still rolling, and had continued to run for a short time while lying on its side. Smoke drifted past the lens, distorting fleeing figures, and finally the screen abruptly went black. That was seem-ingly the end of the tape, because Grael then restored the lights, and cut the projection. "What you saw was the very last engagement between the Allies and the Third Reich. In which we were handed our hats."

Renquist raised an eyebrow. "In 1947?"

Grael said nothing. Renquist nodded. He began to see where this might all be going. In the immediate aftermath of World War II, he had spent a little time in Buenos Aires, as a guest of Juan and Eva Perón, although the charismatic, if megalomaniac, human couple had no idea who or what he really was. Former Nazis were coming to town by every means of conveyance from cruise ship to U-boat, and with them all the gold, diamonds, art treasures, opium, and

Swiss francs they had squirreled away against the fall of their *führer*. Argentine society was in something close to meltdown, with political murders nightly, and Perón's "shirtless-ones" constantly on the rampage. For a nosferatu it was a custom-crafted paradise.

Most of the Nazis that came through had given up the cause and were looking for nothing more than a bolt-hole in which to hide: but rumors abounded of the more fanatic heading north for Brazil and into the Mato Grosso to re-group and contemplate revenge far from the eyes of civilization. Wilder stories also circulated about others who had gone south with weapons or heavy equipment to set up a permanent base in Antarctica. Renquist had assumed that, had there been so much as a grain of truth to the story, they would have frozen to death by the first winter. Then, some two years later, he heard the softest whisper that some kind of Allied task force had gone in to clean them out.

Grael confirmed it without Renquist needing to ask. "It was called Operation Highjump."

"Nineteen forty-seven?"

"That's right. It was a task force led by Admirals Byrd, Nimitz, and Krusen aboard the aircraft carrier the USS *Philippine Sea*. In addition to the carrier, there were the destroyers *Brownsen* and *Henderson*, the submarine *Sennet*, plus support and supply ships. The DC-3s you saw were rigged with JATO bottles to get them off the deck of the *Philippine Sea*."

"JATO?"

"Jet-assisted takeoff."

"Ah."

Coulson added another detail. "Secretary of the Navy James Forrestal was also along for the ride."

That did take Renquist by surprise. "The same James

Forrestal who was supposedly thrown out of a window of the mental ward of Bethesda Naval Hospital?"

"The very same."

"I thought he was murdered for attempting to go public on CIA covert operations?"

"Forrestal wanted to go public with a lot of stuff."

"And I presume that film was a vignette of Highjump getting started."

"That's correct."

"And what was the thing in the sky?"

"A flying saucer."

Thyme looked up. Now all the humans were watching his reaction. He treated them a calculated display of mild surprise. "That was what it looked like. A *Nazi* flying saucer?"

Grael nodded. "The *Flugelrad*, also known as the *Flugkriesel*. The prototype was constructed in a factory attached to Mauhausen Concentration Camp, by a team led by Viktor Schauberger using the liquid vortex propulsion unit designed by Rudolf Schreiver. How ten production models got to Antarctica is still a mystery, but they did, and they proved more than enough to rout Byrd and his boys."

Renquist held up a hand. "Hold it a moment. Is this the Admiral Byrd who was supposed to have flown over the North Pole in the twenties, and seen some kind of huge hidden fissure obscured by clouds?"

"Again the same one."

"Some strange company being kept here. Didn't he, too, have to be muzzled at some point?"

Grael made a regretful, couldn't-be-helped gesture. "There was a lot of muzzling. When the remains of Highjump limped back to Norfolk, the first reaction was that we should fuel up the Flying Wing and go back and nuke the bastards. Unfortunately, Hiroshima and Nagasaki were still quite warm, and President Truman was decidedly less than keen. The geophysicists would have screamed bloody murder if we'd let off a nuclear blast in the Antarctic, and there was also the problem that an atom bomb might not have worked at all."

"Why not?"

"Because the sons of bitches hadn't set up a base on Antarctica. They were under Antarctica. They'd made their way down into the Hollow Earth."

Thyme didn't care much for the history lesson. Some of it she already knew, and the rest she treated on a need-to-know basis. Coulson and the director were teaming Renquist, he understood that, but he was taking it, because he had little or no choice. Thyme Bridewell was aware that Renquist could do things no human could even attempt; but she was also familiar with Deerpark, and for him to make any kind of stand against the Old Man would be about as futile as her facing him down, naked, with two pistols. She at least had the excuse that she was abused, burned out, and crazy. Renquist wasn't crazy, so he had to be biding his time. She hadn't heard too much of this Hollow Earth stuff before, and she didn't have a clue whether it was true or not, and hardly cared. Inside Deerpark, truth was such a relative commodity that Thyme hung little importance on it. Maybe there were Nazis or worse burrowing beneath the crust of the planet, or maybe there weren't. On the level that Thyme functioned, it made very little difference. The entire intelligence community had been forged and fabricated out of threatening shadow-shapes and paranoid fantasies, and everything went at least double inside of Deerpark. To attempt to sort the real from the imaginary wasted time and was wholly without profit.

The piece of film had looked reasonably authentic, but to phoney up that kind of documentation was child's play. The trick that Thyme, along with most other black-op operatives, had long ago learned was not to bother with truth, even as a concept. You accepted it, but, at the same time, you didn't believe a word of it. That way you stayed maybe halfway sane for a while, and still managed to keep with whatever program to which you found yourself drafted. Victor Renquist was clearly being drafted, and, for her, the Hollow Earth preamble only served to indicate that they wanted to deploy and use him in a deeply bad place.

In the old days, when she sat in on these briefings, dutifully playing the role of the decorative and apparently mindless party slut, her task was either to lure the pigeon in the first place or work as the pigeon's handler during the job. The ramifications of a plan had little interest for her. She merely played her part, doing what she was instructed to do, on time and on cue. Unfortunately, since her encounter with Renquist, one thing had changed. She still didn't give a damn about the Old Man's elaborate machinations. She still didn't want to know about the plots and schemes or the extensive backgrounds that went with them, but she had become supremely interested in Victor Renquist.

Thyme doubted she was included in whatever mission Renquist was being pitched into, but she was determined to make herself a part of it. Persuading either Coulson or the Old Man of that was so far out of the question she hardly needed to consider it. Her best chance was to manipulate Renquist into declaring her indispensable. Maybe

later, the Old Man might accept her as an integral part of
the bargain, but in the meantime she had to concentrate
on winning over the nosferatu. And the fastest way to do
that was to learn everything there was to know about him.
Fuck the script, concentrate on the characters. She had noticed the file immediately as they had walked in the door
of the briefing room but had refrained from either com-
menting or letting anyone notice her interest in it. The blue
loose-leaf binder, with red eyes only stickers, and the NSA-
FEMA logos, was almost certainly Renquist's jacket. During the showing of the film, she had surreptitiously moved
it so it was closer to her. Now the two men and the vampire
seemed completely absorbed in their metaphysical poker
game, she picked it up, quietly, and with all the casual lack
of concern of a woman idly leafing through a copy of *Vogue*
because the men in the room were both boring and ignor-
ing her. One thing she'd learned from the nuns was how
to read well in bad light and, since Renquist had had his
way with her, for some reason she didn't quite understand,
she saw even better.

Renquist ran a pensive index finger round the rim of his
empty vodka glass. "So if you couldn't use atomic weapons
on them, what could you do?"

"Why, my dear Renquist, we cut a deal."

As the Old Man answered, Coulson noted that Renquist
was taking this all very much in his stride, but then he had
to remind himself that Renquist wasn't human. The hand-
some and urbane exterior was so damned deceptive. Why
shouldn't he believe their story? Wasn't he, and all of those
like him, themselves the subject of disbelief and skepticism?

"A deal?"

"In a nutshell, they stayed below and we stayed above."

"That hardly seems credible."

"They weren't Communists, and that's pretty much all that counted in those days."

Renquist still seemed less than convinced. As a political thinker he was astute, but with two obvious weaknesses; he tended to overestimate human levels of cunning and not allow for the sometimes deep and brutal stupidity of fools with power.

"Some strange alliances were formed in the name of fighting Communism, but this . . ."

"Defies all strangeness. Don't forget that there were only a few of them and a great many of us. For them to come out and threaten us would have proved fatal, even if they had developed some very advanced technology."

"Like the *Flugelrad*?"

"Like the *Flugelrad*. Which made it also fatal for us to attempt to winkle them out. You also have to remember that they needed things from us. Machine tools, fabrics, pharmaceuticals, luxury goods; cigarettes and nylons, you name it. They might be setting up an underground empire to last a thousand years, but they still needed the stuff they'd become used to and took for granted, up here."

Coulson remembered there had been something in Renquist's file. A note from de Richleau's archives about how de Richleau and Churchill had exhibited some merriment at the news that Hitler had hundreds of crack mountain troops of the Waffen SS climbing all over Tibet searching for the entrance to the Hollow Earth. What he didn't know was that they had, in fact, not only found it, but mapped a number of others before 1945. He looked round for the file to see if he could find the item, but discovered that Thyme Bridewell was leafing through it. She looked up and made a dumb-show gesture. What did he expect? Coulson decided to say nothing. He probably owed Thyme that much. Neither the Old Man or Renquist had noticed. They were deep in Underland.

"So a bargain was struck?"

Grael smiled. "Probably regrettable, but yes."

"And it held?"

"More or less. Their *Flugelrads* came out pretty regularly and were mistaken for alien spacecraft. We shot some of them down, and they blew up some of our aircraft, but more talks were held, and we put a stop to that, although they still buzzed commercial airliners now and again. And there was nothing we could do about the abductions. The real rule was that they didn't hit any ground targets, and we didn't go subterranean. Both sides pretty much adhered to that. There was the unfortunate incident at the Bentwaters Air Base in England, and, of course, the major fuckup that caused the New York City blackout, and the oil companies made some tries at infiltrating below, but, by and large, coexistence was managed."

"So what changed?"

The Old Man raised an eyebrow. "Changed? What makes you think things changed?"

"If the situation had continued to remain stable, you certainly wouldn't be telling me all about it."

Coulson took a certain pleasure in the way Renquist seemed to let nothing get past him. For their first vampire in captivity, they had themselves a distinguished specimen. The creature could have been some drooling, blood-drinking nocturnal cretin, but they had pulled in a thoroughbred on their first try, and all might actually be well if he didn't ultimately prove too smart for them. The Old Man was less pleased at the way Renquist had short-circuited his lecture. His face darkened, and he rang for

Hemple before answering. He obviously needed more cognac. *How the hell much was the director currently drinking, on top of all the life-prolonging, meds?*

"You're right, of course, things have changed. However the Underlanders might have started out, they're now the Mole People."

"The Underlanders?"

"That's what they called themselves. In the early days it was easy. They were Nazis, and we'd been fighting them for five years. We understood each other, and if there was a problem, we could bring in some of the old Gehlen Group, the Operation Paper Clip Nazis from Langley as advisors and mediators. There were enough former SS, Abwehr, and Gestapo in the CIA back in the forties and fifties for everyone to just about speak the same language."

Renquist nodded. "But humans grow old. New generations take over."

"Indeed they do, Renquist. Indeed they do."

The hunger that Renquist had observed when he'd first seen Grael now completely suffused the director's aura. Up close he could see that it was a very primal and desperate hunger for life, completely driven by an equal and opposite obsessive terror of death. Grael feared death in the worst of grand manners. Since his fifties, he had been hagridden by the classic dread of mortal egomaniacs, the dread that compelled kings and countesses to hire alchemists or bathe in the blood of virgins, and billionaires to retreat into climate-controlled plastic bubbles, racked with germ phobia. The director saw death as a vast and infinite emptiness in which he'd find himself screaming and alone for all eternity. The hunger was also tinged with envy. Renquist had the immortality that Grael wanted so badly, and that envy would eventually override all other considerations. Despite all that was being discussed, Renquist knew the director's hunger would spawn any number of underlying agendas, and he should guard himself accordingly.

"So what is this new generation of Underlanders like?"

Coulson was the one who admitted the weakness. "That's the problem, we don't know."

"You don't know?"

Grael resumed his interrupted lecture. "Since the early nineties, communications have made less and less sense. First they became strange and then stranger. It was as though we were no longer relating to human beings as we knew them. The Old Guard, the original Neuschwabenland Nazis, held on to power for far too long. Dissent was savagely repressed, and it started to resemble North Korea down there. In addition, as far as we could tell from some of the stuff that was being shipped to them, a widespread program of genetic experimentation had been going on. We believe that around 1997, some kind of uprising occurred, and shortly after all contact broke down."

"That was during the Clinton administration?"

"Right."

"And did Clinton have a policy on them?

"Clinton didn't know about them."

"Anything about them?"

Grael looked at Coulson, but Coulson wasn't going to field this one, and he had to respond himself. "Since Reagan, the president hasn't been included in that particular loop. This is strictly nonaccountable, deepest black budget material."

Renquist wasn't in the least surprised. "Too delicate to be trusted to politicians?"

"Far too delicate. Especially for that politician. He had

little sympathy for our work at the best of times. He would have certainly have attempted to do a John Kennedy on us, except it had been made clear to him from the start how, in that eventuality, we would have done a John Kennedy right back on him."

Before Grael could elaborate further on the threatening of Bill Clinton, Hemple arrived with a fresh round of drinks. Although Renquist hadn't asked for and didn't need one, he found himself with another frozen vodka, which he held on to, maintaining the illusion of being one of the boys.

"Do you know anything at all about these modern Mole People? Surely there must still be some flow of consumer goods at the very least?"

Grael nodded. "Some trade continues. Lately, the Chinese had been sending them a load of illegal software and microprocessors, but the Underlanders now shun all but the most minimal of direct contact, even with the boys from Beijing."

Coulson added an addendum. "The most we can glean is that not only have some strange things been happening among the Underlanders, but they've been using their *Flugelrads* to gather up some . . . how should I put it . . ."

Grael provided the word. "Some very exotic individuals have been taken down there in the last few years."

"Kidnapping?"

"Kidnapping or recruitment. Probably a combination of both."

"What kind of exotic individuals?"

Grael seemed to feel it was of little importance. "Who knows? Serbian Chetniks, Tibetan Serpent Cultists, on-the-run Hawk Colonels, gunmen from the Aum Shrinrikyo, defectors of all kinds."

Thyme asked no one in particular. "So scum sinks rather than rises?"

"Charles Manson wanted to hide in the Deep Pit in Death Valley, but he couldn't find it."

Coulson eyed Renquist carefully over his brandy snifter. "It's possible some of your kind may be down there."

Without breaking into his mind, Renquist couldn't tell if Coulson was telling the truth on this last point. Renquist had noticed that Coulson lied only when he needed to, and he did it very well. He seemed to be a man who believed lies should not be wasted on trivia. From the scanty description, this Underland might be a place to attract an immigration of nosferatu, but it sounded a little too pat, too calculated to pique Renquist's interest. He knew the bait was being dangled in front of him. Rather than snap at it, he called, if not their bluff, at least their procrastination.

"Am I right in thinking that all this is building to the conclusion that you want me, one way or another, to go down into the Underland?"

When Hemple arrived with the second round of drinks, Thyme had put down Renquist's file and acted girlish and delighted at a second Bloody Mary, as if it was all her little alcoholic pea brain could desire. Coulson had already caught her going through the dossier, but to his credit he had said nothing. Then Renquist had asked if it was the plan for him to go down into Underland and she immediately began to take notice. Instead of answering Renquist directly, the Old Man had slowly turned and looked at Coulson. "Our friend here really likes to cut to the heart of things."

Renquist's eyes glittered, and, aside from giving Thyme something of a chill thrill, it made it clear to her that the Old Man hadn't done himself any favors with this less-than-respectful aside. "And what is the heart of things?"

The Old Man compounded his discourtesy. "Yes, Renquist, you have discovered our agenda. We want you to go down into Underland and come back with a detailed report of the situation down there."

Thyme waited, along with Coulson and Grael, while Renquist gave himself a moment by throwing back half of his second vodka. "On one level I find the prospect of an expedition to a place I never knew existed outside of legend quite fascinating. On the other hand, I find the delivery of your proposition less than acceptable. You really could have met me in a Washington restaurant and put the idea to me over drinks or dinner and saved all the *Sturm und Drang*."

"*Sturm und Drang?*"

"We're dealing with the offspring of Nazis aren't we? I'm merely seeking appropriate language."

"So you'd have no real objection to performing such a service for us."

Renquist made a dismissive gesture. "If I had an objection, would it really make any difference? Your behavior so far suggests I have no choice in the matter."

Thyme decided she'd been quiet long enough, and it was time for her to throw her nine cents into the machinations. "Victor . . ."

Renquist swiveled in his chair and faced her. "Thyme?"

"There's something you might want to consider."

"What's that?"

"If they're doing something as outlandish as recruiting you to go down into this place, they have to be desperate.

They must have already tried it with regular operatives. Ask them how many earlier teams they've sent in, then ask what the fuck happened to them?"

Now she not only had Renquist's attention, but Coulson and the Old Man had turned to look at her. She could see the Old Man's ire rising although he kept his voice deceptively calm. "You're not being particularly helpful, my dear."

Renquist immediately came to her defense. "I disagree. It sounds like a highly germane question." Thyme found herself basking in his approval, but fuck, what was the matter with her? She hadn't acted like this over a man in years, but, then again, Renquist wasn't a man. "How many others have you sent in?"

Grael glanced at Coulson. Coulson took an uncomfortable breath. "There were two other insertions."

"And what *did* happen to them?"

Coulson tossed the ball to the Old Man. "You want to answer that, Director?"

The Old Man didn't know whether to direct his anger at Thyme or Coulson. Thyme would have laughed except she knew it might push him over the edge. "The first team vanished without trace. We believe the second defected to the Underlanders."

"And you believe a nosferatu can do better?"

"Your special capabilities could help you function better in that place."

Now Thyme couldn't help herself. She laughed out loud. "And if you vanish like the others, the Old Man can deny the whole thing."

"Damn you, woman. Get out of here. We don't need your smart mouth."

Again Renquist stood by her. "I'd still prefer it if she stayed."

"Look, Renquist . . ."

An intangible darkness seemed to gather around the nosferatu, and for the very first time in their long acquaintance, she saw the Old Man afraid of something.

"I would prefer it if she stayed."

The Old Man recovered himself and waved an angry but nonetheless yielding hand. "Keep her. Let her stay. She's yours."

Thyme grinned. "You hear him, Victor? I'm yours now. I've been passed from hand to hand to hand in this place for as long as I can remember, but now I'm yours."

"Am I expected to go to this Underland alone?"

Renquist had allowed Thyme her fun with Coulson, but now it was time to get back to business. Grael was still furious at him for insisting that Bridewell stayed, and refused to look at him. Coulson answered instead. "No, you won't be alone."

"Who else will be with me?"

"I will."

"Just the two of us?"

"We'd have a small detachment of trained personnel with us."

"All human?"

"Of course."

Renquist had expected Thyme to remain quiet for a while after almost being thrown out of the briefing, but she seemed to have the bit between her teeth, and again her interruption was right to the point. "I'm still not quite clear what talents Victor has to equip him for an expedition to

Underland. Is it because he can see in the dark, or his strength, or are you just looking to fight evil with evil?"

Grael rounded angrily at Renquist. "You still insist on her remaining?"

Renquist actually smiled. "Now even more so. She seems to have my best interests close to her heart. Why *do* you view me as so suitable for this mission?"

Coulson sighed and glanced at the Old Man, who made the slightest gesture of assent. Coulson leaned toward Renquist as though eliciting his confidence. "The truth is that all of the other divisions of NSA-FEMA have run out of road on this. They don't have a clue. If Paranormal Operations and Research can resolve the Underland situation, it'll make this division king of the hill. The catch is that, by definition, POR has to resolve it by some paranormal means. Hence the kidnap of Victor Renquist."

Renquist's expression was both amused and rueful. "So, as with all things in this part of the country, it eventually comes down to raw politics, and the need to look good."

Coulson nodded. "That is one way of putting it."

Grael stared balefully at Renquist. "Looking good is what gets the funding, and we live on funding. Much like you things live on blood."

"So why stop at one nosferatu?"

"What?"

"This mission team will consist of you, me, and a squad of Thompson gunners, am I right?"

Grael grunted. "Thompson gunners. I haven't heard that phrase in a long time. Not since the old days in the Congo."

"I rather like it, even if it is archaic. They may not still carry Thompson, but it seems apt for mercenaries with automatic weapons." Renquist looked from Grael to Coulson and back again. "So, why just one nosferatu?"

"We went to enough trouble to get you. How the hell are we supposed to come up with more?"

"Just give me a telephone. I'll have any number here in less than twenty-four hours."

Grael seemed almost outraged. "That's preposterous."

"Is it? You think we nosferatu aren't in close contact with each other, Director? What makes you assume that only humans are capable of social organization?"

Renquist was growing angry at what seemed to be Grael's willful stupidity. Coulson sensed this and attempted to head off the clash. "It might be worth investigating the possibility."

"That's nonsense, Jack. I don't trust one of them on his own, let alone two or three of the things."

"You know, Director, if you didn't maintain such a cult of secrecy, you might be better informed and not so ready to disrespect me with your ignorance. In my colony there is one called Lupo."

"Lupo?"

"He has done contract work for numerous branches of your so-called intelligence community over a span of years, and his trustworthiness has never been questioned. You will find reference to him in this dossier you have on me, and, if you look farther afield, you will find out a great deal more about him."

"You say his name is Lupo."

"He uses the name Lupo Leomonte at times, also Lupo Rieti. In other contexts, he is Vincent Satrielli. He is also known to the Sicilian Mafia and some sections of law enforcement as Joey Nightshade. I would suggest you start with the FBI central databank and work outward from there. References to Lupo will not be hard to find. Would you like me to spell those names for you."

The director was speechless, so Coulson quickly filled the vacuum. "You can contact this Lupo?"

"Of course I can contact this Lupo. He is one of my closest associates."

Coulson looked at the director. He either needed more medication or considerable rest. "This might be worth the effort of checking it out."

The Old Man's voice suddenly sounded weak. "How do we know this isn't just some vampire subterfuge?"

"We don't, but we still should investigate the matter." He turned to Renquist. "I will see that Lupo is checked out, and then we can talk again."

"Talk again?"

"After we've done our homework."

"Do I understand this session is at an end?"

Coulson nodded. "I believe so. The director appears to be flagging."

"I would like to sleep myself."

Coulson rose from his chair. "I will have someone show you and Thyme to your new accommodation."

Apparently Renquist and Thyme Bridewell were being considered, at least by Coulson, as two halves of some unholy bond. The man was now treating them like a couple, and Renquist wasn't sure how he felt about that. It might have its short-term advantages, but he could also see a tangle of potential complications should such an idea endure for any length of time.

chapter FOUR

B efore the phone call had come from the congressman, Lupo already knew that Renquist had been taken. Where his don was concerned, his empathy was sharp and precise. Their relationship went back so far that when something traumatic happened to one, the other felt it. Even in the Los Angeles Residence, across the width of the continent, Lupo had sensed a strange constriction and knew that Renquist was in trouble and was somehow confined, deprived of his freedom of movement. The congressman had merely filled in some details. The politician's name was Ralph Bendix, and he was one of the handful, both Republican and Democrat, that Lupo either held in personal thrall, or who had made themselves vulnerable to his remorseless blackmail. Lupo had chosen Bendix because of his seat on the House Intelligence Committee. Bendix had no idea of

Lupo's real nature. All he really knew was that Lupo could, with the most minimal effort, ruin him politically and probably send him to jail until he was a very old man. The human would wake in the night sweating at the knowledge that, deposited in some obscure bank vault that he would never be able to locate, a single reel of film and a number of videocassettes waited, like an undiagnosed cancer, to destroy his life.

Bendix would always return Lupo's calls and comply with what ever demands he might make, because the reel of grainy amateur film showed him as a young gung ho army lieutenant in Vietnam, whose warped and bloody enthusiasm had led him to take the leadership role in an atrocity that was garish and excessive, even by the perverse standards of the time. Lupo, of course, had seen far worse in his long, undead existence, but that didn't negate the impact, should the damning clip ever be aired on national television. The close-ups of the youthful Bendix's unhealthy and unmistakable glee were enough to finish him, as he encouraged his men to Zippo the huts, and rape, torture, and slaughter the old men, women, and children who had turned out to be the only inhabitants of the anonymous village a few klicks outside of Tra Vinh in the Mekong Delta. The videocassettes would never air on national TV. They were too raw and explicit to even edit, showing as they did, in graphic detail, cruel, unusual, and far more recent sex parties with perilously young Oriental women. Lupo's grip on Bendix was made even tighter and more intractable by the fact that the massacre and the orgies were psychologically and inseparably linked in the politician's mind. The horror of rape and murder had been so attractively intense that the human had sought over and over, and even taken suicidal risks for one in public office, to relive the vicious excitement.

Bendix had not been able to tell Lupo a great deal about what had happened to Don Victor. The congressman was too scared of Lupo to attempt to lie or not make every possible effort, but he had run into one of the multitude of brick walls that the intelligence community routinely erected to hide their activities. As he succinctly put it. "I swear, I'm doing everything I can, but you know what it's like. They treat us like mushrooms. They keep us in the dark and feed us shit."

"So what did you find out, Bendix? You know my threats are never idle."

"Some kind of flap went down at the Watergate. A SWAT team sealed off an entire floor, and later came out with a prisoner under heavy restraint. At first it was assumed these were regular DC cops or FBI, but when I checked neither knew anything about it, beyond that it had happened."

Thus far, it had sounded completely plausible. Renquist had indeed gone to Washington, on an overdue excursion to consolidate his own political contacts in the nation's capital, and he had been booked into the Watergate, as had been his habit in recent years.

"Did you get anything from the hotel?"

"I put an aide on it, and the individual who was taken away seems to have been registered under the name Van Ryder."

That again had the ring of truth. Lupo knew that Van Ryder was one of his don's traveling aliases, and even if he hadn't, the initials would have been enough to inform him. "Have you discovered who took this Van Ryder?"

Bendix sounded acutely uncomfortable. "That's where the problem starts."

"You are well aware I don't like to hear the word *problem*."

"I know who doesn't have him. I talked to my insiders at Quantico and Langley, and neither the FBI nor CIA is holding this man. Naval Intelligence doesn't have him either."

"So who does?"

"We're getting into some deep shadows here."

"You should be accustomed to deep shadows, Congressman."

Just because Lupo had the film and videos, it didn't mean that Bendix had totally curtailed his more distasteful erotic games. When the need grew too strong to be sublimated or ignored, he still managed to find the courage to placate it.

"There was a whisper."

"A whisper?"

"There's this very weird area where Federal Emergency Management and the National Security Agency overlap."

"NSA-FEMA?"

"You've heard of it."

"You should know by now that little escapes me."

"There seems to be something afoot there."

"Afoot?"

"I really have no details."

"You are starting to disappointment me."

"As far as I can tell, there's been friction."

"Friction?"

"Ever since Mervyn Talesian became the president's new Special National Security Advisor there have been problems. From the very start there was resentment at how he was able to come out of academic nowhere, jump the pecking order, and move into the very center of power, with his own staff and his own office in the White House. The rancor grew worse as it became clear he had the president by the balls, and as the media hailed him as the new foreign relations wonder boy. More than one attempt has been made to unseat him, but he's always ahead of every coup or conspiracy. It seems pretty certain he has his own private intelligence unit, like Henry Kissinger did way back in the Nixon era, which, needless to say, has pissed off the spooks at NSA-FEMA and quite a few others besides."

Lupo's voice was chill and ominous. "You're giving me background, Bendix. I want facts."

Bendix now sounded frozen with fear. "I'm not sure you're going to like the facts."

"Just tell me, and let me be the judge."

"I keep hearing about a unit called the NSA-FEMA Paranormal Operations and Research Facility, both in the context of the arrest of this Van Ryder character and the head-butting with Talesian."

A breathless, frightened silence ensued as Bendix waited for Lupo's reaction, and Lupo allowed him to sweat. Finally, the congressman could stand it no longer. "I'm sorry. You have to believe that the last thing I want to do is disappoint you, but that's all I've been able to come up with. I know it makes no sense, but . . ."

In fact mention of the NSA-FEMA Paranormal Operations and Research Facility made more sense to Lupo than Bendix could ever have imagined, but the human didn't need to know that. From his unique nosferatu perspective, Lupo had been able to observe how paranormal operations were currently enjoying a deeply secret vogue. In part it had been triggered by the discovery that Osama bin Laden and the other terrorist leaders who had followed in his wake had used the dreams of their followers as an aid to mind control. Lupo doubted that Bendix's inquiries would take him very much further, but he wanted to keep the squirming congressman firmly on his merciless hook. In England, London criminals had an expression that Lupo rather enjoyed. They talked about "putting the frighteners" on people. Lupo would conclude by putting the frighteners on Bendix before he hung up on him and left the unfortunate mortal to scuttle and scurry, desperately trying to ferret out information that, by the time it reached Lupo, it would probably be irrelevant.

The notion of "the frighteners" had bulked large in the almost five hundred years that Lupo had survived. He had been created in the time of the Borgias, and had made his nosferatu bones amid the naked blades and baroque intrigues of Italian city-states, and, as the years passed, and his life extended infinitely, it had seemed only reasonable that he should support himself by marketing his undead skills and attributes to the human power structure, such as it might be at any given time. Popes, presidents, and prime ministers, dictators, captains of industry, bankers, beer barons, and racketeers had all employed him as a nocturnal contract killer, and he was especially sought after for the hits that were thought to be impossible. Other nosferatu, the kind who prided themselves on remaining aloof, like a nocturnal aristocracy, tended to look down on Lupo as a compromised, night-stalking mercenary, but Lupo held such elitists in equal contempt for being unable to face reality and often being destroyed because of their practical inadequacy. No itinerant vampire hunter had ever so much as attempted to drive a stake into Lupo. His killer-fearsome reputation and his contacts in the corridors of mortal power had always protected him.

That was why he and Renquist had trusted each other the very first time they'd met. They both appreciated old-fashioned principles and an old-fashioned sense of honor, and, although both where skilled pragmatists, their pragmatism was at least couched in a veneer of chivalry. When Renquist had become Master of the Colony, Lupo had been the first to pledge him his absolute loyalty and that the focus of his every effort would be the protection and survival of that colony. This was not to say he didn't, from time to time, execute a commission for organized crime, who knew him as Joey Nightshade, or for the intelligence community, who claimed not to know him at all, or that such work did not make a useful contribution to colony's material liquidity.

Even among the members of the colony, he knew there were those who thought him something of an anachronism. They considered his elaborate manners heavy-handed, and secretly laughed at the way he insisted on addressing Renquist as "Don Victor," and at how he was one of the very few who still dreamed away the daylight hours in the traditional coffin, in his case a massive edifice of brass-bound mahogany. They judged the careful gravity of his thinking as slow and ponderous, and he knew that, to a degree, he was even feared by some of his companions as too old and too unknowable. As he walked the night, cloaked in his grim invincibility, some of the newly Changed looked on him as little more than a throwback to times that would never return. They never, however, expressed such opinions to his face.

Lupo had taken the congressman's call seated at his don's

desk in Renquist's spacious if dusty and unkempt library on the ground floor of the LA Residence, in the house at the end of the road-with-no-name off Benedict Canyon. While the rest of the colony slept, and the hazy polluted sunlight of Southern California was shut out by the sealed windows, he had waited silently for the phone to ring. The large antique grandfather clock stood in a corner, the one on which carved wooden demons scaled a carved wooden tower, and green copper dragons and gargoyles appeared at the windows when it tolled the quarter hours. The only noise above the distant freeway traffic and the sudden rustling of an armadillo in among the unpacked and uncataloged books, was the clock's measured ticking, and the worn escapement's faint grinding, and that was again all that remained when the call was over. The library was so much a part of Renquist that it was hard to believe he was a prisoner on the other side of the country. It was as if he might walk in at any minute in one of his dark bathrobes, to be one with the dust and the thousands of antique volumes that Renquist never seemed to finish organizing onto the many yards of shelves, and which were worthy to be in the collection of any major museum. Close to the desk, a large and very ancient volume lay open on a table, as though Renquist had been studying its text before he left for DC, his place marked by a short, jeweled dagger placed in the furrow of the spine.

"Dammit."

Lupo allowed himself a brief flash of anger that once more a human-instigated crisis was upon them, but then he returned to hard practicality. It would be some hours before the rest of the colony woke, and he would use the time to make further calls to numbers with East Coast area codes. He had other connections in the capital, more covert and more potentially useful than just a compromised and corrupted politician. Lupo would learn all he could before he informed the others that their leader was lost.

Renquist surfaced from a dream-plagued sleep to find Thyme Bridewell ready with a large glass of ice water. He blinked and shook his head. "Have you been waiting there for long?"

"No. I also slept for a while. And then I had some thinking to do."

Renquist drank almost the whole glass of water, then handed it back to her. The two of them had been transferred to a new room. They were out of the pod in the underground detention area and above ground, in the west wing of the original house that had borne the name Deerpark. The room had little to recommend it. It was slightly larger than a double room in a midclass hotel. The windows were sealed. The only furniture was a king-size bed over which Renquist had draped his fur rug, two uncomfortable chairs, and a dressing table. A door opened on a minuscule bathroom, and a small refrigerator was stocked with water, alcohol, and ice. The almost regulation TV graced its own movable stand. A telephone stood on the bedside table, but it allowed no outside calls. The color scheme was muted shades of cream and orange, and a van Gogh print hung on the wall. The door was locked from the outside, but a lack of any more heavyweight security measures seem to indicate that they now trusted him at least not to attempt an escape.

Renquist was scarcely awake enough to examine auras, but something in the way Thyme took the glass, plus a definite stiffness in her speech and expression, spoke of all not being well. "You were thinking?"

"Contrary to popular opinion, I am able to think."

It was confirmed. The honeymoon was apparently over. Thyme Bridewell was no longer happy, but Renquist had the good sense and good manners not to probe mentally for whatever troubled her. She would let him know herself soon enough.

"Tell me something?"

Renquist was cautious. "Tell you what?"

"You've fed from me twice now."

Renquist's expression was neutral. "You appeared to enjoy it."

"I did, but after the second time, it was harder to recover. The weakness didn't go away."

Renquist flexed his muscles, easing them to physical wakefulness. "That's only natural."

"If you keep feeding from me, I'll die on you."

Renquist swung his legs over the side of the bed, not really needing to commence this new night with an interrogation. "I thought you didn't care if you died."

"That was then. This is now."

"You've decided you don't want to die?"

"That's right. I don't want to die."

"If that's the case, I'll ask Coulson for a replacement. It shouldn't be a problem."

Bridewell looked shocked. "A replacement?"

"It's the only logical course of action."

"And what happens to me?"

"I don't know. What does happen to you?"

Thyme looked at Renquist as if he was an imbecile. "I'll be taken away, won't I?"

Renquist was still too fresh from the dreamstate to grasp the underlying point. "Why should they take you away?"

"Because you won't need me anymore. And when you

don't need me anymore, that's me fucked, after I pulled a gun on the Old Man."

"Two guns if I remember correctly."

"Okay, two guns. That only makes it worse."

"Just because another is brought in for me to feed on doesn't mean you have to go."

"You think I want to stay here and watch?"

"I imagine a role can be found for you."

"A role?"

It suddenly dawned on Renquist that Thyme was jealous of her theoretical replacement. She was showing the classic symptoms of an extreme darklost a great deal faster than Renquist had ever seen before. It was either because of the implant in her head or some psychological yearning that came from being raised as a Deerpark experiment. "You want to be nosferatu one day don't you?"

"Yes, but . . ."

"But what?"

"She'll have to die. I don't want another moody darklost hanging round."

Renquist looked at her with interest. "Where did you learn the word *darklost?*"

"From your dossier."

"You've read my file?"

"It was laying around in the briefing room, so I picked it up and read it during the history lesson."

"And no one stopped you?"

"In your bloody arrogance, you men didn't give a fuck what I was doing. Remember, Renquist, the ignored bimbo becomes invisible and can do anything she wants. We girls have a lot of practice hiding behind airhead vapidity and substance abuse."

"I'll attempt to remember that."

"So am I a darklost?"

"What do you think a darklost is?"

Thyme frowned. "A human with her nose pressed to the candy-store window of life eternal."

Renquist smiled "That would be one description."

"Do you promise me she'll die?"

"You're totally unscrupulous."

"Totally. And I find to my amazement that I'm still learning."

Renquist turned and picked up the phone from the table beside the bed. The move drew a sharp reaction from Thyme. "What are you doing?"

"I'm calling Coulson."

"But you haven't answered me."

Renquist was growing irritable. "No, I haven't."

"If they send a new girl, will you drain and finish her? Will you kill her so my position is assured?"

This was as far as Renquist was prepared to go. "Be quiet."

Thyme's eyes angrily narrowed. "What did you say?"

Renquist lowered the phone. "Damn you, woman, be quiet while I talk to Coulson, or I swear I'll tell him to remove you."

Thyme's aura colored as she realized by how far she'd overstepped the line. "I'm sorry, Victor. I . . ."

"Quiet."

He found that he'd lost the dial tone. He jiggled the cradle and a human operator answered. "I want to speak to Jack Coulson." He waited for a few moments. "Coulson? This is Renquist. I need another human female. This one can be disposable." A pause ensued. "Bridewell? No, for the moment she can stay. I prefer that she remain alive, and that won't happen if I continue to feed from her exclusively." He looked up at Thyme, whose aura was a kaleidoscope of relief, gratitude, and sudden weakness. As he hung up the phone, Thyme fell to her knees at his feet and hugged his legs. "Victor, thank you, thank you . . ."

"Don't thank me too soon. Neither of us knows what will happen next."

"Victor . . ." For a long time she clung to him, as though deriving a desperately needed comfort from his touch, but when she finally raised her head, a trace of the old sly rebellion had returned. "You know something?"

Renquist raised an eyebrow. "What's that?"

Thyme smiled. The bad-girl persona of Fem-Juv 8-79 had fully returned. "I have come across many oblique approaches to the suggestion of a three-way, but that has to be both the most oblique and certainly the most bizarre."

Renquist could only shrug. "Sex is hardly my concern."

"I'm not so sure about that. You may not physically practice it, but you sure as shit understand it. You understand it better than the majority of humans."

Renquist iced over. Bridewell still needed to be put in her place. "I understand a multitude of things better than the majority of humans."

"Further vampires are totally out of the question."

Didn't the Old Man ever need to sleep? Coulson felt beset from both sides. Renquist wanted fresh blood, and Grael, now that they were back in his private quarters, was close to becoming infantile. "I'd be the one going into Underland with them."

"And if you recruited more of the horrors, you'd be a bloody fool."

"I've run a check on this Lupo, and it's as Renquist said. He may be another vampire, but he's also a highly respected contract killer. His record, one that seems to go back forever, shows a hundred percent success rate and is without a blemish."

"So why didn't we pick him in the first place?"

Coulson was about to censor his first response, but then wondered why the hell he should bother. Why should he kiss up to this irrational and vacillating old fool with at least a bottle of brandy in him and heaven only knew what drugs, and who should have been forcibly retired years ago. "I don't know. If you recall, I wasn't in on the planning stage. I was only called in when everyone else chickened out on handling the vampire. Whoever dreamed up this idea was a bloody fool. It wasn't thought through properly. The right kind of research wasn't done. When I was first turned loose on Renquist, I had no idea what he really was, or what he could do. I was provided with no clues to his character. Basically, you gave me a linear monster, and I had to find out for myself that I was dealing with something far more complex and perplexing. So far, this whole project has been a complete bloody fuck-up, and now you're compounding the original stupidity by flatly refusing to let me examine alternative options. Do you realize that poor fucking Thyme Bridewell has made more progress in getting close to Renquist than any of us? And you wanted to feed her to him."

The director was rapidly turning puce. "You can't talk to me like that. I tolerate a lot from you, Jack, because you're good at what you do, but you can't call me stupid to my face and get away with it."

"So fire me. You think I need this shit?"

"You believe you're your own man, Jack? The independent operative? The hired gun with the hired morality?"

"I'm not one of your flunkies. I know that for sure.

Maybe you should put Schultz or Lustig in with Renquist and see how long they last."

"How long you think you'd last if I put out the word on you?"

"Are you threatening me?"

"No one walks away from me."

"So what's the plan. You summon Vargas in here and have him put a bullet in the back of my head?"

"If need be."

"And what would happen to your Underland operation then?"

"It would continue."

"Bullshit. You've made me an integral part, and without me the project goes to shit."

"Are you challenging me to put that to the test, Jack?" Grael, who was sitting at his desk, reached for the red phone and spoke into the mouthpiece. "In here. Now."

Coulson looked at the Old Man in amazement as he put down the phone. "Are you senile? This is one hand you really don't want to play out."

Grael said nothing. He just sat with his fingertips still resting on the phone.

"I could kill you before Vargas even gets here."

The director shook his head. "You won't. If you were going to do it, you'd have done it. Instead, you're talking about it. That's you're problem, Jack. You always want to know what happens next."

In this, the Old Man was absolutely right. Coulson had waited too long, and now Vargas was coming through the door. His gun was already drawn, and his hackles were up, ready for an emergency. He seemed a little perplexed when he found only the director and Coulson, apparently in normal conversation.

"Vargas."

"Boss?"

"I want you to put your gun to Mr. Coulson's head."

Grael made the request with no more emotion than if he had been ordering a drink or a snack. Vargas exhibited even less feeling as he carried out the order. Coulson said nothing as the cold barrel of the automatic touched his skull just behind his left ear.

The old man flexed his bony fingers. "Get down on your knees, Jack."

Coulson turned slightly, as much as Vargas and his pistol would allow. "No. I'm not going to do that."

"You're not going to do that?"

"I'll die on my feet. At least that choice is mine."

"I could have Vargas put you to your knees."

"That might create a problem. He'd need both hands, and what would he do with his gun?"

"Aren't you afraid, Jack?"

"Yes, but I'm not going to grovel."

"You think I'm bluffing? That I won't have you shot?"

"Oh, no, I believe you. You're fucking crazy enough. Remember, I've seen what you can do."

"What do you want, Jack? Tell me what you want."

"I always want to know what happens next. Isn't that what you said?"

"Just tell me what you want, Jack."

Lupo was filled with a profound sense of relief when Dahlia was the first of the colony to emerge at the end of the day and the start of a new night. Lupo had remained awake through the long afternoon. After making calls to all of his human assets in the twin businesses of espionage and murder, he had waited for the sun to set. He had left Renquist's library and gone to the kitchen. The kitchen was the place, in all normal circumstances, where the colony began each evening. The large ground-floor room was a very odd mixture of the wholly normal and very nearly unthinkable; the American mundane, and what, to many humans, would be nothing short of a bizarre and hideous abomination. Most of the flat surfaces in the communal rooms, particularly the kitchen, were a clutter of the familiar and the unrecognizable; piles of unopened junk mail, a perfectly ordinary Sony TV set, a Gaggia espresso machine, an IBM laptop computer, Max Factor and Calvin Klein cosmetics mixed in with nameless things marinating in jars of unappetizing liquid. Four-hundred-year-old weapons and implements of pain shared wall space with framed photographs and Broadway playbills, and since none of the colony members considered themselves responsible for keeping the place clean, or even marginally tidy, and, for obvious reasons, no human maid came in to perform these chores, the communal area qualified as a chaotic slum.

Lupo sat very still at the long farmhouse table as an armadillo, bolder than most of its brothers and sisters who shared the Residence with the colony, poked a cautious scaly head out from the space between the refrigerator and the freezer in which the colony kept its fresh ice and frozen supply of whole blood for times when hunting live prey was either difficult or unadvisable.

The small and very ancient armored creatures were, according to nosferatu superstition, bringers of good fortune and security to a Residence and its inhabitants, and they had an inexplicable propensity for seeking out the undead and taking up abode with them. Lupo, whose patience was almost infinite, scarcely breathed as the armadillo slipped out from its hiding place and moved across the kitchen floor, inspecting various small objects. He watched with pleasure as it foraged, completely unaware of his presence. Then a sound startled the animal, a movement in the corridor outside, and it scuttled back to the shelter of the refrigerator.

Dahlia came into the kitchen looking scarcely awake, and was surprised to see Lupo there already. "You look like you've been up all day."

Lupo flexed his arms, which had grown stiff while he'd remained motionless observing the armadillo. "I was."

Dahlia knew that Lupo set great store by his rest and was not prone to spend sleepless pensive days doing nothing. "What's wrong?"

"Something has happened to Don Victor."

Dahlia looked aghast. "Don't tell me. Not destroyed? I felt nothing."

"Not destroyed, but a prisoner."

Even among the members of the colony, Dahlia's story was less than clear, and a number of variations were repeated behind her back. The only certain part was that Dahlia had negotiated the Change from human when nothing more than a child, and had then, quite deliberately, arrested her physical development so she had remained a cutely feral ten-year-old Victorian moppet ever since, apparently, at the same time conducting a form of homosexual incest-bonding with her even more bizarre sister, Imogene. Beneath the ringlets, and the Shirley Temple, lollipop exterior, lurked a sharp and devious mind, honed by a solid vein of perverse cruelty, the capacity for blasphemy of a hungover longshoreman, and a sense of humor that took no prisoners. On this particular evening she had emerged from the private quarters she shared with Imogene, with her hair in rollers and still wearing the short baby-doll nightdress, in which she had presumably slept. She put coffee in motion. Dahlia drank coffee in the same way that Renquist now and then drank vodka. It didn't have the same stimulant effect on her as it did on humans, but it provided a symbolic start to each fresh night. With the coffee happening, she turned to face Lupo. The worried gravity of her expression was equal to the concern displayed in her aura. "Did a hunt go wrong? Was he observed making a kill?"

Lupo shook his head. "No, nothing as simple as that. He was taken at the Watergate by agents of some NSA paranormal unit."

"Your telling me the fucking Feds have him?"

"That's right?"

"What about all the bribes and blackmail? I thought we had Washington under control."

"I have humans trying to get me more details."

Imogene was in the kitchen, having entered silent and insubstantial as a ghost. "Details of what?"

Dahlia moved close to her sister. "Victor has been abducted by the Feds."

"I don't believe it."

"I'm afraid it's true."

Imogene shook her head. "The federal government of the United States? What do they want with Victor? Do they intend to test his tolerance to shameless hypocrisy?"

Imogene was a total contrast to her sister. She was almost six feet tall, narrow-boned and corpse-thin, to the point that, at times, her flesh seemed almost transparent. Currently her hair was cropped into a short flattop and dyed a vibrating rock & roll orange. The lenses of her sunglasses matched her hair, while her black leather jeans and cotton roll-neck gave her something of the look of a beatnik tarantula. She carried a small leather-bound notebook in which she habitually wrote with an old-fashioned Parker fountain pen. The pen had a custom nib, so Imogene could inscribe the intricate calligraphy of the Old Speech, and colony rumor claimed that the leather cover of the notebook, and the covers of all the other notebooks that had preceded it, were made from actual tooled and finished human skin: but no one knew for sure because not even Renquist dared to touch one of Imogene's notebooks.

"So far it's less than clear."

Imogene looked from Dahlia to Lupo. "So what are you telling me? That a rerun of the Great Slaughter is about to start and we can expect a SWAT team to come rolling up the driveway at any moment armed with stakes and hammers?"

"I don't think so. I can find no sign of a conspiracy against us. Nosferatu in general would appear to be safe behind the very effective screen of total human disbelief. As far as I can tell, Don Victor is in the hands of some black operations paranormal unit."

"The NSA-FEMA Paranormal Operations and Research Facility?"

Both Lupo and Dahlia stared at Imogene in surprise. "Where did you come up with that?"

"It's a fairly recent gathering-under-one-roof of all the old occult warfare units. Its headquarters are at Deerpark, a large estate in rural Virginia."

Lupo nodded. "I know Deerpark. I've never been there, but I know it. For many years it has been the place of concealment for a variety of things that our government does not wish to have known."

"The odds are that it's where they have Victor."

Dahlia was mystified at how well informed her sister

seemed to be. "How the fuck do you know all this?"

Imogene smiled, opened the refrigerator, and took out a bottle of water. Lately she had been emulating Renquist's habit of drinking water on first waking. "I have warped hackers to my will, and now they do my bidding without question. It's quite astonishing what evil secrets can be disinterred with a computer and the right bending of thralls."

The coffee was ready, and Dahlia poured herself a cup. It was thick and dark. "So what do the Feds need with Victor?"

She offered some to Lupo who declined. "I would imagine they know something of Don Victor's record and are looking to recruit him into their intrigues."

Imogene opened the lid of the laptop. "Wait just a moment, there's something I have to check on." She pulled up some documents and scrolled through them as Lupo and Dahlia watched and waited. "Yes, I thought so. If Renquist is at Deerpark, there could be another agenda. The director of the facility is currently one Herbert Walker Grael. He is nearly a hundred years old and has been on a series of life-extending medications for at least a quarter of a century. It's possible that Victor might have been abducted for another reason. This Grael might be looking for the secrets of immortality."

Lupo made an inhuman rumbling sound deep in his throat. "It's never good when humans seek to be immortal. As a rule a quest for the life eternal creates a great deal of death and very little else."

Dahlia stirred her coffee. "So what do you intend to do about it, Lupo? Rush off after Victor just like you did when he got into all that trouble in Scotland with the Fenrior Clan?"

"If he's in trouble, it's my duty to help him."

"And leave Imogene, Sada, and me to run the Residence on our own?"

"And Nacza."

"Yes, I suppose you can count Nacza now that he at least seems to be housebroken."

Since the colony had first moved to Los Angeles, Renquist had increasingly relied on Dahlia to take care of much of its day-to-day running. The diminutive nosferatu enjoyed the authority, but that didn't stop her complaining bitterly about all the responsibility she felt she was expected to shoulder. "I swear, for most of you, this place is turning into nothing more than a rest stop between excursions."

Lupo looked at her bleakly. "Are you about to tell us we use the place as a hotel?"

"Something in that vein."

As the colony had learned the hard way, it was never a good idea for Dahlia or Imogene to travel too far among humans. Apart from the obvious problem that they both looked outlandish by any set of human standards, even those of Southern California, it tended to be a bad idea to put the childlike figure of Dahlia in any direct conflict with human authority. Her abusive contempt for mankind, its works, and its social foibles was something she had never bothered to check or control, and the scathing, world-weary tone coming from her moppet body was too much for the majority of police officers, customs agents, and even the cabin attendants of chartered jets. Being effectively housebound herself except when she and Imogene forayed out to hunt, she resented those who felt the need and enjoyed the freedom to travel. "I fail to see the point of maintaining a colony if those who make up that colony spend all their fucking time gallivanting round the goddamned planet. Right now we have Segal off bike riding with hu-

mans, and spending the days in his safe-lair. I suppose the
only mercy is that the humans he's running with are so
degenerate themselves, and so heavily drugged, that they
pose no threat to him or us. We also have Brandon Wales
and Miss Dance on some prolonged bonding courtship,
and now Julia's taken it into her head to go after the fucking De Reske woman."

Imogene looked disbelievingly at her sister. "Don't tell
me you wouldn't prefer Julia to be anywhere else but here."

Dahlia sighed. "Yes, my dear, you're right. I much prefer
it when that troublemaking cunt is elsewhere. I all but
pushed her out into the fucking sun when she came back
after her breakup with that Destry Maitland."

Dahlia's irascibility was to some degree warranted. In
theory, a nosferatu colony was supposed to provide a safe
haven in a human-controlled world, and, it was hoped, a
degree of calm and serenity. Unfortunately, theory and
practice never quite seemed to match. While they resided
in New York, the colony had suffered an internal uprising
that had cost two young ones their immortality, and in the
course of which Renquist's longtime consort, the much-
mourned Cynara, had gone violently to the real death at
the hands of a psychotic and defrocked priest. When the
survivors had relocated in LA, all hoped for a slightly less
stressful and intrusive way of life, but all had been quickly
disappointed. The human Marcus De Reske had attempted
to use the wealth and resources of his high-tech mind control cult, the Apogee, to open the way for an inter-
dimensional invasion by the Ancient demon Cthulhu, and
Renquist had insisted that it was the colony's duty to
thwart him in his plans.

Even their victory over De Reske had failed to gain them
any interval of peace and quiet. At Julia's insistence, the

aging movie star Brandon Wales had not only been brought through the Change, but also restored to the appearance of gilded youth. Julia's master plan had been that Wales, freshly immortal and rejuvenated to his former glory, would provide her with the ideal bond partner and hunting companion. Unfortunately, the other females had their own ideas about this, and Julia had found herself in a competition for Wales's attention that would turn the night-by-night routine of the colony into a distorted, undead soap opera. It also turned out to be a competition that Julia would ultimately lose.

Dahlia joined Lupo in his thoughts. "I couldn't stand to be near her after Elaine Dance snagged Wales from under her nose."

Imogene looked up from her notebook. "You think we'll ever see those two again?"

Dahlia shook her head. "I very much doubt it. They really pair bonded. They'll wander the Earth together until something interrupts them. They have no need for a colony."

"Who'd have thought Wales would have bonded with a neophyte like Elaine?"

"He was a neophyte himself."

"But he was so beautiful."

"Still jealous, Imogene?"

"I won't deny I tried."

Elaine Dance had been nothing more than a darklost leftover from the New York adventure, a human with whom Cynara had amused herself, holding her in thrall, promising her the Change, but, with typical nosferatu coldness, never quite allowing it to happen. Dance had arrived in Los Angeles during the conflict with De Reske, and, in the aftermath, Renquist had made her nosferatu out of a sense of duty—a sense of duty that even Lupo considered a trifle overextended in that instance. Dance had then surprised the other females by disappearing with Brandon Wales one fading sunset, and, for a while after, Julia had been totally insufferable. Then Renquist had departed for London and found himself involved in the drama surrounding the waking of Merlin. Lupo and Julia had flown to Don Victor's aid when he had been taken to the north of Scotland by the Clan Fenrior, a primitive pack of nosferatu highland swordsman, who seemed to be attempting to live as though it was still the sixteenth century. Although the escape of Merlin had left this episode without a wholly satisfactory settlement, it also had an aftermath that provided Julia with an interlude of undead romance.

Destry Maitland was at least a seasoned nosferatu, one of the now sundered Ravenkeep troika and the owner of the great Uzbek stallion Dormandu, on which Merlin had effected his escape. Even while the newly aroused Merlin still threatened them, Julia had established a relationship with Maitland that had come as close to sexual as it was possible for two undead. Julia had brought Maitland to the colony, but, for reason's unknown to Lupo, the female bond had failed to hold, and Maitland had moved on, leaving Julia aggressively bereft.

Dahlia again expressed her contempt. "To have Julia mooning around playing the lovelorn human lesbian was more than I could take."

Imogene looked up from her notebook. "I never did understand why, after the affair with Destry ended, Julia decided to go off and track down the De Reske woman. I mean, she wasn't even nosferatu. Just a human with some remarkable powers."

Dahlia sighed. "She's another of Victor's castoff darklost.

Julia probably thought, if she found Philipa De Reske, she could somehow use her to manipulate Victor. Julia has never given up on wanting to replace Cynara as Victor's consort. And don't forget that the last time the De Reske woman was seen, she was making off with the head of . . . what was the name of the mortal whore, the one who turned out to be the real power behind the Cthulhu business?"

Lupo growled deep in his throat. "Tara Swerling."

Dahlia nodded. "Tara Swerling. That's right, and the small living fragment of Cthulhu that was supposed to have hidden itself inside the head, that might also be part of Julia's motivation."

Lupo was about to comment further on Julia's motivation, but he caught himself. He must have been more tired than he had imagined. His don was in danger, and he was indulging in colony gossip. "I thought we were discussing the plight of Don Victor?"

Dahlia shrugged. "Yeah, well, I guess I was sidetracked into bitching about Julia."

In Lupo's opinion Dahlia not only had the body of a ten-year-old, but also the attention span. She seemed capable of going off on conversational tangents no matter how serious the situation. She needed to be reminded of the potential crisis. "The fact still remains that Don Victor is in the hands of humans."

Dahlia also had trouble relinquishing her position of the put-upon, de facto keeper of the colony. "Sometimes I think Victor only gets into these fucking predicaments as an excuse for you and him to act like fifteen-year-old boys, and have breathless fucking adventures, swashbuckling all over everywhere."

Lupo grew stone-faced and stern. "If it pleases you to

think that way, Mistress Dahlia, then please do so, but, at the moment, my major concern is Don Victor, not swash-buckling."

"I would imagine, though, you want to go tearing off to this Deerpark place and bust him out of whatever passes for the slammer there."

"I think I still need more information, but yes, going to Don Victor is clearly where my duty lies."

"So you're about to put your mysterious travel plans in motion?"

"I have already covered that eventuality."

"You're too fucking secretive, Lupo."

"I don't think so."

"Before you charge away to rescue Victor, spare a thought that you'll be leaving three defenseless females and a scarcely civilized Tlacique blood-child alone here in the Residence."

Imogene protested. "Don't be theatrical, Dahlia dear. You, Sada, and I are not in the least defenseless, and we can hold the Residence on our own if need be."

"That's not the point."

Lupo sighed. Why were females addicted to complications? "I will summon Segal back from his motorcyclists."

Dahlia sipped her coffee. "I suppose that's better than nothing."

Lupo rose to his feet. Any moment, Sada would be up and insisting that she turn on the kitchen TV and watch Mexican soap operas. The kitchen would totally cease to be a place of peace and quiet. Like the armadillo behind the refrigerator, he needed a refuge. "I have more telephone calls to make now that it's dark. I'll be in Don Victor's library if I'm needed."

Dahlia looked at him over the rim of her coffee cup.

"Don't forget one thing, Lupo. Victor is like a cat. He falls on his feet. As we speak, he's probably lording it over the spooks and having them feed him live humans."

The room was bloody, red on cream and orange, like the splatter work of a furious and homicidal Jackson Pollock. The bed was bloody, the walls were bloody, the TV was upended and smashed. The woman called Wisteria lay dead, her nude body contorted on the floor, and Thyme Bridewell was facedown on the debris of the bed, unable to move. Many times in her life she believed she'd climbed the towering twin crags of madness and depravity, but, in the torn-sheet aftermath of the terrible feeding that had just occurred, she realized that she had only previously ascended the foothills. The preceding two hours had been such a display of unchecked predator savagery that even the immediate memories so frightened her that she preferred to remain, at least for the moment, in the mindless now, with all thoughts and reflections held at bay. Thyme had tasted blood, but was hardly ready to contemplate the real depths of what that might mean.

"Oh God."

Renquist sat down on the bed beside her. "I believe you've gone a little beyond calling on any Christian God." Renquist paused while he adjusted the cuff of his shirt. "Or any God at all for that matter. Unless you happen to have the ear of some ancient Central American soul-eater."

Thyme groaned a second time. "It's an habitual figure of speech, damn you." Even the movement of the mattress made her head hurt. Renquist, on the other hand, had showered, changed his clothes, and seemed completely unruffled by what had just transpired. She could only suppose that, after a thousand years, he really had seen it all. "What have you done to me, you bastard? And how can you be so fucking suave just moments after?"

Renquist briskly stood up again as though he didn't want to listen to her whining. He went to the fridge, poured her a straight vodka, and brought it back to the bed. "Drink this. It might help restore you your equilibrium."

"What makes you think there's anything wrong with my equilibrium?"

"I just showed you the abyss, Bridewell. No human is so jaded as to take that in her stride."

Thyme rolled over and attempted to sit up. She suspected that Renquist had, in some degree, arranged the raw intensity of the spectacle for her benefit, perhaps as some kind of a test of her eligibility to become nosferatu. She also knew that much of what had happened in the room was pure hallucination created by Renquist manipulating her mind from the inside. On the other hand, the fact that the room looked like an abattoir proved that reality had also played its part. The woman called Wisteria hadn't lasted long enough even to have a history. To say she was escorted to their room by Vargas was an exaggeration. She was little more than delivered. Thorazine, or a prefrontal lobotomy, had made her close to vegetative. Poor Wisteria. She had been a pretty little thing, with her white bikini and high heels, and the cutesy, honey blond looks of a provincial beauty queen or TV anchor; but when Thyme had first seen her, she'd realized that her earlier potential jealousy, was, in reality, nothing short of pitiful. The woman wasn't tangible enough to be a threat, and Thyme regretted that she'd acted so foolishly, especially in front of Renquist. Being a darklost was infinitely worse than being a hormone-pumping teenager, insofar as she ever really was a hormone-pumping teenager, but there were similarities.

"You showed me the abyss, all right."

"Look on it as the commencement of your education."

Taking the glass of vodka from Renquist was hard enough, but getting it to her lips without spilling it was even harder. "Once, in the line of duty, I spent a long morphine, amphetamine, and tequila weekend distracting a dictator by letting him whip me so repeatedly with such a variety of implements that my body was striped like a tiger for a full ten days after. I believed that a triumphant acme in degeneracy. That my share of the take was close to a quarter of a million dollars added a further piquancy to the overall sweat of corruption."

"But now that weekend has been surpassed?"

"I later had the satisfaction of seeing the son of a bitch slowly garrotted by his personal bodyguard and his chief of staff, but, yes, I think you just topped all of that."

"You desire similar revenge on me?"

Thyme downed her vodka and felt a warm numbness. She loved Renquist. He was bathed in violet light. She didn't know she was briefly seeing an aura. "Oh no, Victor, not you. If that was Hell, let me be damned."

"You sound a little purple."

"I feel a little purple." She started to drift. "Purple . . . nightshade . . . belladonna . . ."

Before Wisteria arrived Thyme had protectively rendered herself numb. Not only with booze, but with a couple of Deerpark's exclusive homemade Quaaludes, possibly the last of those pills on the entire planet, the once famous and adored hypnotic having vanished from even the illegal drug market decades before. Thyme had, at that point, really been looking for a buffer against herself, an insulation from such remnants of vestigial revulsion that the coming experience might swirl to the surface. She quickly discovered,

however, that both barriers and possible revulsion would
be swept aside by the seduction of an evil so pumped and
gothic it was anything but banal, and quite irresistible. Except, as she asked herself before things progressed well beyond the scope of language, what was evil in this instance
except a spirited attempt to leapfrog the food chain?

Thyme had seen others like Wisteria, with the same dead
eyes revealing an extinguished will and a readiness for sacrifice. She had seen them on the sets of snuff movies. She
had seen them moments before bullets started flying. She
had seen them being squired on the arms of psychotic torturers and assassins with whom only the near-brain-dead
could form a liaison. In earlier times those who waited on
line, climbing the Aztec pyramids to have their living hearts
cut out by the Priests of the Sun probably had the same
eyes, and the crucified of Ancient Rome after they'd received their dose of opium and vinegar, from the sponge
on the spear held up by the bribed executioner.

From the moment that Wisteria set foot in the room,
Renquist had worked her like a puppet, shaping and inter-
weaving her nervous system, while, at the same time, laying
a wide-screen, patterned scenario in Thyme's imagination,
time-shaping the backgrounds, altering the contexts and
tweaking the details, in a veritable tour de force of mind-
bending illusion and metaphysical destructuring. Victor felt
no need for continuity in the erotic mirage. Wisteria made
love to Thyme amid silk and incense, and the soft splash
of decorative fountains, houris in the seraglio, a perfumed
garden of fourteenth-century Byzantium, naked with jewelry where no jewelry had been before. Gold bangles and
chains at wrist, throats, nipples, and ankles, and pendant
earrings with tiny bells that tinkled as they writhed. The
fantasy Wisteria had a gold-and-diamond stud in the tip of

her tongue. The gold was cool and smooth while the diamond was a pinprick abrasion, reminding Thyme for whom the tiny bells tinkled, and that the body of Wisteria was only a thin disguise for Victor's orchestration.

With a shift in scene, they sprawled under orange flame against a violent, bruise-colored sky, as if the night itself were on fire. The ground trembled, and the earth moved continuously, and, in the distance, towers burned and fortresses crumbled. All round them were fields of poisoned flowers that hid the charred bones of the incinerated dead. Innocent white but deadly blooms that spilled a languorous and addictive perfume, while overhead, flights of carrion black, bats or birds circled, eventually to coalesce into a single sable-cloaked phantasm that Thyme knew was another version of Renquist. The spectre covered the melting-merging lovers, flowing between them like a liquid presence to inflict small but gentle wounds with a glass-obsidian blade, until Thyme felt herself one with the bloodstream, micro/macro, the hunter-killer virus attacking the red, oxygen-gorged cells, or the black hole feeding on the unraveling death throes of a terminal star. And then in a moment of absolutely clear reality, Renquist opened a wound on Wisteria's breast, and spoke softly to Thyme as he forced her mouth to the blood, like a puppy being taught to suckle.

"The darkness enfolded the light, but the light comprehended it not."

She also heard her own dreamy reply. "Is that from the Bible?"

And Renquist laughed. "No, my dear, a far older book."

As Renquist drank the blood of Wisteria, Thyme was shrouded in a new illusion. A razor-sharp crescent moon of corrupted silver rose over a frozen landscape of frightened trees, and the material moment was again gone. The wide-eyed deer sniffed the air too late, and could not flee before the pack was on her. With Renquist channeling the feeling, Thyme became the she-wolf tearing at the prey to feed her hungry cubs. Renquist's purpose was clear. Thyme was made to know the frenzy and the exultation that could be hers. Such shreds of shame that were left to her were being forcibly stripped away. As Renquist tightened his hold on her, he wanted her morally naked, separated from her humanity, clearly seeing what she might become should he so choose. She in no way resented him. She already knew that to become nosferatu would involve no half measures. To look away squeamishly, or worse still, to look back, would not be tolerated. If Thyme was to succeed, she could only be bloody and resolute. To do otherwise would condemn her as darklost forever. She had somehow to make sure that Victor made her just like him.

"Bridewell?"

Renquist's voice snapped her out of the preoccupied reverie. "I'm sorry. I was . . ."

"You were drifting."

She knew he was right, but what the hell did he expect? She was still only human after all.

"I was thinking."

"You were reliving the last two hours."

"Yes. I was." Again, what the hell did he expect?

"I'm aware how you must feel, but this is not time for shocked introspection."

Thyme shook her head and looked round at the room turned slaughterhouse. Her own voice sounded very distant. "I'm not shocked. Unless that in itself is shocking."

"I've called Coulson and told him we need a new room."

It had been enough of a surprise to find Renquist up and

dressed. She hadn't even been aware that he'd used the phone. "Yes, I suppose we do." Her voice was still a long way away.

"Pull yourself together, Bridewell. We are still deep in the woods."

Thyme didn't feel like pulling herself together. If anything, she would have liked simply to come apart and defer reality for a while. "You're nosferatu. You take all this in your stride, but I'm new to the game."

"You wanted her to die."

"I know, but . . ."

"There are no buts. I would recommend you take a shower and ready yourself to move out of here. Coulson is coming in about twenty minutes, and from his tone, I think we will soon be leaving."

"I don't think I can move."

"Just do it. Don't even think about it."

"You made me drink her blood."

"As I said, the commencement of your education."

"You're closing your grip on me, aren't you?"

"The grip is in your mind, my dear."

The snow had stopped falling, the sky was clear, and the moon had come out. Renquist took a deep breath of the crisp, freezing country air, and his head immediately cleared. When he exhaled, condensation billowed like smoke. He also discovered that he could once again hear properly. He was clearly out of range of the microwaves and whatever other radiations to which he had been deliberately exposed. The newly fallen snow on the terrace was fresh and virginal, with a blue shadow-sheen, untrodden by anyone until he and Coulson left their footprints. In the Wardroom, on the other side of the French windows, the denizens of Deerpark ate and drank, talked and laughed, in the warmth and light, bolstering the fiction that they had just completed another day as nothing more than civil servants in government employ. Although only separated by glass doors and velvet drapes, Renquist and Coulson could easily have been on another planet.

At the end of the terrace, steps led down to a sweep of a white lawn terminating after about a hundred yards in a dark mass of trees, and it was toward those steps that Coulson seemed to be headed. He had come to the room as he and Renquist had arranged on the phone. He had unlocked the door, but then stopped dead on the threshold at the sight of the carnage inside. Renquist had to give Coulson credit for controlling his reactions better than most humans might have done under the circumstances. "I fear the party became a little wild. Perhaps a reaction to incarceration. I'm afraid I'm going to need another room."

Coulson could see Wisteria's body from the doorway, and he looked questioningly at Renquist. "And Bridewell? Is she dead, too?"

Renquist smiled and shook his head. "No, she's fine. She's taking a shower."

Renquist was only wearing a lightweight black jacket over his shirt and jeans, and Coulson questioned this. "I was intending to go outside so we could talk privately. Will you be warm enough?"

Renquist had laughed. "I will be quite warm enough. We feel cold in completely different ways."

At first, Renquist and Coulson were content to walk in silence. So far the snow on Deerpark was only three or four inches deep, and they could stroll easily. Renquist was delighted to be out from under the bunker atmosphere inside Deerpark that seemed to swath everything like a shroud.

He realized how much living in California deprived him of weather, and wistful memories of other snow-covered nights down the years intruded, visions of St. Petersburg, the Persian uplands, or the dark woods of Maine. He had to put them aside, however. Coulson wanted something, and Renquist needed to know what that something might be.

"So the time has come to talk privately, away from microphones and spy cameras?"

Coulson nodded and rubbed his gloved hands together. The snow crunched underfoot and the temperature must have been well below freezing. "What about the helicopters?"

"We'll be okay here on the lawn. The choppers mainly work the perimeters. Besides, I have more important matters to consider."

"Specifically?

"Specifically? Specifically a couple of hours ago the Old Man had Vargas put a gun to my head. You might call it a kind of loyalty test."

"That's how they calculate loyalty in this place?"

"That's how the Old Man sometimes does it."

"But since you're here and talking to me, I would have to assume that you passed."

"In a way." Their path crossed the footprints of a fox. The animal seemed to have hurried across the lawn, making for the trees. Coulson had fallen silent again, as though he was unsure about the wisdom of this conversation with Renquist. Renquist was tempted to run like the fox, but both common sense and curiosity restrained him. He simply kept pace with the human until Coulson was ready to talk about what might be on his mind. "I not only passed the test, but I managed to convince the Old Man that we had a better chance of getting in and out of Underland alive if I was calling the shots."

"I must congratulate you. That's quite an achievement for a man with a gun to his head."

"Grael may be crazy, but he's far from stupid. I think if I'd backed down, or gone in any other direction, he would have had me shot."

"He's a respecter of courage?"

"In his own way."

Coulson once again fell silent, but this time Renquist felt he needed prompting rather than time. "So how are we going to proceed if you're now in full command?"

"I'm not in full command. There was this one point on which our director refused to budge."

"And that was?"

"He rejected out of hand any suggestion of bringing in Lupo, or any others of your kind."

Renquist halted. "You were in favor of doing that?"

Coulson stopped, too. "I was coming to believe that it might be a way to get you to trust me."

"You need my trust?"

"Can we go on walking? I feel the cold even if you don't."

The nosferatu and the human continued to traverse the snow-covered lawn. "You and I will be headed for the worst place in the world." Coulson smiled grimly and corrected himself. "The worst place under this world."

"And we need to watch each other's backs?"

"It goes deeper than that. I think we're going down there on a very slim need-to-know basis."

"Grael isn't telling us everything?"

"I don't believe the Old Man tells himself everything. His left and right hands are virtual strangers, and grunts like us are only briefed as far as he thinks is good for us. Like I said, it's all need-to-know. I believe the only thing we can count on is that something is happening down in Underland, something that poses a clear danger to all of us up here on the surface. And it doesn't matter what species we are. We'll all feel the impact."

"You're proposing an alliance?"

"We'll be going into a situation about which we know next to nothing."

"Learning as we go?"

"And I hope the deeper we go, the more we will learn."

"Where does it leave this attempt at mutual trust if Grael has vetoed the idea of bringing in Lupo?"

This time it was Coulson who halted. "I want to bring in Lupo anyway."

Renquist stopped and turned. "Would you mind repeating that?"

"I want to bring in Lupo on my own responsibility. I'd like you to tell me how to contact him."

Renquist scanned Coulson's aura. As far as he could tell, the man was doing his best to be as frank and candid as he could, and doing pretty well for one in the secrecy business. Renquist still felt the necessity, though, to ask the obvious question. "How do I know this isn't a setup. How do I know this isn't just Grael using you to enlarge his collection of live nosferatu?"

"You're welcome to look into my mind."

Renquist had, in fact, already gone that far. Every indication was that Coulson was telling the truth. Perhaps not the whole truth, but certainly his intentions for Lupo were exactly as he said, and to bring Lupo in was entirely his own idea. "I'm not sure I'm entirely taken with the notion of Lupo just walking into Deerpark."

"Lupo doesn't have to come to Deerpark. He can go straight to Andrews Air Force Base. Across the Potomac from Dulles International. I have contacts that can supply him with all the passes and documentation he needs to get him inside. He can meet us there, then travel with us on the same transport."

"When do we travel?"

"As soon as we can. Within the next forty-eight hours. I want to be away from here and beyond recall before the Old Man can change his mind."

"That makes sense except for one thing."

"What's that?"

"Neither Lupo nor I can go to the Antarctic. It may be winter here, but it's high summer in the southern hemisphere. It's getting close to the midnight sun down at the South Pole."

Coulson burst out laughing, as much in relief as at anything Renquist might have said. "We're not going to the Antarctic, Renquist."

Renquist frowned. "I thought that was the entrance to the Hollow Earth."

Coulson got a grip on himself. "There are any number of entrances. The Soviets and later the Russian Mafia had an access point on the Baltic island of Rugen. The Chinese go in through Tibet. I believe there are at least two shafts leading down under the Andes. And there was a rumor Nikola Tesla had his own private entrance through a fissure and bore hole on Long Island, but that one was sealed with explosives back in the 1940s, on Hoover's orders, after the FBI seized Tesla's papers."

"And us? How do we get in there?"

"Ice Station Zebra."

Renquist looked doubtful. "I thought that was the name of a movie."

"It's the name used by the agents who go there. It's a secret base in northern Greenland. Its real denomination is NORAD 40."

"It's a radar station?"

"It was once, but now it's a Cold War leftover used exclusively as a transit point for trade with Underland."

"So we'll be going north?"

"That's right. You'll have hardly any daylight to worry about. And, of course, once we've descended the Arctic Fissure and are inside Underland, you won't have any daylight at all." Coulson shivered. "Listen, can we go back indoors?"

"Of course."

"I'd like to conclude this conversation while we're still out here. Do I get a secure phone number for Lupo?"

Renquist slowly nodded. "Yes, I'll give it to you. And if it does turn out to be a setup, Lupo is more than capable of taking care of himself."

One scene in the film *Lawrence of Arabia* had always stuck in Coulson's memory. It was when, after taking Akabar by land and then crossing the Sinai in a sandstorm, Peter O'Toole as T.E. Lawrence walks into the British officers' mess in Cairo in his filthy Bedouin robes and with his Arab boy companion to the intense consternation of English military conservatism. Coulson had never thought he would have the chance to act out such a scene himself, but walking into the Deerpark Wardroom with Victor Renquist at his side was probably as close as he would ever come. Coulson had always had a secret schoolboy admiration for Lawrence, the misfit outsider who had, by the application of his own unique and unorthodox madness, actually changed the course of history. The man had been the total antithesis of the self-congratulatory spook-suits who now ran the global conspiracies.

The reaction to the entry of Coulson and Renquist was much the same as the one in the film. The entire room fell into hostile silence, and all heads turned. Coulson wasn't sure how many of those present in the Wardroom knew for sure that Renquist was a vampire. Deerpark might be one of the most secret installations in the world, but, within its own closed community, little remained confidential for very long. He was prepared to bet, however, that most were aware that Victor was, at the very least, a homicidal sociopath, brought in from the outside world with blood on his hands. Some probably even knew that he had racked up a body count of four since he'd been there. Renquist had demurred when Coulson had suggested they stop in the Wardroom. He seemed concerned about the risk of walking into a public place among humans who knew he wasn't one of them, but, after deciding to risk all by going against the Old Man and privately recruiting Lupo for the mission, Coulson was in a mood of reckless rebellion.

"Come along, Victor. We'll be out of here soon. Fuck 'em. Let's put you just once among all those Ivy League pigeons and the rest of the pencil-pushing fucks."

Renquist had made a gesture of surrender and followed him into the hubbub of drinking humans. Before they were even halfway to the bar, a short thickset individual called Rampton got to his feet. Rampton, who was nicknamed the Gargoyle because of his slight hunchback, had come to the Deerpark mind control unit after being fired as the assistant warden of a federal prison. Rumor claimed he had beaten and tortured inmates for his own amusement, far beyond what was unofficially considered acceptable. At Deerpark, Rampton was permitted a much freer hand. He looked as though he wanted to make an issue of Renquist's entrance, but two of his drinking companions dissuaded him, managing to talk him back into his seat.

At the bar, Hemple had received them with a hard warning look. "Are you sure about this, Mr. Coulson?"

"Oh, I'm very sure about this, Hemple."

"If you say so."

Hemple probably disliked Renquist being in his bar as much as Rampton did, but his control and sense of place was so much more rigid. "A martini, Mr. Coulson?"

"Please."

"And for your . . . friend?"

"He'll also have a martini, but make his with vodka."

Once Hemple had mixed the drinks, Coulson turned, leaning on his elbow, back to the bar and facing the room, seeing if anyone would openly challenge his bringing Renquist there. Although Rampton continued to glare at them, Coulson found his open provocation had no overt takers. As he suspected, the company men were so chicken-shit it extended even to their prejudice and territorialization. Since no barroom brawl seemed imminent, Coulson indicated to Renquist that they should perhaps take their drinks to a table. Renquist pointed to one away from the main crowd of drinkers, and Coulson went along. As they settled in, Renquist glanced around as though looking for surveillance devices. "Is it safe to talk here?"

"There's too much background buzz, even for a directional mike. One of us would have to be wired to catch the conversation. There are probably three or four cameras looking at us, but if you keep your head down and don't give then the chance to lip-read, they won't know what we're talking about. How's your martini?"

Renquist sipped his drink and nodded. "It's very good indeed." He looked quizzically at Coulson. "You seemed to come in here looking for a fight."

"After the last few days, one might have cathartic value."

"Brawl therapy?"

Coulson laughed. It was so unexpected that a vampire might have a sense of humor. "Brawl therapy. I like that."

"Violence is one way to release excess emotion."

"I'm not sure many psychiatrists would tend to agree with you."

Renquist permitted himself a half smile. "And to even the balance, I tend not to agree with many psychiatrists." The smile faded, and again Renquist looked carefully around. "You are certain we cannot be overheard?"

"I'm certain. You have something on your mind?"

Renquist fixed Coulson with an odd stare. "I believe, when we leave, we are going to have to take Bridewell with us."

This was about the last thing that Coulson had expected. "You're kidding?"

"I'm perfectly serious."

"What possible use can she be?"

"She's a trained operative, isn't she?"

"Yes, but she's burned out and unstable."

Renquist continued to maintain eye contact with Coulson. "Nonetheless I would like her with us."

Coulson was starting to find Renquist's eyes highly disconcerting. "Is this some kind of test? Are you now gauging my loyalty?"

"I suppose you could think of it as a test, but not in the way you imagine."

"Why do you want to take Bridewell? Surely you could find other sources of nourishment along the way?"

"It's not so much that I want to take her with us. I'm more concerned with what might happen if we leave her here. She has become what is known as darklost."

"I read about darklost in the dossier."

To Coulson's relief, Renquist finally looked away. "Well, she is one."

"And that's a problem?"

"Darklost can be compulsive and highly unpredictable."

"Bridewell is unpredictable at the best of times."

"And she has that implant in her head. At times, even a relatively normal human who has become darklost can form a psychic link with the nosferatu who made her what she is. I have no idea how the implant might enhance such a link."

For Jack Coulson to listen to someone talk calmly and seriously about a psychic link as a factor in an enterprise in which all concerned might well be risking their lives would once have seemed far beyond the boundaries of insanity. Except this was Deerpark, and, within its grounds, all deals between the rational and irrational had long ago been canceled. He only had to look round the Wardroom to confirm that. The two attractive women drinking scotch on the rocks at the bar and making small talk with Hemple were Maria Sanchez and Sigrid Karnstein, a lesbian couple who attempted, on a daily basis, to access the spirit world for inside information about Iraqi counterintelligence operations. The group around the billiard table were all part of a remote-viewing team. Across the table from him was a fully documented, undead vampire, and if he entertained the slightest doubt about that, a cleaning crew was already at work in a room in another wing of the building, washing blood from the walls, floor, and ceiling, and removing the furniture, drapes, and carpeting to burn them.

Once again Coulson wished he had a cigarette. If the lunatics had taken over the asylum, that had to make him, at the very least, a visiting lunatic. "So what are you saying? That if we leave her behind, we become vulnerable? To what exactly?"

"I have no idea of the capabilities of her implant, but I believe Grael might very well be able to use her to monitor us."

"Even inside Underland?"

"I see no reason why not. And that's not even taking into account what she might decide to do of her own accord. A darklost can be a desperate creature. The desired prize is, after all, a form of immortality."

Coulson let the madness carry him along. "The simplest solution would surely be to kill her. If she's out of the way, we no longer have to worry about her."

Renquist shook his head. "I can't do that."

"Why not? This is an odd time for you above all to discover a belief in the sanctity of human life."

"As you well know, I don't give a damn about the supposed sanctity of human life."

"So what's the problem?"

"I promised her I wouldn't kill her. It's as simple as that."

"I made no such promise."

"I'd rather you respected my wishes in this."

Coulson stared down at the olive in his martini, avoiding Renquist's eyes. "Is Bridewell a deal-breaker?"

"I'd rather it didn't come to that."

"Do you see her being of any possible use to us?"

"I believe she might be. As we are both well aware, the training she received at this place gives her a unique and uncompromising outlook on the world, and, as a darklost made by me, I command her unquestioning loyalty as long as she believes there is a chance I will ultimately make her nosferatu."

Coulson sighed. "Very well." He wished some miracle might occur by which he'd magically become a shoe sales-man or a bank teller with no memory of any of this, but he knew that wouldn't come to pass. He had made his metaphoric bed, and now he had to thrash about on it. "Be sure of one thing, though. The very first time she takes a wrong turn or does anything I don't like, I will have no compunction about putting a bullet through her brain, im-plant and all."

Renquist raised his still full glass to Coulson. "If such a thing occurs, I won't stop you."

"Then we're agreed?"

"Agreed."

"Then let's get the hell out of here. I think we've caused the natives enough discomfort."

The conversation in the Wardroom had resumed, but grim glances were still being directed at Coulson and Ren-quist. Accordingly, they rose and started for the door, but when they reached it, two further obstacles confronted them in the form of Schultz and Lustig. Both men stopped dead in their tracks. Schultz's jaw dropped, and Lustig blurted out what was obviously the first thing to come into his head. "Does the Old Man know about this?"

Lustig's fear of the vampire was actually exceeded by his fear of higher authority, and Coulson couldn't help but laugh out loud. "Does the Old Man know about what?"

"That you're taking this *thing* out for drinks."

"Would such a thing be possible if he didn't?" Lustig seemed set to go on protesting, but Coulson cut him off.

"If I were Renquist, I wouldn't take kindly to being called a *thing*. Especially not to my face."

Lustig suddenly realized the implication of what he'd done and tuned pale. Renquist, on the other hand, merely smiled and extended a hand. "I believe you two gentlemen are the ones who arranged to have me brought here from the Watergate. I'm pleased finally to meet you in the flesh."

Coulson couldn't quite believe that Lustig had the courage to grasp Renquist's hand and shake it. Either he was sufficiently shocked to have reacted out of blind habit, or Renquist had taken hold of his mind. For a moment, Coulson thought Renquist was going to do something terrible, but then he released Lustig's hand and the contact was over. He turned to Schultz and again offered his hand. Schultz also took Renquist's hand, but then did something incredibly stupid, even for him. Schultz was essentially a low-level bully, with a fondness for crushing the knuckles of the unsuspecting while shaking hands, but to try such a thing on Renquist was so unthinkable that again Coulson didn't know if it was shock or Renquist's influence.

Renquist merely stared at Schultz and smiled. "If I so desired, I could break all the bones in your hand, little man. Do you know how many bones there are in the human hand?"

"I . . ."

"No, you don't, do you? Therefore, I recommend you think twice before trying that handshake trick on anyone else."

He released Schultz's hand and turned as though Schultz and Lustig were dismissed. "It was nice to meet your underlings, Coulson, but can we go now?"

They had walked about a half dozen paces when a terrible, drawn-out screaming echoed from the Wardroom.

Coulson stopped and turned, but Renquist gripped him by the arm. "Just keep walking."

"What's happening? That sounds like Lustig."

"It is, but still keep walking."

They moved on as three uniformed goons hurried past them, responding to the barroom commotion.

"What happened?"

"I implanted a short-delay suggestion. Right now he believes that his flesh is liquefying and melting off his bones. Of course, no one else can see what he imagines he's seeing. It will be assumed that he's in the throes of some very violent nervous breakdown. I imagine the experience will leave him mentally incapacitated for quite some time."

"Why Lustig and not Schultz?"

Renquist laughed. "Schultz is going to have to wait twenty-four hours for his turn in Hell."

Coulson shook his head with the expression of a man who devoutly wished the wonders would cease. "Now we really do have to get out of here as soon as possible."

chapter Five

B y night, Andrews Air Force Base was a place of hundreds of lights — runway lights, work lights, high-mounted floodlights, the marker lights of radio and radar antennae, the lights from buildings and ground vehicles and, of course the lights of the aircraft themselves. Renquist had never had the chance to explore a modern military air base, but it looked like a perfect operating environment for nosferatu, with so many pools of light hard against shadows as deep and black as India ink. Coulson and Renquist had been chauffeured to the base by a blue-uniformed Deerpark Security goon driving a government-issue Lincoln Town Car that, Renquist suspected, judging by the cumbersome weight of the vehicle's ride, was effectively bulletproofed. The driver didn't speak during the entire journey, and rarely even glanced in his rearview mirror at the two passengers in the back seat. The rule among Deerpark Security seemed to be that they saw nothing and said less.

The car was stopped no less than three times by Air Force Security, but the driver carried a folder of credentials that assured their access was not to any degree questioned. At the checkpoints, the man didn't have to speak. He just handed the folder to the equally silent Air Force cops manning each barrier, with their polished helmets, white gloves, and holstered weapons, and, after a reasonably detailed inspection, they waved him through. Each time the driver rolled down his window, Renquist believed he could smell ice on the waters of the Potomac, the chill carried by a wind that gusted across the extensive complex of runways and taxi zones. As they penetrated deeper and deeper into what functioned as the capital's military and government airport, Renquist peered from the backseat of the Lincoln at the parked ranks of military jets and helicopters. Farther into the base he spotted the geometric and matte black shape of what he assumed was a Stealth aircraft, and he thought he saw the tail section of a presidential 747, but he couldn't tell if it was the plane designated Air Force One when the president was on board, or maybe the legendary *Looking Glass,* the command plane in which the president and his staff would ride out a nuclear attack. It was clear, however, that they were entering progressively more secret areas of the facility.

Shortly after they passed the Stealth plane, Coulson had nudged him and pointed ahead. "That looks like our transport coming up."

What Coulson had referred to as a transport was a sleek, black, twin-engined, private jet without markings of any kind. Was it a Gulfstream? Renquist wasn't sure. On the

other hand, he instantly recognized the unmistakable silhouette of Lupo, dressed in a long black overcoat that
flapped in the wind, and with his face partially concealed
by the brim of a black Borsalino. He stood apart from the
ground crew, which was loading items of cargo into the
body of the plane. When the Lincoln came to a stop a short
distance from the aircraft, Renquist didn't wait for Coulson's permission to immediately exit the car and hurry to
greet his old friend. "Lupo. I am extremely pleased to see
you."

"And I you, Don Victor."

Coulson was hurrying to catch up with Renquist, and
Renquist made a gesture of introduction. "Lupo, this is
Jack Coulson. He is mortal, but should be treated like a
friend."

Lupo's response was momentarily drowned out by a military transport taking off from a runway some five hundred
yards away. The two nosferatu and the one human looked
up briefly as the plane climbed for altitude before resuming
their interspecies formalities. Lupo extended a hand and,
without hesitation, Coulson shook it. Renquist wryly noted
that the man seemed to be becoming accustomed to the
company of the undead.

"I am pleased to meet you, Jack Coulson."

"Your reputation has preceded you."

Lupo's expression was unreadable under the brim of the
black hat. "I'm not sure I'm pleased to hear that. My trade
is, after all, one that must be plied in secret."

"It's a reputation known only to a very small and select
group."

Lupo nodded as if, to a degree, mollified. "I can only
hope it remains that way." He turned to Renquist. "I take

it he is not one of the ones who abducted you?"

Renquist shook his head. "No, that was two other mortals."

"And what has become of them?"

"Pay them no mind, old friend. They suffer as we speak."

"I trust they suffer enough."

"I have taken good care of them."

A young officer in a cold-weather flight suit approached the group. "If you gentlemen would board the aircraft . . ."

Lupo hesitated. "There was a young woman, a darklost as I read her . . ."

So happy to see Lupo, Renquist had neglected to ask about Bridewell. "Yes, the darklost. Where is she?"

"She is already on board. She seemed to have the correct credentials."

Renquist reassured Lupo, although he knew later that he'd have to explain to him why Thyme Bridewell was travelling with them. "That's as it should be. So I suggest we board the plane ourselves."

Coulson wondered if he was afraid. Events seemed to be outstripping his feelings. He sat in a private jet, in temporary surroundings of executive luxury, and any impartial, if uninformed, observer might have been forgiven the assumption that he was a Master of the Universe who had reached the very apex of all corporate opportunities. The impartial and uninformed observer, on the other hand, would not have known that two of his companions on the aircraft were not even human, and that the woman who completed the quartet was seriously disturbed and had electronic devices surgically installed in her brain. If that wasn't enough to give Jack Coulson a moment of pause, as the Gulfstream lifted into the freezing sky, with its wheels fold-ing into the fuselage, the matter of their destination also remained. They were cleared for a direct course to a transit point deep inside the Arctic Circle that gave access to a world that most of humanity considered a chimera of fiction, fantasy, or paranoia, if indeed, they considered it at all.

Coulson found himself wishing more and more that he still had cigarettes. As the pilot turned off the obligatory seat belt sign, he wanted to light a Marlboro so badly he could taste the smoke, and feel it catch in his throat. He found himself running down memory's checklist of all the other planes down the years and miles, smoking, non-smoking, and, in one case, actually on fire, that had brought him to the situation in which he now found himself. The DC-9s and DC-6s, the Bristol Freighters, and Piper Cherokees, the scheduled 747s and the wind-whipped, beat-up Huey's, left over from the Vietnam War, in which he'd been too young to fight, but had become his schoolboy obsession. How many times, as a teen, had he watched *Apocalypse Now* and wanted to be as cool as Captain Willard, or recklessly dared to wonder if he had the intensity of resolve it took to become as pitiless as Kurtz? And now, at least, he seemed to have made it to Willard, and maybe Kurtz was still to come. He had told Renquist that they were going to the "worst place under the Earth"—a remark that had been devoid of any implied humor.

Jack Coulson's wanderings had started straight out of college. He had zig-zagged his way through a world of other people's hurt, pretending to be a photojournalist, but in fact following a boyishly amoral need to keep up with the action. Very rapidly he had become addicted to the shit, and where the shit went, he followed. He was soon embroiled, and compromised, and he relished it, with only a minimum of guilt, which rapidly diminished the longer he spent in the bush and the closer he came to the firefight. He had served his freelance apprenticeship in the era of the Contras and Ollie North, Pablo Escobar, and Jeane Kirkpatrick, as the Soviet Evil Empire sagged under the weight of bureaucracy and the arms race, when all that was needed to fill a plane with CIA cocaine was a confirmation that the plane was taking off empty. From La Paz to Medellin, from Havana to Trench Town, and on to Beirut, and back to Bangkok, then home to weird shit in Mena, Arkansas, and then off to Port Au Prince and the fall of the Tonton Macout.

Getting dusted with the zombie drug should have been a turning point, but it turned out to be nothing more than a circuitous detour through peyote ceremonies and Santeria, the Society of Lucifer, and secret meetings with the late Terrence McKenna, John Running Elk, and the venerable Dr. Benway, as he searched for what he thought of as the last remnants of his lost humanity, mislaid during the seventy-two hours of personality extinction he'd experienced in Haiti, before some of Fidel's covert ops boys took pity on him and dragged him out of the underground *Oum'phor* where he could well have been abused all the way to a permanent grave.

The finale of his posttraumatic, extreme-spiritual diversion came in the form of an affair with an older woman, who had persuaded him that he should abandon his quest for his mislaid soul, because, as she put it, "the ectoplasm of lost humanity turns toxic as rapidly as sashimi in the sun." Philipa De Reske had been the estranged wife of Marcus De Reske. And she was now his widow. Between the two of them, they had built the franchised faux-religion known as the Apogee, all the way from nothing more than an insane postpsychedelic concept to a multimillion-dollar corporation with a glass tower in Beverly Hills that had doubled very comfortably as a corporate headquarters and holy temple. Philipa had, at the time, recently broken with Marcus, feeling she was also being eased off the gravy train, and her seat given to Marcus's latest bimbo-of-death mistress, a silver blonde name Tara Swerling. In an impulse of devilment and payback, Philipa had shown Coulson enough of the inside workings of the Apogee for him to fully grasp how mind control, gussied up as New Age faith, could really get freaky with its followers and effortlessly separate them from their money.

Philipa De Reske had probably saved Jack Coulson from being nothing more than another tedious, murder-for-hire asshole, just one more wet-work whore among the Miami Cubans, rabid Serbs and Chechens, IRA Provos, unemployed KGB, and former Green Berets who went in for that kind of thing. From the zombie dust to the Apogee, Coulson's quest for enlightenment had, if nothing else, made him a unique specialist in certain areas of occult combat. Philipa convinced him that he should stop resisting and accept his experience as a pointer to vocation, that he had no real alternative to the role of occult warrior, so he might as well go with what he was good at. She had set him on the course that had led him back, if not to the general rough-and-tumble of international intrigue, at least to the more rarefied conspiracies of men like Herbert Walker Grael, and ultimately to being on this Gulfstream headed for what might just really be his heart of darkness.

He turned and glanced at Renquist and Lupo. He certainly had the right companions. Both nosferatu lay back in their seats with their eyes closed, and he wondered if they were resting or telepathically exchanging information.

Bridewell was staring at the tiny screen of a handheld television, and, suddenly finding himself with nothing to do, he recalled that he'd been living exclusively on alcohol for many hours and that he was really hungry. He rose from his seat and walked back to the small galley. No cabin attendant had been included on this flight for all the obvious reasons, but the galley was well stocked with both food and drink. He poured himself a Kirin and, beer in hand, browsed the selection of TV dinners, selected a tray of teriyaki beef on a bed of rice, and placed it in the microwave. At almost exactly at the halfway point of the preset cooking time, Thyme appeared in the entrance to the gallery. "How're you doing, Jack?"

Coulson shrugged, still watching the timer on the microwave. "I'm fine, how about you?"

"I feel like Dorothy, setting out for Oz with the two vampires and the spook."

"It seems like the nosferatu are taking over."

Coulson wanted to maintain a slim semblance of normality, at least until he'd eaten, so he didn't respond to what had to be bait for some kind of pointless and probably lengthy discussion. "Do you want a drink?"

"Sure, pour me a scotch and give me a Coke to go with it. For some reason I don't quite understand I always drink scotch and Coke when I'm flying. It's probably something to do with the cabin pressure working on the carbonation and the caffeine."

Coulson assembled scotch, ice, a tall glass, and a can of Coca-Cola. All the glasses in the gallery were actually made of plastic, and decorated with logos of various government agencies and departments.

"I'm going to be one soon."

"One what?" This was the kind of conversation that Coulson had wanted to avoid.

"I will soon be a nosferatu."

"Does Renquist know that?"

"Not yet, but he will."

Coulson tried to change the subject. "Are they sleeping out there?"

Bridewell shook her head. "I think they're having some kind of telepathic conference." She grinned. "They're probably talking about you, Jack."

Renquist had boarded the aircraft, again noting how well the keepers of American secrets treated themselves. The interior was plush with darkly muted, self-important colors. It had been decorated for those who needed their sense of power constantly reaffirmed and bolstered. The seats were soft brown leather and, although locked for takeoff and landing, could swivel at will during level flight. The passenger cabin was equipped with personal TV and computers, a chart table, and a large projection screen on the bulkhead that separated the flight deck from the cabin. As the pilot waited for final clearance, the four passengers had remained silent, each in his or her own way locked into the contemplation of embarking for the totally unknown. Renquist knew that, as soon as they were in level flight, and not headed into the sun, or anything else as completely outlandish, he needed to fill Lupo in on everything he knew, everything he'd seen, and everything he theorized or suspected. Where such an exchange would involve humans in a lengthy verbal discussion, nosferatu as intimate as Renquist and Lupo were blessed with the capacity simply to relax, close their eyes, and open their minds to each other.

Renquist could provide Lupo with a visual and highly detailed shared memory of everything that had happened to
him since he'd checked into the Watergate. At the same
time, he could supply Lupo with answers to any questions
he might pose and fill in background details on anything
that was not absolutely clear. And all the time they were
engaged in the transfer, the humans would likely assume
they were merely asleep.

The only point in the exchange where things became less
than clear was when Lupo had pressed Renquist on the
inclusion of Thyme Bridewell in the party. When he'd
talked to Coulson, Renquist hadn't exactly lied about his
promise to Thyme, but his motives for wanting to keep her
alive and bring her with them had been vague, even to
himself. Obviously she posed too clear a threat to be left
at Deerpark, with not only all the conflicts of a darklost,
but also the darklost's near-hysterical rage, should she decide that she'd been deprived, abandoned, or forsaken.
That, however, was merely a fast housecleaning of the negative aspects. If Renquist had only wanted to protect himself against what she might do, he should have killed her
as Coulson suggested. He had broken his word to humans
more times than it was possible to remember, and to cite
any promise he might have made to Bridewell was mendacious to say the least.

The positive side of making Bridewell a part of the expedition was much more difficult to delineate. In Deerpark
parlance, she was a "resource." The surface facts were as he
had described them to Coulson. The woman was a highly
trained if unorthodox operative, with a wealth of experience behind her, some of it abnormal by any scale of values.
She was also, for the time being, absolutely subject to his
command. The combination of those two factors could ob-

viously be put to use in a variety of as yet unknown situations. What he hadn't told Coulson was that, at any given time, it would be relatively easy, especially now that Lupo was with him, to transform Bridewell into full nosferatu and turn her loose on any opposition they might encounter, with all the raw and feral fury of the newly Changed. He supposed one analysis might be that he was treating Bridewell as a weapon that could be armed and primed, should the need arise, but even that was far from a complete explanation. To be completely candid, Renquist was operating on instinct rather than reason where the darklost was concerned. Fortunately, Lupo would be quite prepared to accept that and act accordingly. It wouldn't be the first time that they had embarked on a venture relying on some non-verbal and hard-to-define nosferatu intuition.

With the matter of Bridewell settled, at least for this initial stage, all that remained were the immediate specifics, and, up to boarding the aircraft, specifics had been pretty thin on the ground. What was their objective when they reached this mysterious installation with the nickname "Ice Station Zebra"? What might be expected of them, and what might they expect to confront? Renquist knew that the always meticulous Lupo was less than happy with the dearth of hard facts and stated plans of action. He was also aware that Lupo didn't really see why one or both of them didn't merely rip into Coulson's mind, and drag out all the information they could find. Again a certain level of instinct was at work. Renquist's sense was that, with Coulson, he should resist the violent impulse. It might tell them what they wanted to know in the short term, but, for the longer haul, he wanted Coulson sharp and functional, not a bleary thrall with no ideas or impulses of his own. He didn't want to turn the human operative's mind into a tattered phone book because they'd thumbed through it too carelessly or too often.

That Renquist wanted to keep Coulson's brain intact didn't, of course, preclude using the remainder of the flight to the Arctic Circle to quiz him on all that he knew—and they didn't—and ruthlessly exploit their capacity to read his visible aura to call him on any lies, half-truths, deceptions, or displays of subterfuge. Lupo wanted to get started on the questioning as soon as possible, and Renquist could find no reason to disagree with him now that he himself was no longer vulnerable or needed to employ the caution of a prisoner.

Coulson had no sooner finished his food than the two vampires started in on him. They'd had the good grace to let him eat in peace: but the moment he set down his fork, they wanted to know it all, everything, down to the smallest detail. Bridewell was very glad she wasn't in her former lover's shoes. The way that Renquist and Lupo had borne down on Jack Coulson had been little short of awesome. It might well have been enough to spook her, and the one thing Fem-Juv 8-79 prided herself on was how she didn't spook easily. She had followed Coulson out of the galley, in the waft of soy sauce, with her scotch and Coke in her hand, in a highball glass with a Justice Department logo. While he ate, she had gone back to her handheld TV, and, through all that time, the two nosferatu had remained prone in their seats with their eyes closed.

She didn't know what influence caused her to look up at the very moment that both Renquist and Lupo, in perfectly synchronized unison, opened their eyes, sat up, and stared straight at Jack Coulson: but it was enough to cause the normally self-assured Coulson to blanch white, and

Thyme was gratified to see that he was still capable of experiencing irrational fear.

Lupo delivered the bad news. "We have decided it's time to talk."

Thyme had to admit that Coulson recovered admirably, using only a sip of his beer to cover his shock. "Yes, I guess it is."

The first question came from Renquist and was relatively simple. "I understood we were taking a weapons team with us?"

Coulson nodded. "We are. They'll be flying up separately in about four hours. There's a transport flight coming up with a load of stuff for the Underlanders, and they are on it."

Lupo grumbled in his throat. "So the common foot soldiers don't travel like this?"

"Did they ever?"

Lupo treated Coulson to a long, thoughtful look. "No, I suppose not."

Renquist returned quickly to the point. "So when we first go into this Ice Station Zebra, we'll be looking out for ourselves?"

"We have no reason to expect any trouble there."

Lupo continued to stare stone-faced at Coulson. "Why not?"

"It's an area of neutrality. A DMZ."

"Neutrality between what and what?"

"Between the US and Underland. It's where all the trading is done."

"I thought contact had ceased."

"Trade continues."

"How?"

"There's a trade representative who meets each shipment,

places the new orders, and arranges the transfers of funds."

"That hardly sounds like a total breakdown of communications."

Coulson's forehead had taken on a slight sheen as though he was either beginning to sweat or his collar was too tight. From where Thyme sat, the stares of the two nosferatu were clearly starting to pressure him. Not that Coulson didn't merit or deserve some pressure. Jack was slick, and he could use a challenge. His personal craziness had been honed by some fairly outrageous wheels of fortune to the point that he could be as smooth as polished marble, and bright as the chrome on a new trailer hitch. Thyme had rarely seen him meet his match. He had almost certainly not told Renquist all there was to know about the mission, and this now seemed to be the time of reckoning.

"The breakdown in communications is in that we have no idea what's going on in Underland."

Lupo was looking increasingly unhappy. "So what happens when we get to Ice Station Zebra?"

"I make contact with the Underland trade representative and hope to persuade him to arrange an audience with whoever is now in power."

"And what do we do?"

"Wait and see how he reacts."

"And if he reacts badly, what then?"

"At that point we apply some pressure. He has to be made to understand that our request is backed with the full force of the United States government."

Lupo noisily exhaled. "Wars have started over less."

Coulson sighed. "I'm well aware of that. We will be walking a narrow line."

Thyme found it hard to fault the way Jack was handling Lupo and Renquist. He had the technique of appearing

frank and candid, but at the same time giving away only what was absolutely necessary. He had the added advantage of not only having talked the talk but also of having walked the walk for a considerable distance. In that, he was radically different from the federal career flunkies inside Deerpark, and all the other soulless establishments just like it that the government had scattered around the nation. When handling the hellish, Jack Coulson could be more than just theoretical. Jack Coulson had not just visited his personal hell, he had served a protracted sentence there, and, in fact, might still only be out on spiritual parole. Something had happened to him in Haiti, the details of which he'd securely chained down and hidden behind iron masks somewhere on the far side of denial. During their affair, one time after orgasm, he had attempted to tell her about it in an Italian hotel room. They had both been drunk, intoxicated but still capable. Standing with his back to her, naked at an open window, drinking grappa from the bottle, smoking a Marlboro, and staring into a hazy Roman dawn, he had launched into a confused and headlong story of a Tonton Macout ambush, the forcible use of the zombie drug, and a descent into living death. Seemingly the Tontons had then brought him to some kind of underground Oum'phor or temple, where he became the focus of some outlandishly horrible ceremony. He'd been unable to describe the details of what had been done to him, each time breaking down, unable to continue. He attempted to resume the monologue four times, but had always faltered, ending in inarticulate lip-biting, and, after the fourth try, he had collapsed sobbing like a baby in Thyme's arms. The next morning, and forever after, the incident was never referred to again.

A few seconds of silence ensued while Renquist and

Lupo considered what they had learned so far. "The other teams that went in, they also walked the narrow line?"

"More or less."

"But they lost their footing?"

"So it would appear."

"How much do you know about exactly what happened to them?"

"Not a great deal. Or, to be precise, I haven't been told a great deal."

"Don't your people believe in the maxim forewarned is forearmed?"

"They've never made it past need-to-know. That's why they fuck up so often."

Renquist brought the conversation back to the subject at hand. "So what exactly happened to the previous attempts to penetrate Underland?"

"We touched on that back at Deerpark."

Renquist made an impatient gesture. "I know we touched on it, but the time has come for any and all details."

Coulson rose from his seat, picked up the used food tray and the empty beer bottle, and went to the galley, talking as he opened another beer. "The first group went in the hard way. They were all ex–Delta Force, and they wanted to do the macho ice trek. They left Zebra in a helicopter that set them down close to the Fissure. From there they approached on foot, with intention of climbing down without the Underlanders knowing. We had communication with them until they began the descent of the Arctic Fissure, but that was all they wrote. As far as anyone could work out, they either fell or were intercepted and killed."

"So the second team tried another route?"

"They employed a scenario closer to the one we're using."

Lupo scowled. "That's encouraging."

Coulson continued. "They were met at Ice Station Zebra by a delegation of Underlanders who conducted them below."

"And they, too, were never seen again?"

"We never saw them, but they were in radio contact for the next two weeks, routinely checking in."

"And after that?"

"There was silence for a week, and one final and highly cryptic message."

"Which was?"

"That they'd embraced the Serpent and would make no further communication. They intimated that they would be staying in Underland."

"And was this believed?"

"It prompted a lot of discussion. As far as we could tell, they weren't broadcasting under duress. They certainly used none of the prearranged keywords that would indicate anything like that. I pretty much accepted they'd willingly crossed over."

"And no one theorized why?"

"There were a million theories. None seemed to hold water. That's why we now find ourselves cruising at thirty thousand feet."

Coulson paused and took a hit on his beer. Thyme was pleased she wasn't the one under interrogation. Renquist and Lupo were a prefect team. Renquist was the scalpel, Lupo was the highly accurate blunt instrument. Renquist leaned forward, with the intensity of a rapid-fire, big-money chess player. Lupo sat back and coldly contemplated. Massive and foursquare, he stared over his prow of a nose, through eyes so narrowed that, even though he had never looked into the sun, deep ridges and furors were etched in his face. Where Thyme Bridewell had previously only been enthralled by Renquist alone, she now found herself hopelessly in love with the sheer magnificence of the nosferatu as a breed. They were so formidable, but at the same time so powerfully uncomplicated. Unlike humans, they required no validation of their existence. They did not question why or what they were, and they certainly seemed to have no desire to reshape the world in their image. Indeed, quite the reverse. For Thyme to be reshaped in Renquist's image, she might have to grovel on her knees, begging him to Change her: but she was, now more than ever, completely devoted to the idea of becoming the same as he and Lupo, and all the others that might lurk in the night.

"This Underland trade representative, who and what is he?"

Coulson indicated a pile of folders on the plan table. "There's a short dossier on him."

Lupo slowly but emphatically shook his head. "I am too old for dossiers. I leave them to humans and the young. Just tell me in your own words."

Renquist reached for the folders. "Explain it to Lupo. I'll glance at the dossier while you're talking. What is this person's name?"

"John Tiberius Beauregard."

Renquist sorted through the folders until he found the correct one. "John T. Beauregard Jr."

As Renquist opened the folder, Coulson looked directly at Lupo. "This Beauregard would appear to be second-generation Underlander."

"Second-generation?"

"His family arrived there after the influx of Nazi fugitives, but have been down below long enough for John T. Jr. to have been born beneath the surface."

"And who was his father?"

"His father, John T. Sr., came out of the rotting gumbo of Louisiana politics, and moved from something akin to a Huey Long position, further and further to the right, until he was too fucking crazy even for the Klan. Some even maintain he was hanging with Clay Shaw, David Ferrie, and the rest of the New Orleans Kennedy conspirators. By the midsixties old John T. appears to have gone completely insane. He declared himself a Nordic pagan, which put him at complete odds with the Christian Right, then claimed that the takeover by the New World Order was going to come down at any moment and that he was heading out for the Land under the Earth. After about 1973, he vanished, never to be seen again. The more rational concluded that John T. had finally lost his mind, killed his entire family, then himself out in some impenetrable bayou, where the alligators disposed of the bodies."

"But he really made it to Underland?"

Coulson nodded. "In his madness, it seemed he figured it out for real."

Renquist looked up from the dossier, obviously amused. "That's one of the troubles with the current practice of enfolding secrets in a winding-sheet of paranoid fantasy. Now and again the extremely paranoid discover exactly what was supposed to be kept secret from them."

Lupo was pensive. "He moved to Underland with his whole family, like some kind of paranormal pioneer?"

"The only one of the Beauregards who remained topside was the eldest son, Samuel T., who ran away to the San

Fernando Valley to make gay porno tapes under the stage name Sam Ramm. Needless to say, he and his daddy really didn't get along. In fact, Sam Ramm turned out weird so early that his name was changed and the second son became John T. Jr."

Renquist tapped the dossier. "It says here that Beauregard Jr. sports the titles 'Companion of the Serpent' and 'Stormleader of the Iron Order.'"

"A little disquieting, I admit."

Renquist nodded in agreement. "Was the possibility considered that any entirely new social system might have evolved down there?"

Coulson sighed. "It was by me, but the government suits could only think within the parameters of some variety of twentieth-century totalitarian autocracy."

Renquist warmed to the subject. "Such titles as this Beauregard assumes usually indicate the social order is degenerating to feudalism."

Now Lupo joined in. "And feudalism generally involves the adaption to some form of divinity."

"Or at least a divinely appointed monarch."

The boys were getting to the point of mutual congratulation, and Thyme decided the male bonding, even if it was cross-species, had gone far enough. "And a divinely anointed monarch brings us squarely back to divinity."

Renquist looked at Bridewell as though he had completely forgotten about her. She laughed. "You don't listen to a word I say, do you, Renquist? You're making me the invisible bimbo again."

Then, to Thyme's even greater amusement, Renquist, before he could respond, was cut off by the pilot's voice over the intercom. "Gentleman, Ms. Bridewell, we are starting our descent to NORAD 40. If you are currently moving

around the cabin, it might be advisable to resume your
seats."

The air was so cold that it was devoid of content. Renquist
had never been above the Arctic Circle before. As far as he
could calculate, St. Petersburg was as far north as he'd ever
gone. It was not the climate that had directed his wanderings away from the far north. The temperature didn't
bother him at all, and he rather enjoyed snow. He had
never headed toward the North Pole, or the South Pole for
that matter, because humans didn't thrive in those places.
The Nosferatu were man-feeders. They followed the herds,
and could not prosper in a wilderness where freezing humans feared to tread. The distance from the Gulfstream's
passenger door to the igloolike tunnel that led inside the
NORAD 40 complex of single-story buildings, nine-tenths
buried in the snow, was around a hundred feet. Bridewell
and Coulson had donned heavy coats before stepping out
of the plane, and they still ran, heads down against the
cutting subzero winds, for the sanctuary of warmth and
shelter. Renquist and Lupo, on the other hand, covered the
distance at a leisurely pace, Lupo holding his hat, Renquist's hair streaming wildly, and the coats of their Washington street clothes flapping like demented raven wings as
they paused to look up at the sky where, between masses
of cloud, the starfields shone, brilliant and dense in the frozen sky, so far from the glare and airborne filth of cities.

Inside the base, the atmosphere was radically different,
warm, almost steamy, with undertones of a sauna, and dozens of conflicting smells: baking, alcohol, dirty clothes, aviation fuel, hot metal, and damp leather. In some respects,
it resembled nothing more than a crowded, if makeshift,
and not very well maintained ski lodge, and, like a ski

lodge, it was noisy. Vintage country music played over a less-than-discreet PA system, but as they moved into what was laughingly called the transit lounge, Patsy Cline was forced to compete with the electronic crash of pinball machines and the sound cards of arcade games. An entire community seemed to be gathered in this portal between the above and the below. Renquist didn't see any faces he actually knew, but the collection of human types was highly familiar. Military and mercenary, players and adventurers, crazy scientists and crazier covert operators; with few exceptions, a variety of Joseph Conrad misfits, updated by a hundred years, and modified for the modern world. Ice Station Zebra was populated by the same aberrant personality profiles and distorted genomes that had once manned the far-flung outposts of empires and would, sometime in the future, establish the first colonies on Mars.

By far the majority of auras told of junkie-slaves to the endorphin rush. The kind of brain chemical hunger that could always be found in professional soldiers, war photographers, cowboy drug smugglers, and rough-terrain taxi pilots. They also leaked a nervousness and an anticipation—a fear of what could happen next, and the hope for what might. Collectively it was an emotional combination that caused them to drink a lot and boast of their exploits in a booze-lubricated camaraderie. As human company went, Renquist could have chosen a good deal worse, although the surface of shared adversity hid a more negative lower waft of intrigue, conspiracy, distrust, and suspicion. Spooks, spies, observers, informers, and stone killers were all well represented. Many of these men and women had not only the potential for violence when required, but also a thorough, field-tested grounding in its practical applications. Although they were clothed in parkas, anoraks, and kapok quilting, fancy sweaters, and spandex, they were dangerous professionals, not snow bunnies and their escorts. In the den he was in, sex and hot chocolate might be included somewhere on the menu, but neither was given a particularly high priority without an ulterior motive.

Renquist was immediately aware that he'd been lied to by either Coulson, Grael, or both. If communication between Underland and the USA was as limited and interrupted as they'd claimed, why were so many people at the transit point? The only other explanation was that NSA-FEMA Paranormal was being fed a mess of disinformation, and he wasn't sure which alternative he liked less. He immediately communicated his findings to Lupo, who straightaway looked round for Coulson. "He should be braced on this matter, Don Victor."

Renquist wasn't so sure, and also Coulson had, at least temporarily, vanished. "Leave him for now. I prefer just to get a feel for the place."

Lupo glanced around. "I think I'd prefer to be somewhere a little more private. We are much too noticeable in this mass of humanity."

Renquist and Lupo had realized the same thing at exactly the same moment. Renquist in his leather jacket and Lupo in his mobster overcoat hardly conformed to the unstated, but very obvious, practical dress code at Ice Station Zebra. In their demonstration of bravado at not feeling the cold, they had rather overreached themselves. Not to feel the cold was one thing, to attempt to blend with a mass of humans who did was something else again. Already their outfits, so plainly from a more temperate climate, were drawing curious glances, and Renquist knew it was too late for a dignified retreat, had there even been somewhere to which they *could* retreat. "I think we've screwed up here, my

friend. If anyone here is capable of recognizing us for what
we really are, we have already betrayed ourselves, and everyone in the room at least knows there's something anoma-
lous about us. The best we can do is to brazen it out."

"I don't like this."

"Neither do I, but it can't be helped. We've erred, and
we're going to have to live with it. The only factor in our
favor is that the humans in this place are very far from
normal themselves."

While Renquist and Lupo had taken the time to inspect
the room, Bridewell had headed straight for the transit
lounge bar and was ordering a drink. She appeared completely unfazed by those around her and, as far as Renquist
could read her, she seemed perfectly at home, almost comfortable. She might have owed him the fealty of the darklost, but Thyme Bridewell was among what was still her
own kind. Renquist grasped that, up to this point, he had
been thinking of Ice Station Zebra as the calm before the
storm—a place of rest and preparation before the real chal-
lenges came. In that he had been completely and profoundly wrong. Ice Station Zebra was a challenge in itself.
His inappropriate style of dress and his unpreparedness for
what he was now discovering, had left both himself and
Lupo vulnerable. This had to stop. He had to be far more
careful from there on out. He didn't feel entirely responsible for the mistakes. He had neither been briefed nor
warned as to what to expect when the plane landed, and
that was unforgivable. If Coulson had known, he should
have alerted him and shared the information. On the other
hand, if Coulson had come there with no more clue than
Renquist, then he should not have been leading their expedition at all.

Renquist found himself with no option but to join

Bridewell at the bar, but, as he moved through the crowd, he began wondering, just like Lupo, where the hell Coulson had vanished to.

"Why the fuck wasn't I warned?"

"There was no time."

"You're trying to tell me that everyone and their uncle all had the same idea at the same time?"

Walter Weir was Jack Coulson's contact at Ice Station Zebra, and NSA-FEMA's man on the ground. He had buttonholed Coulson the moment he stepped inside the base entrance and whisked him into an empty office.

"The first I knew of was when we started getting all these requests for landing clearances."

Weir keyed a lengthy code into a computer on the desk in the small spartan room that seemed to double as his office and living quarters, and brought up a breakdown of arrivals and departures over the previous two days. The secret base had been handling a traffic flow comparable with that of a small-town commercial airport. Centerfolds from *Maxim* and *Playboy* pouted down from the walls attempting to humanize the military-issue steel of the highly utilitarian desk, table, bunk, filing cabinets, and lockers. "I've reported all this to Deerpark, but they're demanding explanations just like you."

"Couldn't some of the clearances have been denied, or at least stalled until we could get out of here?"

Weir looked even more helpless. "NSA-FEMA doesn't have the lock on who comes and goes. There's a whole lot of agencies and corporations who kick in for the upkeep of this place, and they expect to be able to use it whenever they want."

Coulson appealed to the naked women in the glossy pictures for some kind of calming influence, but found none. "So where's my transport in all this aerial logjam?"

Weir avoided his eyes. "Its takeoff from Andrews had to be delayed. It won't be up here for at least seven hours. I managed to get your flight priority clearance, but that ain't going to happen for a C3 full of gin and computers."

"Gin, computers, and my backup squad."

"There wasn't a damned thing I could do about it. Deerpark had that information before I did. They should have clued you in."

To go into full agency foul-up so early in the mission was beyond Coulson's worst objective fears, and he found that all he could do was curse. "What the fuck, Walt? Why do we work for these jackass government retards?"

"Yeah well, Jack, before you go into the full shit fit, there's worse."

"There's worse?"

"Something's hotting up down under. There's been encrypted stuff coming from the tower on the edge of the Fissure for the last ten hours."

"Has it been read?"

"I'm a glorified janitor and check-in clerk, not a code-breaker, for fuck's sake. Besides there's a whole manual of protocols about communications from down under. We cut each other some slack up here at Zebra, you know what I mean? We're a subzero facility with polar stress. We fucking live here in Little Claustrophobia. We try and get along. We don't need anyone going critical or maxing out with an Uzi."

"Did you at least find out where all this shit was being sent to?"

"What do you take me for?"

"So far a glorified janitor with a skin mag collection. Enlighten me?"

"Like you said, to everyone and his uncle. A whole lot of extra stuff to Talesian's office at the White House, plenty of petro-chemical, a lot of military industrial, and of course the super-echelon black hole shit going to places that aren't supposed to exist." Weir paused. "There was also a cookie for you."

"Shit."

"A direct word from Beauregard. He's coming in early. He wants you there to meet him when he touches down."

"The fuck he does."

"You've never met him, right?"

"No, but . . ."

"Up here, his wish is your command, and he's one bad motherfucker. We're talking Darth Vader Jr. He could burn this place off the ice if he wanted to. He's C of S."

"What are you talking about?"

"You plan on going down under, and you don't know about the C of S?"

"What?"

"Companions of the Serpent. That's the bottom line. You don't fuck with the C of S. You don't even talk about the C of S."

"Do you know who I have with me?"

"Two heavyweight weirdos and Thyme Bridewell?"

At least it wasn't common knowledge that Renquist and Lupo were vampires. Perhaps he should be grateful for that small mercy. "Fucking a-firm on that. And now I've got to meet with this Beauregard without even my weapons team behind me. It's fucked up, Walt. It's really fucked up."

"That's because your thinking is one-eighty ass backwards, and it's stagnating the process, Jack. Out here, it's not us that run things, it's them. It's their back door, pal, not ours. We just sit here in the snow at their pleasure."

"How long before Beauregard shows up?"

"Twenty minutes. Maybe a half hour."

"This is fucking crazy, Walt."

"Just wait a half hour, Jack. You'll see just how fucking crazy."

Thyme Bridewell was being told nothing, and she was starting to fume. Vampire or human, they all behaved like men, expecting her simply to go along without a word of explanation. When Coulson had come to extract her from the transit lounge she had committed the only act of rebellion she could think of on the spur of the moment. She made Coulson wait while she had the bartender top up her glass with vodka. He didn't take it well. "We've got to hurry, goddamn it."

"Not until you tell me why."

"We have to meet this character Beauregard from the Underland."

"Thanks for telling me that, at least."

"Listen, Thyme, I just don't have the patience to humor you right now."

Drink in hand, she emerged from the transit lounge followed by Renquist, Lupo, and, finally, Coulson, only to find a group of five gunmen waiting for them. Although they weren't in uniform, dressed instead in an assortment of cold weather combat clothing and sporting an unshaven, unkempt, Arctic look, they all wore sidearms. One also carried a shotgun, while another had a stripped down AK-47 at his side. Thyme knew enough to at least put a temporary cover on her disgruntlement and keep her dissent to herself.

The function of this well-strapped crew was far from clear. Were they there to protect or compel, to ensure her safety, and that of Lupo and Renquist, or to make damn sure they all did what they were told on the way to meet this mysterious Beauregard from the Underland?

Thyme knew one of the five. Walt Weir was a light-skinned ex-Marine, another hired gun like Jack Coulson, although he had never matched Coulson's prominence or reputation. Two more of the crew carried themselves as though they had put in their time in the military, while the remaining pair walked with the easy insolence of brigands or terrorists. Her only consolation at finding herself under armed escort again was that at least the escort was made up of her kind of people, not the grim and mindless killer-goon-robot, deathsquad breed that the Old Man employed as Security at Deerpark.

Thyme noticed, as she was checking them out, that Lupo was doing the same, and seemingly coming to much the same conclusion. He saw that any kind of resistance or demand for an explanation was pointless. He nodded to Renquist as though silently communicating his assessment, and both nosferatu fell into step with Weir and his men, as the newly augmented party moved off deeper into the bowels of the secret base. Thyme was starting to see how Renquist and Lupo operated when they were together as a duo. The linked minds of the nosferatu, freed of the human need for clumsy and imprecise language, were awesome in their economy of time and effort. She also observed that they worked to a long-ago-defined pattern. Lupo deferred to Renquist in most things. This had already been made obvious by his constant use of the appellation *Don Victor* as though he was an old-time Moustache Pete mafiosi. Where safety and security were concerned, however, Lupo seemed to make the calls, functioning as Renquist's protector, look-out, and wingman.

Lupo's unhesitating reaction had left Thyme to bring up the rear of the party, but when Coulson moved next to Renquist, and the two started talking, she hurried to catch up and hear what was being said. She was not encouraged when she saw the grim expressions on the faces of the nos-feratu and the man. Then she heard Coulson tell Renquist how there was considerably more going on at Ice Station Zebra than they had expected when they set out.

"I don't have time to explain it all now. We have to meet with Beauregard, but as soon as I get a private moment, I'll fill you in on as much as I know."

Renquist kept pace with Coulson but regarded him coldly. "This is extremely unsatisfactory."

"I know."

"It would seem that we only get the bad news when it's far too late to turn back."

"I'm well aware of that, but we're both in the same po-sition. The Old Man has been concealing stuff from me from the git-go."

"So what do you suggest?"

"We can only hang together and present a united front."

Renquist seemed less than convinced. "A united front?"

"If we fall out among ourselves now, I don't see us get-ting through this."

Renquist glanced at Lupo, who gave the slightest of nods. Apparently when the only remaining option was still less than acceptable, but could not be realistically rejected, Lupo didn't waste time wishing or complaining. He made the best of a sorry situation and moved on.

Like Deerpark, but for very different reasons, most of the base was built under the ground, or at least under the snow. The route taken by Weir and followed by everyone else led them through tunnels, passages, and narrow companionways, uneven and meandering, some still under construction, and lit with neon tubes, hooked in line with a great deal of exposed wiring. Finally, they climbed a flight of steel steps and emerged into a viewing area, a long narrow gallery in which an expanse of double or perhaps triple glazing looked down on a wide concrete apron, lit and marked out like a section of deck from an aircraft carrier. Outside, the weather had changed. A thick overcast had moved in, and small snow flurries were harbingers of more to come. At first it seemed there was nothing to see beyond the landing area, except featureless grey. Then Weir turned to Coulson and pointed out beyond the glass. "There, look over there."

At first it was only a dark shape dropping down from the overcast, but gradually it began to take on a solid form. The same inverted saucer that Renquist had seen in the 1947 film from Neuschwabenland in Antarctica was now materializing out of the fog beyond the double glass, dropping majestically for a vertical landing. As he was able to make out details, he saw it was sleeker than the attack craft that had routed Admiral Byrd's forces back in the aftermath of World War II. That made sense, assuming that new machines had been built, and design improvements had been made. The craft still had the ironclad pomposity of the forties version; even though it came with fewer plates and rivets, it still kept the look of a circular submarine rather than any flying machine. It retained the essential shape of the upside-down dish with the domed superstructure, and an irregular jumble of spheres and steel hoses on the underside that had to be the basic propulsion unit. The new model, however, had more the lozenge/pod look of dark fifties science fiction, a style that seemed to be enjoying a renaissance in modern cyberdesign. The greenhouse panes of the old canopy had been replaced by one large piece of smoothly molded Plexiglas, like the cockpit canopy on a SabreJet, only a hundred times larger. It was tinted the same smoky gold as an astronaut's faceplate, and dark figures could be seen both standing and moving in the dim, lit-from-below control room.

Weir gestured to the machine with something akin to pride. "That's the *Flugelrad*, gentlemen and lady."

Bridewell was the first to react. Her aura blazed with disbelief, shock, and delight. For a moment, she was nothing more than a deranged and wicked damaged child, seeing something that she had always wanted to see. First vampires and now this. "Holy shit. It really is a fucking flying saucer, just like in the film. A fucking Nazi UFO. I don't believe it."

Renquist said nothing, and he noticed Lupo had all but turned to stone. It was plain from his aura that he hardly believed it either. Renquist moved closer to the glass. The twenty-first-century Flugelrad shared more than just a fundamental configuration with its predecessor. Admittedly keeping up with the latest developments in contemporary aviation was not something he did with any particular diligence, and he'd never been in one of the supersecret places like Dreamland, but something about the saucer was, to his eyes, not quite right. Like the vintage model, the craft that was making a leisurely and apparently effortless landing that also gave the impression its designer had made almost no attempt to minimize the weight of the machine, and that could only indicate one of two things. If the *Flugelrad* still employed some improved version of Schreiver's liquid vortex engine, the thing must have a huge power-to-weight ratio. Either that, or the Underlanders had been messing around with some form of antigravity, something supposedly years beyond any current human capability.

How could these complete outsiders, isolated from the mainstream of scientific research and supposedly crippled by the poisonous Nazi ideology that they'd taken down below with them, be able to make such startling technological leaps? Could they have had help? And, if so, from where could that help have come? The USA? The old USSR? Neither of them had antigravity to his knowledge. Renquist didn't want to think what would have been the first thought for any human conspiracy theorist. He didn't want to consider that the Underlanders's help might have originated in some infinite elsewhere. Deep in his nosferatu DNA were the memories of the great conspiracy of fourteen thousand years ago, the conflict that had extended far beyond the Earth, and in which the planet itself, and its monkey inhabitants, had been no more than a mere footnote in an epic power struggle, the history of which was still being laboriously and destructively written across the galaxy. The very double helix of his kind, and also that of the humanity, was the engineered product of that conspiracy. The nosferatu genome still bore the alien splices by which the Nephilim had made him what he was.

Renquist noticed how the emblem emblazoned on the side of the *Flugelrad* had also changed. It was neither the infamous Nazi swastika nor the black Iron Cross of the kaisers. It was now a thick, upright, straight-sided cross, geometrically enclosed in a circle, as though the original swastika had closed its hooks. A stylized snake crawled up the vertical of the cross. For Renquist it was something new. The barbarous Nordic mysticism of the Nazis was a retreat to the lower levels of spirituality, but had their Underland off-spring withdrawn so much further into the murk and shadow that they were now embracing serpent cults? Through the labyrinth of history, in different places and at different times, reptile worship had reigned omnipotent for centuries at a time. The origins of such sects predated the nosferatu, the Nephilim invasion, and the alien domination by the God-King Marduk Ra. The roots of the serpent cults were clouded and concealed, but seemingly went all the way back to the *ultima thule,* the baleful cold of the last ice age.

Just before the saucer touched down, a rainbow glow, like the aurora in miniature, flickered briefly between the *Flugelrad*'s steel skirt and the concrete of the apron. The release of energy was unlike anything Renquist had ever seen. The glitter of color was more than enough to generate further uninformed speculation on what technical advances these Underlanders might have made during their separation from the surface world, but then a two-man ground crew, in thick, fur-lined parkas, wool masks, and goggles advanced on the machine with a long, steel-tipped lance. Thick power cables ran back from the lance to connections inside an open inspection cover on the flat surface of the apron, and the two technicians handled the lance with industrial-strength rubber gauntlets.

Thyme frowned and glanced at Weir. "What the fuck are they doing?"

"Grounding the *Flugelrad*. Those things build up one fuck of a jolt of static, even on the short flight between here and the Fissure."

"This is getting a tad weird even for me."

"Girl, you ain't seen nothing yet." He turned so the next

remark included Renquist and Lupo. "You should all watch your eyes. It can be like an arc light."

The lance touched the side of the machine and created a brief but brilliant flash. Something akin to St. Elmo's fire ran up and down the lance's length, but Renquist didn't see it. Coulson's warning had come too late. He had managed to shield his eyes a little with hastily raised hands, but he still found himself awash in a sea of floating afterimages. Bridewell was cursing. Some darklost developed a sympathetic sensitivity to light. "Goddamn it, Coulson. You could have warned us."

"I did warn you."

"Not fucking soon enough. I'm half-blind."

The men on the landing apron had now put down their grounding lance, and were running out a soft plastic tube, about eight feet in diameter, manhandling its expanding concertina folds until it stretched from a door to the base to an entry hatch in the saucer section of the *Flugelrad*. The tube functioned like a protective jetway, insulating such passengers and crew who might disembark from the wild wind, snow, and freezing cold. When the access tunnel was in place, the hatch slid sideways. Two figures emerged, hurried down the tube, and went inside the base. Renquist looked quickly at Weir. "Is that Beauregard deplaning?"

Weir nodded. "That's our boy."

"And where's he going?"

"He'll be right here to see you guys. It won't take him but a minute to get up here."

Renquist rounded on Coulson. "Anything new about this man that I should be told a moment before he arrives? Is there anything previously forgotten along the lines of non-communication?"

Coulson shook his head. "I swear."

"Okay."

"When dealing with Beauregard . . ."

Renquist's head snapped round as Weir spoke. "Yes?"

"Call him Colonel."

"I thought he was a Stormleader of the Iron Order."

"He's from Dixie and not as into all the Teutonic knights crap as the rest of them. I call him 'Colonel,' and he seems to like it. At least he answers to it."

"Thank you, Mr. Weir."

"You're welcome, Mr. Renquist."

"Is there anything else?"

"If you get the urge to fuck with him, resist it."

For the second time in a matter of minutes, Thyme could hardly believe what she was seeing, but this time she only exclaimed in an under-her-breath whisper. "Does someone want to tell me what the fuck is going on here?"

Was this a costume for a movie? Some Confederate air ace, or one of Quantrill's space pirates? The shiny black, rubberized coat hung clear to the spurs on the inevitable cavalry boots, while the wolf pelt that formed the collar framed his face like a ruff. He wore a serpent ring on the pinky finger of the black glove on his right hand, and a velvet tunic, belted at the waist, showed when the long coat swung unbuttoned. Thyme wondered why he didn't have a falcon on his wrist, as she watched him strut toward them like Prince Prospero in "The Masque of the Red Death." His eyes were hidden behind a pair of black goggles, an elaborate construction that seemed to incorporate different settings and changes of lens, and also a small flashlight lined up to point anywhere the wearer might look; but that feature was, of course, turned off in the neon glare of the base. Thyme could imagine that mole people might have trouble with their eyes, and the complex goggles might be a solution.

"Colonel Beauregard." Weir greeted the approaching Underlander.

"Mr. Weir. Is it cold enough for you?" Beauregard returned the greeting with great affability for one so obviously dressed to intimidate. His accent was strange. His speech patterns and inflections sounded to Thyme as though he had learned by painful repetition to try and speak like his forebears, but a lot of other Underland influences crept in, turning his drawl into a Dixie-fried parody. Below the goggles, his face was narrow and pale. A lifetime in the Hollow Earth seemed to have leached the pigment from the flesh of Colonel Johnny Beauregard, and his lips were almost without color. His hair was either black or dark brown, but plastered down lank, slick, and close to his skull, with a limp lock draped over the right eye of his goggles in an odd confluence of Marilyn Manson, Adolf Hitler, and Spanky from the *Our Gang* shorts.

Thyme noticed that Weir didn't move to meet Beauregard, but remained where he was, and let the Underlander come to him. Doubtless a token display of US truculence. "Indeed it is, Colonel. About as cold as you can expect at the North Pole in the dead of winter."

"We're warm enough down in the Fissure. You should come down and visit with us, Mr. Weir."

"I don't know, Colonel. I have enough to keep me busy."

Beauregard's voice took on a mildly unpleasant edge. "You're not afraid of us Underlanders, are you, Mr. Weir?"

"No, Colonel. Just well aware of my place." Weir quickly changed the subject. "You seem to be a tad early. The supply plane won't be in for a few hours yet."

Beauregard dismissed this with a wave of his gloved hand. "I'm well aware of the supply plane's ETA. Van Pelt here can take care of that." He indicated the other Underlander, who was a less flamboyant version of Beauregard. He wore the same long coat, except without the fur collar. His hair was close-cropped, and his goggles by no means as ingeniously elaborate. "I've come at this time to meet our visitors from Washington."

"Well these are they, Colonel." He pointed to each of the party in turn. "This is Mr. Coulson, Señor Lupo, Mr. Renquist, and Ms. Thyme Bridewell."

Beauregard made a theatrical performance of removing his right glove and ring, taking Thyme's hand and lightly kissing it. She observed that his hand was clammy and that he affected purple nail varnish of a shade she would never use herself. Beauregard plainly fancied himself as the dashing gallant, but Bridewell wished she could see behind the goggles. She had a bad feeling that, although they might be protecting him from the bright light of surface dwellers, they might also be hiding something in his eyes that he didn't wish revealed. She wondered what Renquist might be making of the Underlander's mind. She couldn't believe that he wasn't already up inside it.

After a show of fawning over Bridewell, Beauregard turned his attention to Coulson, Lupo, and, finally, Renquist. He shook hands with the first two, then came to Renquist. As their hands touched, skin on skin, Renquist went into his mind, hard but exceedingly fast, in the hope that he could glean a basic background and withdraw before the human was aware of what had happened to him. On the upper-conscious level, Beauregard seemed to be enjoying himself. His vanity basked in the nervousness he instilled in the surface dwellers. He commanded his own *Flugelrad,* had a wardrobe of gorgeous uniforms, and considered himself one hell of a fellow. On another level he was extremely glad to be breathing the air of the base. Renquist gathered that Underland had a chronic pollution problem.

Going deeper, Renquist found that Beauregard was interested in Bridewell, and already formulating idle and fantastic sexual plans. It would appear that John T. Beauregard was sexually active and highly omnivorous; but, as Renquist had already suspected, the pose of the uniformed fop was merely a defense. The lower depths of the Underlander's mind were a tumor of paranoid fascism dressed up in a corrupted *Gone With the Wind* romance. Down in the murk that was the true John Beauregard, halls of mountain kings became confused with stately antebellum mansions; and he entertained daydreams of furious spectacle in which towns burned, and whole populations were put to the sword, or wiped out in the course of long and formal mass executions, while all the time Beauregard rode at the head of his troops, through smoke and fire, urging them on to bestial glory from the back of a plunging stallion, the bridge of a *Flugelrad,* or the turret of a Tiger tank.

Renquist, however, was not at all interested either in Beauregard's confusion or his schoolboy dreams of conquest and slaughter, so he cut to the area of social order in Underland, as the man perceived it. From what Renquist was discovering, the Stormleader had an imperiously limited perspective. The composite picture drawn by Beauregard's conditioned responses was one of a caste system in which violent young males were the apex. If not in complete power, they were certainly running round armed to the teeth in preposterous costumes. Renquist realized there was nothing new in that, but again the technology was the most compelling riddle. A society that appeared so decidedly primitive, with a definite hint of the barbaric, should not have a machine like the *Flugelrad*. Where, to echo The Joker, did they get all those wonderful toys?

The closest the young man came to providing an answer was the suggestion of a technopriest class who handled that end of things. In his arrogance, Beauregard was neither very interested nor well informed as to where the weapons that fed his macabre visions of grand and passionate triumph and figured so prominently in his tangled appetites for power and destruction came from. He barely knew how these killing tools really worked and had no idea of the mechanics of their production. He was blessed with a skill for operating them, and that was as far as his involvement needed to go. Renquist judged him simplistic even by human standards and swiftly withdrew from his mind.

The intrusion didn't seem to have registered with Beauregard. He was briskly pulling his right glove back on. "Shall we saddle up, my newfound friends?"

"Shall we what?"

He replaced his ring. "Shall we get going? The craft awaits. We are only burning fuel."

Coulson stared at Beauregard in open amazement. "You want us simply to come with you right now?"

"That was the understanding, wasn't it?"

Coulson knew that he was rapidly losing all control over the drama. Not only was he no longer writing the script, but he didn't even have a copy of the one they were currently using. To make matters worse, Beauregard appeared highly amused by Coulson's discomfort. "That was the understanding wasn't it? That you should immediately be brought down to Underland? So you could take the tour and prepare a report for the Yankee security agency?"

"You seem to be better informed than I am."

Both Beauregard and Coulson looked to Weir—Beauregard for confirmation and Coulson for explanation. Weir returned Coulson's questioning stare with a shrug. "That's the way I heard it. Just like the colonel said."

Now Coulson not only didn't know who to believe, but was filled with doubts about Weir. For whom might he be ultimately working? He had been very insistent when Coulson had first arrived that he accept the reality of the situation. "Out here, it's not us that run things, it's them." That's what he'd said. Maybe Weir had made what he saw as a pragmatic acceptance of reality, and transferred his loyalties to Underland. Coulson wondered how many betrayals within betrayals he should now expect. Even as he tried to react without any display of his newfound concern, he was very conscious that Renquist and Lupo were staring at him intently. He knew it was incumbent on him to do something, to make his call on what the next move should be. He could also see that his hesitation was making Weir's backup boys a little twitchy. The hands of the Zebra gunmen were edging toward their weapons, and the one with the shotgun had tightened his grip on the stock. The clear intimation was that if he or any of his party objected to boarding the *Flugelrad*, the refusal would be met with force. Lacking any other option, Coulson decided that giving in had to be the better part of valor.

"I didn't think it would go quite like this, but I guess

our primary task was to pay our respects to Underland, so let's all get on the saucer. Would you care to lead the way, Colonel?"

As they climbed the spiral of steps that led to the bridge of the *Flugelrad*, even Lupo looked around with something close to a childlike awe. Although, unlike humans, nosferatu had never been culturally conditioned through the latter half of the twentieth century to equate flying saucers with alien spacecraft, Renquist still had to admit that the interior of the *Flugelrad* was strange, to say the very least. Except Renquist saw the strangeness as being in the uncomfortable juxtapositioning of the familiar and the outlandish rather than a whole new men-from-Mars style of engineering. Regular commercial computer monitors, probably made in the People's Republic of China were patched into mysterious boxes that might once have been part of a Soviet missile guidance system. They, in turn, were connected to thick, transparent tubes of bright, flowing plasma. Steering was accomplished by the pilot turning a clumsy metal wheel that could have been cannibalized from a Victorian battleship. And what had to be the power controls for the propulsion unit employed both bulky rheostats of a type that would have failed to qualify as state of the art in the 1930s and jog wheel outboards that might have come from a contemporary, and very up market electronics outlet. As far as Renquist could judge, a considerable volume of liquid was needed to put the *Flugelrad* into the air, and much of that was piped via totally incongruous, brass-jointed, copper plumbing. He saw that some sections were white with the hoarfrost of condensation, showing that, at times, the mysterious fluid or fluids flowed at very low temperatures.

A crew of three was required to run this model of *Flu-*

gelrad. In addition to the steersman at the great wheel, an engineer made constant adjustments to the propulsion units according to columns of figures displayed on a bank of small and archaically green monitors. The third of the trio was the navigator, who studied an advanced electronic plot table, but still called verbal instructions to the steersman. Renquist later discovered that the navigator also operated the weapons system when the need arose. The crew and their workstations took up the forward half of the circular bridge beneath the Plexiglas dome. The rear half was dominated by Beauregard's command chair, which was positioned on a raised dais so he had a full three-sixty view all round the dome, and over the heads of the crew. Enough space remained on either side of the chair for at least six people to stand without being uncomfortably pressed together. Renquist could attest to that fact, since on the occasion of his first flight in a *Flugelrad*, exactly that number were occupying the area—Coulson, Lupo, Bridewell, and himself, plus two young men, maybe Beauregard's aides, or maybe his bodyguards, both very like Van Pelt, who had entered Ice Station Zebra with Beauregard and remained there to wait for the transport. They wore the same long, rubberized coats and sported the same severe crewcuts.

Beauregard wasted no time giving his visitors any kind of tour or explanation of the craft. He went straight to his command chair and seated himself, right leg cocked over its arm, in a pose of casual arrogance. Once comfortable, he addressed himself to the engineer. "Hans?"

"Yes, Stormleader?"

"Are we powered up to lift?"

"Yes, Stormleader."

"Then take us up."

He turned his attention to the navigator. "Klaus?"

"Yes, Stormleader?"

"Do we have weather between us and the Fissure?"

"Nothing to concern us, Stormleader."

"Then set a direct course. I wish to touch down at the Templeside landing pad as soon as possible."

"Yes, Stormleader."

The sound of the propulsion unit was little more than a faint hum that rose in pitch as the saucer lifted from the apron. At the same time, Renquist felt a downward pull on his body that he couldn't explain. The lights of the Ice Station Zebra viewing area simply dropped away below them, but there was very little sense of motion. Almost immediately they were into clouds, and, apart from an occasional swirl of grey, they might not have been traveling at all. Renquist only began to perceive a change after about fifteen minutes of looking out of the tinted dome at a blur of nothingness. The clouds began to thicken and darken, and moments later they became streaked with black and red. After maybe a minute, they very disconcertingly began to spiral, as though the saucer was plunging headlong onto a vortex of volcanic fog. The effect was only visual, though. Physically, Renquist had no sense of spinning, and the deck under his feet remained more still and stable than even the cabin floor of a commercial airliner in level flight and clear air. Once again Renquist was forced to think in terms of the Underlanders having some device that nullified gravity. Renquist turned to see how Beauregard was reacting to this vortex that came without a tremor, and found the Stormleader smiling back at him, with spinning reflections of the vortex in the lenses of his goggles. "Antigravity technology, my dear Renquist. It's the secret that makes us so popular."

How did these people have anything of the kind? It seemed so impossible.

"I feel like I'm descending into Hell." Thyme spoke to no one in particular, but the juxtapositioning of the word *Hell* caused Renquist to glance at her. Was it just synchronicity, or was she picking up stray thoughts from him? Beauregard merely laughed. "Maybe you are, Miz Bridewell. Just because so many have fantasized about the pit does not preclude it from existing."

Again with no internal movement, the attitude of the saucer had changed. Now it was running fast between parallel rock walls still with no internal sensation of movement. Beauregard leaned forward and gestured to Renquist. "Baron Renquist?"

Renquist could plainly read the bully hostility in his aura. Colonel Beauregard thought he had them all at his mercy. "I'm not a baron."

"I'm sorry, my friend, I thought all of your kind from topside were counts or barons or lords, or something."

Now Renquist could see himself in the goggles. "I'm just plain Victor Renquist."

"Will you lodge with us, or would you prefer to be among your own?"

Renquist did not like the sound of that at all. Could the human know what he really was? "What do you mean by my 'own,' Colonel?"

"You brought your darklost, didn't you?"

Bridewell chose this less-than-opportune time to assert her independence. "I'm nobody's anything."

Beauregard laughed. "Think what you like, my dear. We're on our way to Underland, and we do things a little differently down there." He turned his attention back to Renquist. "You look surprised."

Lupo was watching Renquist like a hawk, but there was no way to salvage the situation. "You have me unmasked."

"The undead move freely within the Hollow Earth."

"Indeed?"

"They, of course, have their own recognized areas."

"Of course. I suppose they would."

Lupo's thought spoke to Renquist as clearly as a voice. *"He doesn't suspect me."*

Renquist returned the projection. *"Interesting."*

"He knows a great deal about nosferatu, but the information you were one came from Deerpark."

"And the darklost?"

"He's seen similar with Underland nosferatu."

Beauregard, unable to hear the exchange between Lupo and Renquist, assumed the slight fraction of time it took was a hesitation on Renquist's part. "I only inquired as to your preference in lodging so you shouldn't feel out of place. Damn, but I still know how it feels being the lone Southern gentleman growing up in the middle of all those crazy krauts. Yes, indeed, it's always your own kind that you depend on in the end. I'm sure Miz Bridewell would agree, wouldn't you, ma'am?"

"I'm not sure I'd like to exactly define who my kind are right now."

"Oh, Miz Bridewell, I believe you're going to find that out soon enough."

Forward-pointing lights on the skirt of the saucer cut in, and the passengers could now see that they were rushing along a tunnel bored in the living rock, little more than twice the width of the saucer's diameter. The damp and dripping walls of rock seemed so close that Renquist noticed Bridewell more than once cast a worried look in the direction of the steersman. The man, however, seemed totally unworried, making slight adjustments to the wheel as though hurtling through the narrow space was totally routine. Beauregard was leaning forward in his chair as though looking for something. "Klaus, cut the lights. Let our guests see the tunnel mouth and the entrance to the first cavern."

Hans obeyed and the lights cut out.

"Now take down the interior illumination."

Again Hans did as instructed, and for a moment they flew in complete darkness, then a red glow was visible through the clear dome. It was reflected from the moisture on the rocks, and was definitely the light at the end of the tunnel. Beauregard waved a gloved and imperious hand. "Behold, my new companions, your first glimpse of the Underland!"

chapter Six

Renquist had observed many caves in his time. He had lived in at least five, and hidden from humanity and the daylight in dozens more, or even tens of dozens, but he had never seen anything to match his first glimpse of this section of Underland. The sheer size of the cavern would have been enough on its own to make it totally unforgettable, and, as the *Flugelrad* made its exit from the access tunnel, Renquist had walked forward across the saucer's bridge until he was standing beside and slightly behind the helmsman. No one attempted to stop him, and he simply stood and stared in awe, surprising even himself, since awe was not one of his prevailing or regularly used emotions. To call the cave huge, enormous even, did it a grave injustice. From his vantage point on the saucer, it was impossible to see or understand its true dimensions, but it seemed to go on forever. The only real gauge was its easy ability to contain what seemed to be a modest underground city.

This was not to say that the Earth was really hollow. The cavern was maybe as large as the Grand Canyon, but certainly not the whole interior of the planet. On the scale of the Earth itself, it was a tectonic glitch, a seismic pocket where a happy accident had blessed, or perhaps cursed it, with the right conditions to support life. The cavern clearly had the necessary water, a tolerable temperature range, and acceptable ventilation. Nevertheless it was plain to see from the fossil fuel haze that thickened the air through which the *Flugelrad* now drifted, that the ventilation might be struggling. All that it lacked was light, and that apparently had to be manufactured. The only light in Underland was the unnatural light of man, mercifully benign to the nosferatu. The most general illumination came from a system that looked, at first glance, like a geometrically positioned set of artificial moons, high in the roof of the cave. They were, in fact, convex parabolic mirrors, each sixty feet across, with static searchlights aimed continuously at them from the ground.

He would later learn that it took constantly working teams of untouchables and political prisoners to wash and polish the big reflectors, keeping them free from the airborne soot and grime, and that these unfortunates fell to their deaths at excessively regular intervals. By an odd quirk of social perception, the unfortunates who risked their lives tending the mirrors were viewed as the lowest of the low, while the others on the ground, who carried out the far simpler and far less risky task of maintaining the searchlights, had convinced everyone that their task was symbolically close to heroic and merited a high level of social endorsement. He'd find out that these so-called Lensmen were elevated to the status of a paramilitary order, decked out in absurdly lavish uniforms, and performed their duties with needlessly absurd pomp and ceremony. Despite their efforts, however, the light in Underland never seemed more intense than a somewhat dim twilight.

These man-made moon's weren't by any means the extent of the lights in Underland. Thousand of tiny pinpoints defined the terraces of urban terrain on the uneven floor of the cavern, while thousands more twinkled in the smog from structures built all the way up the walls of the great cave. Akin in the most basic way to the tiered homes of the Hopi rock dwellers in the American Southwest, these ambitious constructions far outstripped the work of any primitive tribe, with their hollowed-out grottos and galleries that rose to skyscraper heights, and were served by vertical-track, exterior elevators, and systems of metal stairs that festooned the rock face like geometric lace. One of Renquist's first impressions was that the Underlanders had an almost Victorian fondness for machinery and production line solutions. In addition to the banks of elevators that ran up and down the walls of the cavern, and the arrangement of lights and mirrors that lit the vast space, he could see how the tracks of freight-carrying railcars sliced the city into geometric shapes, while the single spans of an overhead monorail system created its own grid at around forty feet in the air. Fast little ovoids, capable of carrying perhaps twenty passengers at full capacity, sped along their appointed routes, keeping the inhabitants of the city in motion. Despite its overall strangeness, Renquist found some aspects of the Underland oddly familiar. At first, he couldn't see why. After a short while it occurred to him that some aspects of the cavern city were very akin to what in the 1900s had been visions of the next century.

That was where the familiarity ended, though. Freed from the need to provide shade from the sun, resistance to wind, the containment of heat, or even a roof to keep the rain off, the primary concerns of Underland architects were the privacy of occupants and the availability of light, which had resulted in the use of a great many translucent materials. Lightweight paper wall paneling like Japanese screens, Plexiglas and Lucite, even fabrics, were hung on load-bearing frameworks that rose from the cave floor like stalagmites, resembling elaborate scaffolding structures, or a giant child's jungle gym, rather than what any surface dweller might consider a building.

The designers of Underland had gone to great lengths to conserve any possible illumination, and to make each light source do double or triple duty. The light was shared by those inside, outside, above, and below. Entire multistory edifices the size of city blocks glowed from within. Other smaller dwellings and places of work were erected beneath their own canopies of what looked like mirrored mylar, to reflect back light that might otherwise be dissipated overhead to no practical avail. The technique made sense, but Renquist had to smile because, from the air, the things tended to resemble massive mushrooms or toadstools, glowing and lit from beneath. Of course, when he eventually realized the importance of fungi in the Underland culture and economy, he saw how natural it would be to echo it in all areas of design.

While still thinking about the part that light played in the city, he spotted something else that intrigued him. The tracks of both the monorails and freight cars entered tunnels bored into the wall of the cave. He wondered where they went and decided it couldn't hurt to ask about them. At worst he risked being ignored. "Those monorails, Colonel Beauregard, can you tell me something about them?"

In fact he wasn't ignored at all. Beauregard was more than happy to boast. "Are you impressed, Mr. Renquist? Down here we have not neglected our mass transit as you have in your American surface cities."

"I am indeed impressed, Colonel. And also a little curious."

Beauregard's voice became offensively patronizing. "Don't worry. You'll have ample time to ride them while you're with us."

Renquist blinked at the stupidity of the assumption. Did Beauregard think he was a child looking to ride the rides as though the city beneath the ground was an amusement park? He forced down his anger and smiled at the fool. "I'm sure I will, Colonel, but I was wondering about something else."

"What was that, Renquist?"

"Where do the trains and the monorails go after they vanish into the tunnels?"

Beauregard laughed, as though it was the kind of question only asked by strangers or idiots. "Why, my dear nosferatu, after passing through a feeder system, they connect with the major trunk routes that go to the other caverns."

It hadn't occurred to Renquist that all of Underland wasn't laid out in front of him. "This isn't the only cave of its kind?"

"Of course not. There are in fact seventeen caverns comparable to this and hundreds of smaller ones. They are all connected by a network of tunnels."

"That must have been a colossal feat of engineering."

"Indeed it was. In fact it would have been impossible had not the technique of thermonuclear boring been perfected."

Renquist nodded his humble thanks, and Beauregard seemed to think no more of it. Thermonuclear boring? Here was a real conundrum. Thermonuclear boring didn't exist. Not on the surface, not in any form that Renquist knew about. He had arrived in a flying saucer; he had observed mirrors, monorails, and houses made of steel and paper, and now he was being told the Underlanders had nuke-shaping technology. How could this post-Nazi civilization be so technologically advanced? It defied logic, unless some massive extra factor was missing or being concealed. He quickly communicated this non-verbally.

"Lupo, I trust nothing in this place."

"I also have seen nothing in these mole people to engender trust, Don Victor."

It was only when the *Flugelrad* was almost down that the dome came into sight. Anyone who thought the underground cave-city lacked a centerpiece would have to be forgiven. No one had seen the dome because the saucer had been coming down virtually straight on top of it. It suddenly reared up beside them, and Bridewell momentarily started like a kid in a fun house. One didn't expect to look out of a UFO and see a monumental, if begrimed, coiled serpent suddenly rise from nowhere. The structure's circular base, possibly a hundred yards across, was supported on a wide circle of Corinthian columns. It seemed to be constructed out of steel, plastic, and gold leaf. Thyme wondered if the inhabitants considered it art, a holy idol, or a building. It was big enough to be a building. It was sufficiently preposterous to be a holy idol, and had the same dubiously stylized representation. It was a decidedly fat snake with coils that qualified as lumpy, and it did not have a great deal of stretch to its rearing head. As art, it was not at all to her taste. Beauregard had noticed her looking at it and seemed unable to resist an aggrandizing comment. "Observe now the Temple of our Gods."

The way Beauregard spoke the words *Temple of our Gods* made them definitely worthy of capitalization, but Thyme was unsure if this was the product of a rarefied and mocking cynicism, or total self-delusion. From a distance, and with its blemishes minimized by the gauze of smog, it might have been magnificent to behold; but up close and parallel as they were, it really was a fun fair thing, poorly finished in the first place and now in need of considerable restoration. Gold leaf had peeled, and the metal and plastic beneath was pitted and eaten away by the acids in the air. Whole panels were missing, and the entire edifice was covered in a thick layer of soot. Not that it wasn't typical of the entire city as she had seen it so far, with its toy trains and speeding monorails, filled with pretentious gadgets like some polluted Disneyland at the bottom of a mine—a boy's adventure project now falling into final-stage decay behind formative oversights, bad planning, optimistic miscalculations, lengthy neglect, and original vanities. She wondered what the plumbing would be like, but did not hold out much hope. Totally misreading her expression, Beauregard continued to boast in initial caps. "We will land beside the Great Serpent. It is something of an honor to be brought to Templeside."

"I'm flattered."

Representations of a landing pad marked out in interlocking black and red diamonds filled the crew's monitor screens, and Bridewell could only assume they were on their final descent, near to landing. "What will happen once we land?"

"You will all be made comfortable."

Bridewell looked hard at Beauregard. She had encountered so many like him she instinctively recognized him as a son of a bitch. The only question that remained was how big a son of a bitch. "That's good. I enjoy comfort."

An instant of disorientation followed the moment that the *Flugelrad* switched from its internal gravity to the natural attraction of the Earth. Jack Coulson's knees bent involuntarily as a brief downward pull exerted itself, but then all was normal. Beauregard immediately rose from his command chair and headed for the bridge's exit, indicating that Coulson and the others should follow. Renquist and Lupo stepped back, allowing him and Bridewell to go first, then brought up the rear, side by side and silent. The Stormleader's two underlings fell in as a rear guard.

Coulson urgently needed to talk privately to Renquist and Lupo. The few trifles of information that Beauregard had let slip in his boasting were pieces of a puzzle that made no sense unless something of major importance was being kept from them. From what he'd seen of the lightweight monorail system, it appeared to use a mag-lev system which, up on the surface, was years from ever going operational, but looked to have been running in Underland for decades. That the *Flugelrads* had antigrav had been even more of a shock. Antigravity propulsion was another advance that, in the USA, had never gone further than Area 51 and still tended to malfunction disastrously. What had become know as the Philadelphia Effect regularly turned American and NATO test pilots into a living, screaming, and fully conscious chaos of blood, flesh, and entrails, in some cases molecularly bonded to the metal of their machines, who could only be quickly put out of their misery with a bullet.

The remark about atomic boring was as much, if not more, of a shock than the Underlanders apparent possession of a workable antigrav system. If Beauregard's boast had been true, they had nukes. That any kind of nuclear capability should have fallen into the hands of cult-Nazi mole people, who apparently worshiped the Great Serpent, was, to say the least, highly regrettable; but in a world where anyone with a few million, and the secret number to call, could make a small dirty bomb, it shouldn't have been a total surprise. If they could perform nuclear boring, however, the Underlanders were way beyond the small Hiroshima-style A-bomb stage. Their hardware was supersophisticated, and they had players who could operate it. That was the part that called for the hollow pit-of-the-gut chills. Not only in the abstract, but also in the reality that he was, quite literally, down in a hole with these burrowing maniacs, and his only friends were vampires. Damn but how he envied the nosferatus' apparent ability to transfer thoughts and information without a word being said. He didn't like the idea of allowing a vampire in his head, but it left him out of one hell of an advantageous, and perhaps lifesaving, loop.

What he had seen on the saucer flight from Ice Station Zebra, in addition to the unexpected change of loyalties by Weir and his men, only reinforced Coulson's belief that he had been suckered into playing the pawn in some nightmare chess game, where the terrain was alien, and the stakes were perhaps higher than he'd ever known them. He could not even be certain who was really playing the game. He assumed Grael was moving the white topside pieces, but who played black for Underland not only remained a mystery, but one that deepened by the moment. Even that was assuming the game was limited to just a pair of protagonists, and that second and third parties weren't adding their own agendas to the stew.

While the crew remained to carry out a postflight check and lockdown, the party from Washington all followed Beauregard down the spiral steps that led to the lower level of the *Flugelrad*. A hatch was already open. Steps built into what was its underside in the closed position now led down to the concrete of the apron. The first minute on solid ground, even for the nosferatu, was one of looking around and even gawking, marveling at this interior world that seemed to exist in perpetual twilight. Coulson was wondering if the Underlanders preserved the illusion of day and night, perhaps dimming the overhead lights for twelve hours out of every twenty-four in an approximation of night. Then the air hit him, and he could only grasp and rasp, struggling to catch his breath. Bridewell was the first to cough. "Jesus Christ, this is worse than a Texas oil town."

That the air was bad in Underland was a charitable understatement. It didn't quite stink, but certainly had an all-pervading presence. Coulson was fairly certain that sulfur was the prevailing odor in the cocktail, but some of the other ingredients were less easily identified. A variety of exhaust gases were definitely on the list, as was a less-than-efficient sewer system. The reek of soot, hot metal, burning rubber, burned hydrocarbons, and the ozone tang of high voltage also vied for attention, along with a mess of lesser smells that he was unable to put a name to. He glanced quickly at Renquist and Lupo to see how the nosferatu were faring. They weren't clutching their throats and moaning, but they looked considerably less than pleased. Beauregard would have been a total fool if he failed to realize that the atmosphere would come as a shock to visitors from the surface, even city dwellers who were well accustomed to their share of carbon monoxide and PCBs, but he still attempted to shrug it off with an airy gesture. "It's unfortunate. The problem is still being worked on, and, of course, it's always worse in the winter."

Coulson noted, however, that Beauregard didn't remove his goggles, and in this he was not so unique. The *Flugelrad* had landed on one of a half dozen designated landing pads right beside the huge Temple of the Serpent. Two other machines were parked on two other pads, but although the Templeside landing area was plainly restricted and watched over by armed guards, it stood beside a public piazza with a central fountain, and an intermittent stream of Underlanders moved in and out of the Temple. Many of these passersby wore some kind of protection against the air in addition to their regular clothing. Some favored variations on the kind of steel-and-rubber device that Beauregard wore. Others were anonymous behind the same gauze hospital masks adopted by the citizens of Tokyo during flu epidemics. Another alternative was to swath the entire head in a Bedouin-style burnoose, and a number of Underlanders had gone the whole distance and adopted full-face gas masks, with big insectlike eyepieces. A monstrous old man, hugely obese, rolled past in a wheelchair equipped with his own oxygen and wearing a bubble helmet like something out of 1950s science fiction. He was draped in a black, rubberized cape with the cross in the circle emblazoned on the shoulder, and Coulson could only assume that the man was both venerable and elevated. The overall impression of the movement on the piazza was one of an industrial-strength masked ball, made all the more eerie by the fact that everyone accepted the masks, and the need to wear them, as something completely unremarkable. Coulson knew he was experiencing one of the first symptoms of culture shock, and adjusted his perspectives accordingly. After he had accustomed himself to vampires in just a matter of days, masked mole people should hardly be a problem.

Beauregard appeared to be leading them in the direction of the piazza, and presumably on to the Temple beyond. For Coulson the Temple had to be the crowning incongruity. Nuclear rock burners and this monstrosity could not have been at greater odds, or have a greater metaphoric resemblance to the guy with the match in the room filled with gasoline. As they exited the landing area he checked the weapons the guards were toting. He half expected them to have some kind of deathray hanging from their shoulder slings, but mercifully they were only equipped with what looked like some modern descendant of the World War II German machine pistol, the Schmeisser. On the other hand why didn't they have deathrays? If they could cook up antigrav, they could surely build some kind of doom beam. So much was wrong with the picture that it positively shrieked at him.

Led by Beauregard, the party from the *Flugelrad* crossed the piazza. Along the way they passed an area near the fountain, away from the Temple, where street vendors were permitted to hawk their wares. Some offered the expected human food and drink, even hot dogs and Coca-Cola, presumably imported from the surface unless Coke had an Underland bottling plant. The foul air in Underland spurred a brisk trade in hits of oxygen, delivered to each customer, after the payment of some small bills, via a copper breathing mask and a rubber hose, from tall iron tanks on small, wheeled dollies. Other stalls and pushcarts, less easily explained, conducted a brisk trade in live birds and rodents, displaying their merchandise in stacks of piled-up wire cages. The most popular purchases seemed to be white doves and equally albino rats. Renquist had hardly given these vendors a second thought, being focused on observing Coulson's mind from a distance, and watching how he and the human agent seemed to be coming to some very similar conclusions. Bridewell, on the other hand, frowned and looked at Beauregard with a Scarlett O'Hara flutter of her eyelashes that was patently phoney to all but him. "Why, Colonel, what is the purpose of all the animals?"

"It's very simple, Miss Bridewell. They are sold to the common people in order for them to make sacrifice to the Serpents."

"They're killed for the God?"

"The God? Why no, my dear, the common people aren't allowed anywhere near the Dhrakuh. They feed them to the variety of snakes, reptiles, and other serpents that reside in the dry pools and channels in the lower Hall of the Dome. It's an irrelevant process, wholly symbolic; but it keeps the proles happy and promotes the trade, so it's permitted to continue, not to say encouraged."

"Are we expected to make sacrifice?"

Beauregard smiled patronizingly. "Of course not. That would be absurd. You are outsiders."

"I'm grateful for that."

Beauregard had used the word *Dhrakuh* so casually that no one except Renquist had paid it any attention at all. It had even slid past Lupo. *Dhrakuh* was a name that Renquist had not heard for a long time: but, to a student of alternative history such as he, it was far from being unfamiliar. The fables of the Dhrakuh seemed to date back to at least the time of the Nephilim, if not all the way to the ice age that had preceded their colonization. The variations on the legend of the Dhrakuh were as numerous as the alternative spellings of their multiple names. Allowing for local cultural distortions, and the embroidery of millennia of retelling, the Dhrakuh would seem to be a species of sentient reptile. Some tales pictured the Dhrakuh as rivals from space, adversaries to Nephilim in the ponderous colonial era of galactic exploitation that, as far as Renquist knew, still continued, and might well last longer than some of the planets on which the Nephilim and the Dhrakuh had staked their claims. Other variants of the story insisted the Dhrakuh were indigenous to Earth, but still competed with the Nephilim and their genetically engineered cohorts, for the hearts and minds of the smart monkeys that would soon overrun the planet. When the struggle had eventually proved hopeless, the Dhrakuh were said to have retreated into the hollow of the Earth. Down the passage of time, they became confused with dragons, and the historical thread had been even more tangled when the Christians used the Dhrakuh as a model for the Beasts of the Pit, the Serpent of Eden, and all the works of Lucifer.

After the medieval monks were through creating, rewriting, censoring, and burning, little written material that made any real sense remained. In the twentieth century the idea of the Dhrakuh as the source of all fundamental evil was secularized and resurrected under yet another selection of names by some of the more expansive UFO conspiracy paranoids. Whatever the distant truth, the Dhrakuh had long ago departed this Earth, and maybe even this dimension. Of that Renquist was reasonably sure. And yet the idiot Stormleader had spoken as though they not only still existed but were near at hand. Renquist had to concede that an intervention by an advanced and nonhuman outside influence could account for all the scientific anomalies in Underland. But should he really think in terms so incredible? And so soon? When the ancient Dietrich had been his mentor, one of his most firmly held maxims was "when all the plausible options are exhausted, one can only embrace the implausible." Renquist was far from sure that he had in fact exhausted all the plausible options. He might have pondered the problem all the way to the Temple and on inside had Bridewell not halted at the fountain.

Bridewell stopped to look at the fountain. Water gushed from the mouths of four stone serpents. Just before she turned to respond to Beauregard's gesture that she should move on, she saw an orderly, two-by-two procession of children in uniforms. Boys and girls alike were identically dressed in neat little uniforms. Black shorts, white shirts, and scarlet neckerchiefs that currently covered their mouths and noses. The children were accompanied by one adult, a stern-faced woman with the eyes of a prison guard above her smog mask. In her black, rubberized, and hooded coat she resembled a fascist mother superior. Seemingly Underland, like Hitler, had its own organized and militarized youth corps.

The rubber mother superior and the uniformed children led Thyme's eye to a second group of people who were noticeably different from everyone else on the piazza. They were tall, even the shortest being over six feet, but stooped and gaunt, with complexions that were sallow, even by prevailingly pale subterranean standards. The men were dressed in long black coats, shabby, threadbare, and showing the brown of fabric rust on the shoulders. The women were equally shabby in shapeless black dresses, a combination of bankrupt Amish, and distressed, down-at-the-heel crows. They all wore purple armbands, with a red symbol;

two upward-pointing triangles, arranged side by side. The strange group seemed uneasy out in the open among the more regular Underlanders. Bridewell didn't like the look of these people at all. She quickly caught up with Renquist, who had walked ahead lost in his own thoughts. "Victor, do you see those people over there?"

Renquist blinked like a man too hastily woken from a dream. "I'm sorry. What?"

"There are some people over there. They look kind of funky and fucked up, but I get a strange feeling from them."

Renquist turned and looked where Bridewell was pointing. His jaw muscles suddenly clenched and, had he been human, he might have turned white. Without being able to read any aura, Thyme knew that this strange group of people who had given her the bad feeling had come as a profound shock to Victor. She had never seen him look like that before.

Their auras were so degenerate they were scarcely recognizable as any kith or kin of his, and Renquist had to exert a great deal of effort not to show both his shock and his horror. All speculation about Beauregard's use of the word *Dhrakuh* took flight in the face of this new and disturbing revelation. The minds of the creatures were dull and murky, as far as he could read them from a distance, and, worst of all, they contained a foreknowledge of death that should have been impossible. He scarcely wanted to admit to himself that these debased things were nosferatu, but the core of their auras revealed the unmistakable thread of orange psychic fire that defined all of his kind. In each individual it was little more than a smoky ember, but, when they were viewed collectively, Renquist was left in no doubt that the tattered group was a currently unknown, perhaps unique strain of nosferatu. Renquist also wanted to avoid the two very obvious next questions. How had the group reached this sorry state, and how had they come to this place?

The peculiar nosferatu were too far away for details to be clear, and he didn't want to move closer. Even if Beauregard did not object, Renquist certainly didn't want to reveal himself to the creatures until he had learned a great deal more about what exactly they were. As far as he could see, they were uniformly tall and apparently bald, with dead-fish skin, pale and wrinkled like old dry chamois, and he thought he could make out down-pointing yellow fangs protruding below their upper lips. They looked like strange, corrupted throwbacks to the Original Beings, the genetically engineered, self-sustaining warrior caste of the alien conqueror Marduk Ra, who were the primitive ancestors of the modern nosferatu. Down the fourteen thousand years that separated Renquist from the Original Beings, the nosferatu had inevitably changed. The constant recycling of human blood had caused their exterior forms to become more human and more varied. Their minds had expanded and sharpened. Simple Darwinism also came into play. The large, clumsy throwbacks, hairless and frankly stupid, were easy prey to the recurrent outbreaks of human hunt-the-vampire frenzy that seemed to occur at least once a century. Those with a human appearance, greater intelligence, and more highly developed cunning were far better equipped to survive.

The things in Underland appeared to have missed the entire process of refinement and natural selection. They were far from being pure Original Being, but appeared to have reached the developmental state of around ten thousand years ago, when beings known as the Gayal, who looked very like them, only infinitely more powerful, were worshiped as blood gods in the northern river valleys of the Indus. Renquist could only wonder if somehow they had been isolated from all but the most limited contact with the rest of the world. The flaw in that scenario was that if they had not been in regular contact with humanity, how in hell had they fed for so many centuries?

Beauregard made an impatient gesture. This wasn't the time for tourism, and Bridewell and Renquist should move along. Renquist knew that he had little choice. If he wanted to keep the peace, he was going to have to do what Beauregard said and leave speculation and research into the inexplicable Underland nosferatu until later, then he heard the voice.

"Alai akal raanni amastus-ha."

That he was listening to the Old Speech, the ancient language of the nosferatu being whispered to him in a hoarse voice that sounded weak and ill was as much of a surprise as the Underland nosferatu had been.

"Alai akal raanni amastus-ha."

Renquist looked to see from where the voice emanated. It came from close by, definitely not from the mysterious group across the square. Lupo was also scanning the immediate area. A number of beggars sat beside the fountain. Renquist could only suppose that this had to be their designated area on the piazza beside the Temple.

"Alai akal raanni amastus-ha."

One of them gestured weakly, and Renquist looked closer. He had always found it less than pleasant to view the minds of beggars and sample the ill luck, poor judgment, and madness that had brought them to their sorry state: but a beggar speaking in the Old Speech was something that obviously warranted an exception. A weak and unhealthy aura glimmered around the unfortunate, but, as with the creatures on the other side of the square, Renquist could make out the orange core of the undead. Unlike them, however, this being was completely human in appearance. The only feature separating him from the rest of the beggars was that he was clean-shaven, while they all had at least an unkempt stubble on their chins, if not full beards. This nosferatu would seem to have come from the surface, just like Renquist and Lupo; and the sorry condition in which they discovered him only intensified the mystery. Renquist turned his back on Beauregard and the rest of the party from the *Flugelrad* and walked round the base of the fountain.

"*Sha'n limnn nutikla kla?*"

Renquist's reply produced a surge of relief through the nosferatu's aura. "You're real."

"Of course I'm real. Did you think I was an hallucination?"

The beggar nosferatu tried to rise, but then sagged back against the base of the fountain. "Where I now find myself, it would have been the most logical assumption."

Renquist dropped to one knee beside him. "Where you find yourself?"

The nosferatu's voice was feeble and faltering. "You're newly from the surface?"

"That's right."

"Then you wouldn't understand."

"Renquist!" Beauregard was impatiently beckoning to him. "We don't have the time for you to converse with a down and out."

Renquist regained his feet and faced the Stormleader.

The man was becoming a nuisance. "Sir, this is one of my own kind. I am duty-bound to aid him. I really hope you won't attempt to stop me."

Lupo eased into the picture. Hardly moving, he made it very clear that he had Renquist's flank, and anyone who challenged his don challenged him, too. Beauregard's flunkies looked at each other. Did they dare to take on this now-dangerous-looking duo? Beauregard made the decision for them, giving enough ground to avoid an immediate confrontation. "Never let it be said that I didn't respect the concept of duty. But please make it fast. You'll find you really can't do anything for one of those."

To Renquist's surprise, the nosferatu actually agreed with Beauregard. "He's right, you can't do anything for me."

"Can't I take you somewhere?"

"It's too late for me. It may even be too late for you. They'll slip you the funge, and you'll like it, just as I did."

"Funge?"

"Just don't eat or drink anything. Everyone does it to be sociable, but don't. That'll be the end of you."

"I don't understand."

"Look inside my mind."

Aware there was no time for formal niceties, Renquist simply plunged in, only to find that little remained of the individual's consciousness except horror and resignation. Most of the stranger's mind seemed to have been gnawed away: but Renquist had no idea how, or by what. The little that was left was overtaken by a sense of inevitable and closely impending doom. Renquist had seen a similar recognition of ultimate ruin in the rotted-out brains of human addicts, but never in one of the undead. The interior of this mind filled him with a profound chill, as, for the second time in as many minutes, Renquist had read the presence of death in the mind of a nosferatu in Underland. The first and frightening assumption was that, somewhere in this subterranean world, some unknown kill-factor lurked to which the undead were supremely vulnerable. Unlike sunlight or the sharpened stake, which both killed in an instant, whatever this nightmare might be was slow-acting and possibly cumulative, gradually eroding the basic chemistry of their cherished immortality and destroying the mind by stages. Renquist searched such for some coherent thread of memory that might explain how the beggar had ended up like this, but was unable to find anything that made sense.

"What happened to you?"

"There's no time now."

"Renquist!" Beauregard was barking again.

The nosferatu grasped Renquist's arm. "You have to go with him. They'll send the Companions to pick me up now that they've seen me talking to you."

Beauregard advanced on Renquist with his underlings behind him. Lupo moved closer to Renquist to present a united front, but the dying nosferatu weakly waved the pair of them away. "Get going. You can't make a fight of it. Not here. Just remember what I told you. Don't eat or drink anything."

Renquist was suddenly very angry. He couldn't leave even a stranger like this. Lupo took Renquist gently by the arm. "He's right, Don Victor. We have to go."

Renquist looked down at the unfortunate. "I'll try to come back."

"Don't. I won't be here. Just get out of this hellhole while you still can."

Beauregard was by then just six feet from Renquist, and bristling with badly ignored authority. "What the hell is going on here? Didn't I say we had no time for you to be holding conversations with dead-beat vampires?"

Confident that Renquist and Lupo would follow, Beauregard turned on his heel and started back in the direction of the Temple. This time the two undead did follow him, seeing no other immediate option; but Renquist couldn't resist voicing a query to the Stormleader's fur collar and rubberized back. "I'm still curious how that particular dead-beat vampire got to be that way."

"Every society has its dregs."

"I become concerned when I find my own kind among those dregs."

Beauregard again halted, then swung round to face Renquist. All his mannered airs had dropped away, and he had become nothing more than a furious human official. "Are you deliberately trying to waste my time?"

Renquist was, for an instant, tempted to let his own control drop and show this Beauregard the kind of anger a healthy, long-lived, surface-dwelling nosferatu could generate. Simply to take the smug and increasingly annoying human apart would have provided a brief thrill of intense pleasure. Unfortunately, Renquist knew such pleasure would be very brief and its aftermath extremely messy. Thus he restrained himself; stiffening and becoming ultraformal. "No, Colonel, I was merely looking after my own interests. If something down here poses a threat to my kind, I want to know what it is and how to guard against it."

"What makes you think you are under any kind of threat here in Underland, Renquist?"

"The sorry condition of the nosferatu on the piazza."

Beauregard nodded and looking insincerely rueful. "It was a mistake that you saw them."

"A mistake?"

"Yes, Renquist, a mistake. A mistake that you should see those degenerates and jump to the conclusions you're jumping to now. Both man and nosferatu enjoy an equality under the law. They are equal but separate."

"That's the reason for the purple armbands, and the triangle symbols like little fangs?"

"There has to be some kind of regulation. You do, after all, feed on humanity. I don't think we can be condemned for protecting ourselves. On the surface, your kind are slaughtered on sight, from what I hear."

Lupo growled. "They have to find us first, and many don't even believe in us."

"I guess, in Underland, we are more enlightened."

This failed to convince Renquist on any level. "And what about the male at the fountain? He was dying. My kind do not die except under very specific circumstances."

"He was a fungus eater, Renquist. A worthless fungus eater. He knew what he was getting into when he opted for the euphoria and the visions. Now can we get on? We have pressing business elsewhere."

Coulson entered the Temple, relieved that Beauregard and Renquist had not actually come to blows on the piazza. He was developing a healthy dislike for Beauregard, but he hardly thought the time was as yet appropriate for him and Renquist to go head to head. Coulson was certain that Renquist could decimate Beauregard, and probably an entire company of his Iron Order, especially teamed with the even more formidable Lupo. The problems would come in the wake of the confrontation. With no knowledge of the underground city and no place to turn for aid and comfort, they were near-helpless strangers in a very strange land. In theory, had Renquist lost his normally unyielding composure and taken Beauregard out, they might have had a chance at charging back to the landing pads and commandeering a *Flugelrad*, but that was as far as their escape would have gone. Coulson couldn't pretend that he or any of the others was the kind of comic-book, space-opera hero who could jump aboard a totally alien aircraft and fly it like a veteran.

With the potential crisis at least temporarily put on hold by Renquist's good sense, Coulson turned his attention to the Temple itself. His first thought was that, in its overbearing size and extreme pretensions, it shared an inane Third Reich grandeur with the work of Albert Speer. The dome overhead was supported on a cast-iron skeleton that greatly resembled the framework of a nineteenth-century railroad terminal. Like the piazza outside, the floor of the Temple was igneous rock that had been leveled, smoothed, and finally polished to a finished sheen. As though not content that this was enough of an engineering feat by itself, the builders of the Temple had gone on to carve a system of concentric channels in the wide expanse of stone. Three feet across, three feet deep, concave in cross section, and positioned approximately twenty feet apart, these rings of stone trenches were home to hundreds upon hundreds of live snakes. It was to this coiling, slithering multitude that the faithful who came to worship fed the sacrificial animals they had purchased from the vendors outside.

The channels of serpents were spanned by small wrought-iron footbridges, so worshippers didn't have to leap the snake pits if they wanted to progress to the center of the circular edifice. The small rituals of sacrifice were performed on those bridges. The congregation that entered, clutching terrified doves or struggling white rats, took some trouble in selecting exactly the right bridge from which to cast their offerings, and Coulson could only assume that some quasi-biblical, numerical mumbo jumbo had been established that dictated exactly where the rite should be performed. Maybe a dove tossed from one bridge was designed to cure sickness, while a rat dropped from another provided a remission from sin. Although he didn't understand the details, he was left in no doubt that this rigmarole was a device of religious manipulation designed to keep the common people of Underland ideologically in line and metaphysically preoccupied, so they didn't complain too much about how, at the very least, the air was slowly poisoning them or object to anything else that might assail them in this unreal and unhealthy world.

"Some of the more ambitious, or maybe those with more on their consciences, bring live goats to feed to one of the larger pythons."

Beauregard seemed to treat the ways of the common herd with an amused cynicism. He might enjoy the privilege and the power that came with his rank in the serpent cult, but he was anything but a zealot. Coulson doubted that Beauregard was a believer at all, and he wondered how the man maintained his position, unless the whole of the religious elite were merely going through the motions, viewing the prevailing theocracy as merely a means to the end—no more than an exercise in controlling the hearts and minds of the masses. "For a temple, this place seems to be overly well protected."

Beauregard looked at Coulson in surprise. "You think so?"

"There's got to be a dozen of these guys in red coats and hoods, and each one's armed with a machine pistol." Even before observing the reptiles, Coulson had noted the armed men in scarlet patrolling the interior of the Temple.

"They are the Companions of the Serpent. Their assigned task is to defend the Gods, Brother Coulson."

Coulson couldn't shake the feeling that Beauregard was secretly laughing at him. "But you wear the black uniform, like the guards on the landing pad and the crew of the *Flugelrad.*"

"That's because, right now, I am acting as a Stormleader of the Iron Order."

"But, as I heard it, you're also a Companion of the Serpent."

Now Beauregard did laugh. "I'm equally entitled to wear both the scarlet and the black. And that gives me quite a spectacular wardrobe."

Was the size of his wardrobe all that mattered to Beauregard? Coulson didn't think so. He was convinced the pose of the mindless, mocking dandy only served to conceal something more determinedly serious. "You can belong to both organizations?"

"A number of us hold positions in both the Companions and the Order. It assists the balance of oligarchy and theocracy and prevents excesses of internecine strife."

Coulson followed Beauregard across one of the many iron bridges, passing a poorly dressed family dropping a white rat into the trench. Coulson glanced down, idly curious about the fate of the rodent. Coulson wasn't overly fond of snakes, and it seemed, from the rat's point of view, a very unpleasant way to die. The snakes came in literally all colors, subspecies, and sizes. Some could only have been brought from the surface, while others, slithering albino things, that might well have been blind, were plainly indigenous to Underland. The traffic in worshipers seemed to be more than enough to keep the reptiles fat and sassy, and many of the sacrifices, instead of being immediately consumed, scuttled or hopped nervously around for quite some time before attracting the attention of a serpent in need of a snack. Most of the doves had their wings clipped so they couldn't fly away and thwart devotional intentions; but now and again, the job had been imperfectly done and one made its escape. Looking up, Coulson saw whole squadrons of doves perched on the beams high in the dome, where, for generations, they had left visible deposits of dove shit. He wondered what went on in the minds of the true believers when their sacrifice skipped. Did it constitute a sign of holy disfavor?

Coulson was discovering that the more he learned about Underland the less he liked it. A totally subterranean world obviously came with more than enough built-in factors to twist any attempt at social order into a structural pretzel of excess and apparent madness. The simple fact that day and night had been canceled, and that the Underlanders, with the sole exception of *Flugelrad* crews and the elevated like Beauregard, never saw the sun must have had a profound effect. Wouldn't it mean that at least half the population was walking around with something akin to permanent seasonal affective disorder? Closer to home, what about Lupo and Renquist? He knew that the nosferatu needed both to sleep and feed, and could only speculate on how they were going to accomplish that.

Renquist found the Temple of the Serpent repellent and nonspecifically disgusting, but knew he was in no moral position to criticize. As one of the undead, he was judged by many as wholly repugnant; but, no matter how he might want to maintain an impartial and analytical mind, the place gave off a sense of being built on a foundation of hidden horror. It was nothing that he could define or accurately pinpoint, but the Temple made him decidedly uneasy. Thyme Bridewell seemed to share his unease. "I hope we aren't expected to stay too long in this place. It's fucking creeping me out. What the hell are we doing here anyway?"

Renquist shook his head. "I don't know, but I feel it's time to find out."

Up ahead, beyond the next of the concentric snake pits, Beauregard and Coulson were conducting a conversation. Renquist quickened his pace to catch up with them, and when Lupo did the same, Bridewell swiftly followed. "I think I want to hear this."

As Renquist, Lupo, and Bridewell approached the next bridge, their way was blocked by a group of humans who were sacrificing a rat to the snakes. When they saw them, the worshipers pressed themselves back against the guard-rail of the bridge and averted their eyes as though the trio radiated danger. Once they were across the bridge, Thyme looked questioningly at Renquist. "What was their problem?"

"Perhaps they knew what we are. Underland would seem to have its nosferatu population."

"Their own nosferatu came with all the hallmarks of an oppressed minority."

"I know. There's too much in this place that doesn't make sense."

She turned to Lupo. "Do you have a theory?"

"Not a theory, just an observation."

"And what's that?"

"That the mysteries in this place pile up so fast you need wings to stay above them."

Beauregard overheard Lupo's last remark. "You think this place has mysteries?"

Beauregard was his previous affable self, almost as

though the near confrontation with Renquist on the piazza had never happened. Lupo was noncommittal. "Some things would merit questions, even if the answers may not be forthcoming."

"What's that supposed to mean?"

"I think Lupo wishes to know precisely what we're doing here. As indeed do I."

"It is the custom for all new arrivals to visit the Temple of the Serpent and pay their respects to the Dhrakuh."

"And after that?"

"I take you to the meet the Grand Companion."

Thyme found the answer far from satisfactory. "And what's the Grand Companion? One of the most annoying things in this place is that no one seems able to give an intelligible answer to the simplest of questions."

Beauregard's goggles glinted as he regarded Bridewell. He had still not removed them even though he was now back in Underland. "You might call the Grand Companion the high priest of our Gods. I was merely dispatched to bring you to him. I'm sure he will tell you all that you need to know."

Bridewell's eyes narrowed. "What we want to know, or just what we need to know?"

Beauregard's expression was of pure, if implausible, innocence. "I can't speak for the Grand Companion, but I see no reason why he should withhold anything from you."

Beauregard looked as though he was about to say more, but a hiss from the center of the Temple distracted him. Indeed, his head snapped round at the sound. It was the first time Renquist had seen Beauregard exhibit any sign of alarm or anxiety, and he wasn't the only one. Everyone in the public area, around the trenches full of snakes, had turned to look; and a general feeling of nervous anticipation swept across the floor like a chill gust of a diseased wind. All eyes were on the very center of the structure, where, at the focal point of all the concentric rings was a large, metallic object. It was circular, about ten feet across and four feet thick, and it appeared to be made of solid brass. Although it was lavishly engraved around the sides with a wide frieze of Celtic-style intertwining serpents, its construction seemed to have a functional purpose. To Renquist it looked very much like a huge raised hatch or manhole cover. Two tall gushers of steam suddenly jetted into the air from vents set in the floor on either side of the squat metal cylinder, and, simultaneously, high in the dome of the Temple, a pair of large and sonorous bells began to toll, sending all the escaped doves into a white swirl of panic flight.

The combination of the noise and the steam had an immediate and profound effect on the human congregation inside the Temple of the Serpent. The worshipers fell to their knees, then leaned forward to prostrate themselves so their foreheads were touching the cold stone. In their abject obeisance, the sacrificial animals were forgotten. Rats and mice ran free, and doves fluttered away. Even the scarlet guards and Beauregard himself, dropped to one knee, although the guards did keep their machine pistols at the ready. In all of the Temple, only Renquist, Lupo, Bridewell, and Coulson remained on their feet. Beauregard quickly hissed and gestured at them. "Get down. You have to kneel."

Renquist's response was nothing more than a single calm word. "No"

"What do you mean, no? Just do it. It's the law."

"Damn your law. I'm not a snake worshiper, and I don't

kneel to anyone or anything until I'm fully convinced it's worthy of such extreme respect on my part."

Bridewell couldn't resist joining in the mutiny. "Fuck it, I'm with Renquist. I'm not a snake worshipper either. When I get on my knees it's for a wholly different purpose."

Lupo didn't speak, but the way in which he scowled grimly and crossed his arms across his chest was a clear demonstration that he had no intention of bending his knee to anyone or anything. Coulson did the same as Lupo, but with a slightly less implacable demeanor. For a moment it looked as though Beauregard was going to summon the scarlet-robed Temple guards, but then the thick brass cover began to tilt upward, confirming Renquist's first guess that it had a mechanical purpose and was some kind of hatch. At the same time, as the thing rose, a section of floor behind it started to drop downward, as though acting as a massive counterweight. As the cover opened, a large circular hole in the floor of the Temple was revealed, with a flight of stone steps running down into a concealed interior. Steam rose from the opening in majestic billows, and a mist-shrouded red glow became visible, reminding Renquist of a medieval vision of the threshold to the Christian Hell.

Bridewell let out a low whistle. "I'll be damned. There's something under Underland."

Four figures emerged from the ruby mist. At first only their heads were visible; but, as they ascended the steps, it was possible for Renquist to see that all four were seemingly male, and dressed in the same scarlet uniforms as the Temple guards except that, in addition to the hoods, red rubber masks with glass eyepieces completely covered their faces. The devices had to be a kind of breathing apparatus or filter device. Toxins in the hole? The four men reached the top of the steps and stepped out of the circular aperture. The decorative brass cover slowly dropped again, shutting behind them with a series of mechanical sighs, and then a deep and final reverberating boom as it closed completely. The bells ceased to toll. The four took a moment to remove the face masks before walking directly to where Beauregard knelt, and Renquist and his companions continued to stand in attitudes of defiance. The worshipers lifted their heads, but did not rise from their knees. Apparently the figures who had emerged from beneath the floor were worthy in their own right of reverential deference. The faithful were obviously curious to witness what was about to occur, but too frightened of priestly authority to do more than dart covert glances while remaining prone. Beauregard was the first to stand. He welcomed one of the new arrivals with an unusual double handshake, then turned and gestured to Renquist. "Your Eminence, this is the nosferatu Victor Renquist."

The figure that Beauregard had addressed as Your Eminence pushed back his hood and inclined his head. He seemed more interested in Beauregard than Renquist. "You have completed your mission?"

Beauregard stiffened and clicked his heels. "I have, Your Eminence." He turned to Renquist. "May I introduce His Eminence Dr. Heinrich Wessel, the Grand Companion of the Serpent?"

Heinrich Wessel was tall, over six feet, in his early-to-mid fifties, as far as Renquist could tell, chiseled, lean, and distinguished. His ivory, Underlander skin was meticulously clean-shaven, and his iron grey hair was worn close-cropped in the old-fashioned Prussian manner. Apart from his pallor, Wessel's only physical peculiarity was his extremely pale blue eyes, that gave him a less-than-human stare. He had more the air of a general than a theologian. His ramrod posture under the flowing scarlet robe was wholly military, and the large, jeweled cross-in-the-circle he wore around his neck was displayed more like a decoration for valor than a devotional symbol. Renquist conceded that was only to be expected in a land of warrior-priests and militant holy orders. Directed by a sudden intuition he didn't quite understand, Renquist pulled back from physically touching the Grand Companion. Instead of shaking, hands, he stiffened to attention, much the way Beauregard had done, and bowed from the waist. "I am honored to meet any religious leader, Dr. Wessel. Even one who appears from beneath the ground."

Wessel returned the bow, seemingly content that it was a fitting gesture of respect, and showing no outward reaction to the overt ambiguity of Renquist's greeting, and its slightly mocking tone. "And I am honored to meet you, Herr Renquist. Many stories of your exploits have preceded you."

Renquist nodded and also remained expressionless. "Stories told second and third hand tend to be heavily seasoned with exaggeration."

"So you would advise me to judge for myself?"

"I've observed that, in the end, it's the only guarantee of accuracy."

Outwardly Renquist appeared calm. He even had his aura tightly in check so as not to worry Lupo, but his thoughts were in a turmoil. He had no idea what experience the Grand Companion had of the nosferatu mind, or the undead's' natural skill at reading auras; but he didn't feel inclined to attempt so much as a shallow scan of this leader of the serpent cult. He had not wished to touch the human, and certainly did not want to enter his mind. That Wessel had psychic powers of his own was a possibility that had to be seriously considered. The man's abilities were unlikely to be anywhere as forceful and focused as Renquist's, but they might be enough to give access to details that Renquist would rather keep from His Eminence for the time being.

Renquist was rapidly being forced to the conclusion that he was going to have to revise a number of his earlier assumptions about Underland and its snake-venerating religion. He had previously believed that it was nothing more than smoke and mirrors, the trappings of crude exploitation with no basis in reality. Now it would appear that this Temple of the Serpent could be more than merely an oversize architectural deception. The vast and sculpted dome above them and the mysterious chambers of red fog that appeared to be hidden beneath their feet might actually serve a purpose, providing sanctuary and concealment to something that was real and physical, at least in the most general sense.

One other detail bothered him possibly more than any of the others. Seconds before Beauregard had introduced him and Wessel, there had been a silent exchange between the two of them. Nothing that came close to the thoughts that he and Lupo were able to share, just a combination of facial expression and movements of the head, but enough to cause Renquist to try and lightly intercept the gist of what was being communicated. Beauregard had apparently wanted to know if the Dhrakuh was ready, and Wessel had responded that it wasn't. If Renquist had read Beauregard's question correctly, he had referred to the Dhrakuh as though the ancient fable of the godlike reptile species were neither ancient nor a fable, and that something, or things, called Dhrakuh actually existed somewhere in subbasement chambers, caverns, dungeons, or whatever, and the tunnel from which Wessel had emerged provided access to them.

Again, however, Renquist was left without time to think through the fresh revelations. Wessel was making it plain that Renquist and the others should follow him. They were once more on the move, and it was starting to seem as though they would never reach any real destination. "We have arranged a modest reception in your honor, Herr Renquist. An introduction to the hospitality of our mysterious country."

"Watch out for the scarlet women. They are known as the Brides of the Serpent—reptile nuns with weird ways and equally weird appetites." Thyme Bridewell had taken a glass of champagne from a waiter and turned to find herself accidentally next to Beauregard. At the reception he had finally removed his goggles. Nothing appeared to be physiologically wrong with his eyes except that one was green and the other brown. Unless he had a psychological problem with the mismatch, the goggles hid nothing that Thyme would have considered in need of concealment. If his eyes were windows to his soul, they remained heavily curtained and certainly revealed nothing about why he felt the need to make snidely suggestive remarks about the women in the scarlet robes, who were presumably highly placed clerics in his professed religion.

"You think they may take advantage of me, Colonel Beauregard?"

Beauregard shrugged. "There's really no predicting the behavior of the Brides, my dear. And no knowing of what they might decide to take advantage." He dropped his voice. "I've heard it goes much deeper than simple lesbianism. The gossip about what they get up to in the privacy of their cloisters is quite baroque."

"Are you trying to warn me or excite me?" Bridewell sipped her champagne. It tasted excellent, and could only have come from the surface. The elite in Underland seemed to have no compunction about importing their creature comforts. On the buffet table, which she had yet to fully investigate, she had seen Beluga caviar, truffles, and a very fine Canadian smoked salmon.

"So what are your first reactions to our underground world, Miz Bridewell?"

"I have yet to see very much of it, Colonel . . ." She looked round at the party. ". . . but I'm definitely enjoying this part."

Beauregard must have worn the goggles for long periods of every day. Up close, she could see two pandalike circles of rubber, deeply ingrained in the skin round his eyes from the cushions on the inside of the eyepieces. Compared to the other uniformed men at the reception, Beauregard looked like the dashing field commander straight from combat and deeds of heroism. The others also wore either the black or the red, but most were too crisp, too steamed and pressed, and too decked out with medals and gold braid to resemble anything but players in an eccentric production of *The Student Prince* with an overly gothic costume designer.

"So we're not boring you?"

She knew Beauregard was coming on to her, and she had to assume that her being from the surface rendered her, in his terms, something special and exotic. In a way, his attitude verged on insulting. He wasn't attracted to her as a woman, just as a novelty. Under normal circumstances, she would have walked away from the man right then and there, but these circumstances were far from normal, and she decided to string him along and see what he might let slip about himself. Lacking the nosferatu capacity to scan minds, she had to do her research into Underland the hard way. She leaned a little too close to him and opened her mouth a little too wide when she laughed. "I've not been bored yet."

Although she would never have admitted it to Beauregard, by the time that Wessel had announced the reception, Bridewell was well past the threshold of boredom. She had become heartily sick of being shuffled from one place to the next. Okay, so Victor Renquist represented the ultimate prize, but the way she was expected to trail behind and tolerate being treated like a combination of a spare part and a stray dog had been pushing her close to the limits of her endurance. She knew the condition of the darklost was not an easy one. She would be subject to mood swings and bouts of dark and terrible yearning. Incomprehensible words, and strange, half-formed visions would echo in her head, while, beneath it all, a constant anger fumed and smoked like a volcano in the prelude to eruption. She knew that this latent rage came with the territory, and that it was a product of the intense and all-but-unbearable desire to cast off the imprisoning bonds of human mortality and be one with Victor, Lupo, and all the other night-walking predators across the world. She couldn't see, though, that it invalidated her feelings of being ignored and taken for granted. She had been tempted to halt the whole process, to delay and even sabotage this Underland welcoming party for Renquist, by throwing a loud and totally uncontrolled tantrum. It might have had major and maybe even fatal repercussions, but at least it would get her noticed.

She had known, however, even with the chips pretty

much down, she was not going to do any such thing. She was still Thyme Bridewell. She was a pro, an operative, and a team player. A lifetime of conditioning couldn't be thrown off even by the prospect of a bloody immortality. She had also been curious to see this reception. She'd been intrigued to discover how the Underlanders managed their private affairs and personal manipulations, and what constituted formality and fun in their subterranean madhouse. All she had seen so far led her to believe the ruling elite were brutal narcissists, who used the trapping of their quasi-feudal Nazi religion as a cover for fetishistic sadism and playing dress-up with guns. Logical projection seemed to suggest that, behind closed doors, one might reasonably expect a velvet labyrinth of callous decadence and well-rehearsed vice. If vice turned out to be the coin of the realm, her credit was solid. Drinks, drugs, perversion, and mind games had long been four of her favorite things, and she considered herself highly skilled in all of them. She didn't expect to discover too much that was radically different from the near-limitless excesses that could be found in cities on the surface, but she would be interested to evaluate the different local nuances and examine how the natives set their boundaries, if any.

The party had also posed a second intriguing puzzle, over and above the simple question of how the Underlanders conducted themselves. She hadn't missed the very crucial point that the Grand Companion had said the reception was for Renquist. It wasn't for Jack Coulson, or so-called representatives of the US government. Fuck no. It was for *Renquist*. In that one statement, the Grand Companion had turned the whole picture on its side. They had left Deerpark with Coulson firmly in command, with Victor and Lupo along for the ride as paranormal muscle, and Thyme bringing up both the literal and metaphoric rear as Renquist's plaything. The first change had come at Ice Station Zebra when Weir had sold out Coulson to Beauregard and the Underlanders. By association, she, Renquist, and Lupo had been sold out, too. In the saucer she had assumed that they were once again prisoners. Maybe not overtly chained and restrained, but certainly in the discreet custody of Beauregard and his Iron Airmen. Too many orders had been given and too many weapons had been significantly displayed for her to think otherwise. Weir's crew had made certain they'd boarded the *Flugelrad* (stupid Germanic name), and, when they landed, Beauregard had shepherded them all to the Temple. Again they had not been subject to any obvious force or coercion; but she would not have given much for her chances of survival if she, or any of the others, had refused to follow his directions.

That Wessel, the Grand Companion, should shift the spotlight fully onto Renquist had come as more of a surprise than any of the other changes in the power dynamic. Wessel had spoken as though bringing Victor to Underland had been the plan all along. To take him on face value immediately posed the questions "why," and "for how long." Had the delivery of Renquist to the Underlanders always been the objective of Grael and NSA-FEMA, or had they simply been conned by Wessel and cohorts? Either way it would seem that the intention was for Renquist to play some yet undefined part in a much larger design or conspiracy, and, having learned long ago that it always pays to look out for number one, Bridewell wondered where that would leave her. That she not be separated from Victor, and her chance at conversion to nosferatu, was the most important factor in her world, but she had no idea where, if at all, she might figure in the latest scheme of things. She still wasn't certain if she was only now in Underland because, as a darklost, she was too much of a security risk to leave on the surface, or did she, too, have a practical if as yet unrevealed part in all that was going on? If she did, that would suggest that Grael and Wessel had been in cahoots from the very start. It was so far beyond bounds of coincidence that she had been deliberately made a part of the scenario without Grael having some measure of involvement. Was she perhaps intended to be his spy or monitoring device? For all she knew, the Old Man was already watching their progress via the implant in her head. Of course, that function of the damned thing hadn't worked during the experimental trials, and no reason existed to think that it would work now, but that didn't preclude Grael playing her as a long shot.

She was racking her brains for anything that might shed a glimmer of light on the mystery that seemed to expand with every turn when Beauregard again interrupted her speculations. "You seem preoccupied."

She had resolved to be nice to this asshole, but she could not totally keep an undertow of irritation out of her voice. "Wouldn't you be? I'm still trying to figure this place out."

"What's that expression that's used on the surface? Something about going with the flow?"

"Right now I'm more concerned about the flow going with me."

"Just enjoy the experience of Underland. I promise you it won't be hard."

She decided to pout. That ought to disarm the fool. "If there was a party planned, someone could have given me a chance to change for it. I feel like I just climbed Everest and have now been thrust in with the cocktail crowd. You think that's an easy experience to enjoy?"

Let him believe her only airhead concern was for her appearance. In one respect, what she was saying was, in fact, perfectly true. Of the hundred or so guests at the reception, a high percentage were attractive women. Like the champagne and the caviar, the alpha males of Underland seemed to settle for nothing but the best in their choice of wives, mistresses, courtesans, concubines, or whatever they had in the way of sexual partnerships down in these snake-worshiping caverns. Most of the women had the unique subterranean native pallor showing that, unlike the champagne, they had not been recently imported from the surface, but were largely the cream of the underground crop. Although the majority of the men were in religious or military uniform, and the crowd was certainly laced with a representative selection of the Brides of the Serpent that Beauregard had jokingly warned her about, by far the majority of these babes in Underland were dolled up in civilian evening dress. In some respects it was fortunate that she hadn't been able to change her clothes. If she had shown up in something like a leather minidress, she would have been completely out of place. In her jeans, T-shirt and scuffed flight jacket she at least looked like Hannah Reich action-gal, and not some out-of-step style aberration. In Underland, they certainly didn't follow surface fashions, and in many respects it was as though the 1940s had never gone away, merely mutated over and over.

The current underground vogue was for softly flowing, draped-to-the-body silks and chiffons that left almost nothing to the male imagination. Some of the younger women had gone even further with sheer, almost transparent fabrics that were little more than a floating, see-through wrapper for decorative lingerie, with stockings, garters, garter belts, and sculpted corsets making their time-honored sensual impact. The young women wore their hair short and severely styled, and Thyme could only think that it was supposed to be a contrast to the soft contours of the rest of the desired look. The word *desire*, however, caused her a moment of irrational panic. Suppose Victor should desire one of these Underland beauties? Fairly soon, Renquist would need to feed. He would feel the hunger, select a new victim, and she would be forgotten. She would be cast out and doomed to an eternity of wandering and longing. The panic grew worse. She quickly exchanged her empty glass for a full one, but then addressed herself sternly and silently. *Get a grip, sweetheart. You've come this far. You can stay the rest of the course.*

Beauregard must have noticed some part of this sudden anxiety, because he looked at her questioningly. "Is something wrong?"

Bridewell quickly shook her head. "No, no, it's probably just the champagne after all the travelling. The North Pole and a ride in a flying saucer, all in the same day, can be quite exhausting."

"Would you prefer to leave?"

Slow down there, Johnny Beauregard. You're getting overeager, boy. I have no intention of leaving this place anytime soon, and, if I do, I will endeavor to see that it's not with you. "I don't think that would be too appropriate. We really only just got here."

"Perhaps you should eat something. I hear the buffet is quite acceptable."

For once Beauregard was right. She was hungry. In fact she couldn't recall when she had last eaten. Another symptom of her darklost condition was that the simple human needs like food and sleep were pushed aside by the single-minded and all-pervasive ache to be something other than mortal. "Yes, I think that's probably a good idea."

She allowed him to take her arm and steer her through the crowd toward the long buffet table. When finally faced with food, she realized just how starved she really was. Although she considered caviar little more than a seafood novelty, the smoked salmon looked good. She noticed a platter with an artfully arranged display of sautéed twists of some substance she didn't recognize. She turned to Beauregard. "What are those?"

"A kind of mushroom."

"They don't look like mushrooms."

"Our mushrooms grow much larger down here than they do on the surface. In fact, a good deal of fungi find their way into Underland cuisine. They are, after all, one of the few things that thrive naturally in this sunless realm." He smiled, and the mockery was back. "Of course, there is one strain of fungus you might treat with some circumspection."

"I don't understand."

"There's a variety of fungus that has a profound hallucinatory effect on our local nosferatu. They become dangerously addicted to it."

"But I'm not nosferatu."

"But you're darklost."

Something in the way Beauregard used the word *darklost* caused another piece of the puzzle to fall into place. So that was why the Stormleader was all over her with his cloying attentiveness and forced charm. It wasn't just coming from the surface that made her exotic. The likelihood was that he regularly sampled surface women in his trips to Ice Station Zebra. He was sickly fascinated by the idea that she had been with the vampire. For the first time in years, Thyme Bridewell felt her flesh crawl.

*   *   *

The large room could best be described as one of Temple's ancillary chapels, off-limits to the general public, but used when the Grand Companion needed to host a private function or, apparently, greet a visiting vampire. It had the same ecclesiastical, train-station architecture as the rest of the Temple, a high gothic ceiling and stone walls, with a colonnade of pillars along one side, that could comfortably accommodate the hundred or more guests who seemed to have been pressed into service to welcome Renquist. The one thing that could be said in the gathering's favor was that, although he was in the company of a crowd of humans, Renquist didn't need to pretend that he was human himself. Many years had passed since he had felt such a freedom, but he would not have described it as a happy experience. He was pleased at not having to conceal his true nature. Underland presented more than enough problems without that extra addition. The truth had set him free but, as the nosferatu guest of honor, he found himself the center of attention, something he disliked at the best of times. He wondered despondently exactly how long Wessel would require him to behave like a walking sideshow. He would much prefer to go to some private sanctum and let Dr. Wessel explain what was really required of him in the caverns, but it didn't look as though that was going to happen for some time. Meanwhile, he would just have to nod, shake the offered hands, smile nicely, and bear it.

He quickly discovered that a guest of honor had virtually no freedom of movement. He would have liked to speak briefly to both Lupo and Coulson, but it was impossible to do either without completely drawing attention to the conversation. Jack Coulson was drinking and making small talk with a group of officers in the dress black of the Iron

Order and civilians in dinner jackets and starched and ruffled shirts. Lupo was on the other side of the room, corralled against a pillar by a platinum blonde dressed provocatively in a man's white tie and tails and tinted diamond sunglasses, who stood too close to him, moistening her red gloss lips with a small pale tongue and laughing too readily, as though she was under the misapprehension that a nosferatu, particularly a nosferatu as rigid and hidebound as Lupo, could be seduced. A second seduction was being attempted at the buffet table, where Beauregard was leaning close to Thyme Bridewell, but Bridewell's aura showed a revulsion so intense that it must have been caused by more than just the human's obvious character defects. Beauregard could only have said something that had truly horrified her, and Renquist knew from experience that it took something really exceptional to horrify Thyme. He tried to scan Beauregard's mind to see what it might have been, but Beauregard's consciousness was entirely taken over by sexual fantasies, some of which, even by the furthest extremes of the human boudoir, were little short of out-and-out torture, thinly disguised with some decorative if fetishistic trappings.

Either by design or accident, the group with which Renquist had arrived were effectively separated. Since Dr. Wessel, the Grand Companion, had made his commanding entrance, they had been given no measure of privacy in which they might attempt to absorb the rush of new, and in some cases, almost unbelievable developments, and it looked as though their enforced isolation was going to continue for some time to come. Renquist reluctantly turned his attention back to the young Underland female who was at that moment talking to him, but, at the same time saying almost nothing. She had the same ultrapale blues eyes as Wessel, and Renquist wondered if inbreeding was a problem among the humans of

Underland. Were their numbers so relatively small, and their gene pool so shallow that genetic oddities were already occurring after only a few of their short-lived generations? Aside from the eyes, Renquist could see no other physical abnormalities, and since the woman had done absolutely nothing to conceal a body of which she was clearly very proud, he accepted that she was, in all other exterior respects, perfectly normal. Her calf-length satin skirt was cut so exceedingly tight that it all but functioned as a second skin, and the pale fabric of her blouse was so filmy and diaphanous her pink nipples showed clearly against an almost albino skin. As if that wasn't sufficient, she appeared to be positioning herself deliberately for Renquist, continuously moving to display herself to best effect as she talked. She was yet another in the oh-so-many who mistook the deadly lure of nosferatu predator strength for sexual attraction.

Although the symbols and the uniforms had changed, and a strange coating of retrograde religion had been laid over the ideological excuses, the Underlanders' Nazi heritage was very plain to one such as Renquist, who had seen both the old and the new in action. This reception of Wessel's shared many commonalities with the formal dinners and stilted embassy balls he had attended in Berlin in the 1930s, at which party officials and SS officers performed their charades and acted out the prim pretenses of civilization that they believed would conceal the bastard brutality that drove them. Here in Underland, the forced chatter and starched manners were the cover for an equally lurid and decadent hunger that practically guaranteed the gathering would have some unholy aftermath, in which the pearls of etiquette would be ripped from their strings, the uniforms discarded, medals mislaid, and the warped truth of these humans might stand revealed. Renquist devoutly hoped that he would be gone from the place before this culmination came.

He was not, on the other hand, exempt from his own variety of hunger. He found he was unconsciously staring at the young woman's throat and contemplating the veins beneath the skin. His unconscious was reminding him that he would, sooner or later, have to both feed and sleep, as indeed would Lupo. He suspected that feeding would be comparatively easy. These humans knew what he was, and must have expected to provide for his sustenance in some way, at least while he continued to serve their undisclosed interests. Judging by the collective auras all round him, he could quite imagine this crowd being sufficiently sick actually to want to watch and applaud while he drained the blood of one of their number. Although he had not the slightest intention of providing them with any such spectacle, he did not expect that the need to feed would be hard to satisfy. Sleeping, on the other hand, might present much more of a problem. On the surface, his sleeping and waking were rigidly governed by the rising and setting of the sun. What did he do where the sun never shone? The temptation would be to keep on until he exhausted himself, but, if he misjudged his levels of endurance, he was aware that his perceptions could become dangerously distorted.

A waiter passed with a tray of yet more champagne. The young human helped herself, but Renquist declined. He was heeding the warning of the derelict nosferatu and neither drinking nor eating anything merely to humor humans. Since he didn't have to disguise himself, he could refuse all that was offered without being forced to make idiotic excuses. Although he didn't usually take the advice of bums, he had never, in his whole thousand years, met a nosferatu bum. Indeed, such a thing would have been both impossible and unthinkable outside of a place as grotesque and distorted as Underland. He also had one extra piece of information that gave everything else that he had heard a definite plausibility. The derelict had cautioned him that they'd slip him "the funge," and Beauregard had dismissed the derelict as a "worthless fungus eater." It might have sounded like nonsense, except Renquist had previously come across one other solitary example of nosferatu using fungi as a means of intoxication.

During his time in the north of Scotland, with the Clan Fenrior, he had been introduced to the *Uisge Beatha*. It was a practice of the clan, at feasts and festivals, and at many random times in between, to drink themselves crazy on a form of fierce firewater whisky. Normally alcohol would have had no lasting effect, even on these wild Highlanders. The inebriation was achieved when a unique strain of microfungi was introduced into the raw spirit by process of filtering it through a bed of peat moss. Once processed in this way, the *Uisge Beatha* made the nosferatu who drank it fighting drunk for a few hours, but then it wore off, and they returned to normality with little more than a foul headache and a worse temper.

Whatever the fungal intoxicant might have been in Underland, it would appear to have far more lasting and damaging effects. The derelict's whole genetic structure had been altered, and mortal death had somehow been reintroduced. In his case, mortal death had seemed extremely imminent. He had showed the same cumulative buildup of cellular imperfections that normally occurred in humans and were the cause of their rapid aging process. The cells of the undead, as long as they were constantly fed with fresh blood, reproduced exactly, perfection, time without end. That had been the original design of the Nephilim, and that was the real gulf that separated Renquist from the humans all round him. In Underland, Renquist had not been given a chance to examine the indigenous undead, but the odds would dictate that they must have suffered similar damage from use of the as yet unknown, and presumably highly attractive, psychotropic fungus. Had it not been for the unfortunate by the fountain, he and Lupo might have walked blindly into the end of their personal immortality and genetic advantage over mankind.

The more Renquist considered the problem, the more urgently he felt the need to get away from the pointless reception, out of the Temple, and explore on his own. If his fungus theory was correct, they were at risk from something as potentially deadly as direct sunlight. It might be a slower process of destruction, but it was also far harder to detect. *"Lupo!"*

"Don Victor?" Lupo answered immediately, but even his powerful thought was not totally clear through the disorganized thrash of human minds at their most pretentiously social.

"I'm hemmed in here. Can you work your way over here without being too obvious about it? I have something a little complicated to communicate, and I need you to be standing close to me."

"It will not be a problem."

Lupo made some excuse that Renquist couldn't hear and stepped around the woman in the man's tuxedo. As if circulating, and working the crowd, he eased his way closer to Renquist. Mercifully, the party had now been going on for long enough that the novelty of the visitors from the surface was wearing off. The Underlander's were going back to their routine priorities of gossip and sexual pairing, and Lupo was able to move fairly freely with only a few humans attempting to engage him in conversation. Renquist suddenly realized that a gathering like this was probably a form of psychological torture for the withdrawn and reclusive Lupo, although his undead stoicism prevented him from showing it. In less than a minute, Lupo was just a few feet from Renquist, close enough to absorb the unfortunate tidings. Renquist opened his mind, giving Lupo both theory and detail of the supposedly deadly fungus and their local kin. When he was through, Lupo was sufficiently disturbed to frown visibly. *"This is serious."*

"I need to get out of here. We're learning nothing. We are being told only what we need to know, or what they think we want to hear."

"How do you intend to get away?"

"I will wait for a distraction and simply vanish."

Lupo approved. *"That's the best way with humans."*

"Will you remain here and take care of Bridewell and Coulson?"

"I will do what's needed, Don Victor."

"Am I boring you?" The woman in the sheer blouse had noticed something, but interpreted it as Renquist growing weary of her.

Renquist shook his head. "Not in the least."

"It looked like you weren't listening to a single word I was saying."

Renquist laughed. "I was listening to every word."

The young woman grimaced as though she didn't believe him. "I'd hazard a guess you can't tell me the last thing I said."

Fortunately, Renquist was blessed with a perfect front-brain recall, and it had continued to operate quite independently while he conversed silently with Lupo. It was a form of mental exercise that essentially enabled him to do two things at once. "You were saying how you'd always wanted to visit the surface, but it wasn't permitted."

The woman raised an eyebrow, as though she still didn't quite believe him, but gave him credit for a deft and verbal sleight of hand. "I suppose I have to forgive you for being preoccupied. I imagine you are looking forward to the arrival of the others."

Renquist frowned. What was the vapid woman talking about now? "The others?"

"The other two nosferatu from the surface."

Now she had Renquist's full and undivided attention. He all but ripped into her mind and damn the consequences. "I don't understand."

The woman blinked, as though she considered him stupid even by Underland nosferatu standards. "Hello? The two females?"

"I know nothing about two females."

The young woman's aura was suffused with worry and concern. She even looked around to see if anyone had overheard her. "Oh dear. I may have said the wrong thing. Perhaps it was supposed to be a surprise."

Renquist continued to resist the temptation to drag the information out of her by force. It would have caused too much disruption at the crowded reception. "It certainly is a surprise. You'd better explain."

"I don't know if I should. I don't want to get into trouble with the Companions."

"No one will hear you. I find, at events like this, people are too enamored with the sound of their own voices to listen to the conversations of others." Damn her for thinking him stupid. As he spoke, he applied gentle but irresistible pressure to overcome her fear and make her talk, but still allowed her a moment to waver, and believe that the admission, when it came, was entirely a result of her own free will.

"I suppose it won't matter if I tell you. Everyone else seems to know. That's why so many are still hanging around and not already away seeking the pleasures. The rumor is that one of them is a great beauty and actually knew the late Adolf Hitler, the Great Führer of High Germany."

For a moment, Renquist seriously considered the possibility that he had somehow died and gone to Hell. First a potentially deadly fungus and now this. "Would her name be Aschenbach?"

"That's right, Julia Aschenbach."

What the devil was Julia doing in Underland? Back at Deerpark, Julia's name had appeared in Coulson's files as a source of information, and Renquist knew it was possible that she could have been part of another NSA-FEMA mission. A second string, perhaps? Renquist knew so little that it was hard to speculate. Had Coulson been in on it? Somehow he doubted that. Despite his promise, Renquist had seen enough of the inside of Coulson's mind to be convinced the man was, by this point, as much in the dark as he. Julia could easily be working for Grael on a parallel assignment, related, but separate. On the other hand, Julia could just as easily be working for some other organization with a possible interest in Underland. Her arriving here under her own steam was not impossible. Julia had her own Nazi heritage. Before Renquist had Changed her, she had been a budding starlet in the Nazi film industry and reputedly one of Joseph Goebbels's countless mistresses. On reflection, it was almost surprising Julia had not been drawn to this place a long time ago. Unless, of course, she had, and Renquist hadn't known about it. Although Julia had been a member of the colony for almost a half century, there were periods in the aftermath of World War II when she had taken part in adventures he knew nothing about. He was aware she'd had her share of totalitarian escapades, and was fairly certain she had worked in the NKVD's paranormal division. Then, a little later, she had switched sides, involving herself in the very darkest end of CIA counterinsurgency and performing tasks at which even the majority of case-hardened humans drew the line.

"De Reske."

Renquist was thinking so hard and fast that he didn't hear the young woman the first time. "I'm sorry, what was that?"

The woman again regarded him as close to retarded. "That was the name of the other one, the other female. She's called De Reske, Philipa De Reske."

"Damn it to Hell!"

Although Renquist did his absolute best to minimize his shocked outburst, it was enough to convince the young Underlander that she might be well advised to move away from him. She tried for a bright social smile, but only managed to look flustered. "Just as long as you act surprised when they make their entrance."

"Don't worry. I will look extremely surprised."

"Well, it's been nice talking to you."

"Yes, indeed."

No sooner had she retreated into the crowd than Renquist opened the mindline to Lupo. *"Did you catch all that?"*

"I did."

"And?"

"The situation is going to prove extremely interesting." Lupo

used the word *interesting* in the Chinese sense of being one component in the old and hideous curse.

"*If I wait for those two to arrive, I'll never get out of here.*"

"*You must go, Don Victor. I can contain matters here.*"

"*All hell could break loose when they find me gone.*"

"*My experience of hell breaking loose is extensive.*"

"*It's not only these Underlanders. There's also Julia.*"

Lupo took it all in his stride. He didn't have the same problems with Julia that Renquist had. "*Julia knows better than to cross me. I didn't Change her, and she knows I won't play her game.*"

"*And De Reske?*"

Lupo's thoughts were becoming impatient. "*Philipa De Reske and I are hardly strangers. I was there when she gave the blood that saved you.*"

Lupo was absolutely correct. After Renquist had all but been destroyed in the basement of the Apogee building by one of the first energy flows from Cthulhu, Philipa De Reske, human, but with considerable psychic abilities, had allowed Lupo to open one of her veins to feed the fading Renquist. By so doing she had become a darklost, and, ever since, Renquist had felt a certain guilt regarding her, as far as it was possible for a nosferatu to feel guilt. She had not been a victim, but one who had willingly given of herself. Immediately before the incident, she had formed an alliance with Renquist and Lupo to prevent her estranged husband Marcus from opening a portal, and giving the squid-headed Cthulhu, the most ancient, terrible, and best known of the Ancient Ones, access to the current Earth and its entire home dimension. Renquist felt that, by any standard of honor, he should have brought her through the Change, if that had been her desire. Now it appeared that someone else, presumably Julia, had done it for him, if the Underlander in the see-through blouse was to be believed.

"If she is now one of us, it could further complicate matters." Lupo also needed to know one other crucial fact. Renquist swiftly enlightened him. *"I discovered something in Coulson's memory. Our connection with her is not the only one. Before we first encountered her, she had already been involved in an affair with him."*

"She and Coulson were lovers?"

"That's right. It's one more reason I hesitate to leave."

"Your indecisiveness and concern is starting to irritate me, Don Victor. You are creating fresh complications when we have quite enough already. Will you please just take my word that I can contain things here?"

"I'm sorry, Lupo. I will vanish as soon as a suitable diversion presents itself."

"You want me to create one?"

"No, I doubt we'll have to wait too long before one presents itself."

In fact, Renquist didn't have to wait as long as he expected. Within a matter of minutes, a buzz started at the far end of the room, the one closest to the entrance from the main body of the Temple. The crowd reacted by commencing a slow inquisitive surge in that direction. The humans were so focused on seeing who might be arriving, and if it was the two other guests of honor, all Renquist had to do was to let them ebb around him, take a couple of steps back and, to all human perception, disappear into thin air.

"Brides and Companions, ladies and gentlemen, may I present Fraülein Julia Aschenbach and Ms. Philipa De Reske."

Coulson spun round as though he'd been shot. He moved toward the entrance to the room, but found his way blocked by party guests. Even by craning, he could only manage a brief and interrupted view of Philipa over the heads of the crowd. When the majority of the guests had made their way toward the exit, he had hung back and found himself another drink. Now he was in the rear of everyone who was crowding in on the new arrivals. He forced his way closer, drawing hostile looks from some of the Underlanders. He didn't care. He had to see if it really was Philipa. It seemed totally impossible, except, he had been running on very little but impossibilities for a long time now. Finally, he found himself a clear line of sight, and he was left with no further need to wonder. It was Philipa, but not Philipa as Jack Coulson in any way remembered her. If nothing else, she looked a good twenty years younger. When he had known her she'd been in her early fifties, now she looked scarcely twenty-five, certainly no more than thirty. Her thick, luxurious hair, which tended to fall in her face and created her trademark mannerism of constantly brushing it out of her eyes, had been grey when they had first met, and indeed he could remember burying his face in it just to savor her perfume. Now it had reverted to a youthful ash blonde. It took him a few moments to accept the other equally obvious change. Philipa was no longer human.

Julia Aschenbach was tall, commanding, and model-thin. She was the perfect Nordic goddess, with near white hair, high cheekbones, and deathly pale skin. Her eyes were a bright and diamond-hard blue, and she was obviously dressed for Ice Station Zebra or some other frozen transit point, in a neat and efficient, white designer ski suit. Philipa was shorter, had more curves, and wore a bulky sweater and flowing scarves. Underlanders, in the same black field uniforms as Beauregard was wearing, moved behind and beside them like an escort, strongly suggesting that they, too, had just arrived by *Flugelrad*. Coulson already knew that Aschenbach was a nosferatu, and now it seemed that Philipa had also become one. He would dearly have liked to pretend otherwise, but he had been around Renquist and Lupo too long for that to be possible. He had no choice but to accept that the woman he had once known in exquisite carnal detail was gone. The one who had taken him to her bed, and perhaps saved his mind, when he had mentally crashed and burned in the aftermath of the horrors in Haiti, was no more. It remained to be seen what this new being would be like. Coulson was suddenly torn. Part of him wanted to greet her anyway, to see if any trace of the previous Philipa might remain. His more practical and professional side cautioned against it. Philipa was a vampire, and although, after the time he had spent with Renquist and Lupo, he had become accustomed to vampires, having them as his allies, and also being exempt from their depredations, there was no guarantee that this would be the way in Philipa's case. He had no idea where her loyalties, if any, might lie.

All of Coulson's hard-won experience cautioned him against vacillation. "Decide fast and do it immediately" was a rule to live and stay alive by. And yet Coulson found himself hesitating. To accede to the existence of nosferatu was one thing, but to confront one whom he had known when she was human was entirely another. The other part of the rule was "he who hesitates has his decisions made for him," and, within a matter of seconds, the decision was made for him. Philipa spotted him. "Jack! Jack Coulson! I don't believe it. Is that really you?"

*   *   *

Thyme Bridewell saw Renquist vanish like a piece of simple trick photography. One moment he was there, and the next he wasn't. No puff of smoke, no shimmer like a transporter on *Star Trek*, he had simply winked out and was no more. The weirdest part of all was that none of the other party guests seemed to notice a thing. She had almost cried out in horror, wondering if it was the result of a new Underland weapon or some other fresh perversity, but then she gathered herself. Fuck it. She was Thyme Bridewell, late of Deerpark and other wholly unholy places. She had been, and seen, and done. Didn't she pride herself on being one tough cookie? Her training, upbringing, and thoroughly molded character expected her to remain silent even on the rack, or with electrodes clipped to sensitive parts of her body. Being darklost was making her soft. She probably shouldn't have turned to Lupo, but she did, and found that he was way ahead of her, probably reading her thoughts as she plunged close to panic. She turned and looked at him, but he placed a silent finger to his lips, and his voice was suddenly inside her head. *"Be still, girl, Don Victor has only gone exploring."*

Considerably reassured that Renquist had disappeared at his own behest, and presumably knew what he was doing, rather than being the target of some new Underland nastiness, she turned her attention to the new arrivals. Now that she knew Victor was presumably okay, the two female nosferatu became a major cause of pragmatic unease for Bridewell. What were they going to bring to an already highly confused situation? Indeed, were they friend, foe, or just a further complication? At the same time, a strong undercurrent of jealousy reached up from her new darklost persona. They were the first female nosferatu she had ever seen, and she could only react with a furious envy. *Why them and not her, goddamn it?* They were everything she wanted to be, and they had everything that she wanted, while she continued to wait and hope like the pathetic dark-lost she had become at the hands of Victor. The fact that one of them was Philipa De Reske only intensified her resentment. She knew a little about Philipa De Reske. She hadn't been nosferatu for a thousand years like Victor. A few short years earlier, De Reske had been as human as Thyme was, and just as vulnerable. She was reputedly another dabbler in the paranormal, but completely mortal. As if that wasn't enough of a connection and a fresh puzzle, De Reske, like Bridewell herself, had once had a fling with Jack Coulson. Coulson himself had told her that. She had, according to his account, nursed him back to health after the Tonton in Haiti had zapped him with the zombie drug.

At first, De Reske did not see Coulson in the crowd, but then she spotted him. "Jack! Jack Coulson! I don't believe it. Is that really you?"

They moved toward each other as though a genuine affection still existed, but Bridewell watched the reunion with a bleak expression. *Have a care, Jack Coulson, she might be kissing you now, but very soon she could just as easily go for your throat.*

Coulson's other initial reaction, running in tandem with the shock of seeing the new Philipa, was that now Renquist had betrayed him. As far as he could tell, everyone else involved in this business had double- or triple-crossed him. Weir, Grael, and all the rest of them had been playing their own devious and deceitful games, so why not Renquist? All the signs pointed to his being the author of this new surprise. Wasn't Julia one of Renquist's own colony?

Hadn't Renquist admitted that he'd actually made her what she was. Other thoughts and questions churned through his head. Was it Julia who had turned Philipa? How long ago had it happened? Had this also been arranged by Renquist? And why? And how?

Renquist seemed like the obvious culprit, but Coulson had learned that only a fool immediately accepts the obvious. When had Renquist had the opportunity to rig such a surprise? Coulson was certain the nosferatu had known nothing about any of this before he was lifted from the Watergate, and, since then, Coulson had pretty much either watched him or had him watched. Coulson was left no time, though, for theories, answers, or even all of the questions.

"Jack! Jack Coulson! I don't believe it. Is that really you?"

Philipa had quickly disengaged herself from the Grand Companion and the rest of the Underland dignitaries. One of her escorts tried to intercept her, but she easily eluded him. The crowd between the two of them parted as though she had willed it to make way, and she was coming toward him. They almost embraced, as would be natural for one-time lovers who had parted friends, but a sudden awkward barrier dropped between them. It hardly seemed appropriate to throw one's arms either around a woman who was now undead, and, from the reverse perspective, how did one clasp the body, of a man who qualified as a potential victim? For a moment they seemed to hang motionless, both the move and the emotion frozen and uncompleted, then they both halted, almost touching each other, but not actually making physical contact. "Jack . . ."

"Philipa."

"A lot has happened to me."

"I can see that."

"You can?"

"Of course I can. I'm traveling with Victor Renquist, aren't I?"

At the mention of Renquist's name, Julia Aschenbach impatiently, and somewhat rudely, left the reception committee and was quickly beside them. She had no time for any tender reunion between him and Philipa. All Julia wanted was answers.

"You're Jack Coulson?"

"I am."

"So where's Victor?"

Coulson resented her interruption, but knew he could do nothing about it. He was a mere mortal, and a mortal who clearly saw that deceiving or even stalling this Julia Aschenbach was pointless, and to try might be risking more than he was prepared to sacrifice. He looked around, but suddenly Renquist was nowhere to be found. He turned back to Julia, sheepish and more than a little anxious. She wasn't Renquist. She would rip his mind out without a moment's consideration for the possible consequences. "He was here a moment ago, but . . ."

"Don't fuck with me, little man."

"I . . ."

Lupo moved quickly into Julia's line of fire. "Leave the human alone, Julia. He doesn't know where Victor is."

"Lupo, so where is Victor? Why aren't you with him?"

"Don Victor is doing something on his own, Julia. He'll be back."

A stir started among the Underlanders but Julia glared at the Grand Companion and it temporarily subsided. "How long ago did he leave?"

"Very recently, Julia. Very recently. Maybe he received

news of your arrival and decided it was time to make his exit."

Julia glanced at De Reske. "Did you hear that, my dear? The great Victor Renquist would appear to have run away from us."

chapter Seven

Renquist was out. He was on his own and that was a wonder in itself. He couldn't remember how long it had been since he'd found himself alone, unfettered by humans and the constant compromises needed to keep them at bay. Let the Underlanders deal with Julia for a while and see how Wessel and Beauregard, and the rest of the dressed-up clowns, liked that package of tooth, claw, ego, and ambition. In the meantime, he would prowl under the multiple mirror-moons, and satisfy all of his curiosity. The air smelled vile and was all but unbreathable, but at least he was out of that absurd Temple, with its reptiles, its champagne, its animal sacrifices, and its young women who liked to show off their nipples. His vanishing act had gone rather well, and he had pulled it off to perfection, even if he did say so himself. It had been a fairly complicated piece of mass deception, involving a general suggestion to the entire room that he was there, but each individual just didn't happen to be looking at him at the given time. This was followed by a more direct tampering with the minds of those in closest proximity to him. He implanted a half dozen or so of them with the fabricated idea that he was still in the room, and it would take some time before the psychic mirage faded. After that, he had simply stepped back, walked from the reception, and out of a small door behind the line of pillars that ran along one of its walls.

Once out of the Temple, he had found himself on the edge of the piazza, not far from the *Flugelrad* landing pads. The intensity of light was the same twilight gloom Renquist had observed when they had landed with Beauregard, and, as far as Renquist could tell, no attempts were made to provide any kind of surrogate night and day. That suited him just fine. A nosferatu could move easily through the numerous and various shades of shadow. The one problem that did need to be solved was that of his attire. In his long leather jacket and stovepipe jeans, Renquist did not in any way resemble a denizen of the caverns. His clothes defined him for exactly what he was, a visitor from the surface who was creeping around where no visitor ought to be. His very first task was to find a more plausible outfit in which he wouldn't draw instant attention to himself.

Guards were posted around the parked saucers, but they seemed more lax and unconcerned than they had been when Renquist and the others had followed Beauregard out of the saucer. Renquist smiled to himself. This was both to his advantage and very much what he should have expected. The Iron Order rank and file might have looked alert and formidable, snapping to attention when an officer was in the vicinity, but, on their own and unobserved, they reverted to the careless indifference common to all bored soldiers on routine peacetime guard duty in all places and at all points in history. Underland was not at war, and the only danger to the flying machines, as far as the grunts were concerned, was probably pilferers and idle sensation seekers. The guard nearest to him had a cigarette cupped in his hand, and he looked round furtively each time he took a drag on it, but the eye he kept open for the approach of authority in no way warned him of the nosferatu silently stalking him.

The human had known nothing about what happened to him. One minute he was bored, tired, and wistfully anticipating the four or six liters of cheap Underland beer that awaited him when his watch was over. The next minute he was in complete vegetative oblivion. With absolutely no time to waste, Renquist had simply fused the guard's mind, then caught him when he dropped, like a puppet with its strings cut, no brain function and no resistance. He hauled the man swiftly into the deep shadow under the apron of the nearest *Flugelrad,* and began stripping off his long uniform coat. Renquist could not remember for sure, but he thought it was the Chicago film critic Roger Ebert who had pointed out the cinematic anomaly of how, whenever an action movie hero disguised himself in a stolen enemy uniform, it miraculously turned out to be a perfect fit. In reality, the guard was slightly shorter and heavier than Renquist, but that really didn't matter. The rubberized coat was so large and voluminous that it was almost a case of one-size-fits-all. He was reluctant to abandon his leather jacket. It had come a long way with him, but he would be uncomfortably hot and constricted in rubber fabric over leather, so it had to go.

As he pulled the man's lifeless arm from the sleeve of his

coat, he realized he was overlooking the perfect opportunity to maintain his strength by feeding. That had not been his intention when he first set his sights on the man. His only motives had been haste and some natural camouflage, but, feeding, now he considered it, was a very good idea as long as he was quick about it. He didn't doubt that some civil or sacred ordinance existed against killing and draining members of the Underland military, but since he was now, for all practical and probably legal purposes, a fugitive, he might as well be hung for a sheep as a goat.

A nosferatu on the run took his sustenance where he found it, and this was too good a chance to pass up. A part of him felt that he might somehow be betraying Lupo, who, Renquist knew, hadn't fed since he left California. To feed, while his most loyal henchman went without, was totally against the grain of their relationship, but, right then, that could not be helped. Lupo would be the last one to expect Renquist to weaken himself out of a perverse sense of duty. He snapped open the steel spike, which was mercifully still in his pocket, and went to work, bending over the man, making the incision in his throat, with the tubes and sphere's of the *Flugelrad*'s propulsion unit only a foot or so above his head.

Immediately after he had fed and the guard was dead, Renquist was on his way. He took the shortest route off the exposed piazza and away from the Temple, but he didn't give in to the temptation to hurry. He wanted to look like exactly what he was pretending to be, a simple soldier pleased to be going off duty. The faithful were still buying rats and doves, and filing into the Temple. None of them so much as glanced at him. He had been in Underland long enough to realize that it would take a highly extreme circumstance before any of the civilian lower orders would confront a man in uniform. He risked, of course, being subject to a possible routine check by the local equivalent of the military police or the shore patrol, but that was a chance he was going to have to take. Nothing came with a guarantee, even in an eternal life. Renquist's final thought, before slipping on the dead man's coat and ducking out from under the saucer had been whether he ought to take the guard's machine pistol with him. The idea made a certain sense, but, like so many other of the undead, he shunned all contact with firearms, and he did not intend, even in this emergency, to familiarize himself with them now. He left the weapon on the ground beside the desanguinated corpse.

Off the piazza, Renquist found himself in what was the Underland equivalent of a shopping street, where open front stalls hawked their wares. The roadway was the same ground-flat bedrock as the piazza, but definitely not finished to the same reflective gloss. Even if it had been, the sheen would have long since disappeared under the street's thick layer of impacted dirt and garbage. A deep stone trench ran down the center of this Underland thoroughfare, with a sluggish stream of oily water in the bottom that bore an unpleasant resemblance to an open sewer. In addition to his disgust at the rudimentary sanitation, Renquist was surprised that he saw no vehicular traffic, no cars, no trucks, not so much as a bicycle, but he did spot tire tracks in the coating of dirt, and he could only conclude that the use of motorized ground transport was most probably restricted to the elite, the military, and what passed for law enforcement in this place.

The Orwellian drabness of the booths he passed was totally at odds with the scene he had just left. The oppressive and tawdry-gilded bulk of the Temple of the Serpent still loomed behind him but he found he had moved from an environment of lavish uniforms, gourmet catering, chic and expensive young women, and champagne that cost five hundred dollars a bottle in any city on the surface, to a proletariat world of ugly and cheaply made clothing, badly printed pornographic magazines, threatening propaganda posters, and foodstuffs that only came in generic packages, all uniformly stamped with the circle, the cross, and the serpent. The poor of Underland were as dreary and colorless as the elite were flamboyant. They dressed in browns and greys, and the garments they wore were baggy and shapeless, reminding Renquist of the way the unemployed had looked during the Great Depression of the 1930s. They even seemed to be deprived of the drama of black. That was presumably reserved for the Iron Order. The only spots of spontaneous color were the odd ragged, if proudly worn T-shirt's advertising a product, movie, or sports team from the surface.

He wondered what route the garments might have taken to get there. Was this trickle-down economics at its most minimal? The structures themselves were as shoddy as the goods on display, badly made from cheap plastic and paper products in the first place, then crudely repaired ever since.

Renquist found, however, that he could move with complete ease. Most of the sorry humans on the streets, faces muffled against the foul air, either paid him no attention at all, or, if they did acknowledge his presence, it was to avoid his eyes and step out of his way. To Renquist's thinking, Underland was a culture well overdue for an uprising by the lower orders, and, the more he rubbed shoulders with them, the more disgusted he became at the ease with which men like Wessel and Beauregard were able to keep them in their place, and at the passivity with which they accepted their oppressed condition. They were clearly in need of a charismatic liberator, but he couldn't see how one could arise. Underland was too small and too closed, altogether too simple to control and police.

He could feel some things in the pocket of his borrowed coat, and he pulled them out to see what they were. They turned out to be the pack from which the dead guard had taken his last cigarette and the lighter with which he'd lit it. The pack was almost full, and he decided he would keep it for Coulson. He'd been in the grip of an intermittent nicotine craving at least since Ice Station Zebra. Even the cigarette pack carried the symbol of the cross-in-the-circle with the snake crawling up the cross. Totalitarianism, be it religious or political, or any combination of the two, always proved so tediously short on creativity.

Lupo watched the hue and cry gather momentum. In typical fashion, Don Victor had laid enough of a psychic smoke screen that it took the Underlanders a little while to work out that he had really gone. Many believed, even after ten or more minutes, that they had seen him on the other side of the room just moments before, and as Wessel directed his scarlet guards to commence a search, they were hampered by well-meaning but erroneous and completely conflicting information. While confusion still reigned, Julia stayed close to Lupo.

"What the hell does Victor think he's playing at?"

Lupo was not about to be questioned by Julia. He was very careful of the dignity of his position in the colony, and in the hierarchy of the nosferatu in general. Julia was less than a hundred years old, little more than a neophyte from Lupo's perspective, and she was in need of a persuasive reminder that she should address one of his age and reputation with considerably more respect. "I might counter that by asking you to explain why you have brought Philipa De Reske to this place?"

"I didn't bring her to this place. She brought me, very much as Victor brought you. She needed someone to watch her back. Now what about Victor?"

Lupo ignored her question. "And I suppose she also turned herself into one of us without any help?"

Julia hissed angrily. "Of course not. Don't be ridiculous. I did that."

"By what authority?"

"I don't need any stinking authority."

"You do while you remain a member of the colony. All new Changes must be approved by general consent. That has always been the rule, as well you know."

"Have you seen me spending time at the colony lately?"

"No, but I have also not seen any formal resignation from you, and you did return to recuperate after your adventure with the Maitland female."

Julia was becoming angrier by the moment. "Okay, okay, let's say that I felt bringing her through the Change was warranted. It was an emergency situation."

The angrier she became, the more Lupo knew he had her backed into a corner. Julia would never, if she could possibly avoid it, admit she might be wrong. If pressed, she would retreat into a show of fury. In a lesser matter Lupo might have given up, deciding she was not worth his time and energy, but this was not a lesser matter. Their very survival might be at stake. "You are devious, Julia, but this is not a matter of simply winning the argument. I need to know what the De Reske woman is doing here, and I need to know now."

He had promised his don that he would contain the sit-

uation in the Temple, and the reason for De Reske's presence was currently, as he judged it, the most crucial
unknown. He knew he had little time left to find out. Julia
must have sensed this, too, because she sighed and surren-
dered. "You remember in the basement of the Apogee, after
Cthulhu was put back in his box and that whore Tara Swerling was decapitated?"

Lupo's patience was wearing thin. Wessel was organizing
his troops, and Beauregard was already questioning Coulson while two of the scarlet-coated Companions stood on
either side of him. "Of course, I was there. We were all
there."

"When the head went rolling across the floor, one of
Cthulhu's little miniature clones crawled inside it and hid
there."

Lupo stared bleakly at her. "I didn't know that."

"And then Philipa grabbed the head and took off."

"What did she think she was going to do with it?"

"I don't think she knew at the time, but later she tried
to find a buyer for it among those who appreciate such
things."

Lupo blinked. "She tried to sell a piece of Cthulhu?
What, in the name of all that's unholy, was she thinking?"

"She was probably thinking how she was a woman on
her own after we brought down the Apogee. She needed
money to survive. When the Apogee went, all her means
of support went with it."

"It couldn't have been an easy transition."

"After being the top woman at the Apogee, she had all
the right contacts."

"And what happened?"

"Wessel was the highest bidder."

Lupo shook his head. *Are all humans insane? Why should*

anyone want a remnant of Cthulhu? He noticed that Wessel was now pointing to him and Julia. Guards were starting to move in their direction. Lupo knew he only had time for one more question. "So why did you Change her?"

"I thought our chances of getting out of here intact would be better if we were both nosferatu, so I Changed her before we left the surface."

"And she agreed to that?"

"She was darklost already, one of Victor's bloody darklost. She welcomed the Change with open arms."

Scarlet guards surrounded them. At the same time others of the detail were moving out the party guests. Very soon only he, Julia, Coulson, and Bridewell would be left in the room, on their own with Wessel and his armed retinue. Lupo suspected that would be the time at which matters would become unpleasant.

A *Flugelrad*, a smaller, two-man version of the one in which they'd arrived, was making systematic, block-by-block passes over a nearby area of the city, sweeping the ground with a searchlight at regular intervals. Renquist's first reaction was that the hunt for him had begun already. Then he spotted two more, both in the far distance, but widely separated from each other performing almost identical maneuvers, and he knew they could only be conducting routine patrols, much in the manner of the LAPD helicopters that made such a nuisance of themselves over the city of Los Angeles. Any hunt for him would, unless those conducting the search were acting on some totally illogical orders, commence at the Temple and its immediate environs, and fan out in an expanding pattern from there. It would not start with a detailed search of three isolated areas. This was not to say that an all-out dragnet for him would not be instituted very shortly, and he hurried on through the poverty shacks of the Underland underclass.

He reached an intersection where the narrow track of the monorail system passed overhead. One of the podlike cars was approaching, and he halted and stared up at it as it sped by with a high-tension, electrical hum. A strip of narrow windows ran the length of the car about two-thirds of the way up the side of its silver ovoid body. Behind the glass he saw blank, tired faces just like workday commuters on the buses, trams, or subways in any city on the surface. He noted that even the monorail cars carried the insignia of the cross-in-the-circle, along with a set of initials that were presumably those of the underground city's transit authority. The cross-in-the-circle, with its crawling snake, had taken over from the swastika in the worst possible way. Three scruffy young idlers, obviously sons of the proletariat, eyes hidden behind black goggles, but with limp cigarettes hanging from the corners of their mouths, crossed the intersection. The youths' route took them within a half dozen yards of Renquist, and, as they passed, they looked at him curiously. They said nothing and kept right on going, but Renquist realized that a guard of the Iron Order would not be gazing at a passing monorail car like a rube tourist, as though it was the first one he'd ever seen. The adage was that curiosity killed the cat. If he didn't modify his behavior and do more to blend, it might be curiosity that killed the undead.

He noticed that the first of the two-man *Flugelrad*s was over an area noticeably less well lighted than those around the Temple. This meager shopping precinct might be gloomy, but the section of the city where the nearest saucer stabbed down with its searchlight was in near-total darkness, serviced by little more than the artificial moonlight.

It only made sense that, with light at a premium in this enclosed and sunless subworld, the localities with the least illumination had to be those of the poorest, the most furtive, the criminal, and the terminally underprivileged. Since, in Underland, the local nosferatu that he'd seen had been both furtive, underprivileged, and close to being classed as criminals by their purple armbands with the symbol of the red triangles, this would seem to be as good a place as any to start looking for them.

When he'd decided to vanish from the reception, he had no specific purpose in mind. He only knew that he was neither learning nor achieving anything by allowing himself to be confined in the vapid society of the ruling hegemony. Once the idea had presented itself, he decided to go with it. The condition of the nosferatu could tell him more about the true condition of Underland than any champagne gala with the self-styled aristocracy. Now that he had a purpose and an initial destination, he moved on with considerably more resolve.

His new sense of determination took him very rapidly into increasingly dilapidated streets, and a stronger stench of human waste and filth. He was very aware of surreptitious eyes watching from the darkness of makeshift structures, some of which were nothing more than rudely nailed together shacks constructed out of any waste material that came to hand. Seemingly without electricity and plumbing, these shanties were lit by smoky and guttering grease candles, and dangerous-looking, homemade gas lamps. Of course, the darkness in no way hampered Renquist, or concealed these watchers, and he saw clearly that their poverty was all the way down to a third world condition of near starvation. The only consolation in their wretched lives seemed to be in the oblivion provided by a cheap and nasty form of locally distilled bathtub gin. Renquist couldn't understand why Wessel and his ruling power clique condoned an impoverished underclass. He could see that a low-maintenance labor pool would be needed as part of the their social structure, but the only necessity for these ragged destitutes was to serve as a warning and a spur to keep the workers in line. It was the old and time-honored threat made by exploiting employer to exploited employee, ever since capitalism had replaced feudalism, that there were a hundred out there waiting for his or her job; in other words, a planned devaluation of the labor market by maintaining a permanent and calculated level of unemployment among the workers. The further Renquist ventured into the city, the more his dislike of both it and the religious oligarchy that controlled it grew.

He cast around for traces of nosferatu and almost immediately picked up an orange psychic glow in roughly the direction he was already headed. Again the color was not the clear radiance that emanated from the undead on the surface. It was corrupted, as though stained by disease and a desperate and hopeless ignorance. If he was to judge them merely by their merged collective aura, and that was usually an accurate gauge of both the living and the undead, they would be of very little use to him. On the other hand, some accurate input on their origins, how they came to be in Underland and how they had fallen into the seemingly sorry state in which he now found them might just provide him with some working advantage.

Having already passed under the monorail tracks, he found that he was approaching a second section of Underland's internal transport system. If he followed his present course, he would need to traverse a raised embankment with concrete walls that supported the rails of the ground-based freight car system. Apparently the local nosferatu lived on what looked to be very much the wrong side of the tracks. The steep slope of the embankment rose at an angle in excess of forty-five degrees. It would be a hard climb for a human, but should prove no challenge to Renquist's nosferatu strength. He swiftly scrambled up it, and, at the top, he found he had an almost uninterrupted view of what lay beyond. And what lay beyond proved to be an even more depressing prospect than the parts of Underland he had seen already. On the immediate far side of the embankment was an open area of waste ground, strewn with litter, garbage, junk iron, discarded machinery, and strange outcrops of misshapen fungoid growth that were probably the subterranean equivalent of the rank urban weeds that, on the surface, grew in vacant lots and around abandoned industrial sites. The open space terminated in a long and crudely built stone wall, about ten feet high, topped with rusty steel spikes and broken glass that enclosed a dim, grim, shantytown.

The collective nosferatu aura clearly indicated that this township was where they lived, and Renquist could not muster sufficient objectivity to avoid feeling thoroughly sickened. If their weakness was such that they could be confined by a comparatively low wall, they must be too enfeebled and demoralized to be aided by any kind of intervention on his part. The place was clearly an enclosed ghetto, proof beyond any reasonable doubt that the undead of Underland had allowed the humans to reduce them to a state of complete subservience. Renquist was certain that, faced with a choice between the kind of brute existence that was laid out in front of him or perishing with dignity by his own choice, he gladly would walk out into the sun. He might experience a certain reluctance at destroying himself, but he would go with his pride intact. If the Great Slaughter of 1919 had taught him anything, it was that there were limits to self-preservation, and one could only hide and cower from rabid humanity for a finite length of time.

The only charitable question that might remain was whether the wall was designed to keep the nosferatu in or humanity out, and even that was a fairly moot point. The human position in all this was easy to read. Wessel and his people were playing the old and ugly game of scapegoat politics, in which all the ills of the society were blamed on some definable minority. The only unique aspect below ground was that, instead of diverting the rage of the poor and powerless against a group of supposed human inferiors, they used another species as the tool of their elementary mass manipulation.

Over to his left, Renquist saw a set of iron gates festooned with coils of razor wire. Red-on-white signs were posted. He was too far away to read the print, but he could see the twin red triangles — what he had started to think of as the fangs symbol. It was the entrance to a ghetto or restricted area if ever he had seen one, and Renquist had seen far too many in his thousand years. The use of the scapegoat as a means to power was as old as humanity's very first prehistoric attempts at social organization. He didn't doubt that Cro-Magnons had pointed to the Neanderthals as the source of every evil that beset them. All that could be said in mitigating favor for the situation in Underland was that it appeared stable and totally accepted. Armed guards weren't even needed to man the gates. The thing Renquist didn't understand, however, was how these nosferatu fed. Looking at the size of the area boxed in by the wall, it would appear that, unless the ghetto was all but empty, as many as five hundred of the undead could be residents there, which made the proportion of nosferatu to humans impossibly high. In the entire city of Los Angeles, Renquist's colony, which rarely numbered more than ten, were the only undead in town. New Orleans was dangerously famous for its vampire population, but even in that city of excesses, perhaps a hundred nosferatu lurked among one and a half million humans. For Renquist's kind, safety was not in numbers, but in modesty, circumspection, and not pressing their luck.

And then the most hideous of thoughts occurred to him. A colony of such unprecedented size could survive, but only under one unthinkable circumstance. If the Underland nosferatu fed primarily on each other, and only occasionally took humans, they could create a closed loop that would guarantee they continued to exist, but only on the most wretched and debased level. Loath as Renquist was to entertain such an abhorrent theory, it appeared to fit all the available facts. His first instinct was simply to turn and walk back the way he'd come, and he might have done exactly that, had not one of the iron gates opened a cautious fraction and a quartet of nosferatu, three males and a female, slipped stealthily out. Renquist still didn't feel like confronting these things face-to-face until he knew more about them, but he felt he owed it to himself and the others he had left back at the Temple of the Serpent, particularly Lupo, to wait and see what the four would do next.

The nosferatu looked cautiously around, then sprinted for the cover of an abandoned container truck that lay on its side in the open area between the freight car tracks and the wall. It had apparently been left there to corrode away to nothing, but it provided them with a serviceable first piece of cover. The undead from inside the gates had the look of scavengers, and moved as though all the savage predator pride had been knocked out of them generations earlier. It would also appear that they were either incredibly stupid, or they had also totally lost the power of psychic seeing. Although, when Renquist had decided to remain and observe the fugitives from the Underland ghetto, he had sunk into a crouch beside the freight car tracks to make himself a less conspicuous silhouette in the twilight, any surface nosferatu would have instantly spotted his aura. These four, who now lurked in the shadow of the container, probably debating what to do next, appeared to have no clue that he was silently watching them.

Renquist could, however, easily read the auras of the four fugitives, or whatever they were, and when the four drab flickers became suffused with fear, he looked around to see what had prompted this reaction. A short distance down the tracks, human auras had become visible. As Renquist read them, they belonged to a half dozen, resentful and illiterate young men from the slums. The auras were primarily colored by cheap gin and an unpleasant bravado. Moments later, he could hear the voices and uncouth laughter of these drunken bullyboys. At least the local undead still had their hearing, which Renquist assumed had provided their early warning.

As the humans approached, an urgent and fearful discussion took place within the upended container. The minds were murky and hard to read, but, as far as Renquist could tell, three out of the four wanted to cut and run back inside the gates, but the fourth and dominant one, in this instance the female, insisted that they should lie low until the humans had gone, and then go on about their business. What that business might be was less clear than the rest of the argument. Auras relayed prevailing emotions rather than specific details. The dominant one managed to sway her companions, and the four remained concealed, motionless and scarcely breathing. Satisfied that these four Underland undead were able to demonstrate at least a minimal cunning and a degree of courage, Renquist turned his attention to the four humans, and, by extension, his own situation. They were now about fifty yards from him, and he could clearly read them as six epsilon males, thoroughly marinated in Underland's societal disease culture, fueled on inculcated hate and adulterated alcohol, and looking for someone or something to hurt. They were the perfect product of a leader like Wessel. They had been raised and maintained in such watertight ignorance that they sought to vent all of their miserable fury on those they considered to be lesser beings. It had never, even for the slightest moment, occurred to them that their rage might be much better directed at the rulers who kept them chained to their cycle of hopelessness and distress.

Of course, the humans had no idea that Renquist was just in front of them, functionally invisible and watching with interest. The young men had about as much testosterone swagger as they could muster in their deprived and rotting environment. They were proud of the steel-toed boots that were worn by all but one of them. It seemed that steel-capped boots were a prestige accessory that merited a level of cheap respect among the local louts, and, as if the aggressive footwear was not enough, all six carried homemade but very serviceable bludgeons, lengths of iron pipe, a plastic beam wrapped in a vicious garland of razor wire, a large industrial wrench, and a baseball bat, a wooden Louisville Slugger that could only have, long ago, come down from the surface by some devious route.

Renquist knew that all he had to do was remain motionless and this crew of violent yahoos would walk right past him, without knowing he was there at all, even when just short yards away from him. This would have been a perfect strategy had the four undead been able to do the same, but, unfortunately, they were not. When the human crew was no more than ten or twelve yards from where Renquist crouched, one of them noticed that something was not right with the abandoned freight container. A creak and a slight movement came from inside. The one who wasn't sporting a pair of the lethal steel boots pointed and slurred. Although all but inarticulate, it proved all the suggestion his companions needed. Suddenly they were whooping and yelling, charging down the side of the railroad embankment at something between a stagger and a dead run. One tripped and fell, rolled for a few feet, then recovered himself at the foot of the slope, so numb from the gin that he felt no pain. The others just kept rushing toward the container.

At the last moment, one of the nosferatu males lost his nerve. He ducked out of the container and ran, hoping to reach the safety of the gates before the humans could reach him. Three of the louts changed direction and went in pursuit. The nosferatu had no superhuman turn of speed, and it was clear to Renquist that he wasn't going to make his objective. The remaining humans had reached the container and were beating on it with their bat and pipes, attempting to flush out the remaining three undead. By any one of the many nosferatu codes, Renquist was honor-bound to intervene. His only question was did any of the nosferatu codes apply down there beneath the surface? And his self-supplied answer was, naturally, exactly what he feared. Of course they applied down there. Since it was all so mysterious and alien, perhaps they even applied doubly. He despised the local undead as almost unrecognizable as any kin of his, but he could not simply stand by and watch them stomped, possibly to a very real death.

"So is anyone going to enlighten me as to what became of Victor Renquist?"

A half circle of robed Companions had formed and was advancing on them, weapons leveled at the hip in the formal style of the former Red Army. Lupo wondered who had introduced that piece of formation drill to the Companions' repertoire. As they were descendants of Nazis, the moves of their onetime enemy should have been anathema. He could only assume that things must have changed with time. The guests were gone, and the party was very definitely over. Having cleared the room, the Companions of the Serpent turned their attention to those who were left. Coulson and Bridewell retreated to where Lupo and Julia were standing, Philipa De Reske did the same. De Reske had the look of someone for whom the world had taken a sudden and totally unexpected turn for the worse. Lupo almost felt sorry for her. The newly changed nosferatu is a blindly optimistic creature as it first realizes its near invincibility.

"I asked what became of Victor Renquist."

Beauregard was the first to approach the group, and Lupo noted that the cocky young human's growing familiarity with nosferatu seemed to be making him a little reckless.

"Is no one going to answer me?"

The semicircle of Companions halted, but Beauregard stiffly strutted until he was standing directly in front of Lupo. "I will have an answer, one way or another."

Lupo had promised his don that he would contain things here in the Temple, and now the containment had to begin.

Working on the principle that, when no alternative presented itself, the direct approach is the best one, his face was expressionless as he answered with the single simple statement. "Don Victor has gone."

Beauregard's eyes narrowed. "I can see that for myself."

Lupo allowed contempt to show in his eyes. "You asked."

Beauregard appeared not to notice. "I was hoping you might volunteer some more specific information."

"Specific information?"

"That's right. As in where he's gone and why."

"Don Victor provided me with no specifics."

"You call him Don Victor? You are his servant, or something of the kind?"

Now Lupo's eyes were like flint. He hoped Beauregard could detect the effort he was making to keep his anger in check, but he doubted it. Lupo had suspected that Beauregard was a fool, but now his insulting tone confirmed it. Did he believe that Lupo would simply accept his arrogance. "I am no one's servant."

Beauregard's mouth twisted in a sneer. "But he didn't feel the need to confide his plans to you, did he?"

Lupo measured his words. It was not yet time to strike down the insolent puppy. He should wait until the weapons of the Companions were no longer pointed at him. "I'm not even sure that he had formulated any plans before he left. All he told me was that he was leaving because the reception was making him claustrophobic."

"That's all?"

"He also complained that he was learning nothing while he remained confined to some set, if so far unstated, itinerary."

"Itinerary?"

"That was the word he used."

Beauregard's aura was suffused with anger, and, for a moment, Lupo wondered if the human was going to be idiot enough to strike him. Then the ranks of the Companions parted to allow His Eminence Dr. Wessel to enter the immediate picture. "It would seem that Renquist found you less than satisfactory as a tour guide, Stormleader."

Beauregard spun round. His anger now blazed, but he had to bridle it in the face of his superior. "I wasn't aware that I was acting in the capacity of tour guide, Eminence."

"You knew his cooperation was crucial."

This was news to Lupo, and he filed the item for future consideration. Beauregard took a step back as the less-than-pleased Dr. Wessel advanced on him. "I thought, Eminence, I was merely required to deliver him here and act as his escort."

Despite the tension of the confrontation, Thyme Bridewell began to laugh. "Then, John Beauregard, you have fucked up on just about every level. As a tour guide you bored Renquist into making an exit, and as an escort, you allowed him to escape."

Beauregard's temper snapped, and he reached for his sidearm. "Damn you, you darklost whore, I should shoot you where you stand!"

Lupo took a step forward. "Stay your hand, human, or I will stay it for you."

The semicircle of Companions tightened their grips on their machine pistols, one flicked off the safety, and they all looked to Wessel. Wessel ignored them, staring instead at Beauregard with nothing short of open disdain. "Shut up, man, before you dig your grave even deeper."

Beauregard seemed about to say something, but then

common sense asserted itself and he closed his mouth. Wessel nodded as Beauregard finally received the message, then returned his attention to Lupo. "You and Renquist have a form of psychic rapport, am I correct?"

Lupo didn't like the sound of that. Wessel was no uninformed fool like Beauregard. He understood Lupo was undead. "That's not something I'm prepared to discuss with a human,"

"I'm not just any human."

"Nonetheless . . ."

Wessel cut him off. "You don't have to answer. I have a fair idea of your capabilities. Indeed, for all I know, Renquist could be listening to us right now."

"He isn't. I haven't heard a word from Don Victor since he left this room. You have my word on that."

Wessel's expression was one of studied disbelief. "Your word?"

A rumbling anger, like the vibration of a distant railroad train, grew inside of Lupo. "I am not accustomed to having my word challenged."

Without so much as a mental warning to Lupo, Julia suddenly entered the conversation fully on the offensive. "You'd do well to believe that, Dr. Wessel. Lupo is not only Italian, but from the oldest of schools. He treats topics like honor and the keeping of an agreement extremely seriously."

Wessel turned to Julia. "And where is the honor in Renquist running out and leaving the rest of you all here to deal with the situation?"

Lupo answered before Julia could say anything more. "He will return."

"You trust him?"

"Victor Renquist and I have known each other for a number of your human lifetimes. Over such a period trust becomes something beyond all question."

"Suppose you were to contact him and tell him you were in trouble. Suppose you told him it was imperative he return?"

Lupo's face was like stone. "I wouldn't do that. It might distract him from what he is doing."

"You're in a very vulnerable position here."

Julia smiled at Wessel. "I would say it was more of a standoff."

"You do realize that I can order my guards to open fire on you anytime I like."

Julia's smile broadened. "Then you'd be a fool. We can't be killed by bullets."

Wessel sighed. "I'm well aware of that, Fräulein Aschenbach, but I do know you can be hurt and even temporarily incapacitated by them. Even nosferatu from the surface need time to recover from multiple gunshot wounds." Wessel allowed a little time for his words to sink in before he continued. "And, of course, two of you are human. Does Renquist's honor extend to the merely mortal? If you informed him that I was going to kill Coulson and Bridewell, what would be his reaction? Would he run back to save them? Or suppose I threatened Ms. De Reske, would that motivate him? During the Apogee crisis, I understand your don was quite taken with her."

Philipa De Reske hissed angrily, but Julia quickly put a restraining hand on her arm. Lupo believed that he had preferred De Reske when she was human. She had seemed to possess a cultivated maturity, and had amassed a solid foundation of pragmatic wisdom. Now, as a nosferatu, she seemed giddy, foolishly drunk on the discovery of her newly obtained power. Perhaps she would improve, and some of her good sense would return as she grew into their ways, assuming, of course, that she survived to grow at all. Lupo shrugged. "Those are wholly academic questions, Dr. Wessel. I have no intention of contacting Don Victor."

Wessel turned to Jack Coulson. "How do you feel about that?"

"I don't like it, but it's Lupo's call."

"And you, darklost?"

Bridewell signified indifference. "I have been living on his sufferance ever since our first encounter."

"Your humans show great courage, Lupo."

"So I see."

"Perhaps it might get Renquist's attention if I was to start by shooting the darklost?"

Julia shook her head. "I doubt it. Victor leaves darklost all over the place. He allows far too much of his food to walk away alive."

Bridewell's face darkened. "Fuck you, Julia."

Wessel ignored the flurry between Thyme and Julia. "Suppose we put the idea to the test?" Wessel gestured to Beauregard. "Shoot the darklost, Stormleader. Make up for your recent inadequacies."

Beauregard nodded, unsnapped the flap on the holster of his sidearm, and drew the pistol.

The drunken Underland louts caught the male nosferatu who had run in panic when he was less than ten yards from the gates of what Renquist now thought of as the ghetto. One of the young men swung a pipe at the male's head. The nosferatu staggered but didn't fall. Another hit him hard across the back with the same result. The undead of Underland might be debased and stupid, but they did retain a certain durability. After two such blows a human would have been on the ground, definitely stunned and maybe dead. The nosferatu was dazed but he kept on going. The six young humans, so bent on causing pain, and so seemingly confident that they would encounter no resistance or retaliation, had split their numbers in half. Three chased down the nosferatu who had sought to escape to supposed safety inside the gates, while the others had continued on to flush out the remaining trio of undead, the two males and a female, hiding inside the abandoned freight container. On the top of the railroad embankment, Renquist got to his feet. He was both appalled and resigned; appalled that his Underland cousins had turned out to be so powerless to defend themselves, and resigned because he knew that, sooner or later, he would have to abandon his role as the detached observer and intervene on their behalf.

The three by the container were yelling and beating on the rusty metal with their cudgels. In their gin rage, they were full of bravado, but their bravado didn't appear to extend to actually crawling inside the container and pulling the nosferatu out. At least the local undead commanded that minuscule level of respect. The one who had run finally went down. After stumbling and zig-zagging and almost making it to the refuge of the gates, he took a blow to the back of the knees with the baseball bat and he finally fell. The humans were on him, kicking with their steel-toed boots and pounding with their bludgeons.

Renquist knew that if he was going to step in, now was the time, but, just as he gathered himself to make a move, a side panel fell out from the frame of the container. It was unclear from Renquist's viewpoint if the panel had been dislodged by the hammering of the yahoos, or if it had been kicked out by the nosferatu inside, but now the three remaining young ones were making the dash for the sanctuary of the compound, going in all directions, trying to elude the humans and their swinging clubs. The humans were drunk, slow, and stupid, and the two undead males and the single female managed to duck and weave around them. Dodging blows from the lengths of metal pipe, and the baton wrapped in barbed wire, they sprinted for the gates. Unfortunately, the direct path to their objective, and supposed safety, also led them straight toward the other three humans, still gleefully kicking their fallen companion, who could do nothing but roll with the blows and moan piteously.

At the prospect of fresh prey, these three turned their attention from the prone and fetally curled figure and attempted an interception. Again the agility of the nosferatu held them in good stead. They skipped and sidestepped, managing to avoid the wild swipes from the humans. Renquist held back on his intervention, since it seemed that all three of them were going to win the race to the gates and vanish into the enclosure unscathed. Then a human hurled his pipe with more skill than Renquist would have expected, or perhaps with more luck than the thrower deserved. He threw it low and hard with a great deal of spin. It struck the legs of the female, tripping her and sending her sprawling. She tried to rise, but, before she could regain her feet, the humans had formed a circle around her. Now they were taking their sadistic time—the socially powerless savoring their moment of power. The female rose to a defensive crouch, clawed hands protecting her face, knees bent, turning as the boys laughed and jeered, each trying to top the others of the crew with the lewdness of their suggestions and the creative foulness of their gutter obscenities. One thrust at her with his pipe. She hissed and backed away, but that brought her into range of the clubs on the other side of the circle, and she was forced to perform a fast, twisting dance to avoid them.

A human hand reached out and grabbed for the female's shapeless garment. The fingers made contact, twisted, and pulled. The threadbare fabric, that had been cheap and flimsy in the first place, ripped at the first tug, leaving her naked to the waist. This involuntary exposure caused the humans even more merriment than simply having her helpless, and at their nonexistent mercy. They grew slack-faced and even more ugly as her pale torso twisted and her breasts jiggled. Now the only outcome that would satisfy them was a brutal and inevitable gang rape, and Renquist knew that, once again, he was the only possible savior of the situation. He concentrated on a first-phase illusion, and white fire danced along the top of the railroad embankment. That was sufficient to halt the humans' grotesque game with the female. The six young men stared up at the inexplicable white fire, and then at each other as though one of their number might miraculously be able to provide an explanation. At first the fire had been silent, but gradually a high-pitched electric hum augmented the dancing flames. This surprised Renquist as much as it did the humans, since the sound was not of his creating. He looked round quickly and saw a *Flugelrad*. One of the small, two-man patrol vessels, of the kind he had seen previously, was coming up fast, following the line of the freight car tracks. Renquist doused the illusionary fire. Helping a distant relative was one thing, exposing himself to the weapons of the saucer was entirely another.

The *Flugelrad* was overhead in little more than an instant, and Renquist saw that the craft had an impressive turn of speed when needed. It came to an impossibly sudden stop, directly above the small but nasty display of human viciousness. A blindingly bright light on the underside of the patrol ship cut in and a voice boomed from some kind of amplified PA system. "Okay, boys, leave the bitch alone. You all know the rules."

Apparently assaulting and raping the local vampires was at least technically illegal. As the light hit them, the humans froze, shielding their eyes, while the undead female simply fell to her knees. The boys' reaction clearly wasn't sufficient for whomever was issuing the orders. The voice from the PA boomed again. "Get back to your homes right now."

Again the humans hesitated. The voice on the PA took on a tone of impatience. "Get going or I'll call up a ground unit, and you all know what that means."

With hangdog spines and a sullen hunch to their shoulders, the six humans broke their circle and began to walk resentfully away. The *Flugelrad* didn't move, but the light swiveled, following the gang until they began to climb the railroad embankment. They went up the steep concrete slope much more slowly than they had come down, constantly sliding back and, Renquist hoped, grazing their worthless flesh. As he again made himself effectively invisible, the light switched back to the female on the ground. "You there on the ground, get back in the compound or you'll be arrested, too. Think yourself lucky we came along."

The female rose painfully to her feet, and started back toward the gate along a path that would take her past her fallen companion. The light cut out, but the voice had one final instruction. "And drag that other thing inside with you, unless you want the cleanup crew to get it."

With that, the *Flugelrad* accelerated away, and was rapidly gone, on down the tracks and out of sight. The female reached the fallen male and knelt beside him searching for vital signs, any indication of continued animation. The vignette was both sad and pathetic. Renquist could tell from a distance that the male was unconscious, but still clinging weakly to the core of his existence. The female, however, couldn't see that. She tried to lift him, but had difficulty. For Renquist this was yet another sign of these beings' disastrous weakness. He moved rapidly down the embankment and was at her side in a matter of seconds. "Let me help you."

She hadn't heard him approach and snapped round in panic, snarling with fangs bared. Her first assumption was that the humans had returned. At second glance though, she realized that Renquist was a long way from any humanity, and that could only be a minor mercy. "What are you?"

"I'm the same as you."

The female's mind was an indecipherable turmoil. "You're not."

"I am, except I'm from the surface."

She spoke with an accent that, even to one as traveled as Renquist, sounded decidedly odd. "But you wear the coat of the Iron Order."

"I took it from one I killed." Before she could respond, Renquist smiled urbanely and easily lifted the unconscious male with one arm while gallantly offering the female the support of the other. "Shall we go?"

Without thinking, she took his arm. "You're from the surface?"

"That's right."

He could feel her confused marveling, but she started to walk without any further questions, and together they entered the gates of the Underland nosferatu compound. It was called the Gayallag, but Renquist had yet to learn its name.

"Stop!" Suddenly Philpa De Reske was in front of Beauregard.

Beauregard snarled at her. "Get out of my way."

"No, I won't get out of your way. I'm not going to allow this."

Beauregard was outraged. "You're not going to allow it? You don't give the orders here."

Lupo had assumed that De Reske was going into full, tooth-and-fang, feral fit, but she surprised him by turning on Wessel with complete calculation instead of snarling violence. "If you want to know anything about the head of Tara Swerling . . . and the thing inside it . . . you'll call off your overdressed dog."

Beauregard all but turned his gun on De Reske. "You dare to call me an overdressed dog?"

"I'll call you what I want to call to you, little man."

Lupo gestured to Julia to rein in Philipa. At the same time, Wessel motioned curtly to Beauregard. "Back off, Stormleader. Holster the pistol."

Beauregard scowled but obeyed. Julia looked at De Reske with an arched eyebrow. "Aren't you rather championing the cause of the trivial?"

"I was a darklost myself, Julia. Don't forget that. I know how it feels."

Lupo's detachment was such that he found himself mildly amused to watch nosferatu and humans fighting like cats and dogs. Renquist had worried about the combination of Julia and De Reske, and, indeed, it was proving a volatile mix, but, as Lupo saw it, far more positive than

Don Victor had anticipated. Renquist's caution was legendary in undead circles. The two females could be allowed some freedom of action. They were busily creating a high degree of chaos, and, in a rigidly authoritarian system like the one that prevailed in Underland, such disruption could be a potent weapon. Lupo decided, however, that it was high time he assumed the leadership role. He stared hard at Wessel. "So, *Dottore*, how do we resolve this confusion?"

"You believe Renquist will return?"

"He said he would, and, to me at least, his word is his bond."

Julia directed her thoughts at Lupo. *"Between you, me, and De Reske we could easily scramble their minds for long enough to get us out of here. De Reske is not skilled, but she has the wild energy of a young one."*

Lupo silently responded. *"That would only be a very temporary solution. As things stand we could get out of this building, but not out of the cavern. We could not commandeer one of the flying discs."*

"We could put a crew under mind control."

"A crew under mind control would be more of a danger than an advantage. A thrall could not summon the same precise skills. In all probability the machine would be wrecked as soon as it entered one of those access tunnels."

"So what's your alternative?"

Wessel eerily echoed Julia's last question. "So, Señor Lupo?"

"I can only suggest that we await Don Victor's return, and, while doing that, we attempt to defuse the current potential for violence and bloodshed."

"That would require a certain level of trust."

"You have the guns, Grand Companion."

"Indeed I do."

"But you need the information about the head, and it would seem you also need Don Victor's willing cooperation, for some reason you refuse to reveal. Could that be a basis on which to open negotiations?"

Renquist listened with a growing sense of dismay as the Underland nosferatu recounted their strange and frightening history. He sat on a low bench in a structure that he had learned was known as the House-Home. It was the largest building in the nosferatu compound. When he entered with the female whom he had just saved from forcible interspecies rape by the six human thugs, he had discovered that the community that lay beyond the wall resembled a tribal village. Rectangular rows of miserable huts, wickiups, and structures that were little more than crude tents, had been constructed around a central square.

Renquist had seen the *barrios* in El Salvador, and the Palestinian refugee camps in Lebanon. He had been in the slums of London and Paris in the nineteenth century. None equaled the squalor of this enclosure in Underland. Pale scarves of discolored mist drifted in the permanent twilight, and peculiar, almost hairless dogs, and large albino rats with blood red eyes, foraged in the deposits of trash beside the oily water of what could only be open sewers and among cancerous growths of unhealthy fungus. The enclosure lay under a cloud of permanent stench so putrid it disgusted even Renquist, who did not disgust easily. He noticed a complete absence of children and also of the cooking fires and food preparation that would have both been prominent features in any human habitation, no matter how wretched, and he observed that the exclusively adult inhabitants seemed to be so beaten down they suffered from a visible and probably genetic depression.

About the only redeeming feature Renquist could see was that, mercifully, everything wasn't stamped, stenciled, or engraved with the cross-in-the-circle. He did note, however, that another symbol seemed to be repeated throughout the village, a crudely daubed, downturned half circle like a horseshoe. Renquist could only assume it was a simplistic graphic representation of the exposed fangs of the local undead. Maybe a countersign to the two triangles.

A somewhat more substantial A-frame structure with decorated supports at each end, not unlike totem poles, stood in the middle of the central square. It had proved to be the House-Home, a kind of all-purpose meeting hall and symbolic center for all aspects of life in the compound, both material and spiritual. On top of all the other defects that had reduced the Underland nosferatu to an almost subhuman level, they appeared to conduct themselves according to the dictates of an excessively primitive social order. Had the population been human, he might have called it a house of worship; but nosferatu, no matter how debased, did not worship.

The name of the female he had rescued was Nerrilnahathla. Seemingly she and her three male companions had broken the laws of both man and vampire when they had sneaked out of the steel gates of the Gayallag, but such illegal sorties were also far from uncommon. Once she had recovered from the shock of Renquist appearing, seemingly out of nowhere, and grasped the fact that, despite his human appearance, he was her distant kith and kin, she had explained that the survival of the tribe depended on such forays into the forbidden.

"If we do not take the blood of humans, we would be no more. The few men and women that the Companions and the Iron Guards bring to us; the condemned—the criminals, the heretics, and the political prisoners—on whom they benevolently allow us to perform their executions for them; they are never enough to slake the Everlasting Thirst. If we didn't regularly transgress, if we didn't hunt outside the Gayallag, our people would surely wither and perish."

Renquist hardly wanted to hear the answer, but he still had to ask the obvious question. "And how do you slake the Everlasting Thirst the rest of the time?"

"We are forced to resort to each other."

It was as Renquist had expected, but it didn't mitigate his ingrained abhorrence. He did his best not to show any outward signs of disgust, but the idea of nosferatu feeding on nosferatu was such an abomination to all on the surface, an anathema to what Renquist was rapidly coming to think of as the "real" undead, that concealment of his feelings was not easy. He was relieved that Nerrilnahathla was completely unable to read auras. At that point he might have simply left both the House-Home, and the Gayallag itself, never to return, but instinct told him that he had to continue to find out as much as he could about these creatures if he was going to solve the puzzle of Underland and why he was there.

Immediately he and Nerrilnahathla had entered the gates of the Gayallag, Renquist had set the still-unconscious male on the ground. Four females had quickly hurried up with a rough litter and lifted the limp and battered victim onto it. Renquist glanced at Nerrilnahathla to see it this was okay with her. She seemed to catch the fairly simple thought and nodded. "They are his Homeshares. They will tend him."

Renquist didn't even ask what a Homeshare was. He suspected that it might involve some repellent bond that legitimized a form of incestuous rotation-feeding on each other, and he really did not want to know the details. As they carried away the male, more of the tribe began to gather round him. Up close he could see more clearly how far they had sunk, and it was worse than he had imagined when observing them from a distance. They seemed uniformly emaciated, with skin like cheap, white, worn-out leather. Nerrilnahathla was one of the very few who didn't have the exposed upper fangs, that, in many cases, were cracked and yellowing like abused and neglected ivory. Of all their physical features, the eyes of these beings actually made Renquist the most uncomfortable. They were uniformly large, with varying degrees of protuberance, and almost all were the same shade of deep brown/green. They all stared with an air of inherent sadness, as though they had some instinctive if unfocused knowledge of how much they had lost. The high proportion of grotesques should, on its own, have been proof of the parlous condition of the tribe's DNA. They came with all the classic symptoms of a miscarried Changing; the lack of hair, the corkscrew fingernails, the upswept and slitted eyes, the pointed "demon" ears, and sets of upper and lower teeth that protruded like tusks.

The tribe gathered round him, cautiously at first, unsure as to why Nerrilnahathla should have brought this supposed human in among them. Even after she had explained who he was, what he was, and why he was dressed the way he was, they still seemed unsure. Then he heard the words "Surface-guy! Surface-guy!" repeated excitedly. The language proved to be a problem. A few, like Nerrilnahathla, spoke English, German, or both, and he guessed that they were the ones who prowled the human streets and were probably smarter and healthier because they had more access to the most human blood. Among themselves, the tribe talked a kind of a pidgin that came with distinguishable words of English and German, but also other phrases and expressions that seemed familiar to Renquist, although he found himself confused by the constant use of long, rolling vowels. It took him a few minutes to realize that the reason he found some of their words familiar was that they were a distorted and bastardized form of the nosferatu Old Speech, bent out of shape by the weird pronunciation that gave their conversation a booming, alien quality.

While he was still figuring out the confused vocabulary, another word started to be repeated by the assembled crowd. "Hetjarl! Hetjarl!" This was uttered with trepidation, rather than the excitement with which they'd chanted "Surface-guy." When the crowd parted, making way for this Hetjarl, he discovered why. The Hetjarl was a tall grotesque, bare-chested in a leather vest and baggy corduroy trousers held up by a wide, studded belt. His arms were covered by swirling and multicolored abstract tattoos, and he had two of the longest canine teeth that Renquist had ever seen. Rather than making any attempt to disguise them, he consciously flaunted his fangs by having had the points capped with engraved silver. Renquist didn't have to read the grotesque's mind to deduce that Hetjarl was a title rather than a name, and the male held the rank of a tribal leader, selected—Renquist could only presume—for his size, strength, and brutality, rather than his charm or intelligence. The Hetjarl had two or maybe three inches height over Renquist, and he leaned forward to peer into his face, close enough that Renquist could smell his highly unsavory breath. Seemingly learning nothing from this scrutiny, he turned to Nerrilnahathla. *Dvooelii qa-aabiteelaa. Urplaandeer peegi, alsioo bi-aadinmuu dina, Nerrilnahathla-soodi don draag Eisen Oord?"*

The Hetjarl spoke as though he expected Nerrilnahathla to be intimidated, but she stood her ground. *"Ntyyaa urplaandeer peegi. Renquist sii Noz-Fu-Va."*

"Ntyyaa Noz-Fu-Va. Ntyyaaa."

"Dvaa Noz-Fu-Va. Suuloo limuutookla kalee ffridaa sumjoor abutii iqeerrh."

As far as Renquist could follow the misbegotten patois of the compound, the Hetjarl had demanded, using highly uncomplimentary terminology, to know why Nerrilnahathla had brought not only a human to them, but one in the uniform of the Iron Order. Nerrilnahathla, responding in like manner, was seemingly unafraid of him. She curtly informed him that, far from being a human, he was a nosferatu from the surface, with great strength and magical powers. The crowd began murmuring again, "Surface-guy! Surface-guy!"

The Hetjarl frowned as though confused by the news. Renquist saw from his aura that he considered Renquist a definite threat to his position if there was any truth in Nerrilnahathla's claim about Renquist's strength and magic, but he wasn't exactly sure what to do about it. Strength he understood, but magic was a whole other territory. *"Oolsi au ussheetu ynallaatum? Alai kuuoo aattifa wkunoo-akk suna aaqoleembn aysh xoomm nuuobu-uht?"*

Renquist had trouble understanding the Hetjarl's question, and he looked to Nerrilnahathla for a translation, but when he heard it, he wished he hadn't. "The Hetjarl wishes to know if you care to pass along the blood you carry with you in your veins."

Suddenly Renquist realized that the feeding here was more perverted than he had previously imagined. He saw the repulsive transactional system laid out in Nerrilnahathla's mind. Not only did the undead of Underland feed on each other, but the ones like Nerrilnahathla, who dared to hunt among the human population, would, on their return, give up a portion of their own replenished and energized blood to those who had remained behind. Renquist could see that it might be a practical solution under the prevailing circumstances, but he could not get past what, for him, was the excessive ugliness of the practice. Renquist immediately shook his head. "I don't think so."

The Hetjarl let out an animal snarl. "Suppose the Hetjarl think to *take* your fresh blood?"

Renquist stared at him in surprise. "So you speak English?"

"I speak with many tongues."

"Indeed?"

"You think you stop me with your magic? You think you could . . ." The Hetjarl searched for the appropriate word. ". . . *prevent* me from taking your blood?"

"I know I could stop you. It wouldn't even require magic."

The Hetjarl made the mistake of reaching for Renquist. With lightning speed, Renquist seized his hand and, with no compunction about crushing bone, bent it back against the wrist and slowly forced the Hetjarl to his knees. The grotesque resisted, but he was only marginally stronger than any hulking human, and it was an absurdly uneven contest. Renquist's single dilemma was how to end the trial of strength without killing this idiot male. He might hold these beings in total contempt, but they were, at root, nosferatu, and for one nosferatu to destroy another was a taboo that Renquist only violated under the most extreme provocation, and according to the most stringent protocols, as when he had driven Kurt Carfax out into the sun during the internecine strife in the New York Colony during the time of Feasting. Neither ignorance nor stupidity was a capital crime, but Renquist wasn't sure if the Hetjarl's low arrogance would allow him to admit defeat. Fortunately, the problem was solved for him by a new outbreak of murmuring among the onlookers. "Altjarl! Altjarl!"

Now the crowd parted to allow a new figure to make his way to where Renquist and the Hetjarl continue their variation of arm wrestling. This new arrival was stooped and bent. Had this old one been from the surface, he might have seen the fall of the Roman Empire, or even its foundation by Romulus and Remus, and still not have looked as ancient or decrepit. As close to human as Nerrilnahathla, the Altjarl was thin to the point of emaciation, his cheeks were sunken, his bony nose jutted like the beak of an august vulture, and his spine bent in a way that, in a human, would have been a sign of advanced osteoporosis. He needed the help of a cane in order to walk, and dragged one foot behind him; but, for Renquist, the most distressing feature, was once more the eyes. They were filled with an infinite sadness as though he had personally witnessed the decline and deterioration of his tribe. Renquist released the Hetjarl and stepped back. The Hetjarl snarled and looked as though he was still under the illusion he could best Renquist in a trial of strength, but the Altjarl waved him curtly away. *"Hetjarl, nku uzooshi xmjulannool heetii."*

The Altjarl's breathing was labored, his voice weak and faltering, but, at the same time, it contained the power of absolute authority. The Hetjarl got to his feet and slunk away, hissing as though vowing that his business with Renquist had yet to be concluded. When the Altjarl spoke English it was as though he had not used the language in a long time and had trouble bringing it to full recall. "You . . . are . . . Noz-Fu-Va from . . . surface?"

"Yes, I am nosferatu from the surface."

The Altjarl repeated the word as though he remembered it from a long time ago. "Nosferatu. Yes, nosferatu."

Nerrilnahathla leaned close to Renquist, and whispered, "The Altjarl is over two hundred years old." She made it sound as though it was a matter of collective pride.

So even now, in their sorry condition, these Underlanders lived longer than humans. Renquist could imagine how that must irritate Wessel and his followers. Nerrilnahathla seemed very proud of the Altjarl's great age, and Renquist did not have the heart to tell her that he himself was almost a thousand years old, and, barring disaster, expected to survive for another thousand. Fortunately, he was left no time to respond. The Altjarl gestured with a rope-veined claw to the building in the center of the compound. "We go to the House-Home, surface-guy nosferatu. We go to the House-Home and talk."

"My name is Renquist."

"Ren-quist?"

"That's right, Renquist."

"My name is Zarralhapad. I am the Altjarl of these Gayal."

Since all wood had to be brought down from the surface, none was wasted on the undead. Renquist would later learn that even the Altjarl's wooden cane was rare and a prized heirloom. The House-Home was built from a dried and impacted fibrous material that Renquist surmised had started out as some type of fungus, and it gave the interior a cloying, claustrophobic spore-smell. The circle of low benches and the tall presiding chair made it clear that at least one of the central building's primary functions was as a place of meeting, discussion, and maybe judgment.

Nerrilnahathla and Renquist followed Zarralhapad inside. A dozen other apparently senior members of the tribe came after them, while still more remained just outside, peering in through the open door. Nerrilnahathla indicated to Renquist that the Altjarl would seat himself first, and once the old nosferatu had bone-creakingly lowered himself into the high chair, the rest would take their places on the benches. She showed Renquist a place close to Zarralhapad's chair, then sat down beside him. As he read her aura, he saw that she already felt an attachment to him. Since she was the first to encounter him, she had decided they had some kind of special relationship. Renquist hoped that she was not cultivating some strange undead affection for him, as she might be forlornly disappointed. He was not a missionary come to save the savages, and he was certainly not going to bond with her. The moment he had learned all he needed to know about these people, he would be gone, hoping never to return.

The House-Home was lit by candles that burned with such a disagreeable reek Renquist had no desire to know how or from what they were manufactured. The lighting of them constituted a small ceremony before the conversation commenced, as did the females who entered bearing platters of assorted fungoid finger food which Renquist declined to so much as touch, even though the refusal might constitute a serious breach of etiquette. Any of the morsels could be the deadly "funge" against which the dying derelict on the Temple piazza had warned him. Already, while walking the short distance from the gates to the House-Home, he had seen a number of undead slumped against walls or squatting in the dirt staring with bleary concentration at their boots or, if they lacked boots, their gnarl-nailed feet, obviously completely out of their minds on some powerful hallucinogen.

The tribe was an unmistakable patriarchy, although it certainly didn't appear to exclude females like Nerrilna-hathla from performing as hunters. Zarralhapad partook of the prepared fungus, then paused for a long time, letting his mind drift along avenues of pleasant illusion before rousing from his short stupor, and rapping his cane on the ground to bring the assembly to order.

"Welcome, Ren-quist."

"Thank you, Altjarl Zarralhapad."

"You have the gratitude of the Noz-Fu-Va, the People of the Home, for delivering our sister Nerrilnahathla from the depredations of the humans."

"Again I thank you, Altjarl Zarralhapad. It was nothing more than my duty as a nosferatu."

"Is there a reason that you have come from the surface, Ren-quist?"

"I very simply wish to learn the story of the Noz-Fu-Va and how they came to be here in these sunless caverns."

"Do you on the surface not shun the sun?"

"Of course."

"Then have we not found a place of great safety?"

Renquist avoided answering the question by posing one of his own. "And how long have the Noz-Fu-Va been here?"

"We have always been here."

"I would like to learn the story of the Noz-Fu-Va."

"The story of the Noz-Fu-Va is a long one. Some say as old as time."

"Alas, time is something I do not have. Already the humans, those who call themselves the Companions of the

Serpent, may be looking for me. I would hear as much as you can tell me in a short time."

Zarralhapad nodded as though he understood. "Then I will endeavor to tell you what I can in the time that you have."

The story that Zarralhapad recounted was little more than oral folklore, obviously handed down from generation to generation as the life span of the Noz-Fu-Va shortened, the fungus corrupted them, and their closed society turned in on itself. The narrative was often contradictory, and frequently at odds with nosferatu history as Renquist had studied it. The Altjarl had no knowledge whatsoever of their creation by the Nephilim, or the subsequent uprising and flight. Zarralhapad's genetic make-up was so tainted he had never experienced a DNA vision of the Original Beings. He seemed to pick up the story of the nosferatu some eight thousand years ago, when brute beings, at a stage of development roughly halfway between the Original Beings and modern nosferatu, had ruled as blood gods, sometimes called the *Bramaparush,* in the river valleys of northern India. Also know as the Gayal, they had been very similar in appearance to the oafish Hetjarl.

"In the days before time, we of the Gayal dwelled in the night by the wide and dark waters. We were content until the humans learned the Secrets of the Sun, and came to our caves to slay where once they'd offered themselves to us. In those times of suffering, many perished until the Great Trek started and we crossed the High and Frozen."

That was all very much as Renquist had theorized when he'd seen his first vampires of Underland outside the Temple of the Serpent. The Gayal of ancient India were recorded in some of the oldest of nosferatu texts, and usually credited as the immediate ancestors of the contemporary undead. What went unrecorded was how, when the local humans had evidently overcome their awe, and figured out the nosferatu's fatal vulnerability to sunlight, the Gayal had fled north, presumably into the Himalayas. Undead historians had always believed that the Gayal had been wiped out, supplanted by the first moderns.

"For long nights we wandered the High and Frozen without air and without blood, and then the Great Lamia found us . . ."

Renquist was halted in his academic tracks. "Lamia?"

Zarralhapad stopped and stared. He was plainly not accustomed to being interrupted while he was telling tribal stories. His voice sharpened as he repeated himself. "The Great Lamia found us and took pity. She led us to the Starting Place from where we descended into the Darkness of the Earth."

"Please pardon my interruption, Altjarl, but am I to understand you to say that the Great Lamia was one of the Gayal? That she came down into Underland?"

Under normal circumstances Renquist would never have been so ill-mannered as to interrupt the flow of what had to be a long-learned and well-rehearsed recitation. Zarralhapad's tired eyes narrowed as he realized that Renquist was interested in more than just hearing the ancient stories told by rote. "You have a concern with the Great Lamia?"

"Indeed I do, Altjarl. I was created by the Great Lamia."

Although he knew that Zarralhapad might have difficulty believing it, this was the absolute truth. In the twelfth century Renquist had still been human, a mercenary soldier who went by the name of Victor of Redlands. More by bravado than good judgment, he had rented his sword and his services to the heretic Albigensi-Cathars. When overrun by the forces of Pope Innocent III under the notorious

Simon de Monfort, Renquist had been among those who made a final stand at the Castle of Montsegur in the foothills of the Pyrenees. To buy precious time so priceless books and artifacts could be saved from the Christian fire and spirited away over the mountains to safety, Renquist and three other young hired blades had volunteered for a desperate and suicidal rearguard action. Four against hundreds would have been totally pointless had the Cathars not revealed they possessed a process of necromancy whereby the four young men could be endowed with superhuman strength. For some years, the Cathars had secretly protected a being known to them as Lamia, the Great Vampire. She would now return the favor by Changing the young men, but the price of their new power would be that, once so endowed, they would no longer be human. By a near miracle, Renquist had survived the extraordinary battle at Montsegur, but, in the aftermath, Lamia had vanished. At regular intervals during the rest of his days he had made regular attempts to locate her, but those had always ended in failure. Sporadic reports of her activities had continued until around 1650, when she had disappeared without any further trace. The one time he had seen her, in the moments before his Change, she had appeared a mature but stunningly beautiful woman with raven hair, ivory skin, and the strangest violet eyes. If what Zarralhapad said was true, and he had no reason to doubt the Altjarl, she must, even in the twelfth century, have already been walking the Earth for thousands of years.

Zarralhapad stared at Renquist curiously. "If you are the changeling of the Great Lamia, my lord, you must be extremely old."

Renquist nodded and half smiled. "I am old, Altjarl, but I am not a lord."

"Surely any changeling of the Great Lamia must be a lord?"

"I come from a place where there are no lords."

The Altjarl had difficulty grasping this. "That place must be passing strange."

"In some ways it is. But please enlighten me. When the Gayal entered the Darkness of the Earth, did the Great Lamia accompany them?"

Zarralhapad frowned. He was so used to telling the tales of his tribe exactly as he had always know them, they had become little more than sequences of ritualized words governed by rhythms and inflections. Over the years of telling, the actual content had been rendered almost meaningless. He had to think hard, silently mouthing the words over to himself before he answered. "The Great Lamia found us and led us to the Starting Place from where we descended into the Darkness of the Earth . . ."

"And then?"

"No."

"No?"

"The story does not tell of the Great Lamia entering the Darkness of the Earth with the Gayal. She was our savior in the days before time, but she was not one of us. She helped us, but then went her own way. The story unfortunately does not say where."

Renquist nodded. He could not show his growing frustration at the stupidity of these throwbacks, so he resorted to a polite formality. "Thank you, Altjarl. Please go on with your story. I fear time is still pressing."

It took Zarralhapad a few sentences to regain the familiar cadence of his story, but then he hit his stride once again, and the words of the litany flowed according to the age-old pattern. "And the Gayal entered the Darkness of the

Earth and time began. And the Gayal remained in the perpetual night until the Dhrakuh, the Serpent People, came upon them, and the Gayal rejoiced because the Dhrakuh brought them men."

At the mention of the Dhrakuh, Renquist again wanted to stop Zarralhapad and question him, but he knew it would probably do very little good.

"But the men came in numbers, and with them the twin curses of the funge and the machinery. Men flew in the caverns, and they made light. More and more of the men came, knowing the Secrets of the Sun, and the Gayal grew weak from the funge and were cast down low, into a misery of bondage and servitude, and the Time of Wailing was upon the Gayal."

That the addictive fungus had contributed to what the Gayal had become was obvious, but how much they had deteriorated since they had been chased out of the Indus valleys by a comparatively small population of humans was starting to seem somewhat debatable. They might lurk in Underland confined to a ghetto, victimized by the local yahoos, and all the while gnashing their teeth at how the once mighty had fallen, but, on one level, it was only their strange underground confinement that was keeping them alive as a subspecies. Everywhere else on Earth, the Gayal had become extinct, replaced by the smarter and more adaptable modern nosferatu. The Time of Wailing might be upon them, but at least they were alive to wail.

"I'm sorry, Altjarl, but once again I must seek some clarification. I need to know all I can learn about the Dhrakuh."

"And the Gayal dwelled in the country of the Dhrakuh, night without end, turning upon their own for sustenance when unable to hunt in the ancient ways."

Zarralhapad seemed not to have even heard Renquist, who was impatiently wondering if it was because the Altjarl was too old, too stoned, or too stupid to be aware of anything but the endless singsong recitation once he got going.

"Altjarl . . ."

Zarralhapad abruptly stopped and stared blankly. "The Dhrakuh?"

"That's right, the Dhrakuh."

"The Dhrakuh are all round us, Ren-quist. That should be self-evident."

That was exactly the answer Renquist did not want to hear. Did they still exist in physical reality as Wessel's behavior seemed to imply, or were they only a figment of legend and the prevailing belief system? If the unbelievable was true, and some kind of reptile beings really did cohabit this underworld with men, women, and the Gayal, they might be the key to why he was there. Renquist's problem was how to frame the question in a way that Zarralhapad would be compelled to give him a straight and factual answer. Perhaps he should have allowed these fools to believe he was some kind of magical lord and let fear prevail where courtesy could not.

"I do not quite understand."

"What would a surface-guy need to understand?" The Hetjarl, miffed at being excluded from the gathering, was in the doorway of the House-Home, still nursing his injured hand. "Why do you waste time here, Ren-quist, when the Companions and the Iron Order are right now searching the city for you?"

"Searching for me?"

The Hetjarl appeared to view the bearing of bad tidings as some compensation for his earlier humiliation. "See the

Flugelrads for yourself. They are all over the homes of the humans. Soon they will be here."

Renquist attempted to stand, but his legs suddenly felt spongy and a wave of dizziness washed over him. He sat down abruptly. Nerrilnahathla's aura radiated concern. "Is something wrong?"

Strange colors-without-names from a deviant spectrum spiralled at the periphery of his vision. "I can't see properly."

"Have you fed since you came to this place?"

Renquist's throat was now constricted, and he had difficulty speaking. "I . . . killed a guard and . . . stole his uniform. I . . . took his . . . blood."

"You fed on an Underlander."

"Yes."

"The funge was in his blood."

"The humans use the funge?"

"Of course. You didn't get a full dose, but enough. You now embark on your very first *eztzaama*."

Suddenly all the colors closed in on him, and reality was no more. The Hetjarl burst out laughing, but Renquist did not hear him.

Wessel's specific order had been to confine each of the party separately but, as the Companions took them away, Lupo had rearranged that command in the minds of the escort so the entire party from the surface would all be locked in together. Julia had been fully in favor of violently mind-stunning the guards, but Lupo had vetoed anything so overt. Until Renquist returned, they would allow the humans to believe that they were docile and cooperative. Julia had grudgingly bowed to his judgment, but that didn't stop her fuming with a barely suppressed rage. As the door was closed behind them and the key turned in the lock, she snarled at Lupo. "Damn you. Now we're fucking prisoners."

"Only because we choose to be. I could forcibly remove that door at any time. Or pick the lock. Whichever you prefer."

As prisons went, the large windowless room with the inevitable Underland stone walls, stone benches, an iron door, and a total absence of wood where wood might have been expected, had they been on the surface, was neither particularly appealing or overly inhumane. The hole in the floor that functioned as a human toilet was less than appetizing; but there were no rats, or roaches, or any other parasites. They weren't forced to share the place with the skeletal remains of any previous occupant, and no madman was screaming in an adjoining cell. Although largely medieval in appearance, it was not equipped with chains, stocks, iron masks, or instruments of torture. The room was dry and warm, and the air that wafted through a narrow vent in the ceiling was as fresh as any air in Underland. The primary discomfort, after so much had happened at such speed and intensity, was having absolutely nothing to do except look at each other or stare at the walls. Lupo had been held in enough lockups and confined in enough dungeons, down the long years, to treat confinement as a tedious interruption of his life during which reality had to be put on hold. An awareness of time was the archenemy, and to count the minutes was a first step on the path to becoming stir-crazy.

Everyone seemed to share his experienced resignation. Even Julia, with all of her unchecked rage, accepted the situation for neither more nor less than what it was. She had, of course, during her comparatively short existence, journeyed, at the very least, to the Soviet Gulag and back, so she was no stranger to doing time. The two humans, Coulson and Bridewell, were professionals and had both seen the inside of more than one cell in the course of their careers. Even De Reske, during her hippie days, had been tossed into a couple of jails.

All settled on the chill, unyielding benches and prepared to wait for what might happen next, but De Reske tended to fidget, something Lupo guessed was only to be expected. He remembered her as a human who would have taken the situation in her stride. Back when he and Don Victor had come into confrontation with the Primary Church of the Apogee, the woman had possessed nerves of steel. Four-square beside him and Renquist, she had coolly confronted the first emanations of Cthulhu conjured by her husband Marcus. She had not even flinched from what had to be done when Don Victor, all but destroyed by a massive jolt of psychic energy, had needed her blood to survive. Her current discomfort was easily explained. She was simply a very new nosferatu, and, like all very new nosferatu, was consumed by internal surges of energy that made it very hard for her to keep still for any length of time.

That she was in the holding cell at all was still a puzzle to which Lupo had yet to fill in all the blanks. Earlier, back at the reception, she had presented the briefest of thumbnail sketches of what had happened to her since their previous association. Lupo had already known most of it. He was unlikely to forget the momentous challenge of that deadly afternoon, when Marcus De Reske had almost succeeded in assisting the Great Cthulhu to break into their dimension, and the terrible supernatural fog had descended on West Los Angeles, so thick that it hid the sun and allowed the undead to walk by day. The most dangerous of the Ancient Ones had only been repelled after a lethal confrontation in the deep subbasement of the Apogee building during which Marcus De Reske and Orton Ghast, the other cofounder of the Apogee, had been killed, and Tara Swerling, Marcus's mistress, whose pornographic plaything exterior had turned out to be nothing more than a cover for a dark and dreadful ambition, had been decapitated by a whirling undead sword.

In the heat of the moment, Lupo had not seen the tiny squid-headed replica of Cthulhu seek refuge inside the severed head. He had also not noticed that, in the grisly aftermath, Philipa, in an instant of inspired opportunism, had seized the head and fled the building, and, it would seem, also left the city of Los Angeles and the entire United States behind in her run for cover. She had admitted that she'd used her Apogee connections to put the head, and its small but still vastly powerful resident, up for sale in the shadowy international marketplace where deals for paranormal weapons and artifacts were transacted by would-be necromancers, government agencies, and black-arts research scientists. She had also admitted that Grand Companion Wessel had been the highest bidder, and that the head was in Underland, quite probably right there in the Temple of the Serpent, and she had been brought down there for some kind of buyer/seller debriefing. The story, as told so far, left Lupo with many unasked and unanswered questions, and, in search of resolutions to them, and also to pass the time in the cell, he very gently entered Philipa De Reske's thoughts. To his surprise, she detected him almost immediately. "Stop reading my mind, Lupo. If you want the story, I'll tell you."

It was unusual for a freshly changed nosferatu to be so in control of her new and expanded mind that she had that kind of sensitivity to intrusion, but then he remembered that, even as a human, De Reske had the psychic power known as "the sight." Lupo apologetically retreated. "Pardon me. I was just curious about some things."

"You want to know about the head?"

Lupo spread his hands in a wide Italian gesture of the man caught peeking. He didn't regret what he'd done, but he needed to put De Reske at her ease. It was not something he did often, but he could muster a certain charm when it was required. "It might be relevant to our current situation."

"You're wondering why I sold it to Wessel?"

"I'm wondering why you took it in the first place."

"I suppose that you might call it an act of desperation. I was vulnerable on all fronts. Ghast was dead, Marcus was dead. The Apogee was in chaos, and I knew, after what had happened, everyone from the FBI to the IRS was going to come down on the operation, and I was the only poor sucker left alive to take the rap. My only allies were you nosferatu, and I knew you would all melt back into the night at the first hint of trouble, so I grabbed the first thing of value I saw and ran with it."

"Did it occur to you that your actions might have been prompted by the little Cthulhu?"

She avoided his eyes. "Yes." She paused. "Of course. I considered that."

"And?"

"I don't think it exerted any influence. I couldn't detect anything either then or later, but I knew I had to face the possibility. The nasty thing probably felt as vulnerable as I did."

"And why did you sell it to Wessel?"

"That's very simple. As I said, he was the highest bidder."

"There were other bids?"

Philipa laughed. "There were plenty of other bids, but Mervyn Talesian, the president's Special Security Advisor, was the only other one in the ballpark with the kind of money I was looking for. I mean, I wasn't selling *Star Trek* memorabilia or vintage comic books. This was a piece of Cthulhu, and I wasn't about to settle for chump change, no matter how desperate I might be."

At the mention of Talesian, Lupo stared at Julia, who, in turn, looked sharply at De Reske. "You never told me that Talesian put in a bid."

Philipa's expression was blank. "I didn't think it was relevant."

Lupo and Julia exchanged glances. They were both well aware from personal experience that the real Talesian was something totally and absolutely different from his public image of Special National Security Advisor and the apparent power behind the current president, but they didn't want to discuss him in front of Coulson and Bridewell, or Philipa De Reske, for that matter. Instead they merged their memories. When the media lionized Mervyn Talesian as the new Henry Kissinger, the latest genius of US foreign relations, with his much vaunted "tough line" in international diplomacy, they knew better. When he suddenly, and without warning or buildup, stepped from nowhere into the full spotlight of global politics, the official story was that Talesian was an Armenian-American who had previously been a cloistered academic at either Harvard or Princeton, although the press and TV seemed confused over which. He'd only emerged from academic obscurity when the incoming president had selected him to author the first draft of NACT, the Nuclear Arms Containment Treaty. From that point on, he had moved with almost uncanny swiftness into the very center of power, with his own staff, his own suite of offices in the White House basement, and, some said, his own private intelligence force and an extensive enemies list.

Lupo and Julia recognized that Talesian's White House-generated biography was a total fabrication, because Mervyn Talesian was not even human. On what they both thought of as the Scottish adventure, they had seen him wake from a fifteen-hundred-year sleep. In England, in the sixth century, he had been known at the royal court of Arthur Pendragon as Taliesin the Merlin, and he was one of the last, maybe the very last, of a species called the Ur-shu. As Renquist had explained it, the Urshu—later called the "Watchers"—were the most successful product of the entire genetic program of the Nephilim colonization. The Urshu were effectively immortal. They had no problems with sunlight and, as far as anyone could tell, they were of superior intelligence. Just as the ancestors of the nosferatu had been designed for combat, the Urshu were administrators and negotiators, specifically, in the context of Earth, designed to act as mediators between humanity and the Nephilim, whom the humans presumed to be gods. They had massive powers of mass mind control, which more than explained how Mervyn Talesian could get away with his blatantly fictitious résumé, and why no one seriously dug into his background. Like the nosferatu, though, the Urshu also had a weakness. Just as the undead were destroyed by sunlight, the Urshu had to hibernate. They would enjoy a life span of three, four, maybe even five hundred years, and then suddenly they'd vanish, retreating into a kind of suspended animation for a very long period of time, not to reemerge until centuries later.

After the Nephilim had abandoned their colony on Earth, the Urshu had constantly involved themselves in the politics of humanity. Quetzalcoatl would seem to have been an Urshu who intervened in South and Central America. In other areas there was Osiris, Ahura Mazda, the Summerian Uan, the Norse Loki, Gilgamesh, Viracocha in the high Andes; the Greeks had Deucalion and Prometheus. Some even say Confucius was a Watcher, others Pericles, some claimed Jesus Christ as one of them. According to some accounts, they attempted to eradicate cannibalism, human sacrifice, and the drinking of blood. In the Christian era they seemed to have all but died out until the recent waking of Talesian.

Where his cousins in the ancient world had mainly spread a quasi-divine harmony, Talesian had a much harsher agenda. Lupo recalled how, in the Scottish castle of the nosferatu Clan Fenrior, this more-than-mortal creature had presented Renquist with the disturbing idea that the only way to save the planet from human overpopulation was by instigating a major cull of the human race. By means of either plague or nuclear war, Talesian had proposed wiping out 90 percent of humanity. When Lupo had seen the Urshu on CNN, in a public, photo-opportunity consultation with the president, Talesian had seemed to be going for the nuclear option. His hard-line policies kept pushing nations like India and Pakistan, Argentina and Chile, or Iraq, Iran, and Israel, closer to a nuclear showdown. Although they tended not to discuss it, Renquist, Lupo, and Julia were afraid of him and what he might do.

The exchange took only a few seconds, but it was

enough to cause De Reske to look at them suspiciously. "Why are you two doing the collective memory thing?"

Caught unexpectedly in full tandem recall, Julia's answer could only sound lame. "We were wondering how Wessel managed to outbid the White House for the head."

De Reske clearly didn't believe her, but let it slide. Lupo quickly covered for Julia. "What I don't understand is why you went through the Change."

"I was darklost already. You know that."

"But surely it was Don Victor who should have Changed you?"

At this Bridewell looked up sharply, but said nothing. De Reske nodded in response to Lupo. "I didn't think it was a very good idea to come back to California. I was still on the lam from the Apogee fiasco, and, besides, I'd learned that your don could be very . . ." She smiled wryly. ". . . changeable about Changing."

Bridewell's aura showed major anxiety, but Julia didn't notice as she explained why she had Changed Philipa. "It was part of the bargain. We were both in Warsaw. I had just broken the bond with Destry. Sure, Philipa's real desire was to be Changed by Victor; but, in the end, she settled for simply being Changed, especially when I told her the story of how he had Changed and then deserted me in Berlin. I also had to know if Cthulhu had a hold on her before I came down here with her."

Clearly Julia's thinking was closer to his own than Lupo had ever expected. "So we have no fear on that front?"

"Not as far as I know."

The conversation was halted by a key turning in the door. Coulson, who had been silent, locked into his own thoughts, glanced at Lupo. "Is that Renquist?"

"I don't think so."

The door swung back and revealed just two Iron Order guards armed with machine guns. "Thyme Bridewell?"

Bridewell looked up. "I'm Bridewell."

"Come with us."

"Why?"

One Iron Guard laughed nastily. "Because we will shoot you if you don't."

"Just me?"

"Just you."

"What about the others?"

"They stay here."

Julia flashed a message to Lupo to jump the two Iron Guards and go, but again Lupo rejected the ideal. Bridewell, unaware of this, looked to Lupo for some sort of lead. Lupo sighed. "You'd better go with them, my dear."

Bridewell stood up, but then again stood her ground. "Who gave these orders?"

"Stormleader Beauregard wants you."

Bridewell sighed and looked at the others. "On past observation, he either wants to kill me or fuck me, and I suppose there's only one way to find out which."

An Iron Guard pulled her arms behind her and snapped a pair of handcuffs onto Thymes' wrists. Instead of resisting she forced a smile. "Now that could be a prelude to either."

She grinned a little too bravely at her own cynicism and followed the Iron Guards outside. When the door was closed and locked again, Julia hissed angrily. "I hope you know what you are doing, Lupo. First Victor vanishes, now they take away the darklost. Our numbers are being rapidly whittled down. Plus, I don't know about you, but, very shortly, I have to feed."

Lupo noticed Coulson's aura change. Now that he was the last human in the room, the man had become profoundly and understandably uncomfortable at Julia's talk of feeding.

chapter Eight

Her escort knocked hard on a door made from a molded sheet of cast iron, decorated with bronze dragons contained in the outline of a shield, and curlicued hinges of the same material. It seemed too fancy for a place of execution, and Bridewell was minimally encouraged by that thought. For almost a minute, Thyme and the two men waited. Then the muffled click of bolts being shot back, and the scrape of a key turning in a lock came from the other side. The door swung open with a suitably dramatic creak of hinges.

A tall, dark-haired woman, in the robes of a Bride of the Serpent, stood in the doorway, silhouetted against the dim yellow light within. She was one of the distaff elite that Beauregard had previously described as "reptile nuns." This one, however, differed from the Brides that Thyme had observed earlier at the reception in that she held a glass of red wine in her left hand, she was probably drunk, and her robes were unfastened and open, revealing that she was naked beneath, save for stockings, the same scarlet as her robe, and matching platform shoes with high and cruel stiletto heels, confirming that Beauregard, as she had already half suspected, must have ordered her brought there for some carnal purpose—and not for any political, military, or conspiratorial objective. At first the Bride made no move to step back or usher Bridewell inside. She merely looked her up and down in dispassionate inspection. "You must be the one from the surface."

"I'm Thyme Bridewell."

"I thought you'd be taller. I thought you all grew taller on the surface, with all that sun and air, vitamin C, and fresh meat."

Thyme met her cold stare with an equally chill gaze. "We come in all sizes."

The women still didn't step aside, or motion for her to enter. She simply glanced back into the room. "Your new plaything's here, Johnny."

Beauregard's voice came from somewhere in the room. "Then don't just stand there, bring her in."

The Bride gestured curtly for Bridewell to enter. "Now it's your turn to keep the hero amused."

It was a large turret room, forty feet across, completely circular, and decorated in the inevitable black and red. *When the hell are these people going to get past the easy symbolism?* Because of the curved stone walls, most of the furniture had been custom-made, from carved and decorated rare woods that must have been imported at great cost from the surface. The floor was flagstones, harsh for a boudoir or even a playroom, but softened by a scattering of fur throw rugs that were most probably all that was left of a number of endangered species. Apparently the Underland serpent cult set no store by self-denial, poverty, or chastity, and Bridewell's disposition toward Beauregard grew even less charitable. She noticed that the walls of the room were uncommonly bare—no pictures, no paintings, no engravings, no framed photographs, no pornographic prints. That struck Thyme as a little odd when everything else was so overly lavish, and then she realized that it was very hard to hang pictures on walls that were consistently curved.

Beauregard had three playmates with him already, and Bridewell seemed destined to complete the quartet. The Bride who had admitted Thyme immediately proceeded to ignore her and went to a Moorish table of patterned marquetry and inlaid mother-of-pearl, where the refreshments for Beauregard's private orgy had been laid out like a buffet. A small phalanx of bottles presided, all top-shelf booze, straight from the surface; single malt scotch, cognac, designer vodka chilling in a bucket of ice, George Dickel bourbon, and semilegal absinthe. A mound of white powder and some partially consumed lines of what could have been heroin or cocaine, or some recreational chemical completely unique to Underland, reposed on a dark green, hexagonal sheet of glass. One plate held a neatly arranged selection of small snacks that looked like they might have been brought from the reception. A second contained twists of what had to be the intoxicant fungus. The Bride poured herself a shot of vodka and drank it down in one swallow. Bridewell walked a few paces into the room and stood waiting. She would have poured herself a drink, but her hands were still cuffed behind her. The handcuffs alone should have been a clue that she was being taken to Beauregard, rather than hauled away to be shot, interrogated, tortured, or moved to another cell. They were custom-made with cushioning pads of soft leather.

Beauregard greeted her from his bed. She observed that at least he was not wearing his goggles here. "So they brought you, Miz Bridewell?"

"They brought me."

"Good. I always have my way in the end."

"What you can't get by persuasion, you take by force?"

"If need be."

The second woman of the trio was a blonde, and she lay beside the reclining Beauregard, facedown on the bed that was the dominant feature of the room. The vast bed was not only custom-made, but must have been assembled right inside the room. Its huge headboard, that was curved exactly to fit the wall, was a backdrop for drama, rather than a mere piece of furniture. It towered a full twelve feet over the pillows, and, above that was a tented canopy of black silk. The carving on the headboard—serpents, naked women, and grinning, bat-winged demons in lewd and impossible poses—must have taken months to carve out of the dark African hardwood.

The blonde should probably have been described as naked, since the few tatters of ripped lingerie that were bunched around her waist hardly qualified as clothing. She looked mauled, and two distinctive sets of marks on her buttocks showed that she had recently been beaten with both a broad paddle and a thin cane or whip. Damn but Johnny Beauregard was one highly unoriginal motherfucker when it came to perversion. The paddle, like a wide leather table tennis bat with squared-off sides and an ivory, penis-shaped handle, lay on the floor at the foot of the bed; but there was no sign of the whip. A fur rug was beneath the woman, partially hanging off the side of the bed. Only the woman's weight was stopping it from sliding completely to the flagstones. Bridewell thought she recognized the fur. It looked exactly like the one that Renquist held in such high and fetishistic regard when he and Bridewell had shared a prison back at Deerpark, and he had made her a darklost. God, but that seemed so very long ago, and so strangely normal compared to what had happened since.

The third woman was a set piece of abnormality. She was manacled to a red velvet chaise longue. Her head was shaved and, aside from the numerous stainless-steel rings and studs that penetrated her flesh, her only adornment was three straps, studded along their length with sharp, two-inch, steel spikes. One of these was round her throat like a choker, while the other two were buckled halfway down the whiteness of her thighs. Beauregard saw Thyme looking at her and laughed. "Puzzled?"

"I'm not sure."

"Tell Miz. Bridewell what you are, Odonatta."

The woman's voice was slurred and bleary. "I represent a sexual predicament."

"Explain."

"As you see, I cannot close my legs. I am open and available, but any man or woman who places themselves between my thighs would be lacerated."

Bridewell glanced at Beauregard. He wore a black silk robe with the cross-in-the-circle on the breast and nothing underneath it. He'd neglected to tie the belt, and she was able to observe that his penis was, in fact, rather small. "It all seems a bit pointless."

"Pointless? I need no point if it amuses me. I am celebrating here, Miz Bridewell. Tomorrow I leave here on an historic mission."

"And you wanted me to join you?"

"Indeed I did."

"For the party or the mission?"

"For the party, my darling. You have no place on the mission. Right here, right now though, you could be a positive addition."

Thyme looked at the motionless Odonatta. "Why do you let him treat you like this?"

"He's a national hero. We do anything he wants."

Thyme turned back to Beauregard. "I'm not going to be able to do much with my hands cuffed behind me."

"I wouldn't totally agree."

"Give me a fucking break."

Beauregard gestured to the Bride. "She's right. Give her a break. Unlock her hands, Natasha."

Natasha, the reptile nun, was cutting out a line of the unidentified white powder. "I'm busy. Either unlock her yourself, or get one of your whores to do it."

Odonatta's slurred voice came from the chaise. "I'm not a whore."

Natasha inhaled the powder through a silver tube and sniffed loudly. "Take a look at yourself."

"I submit because he loves me."

"Right."

Beauregard nudged the woman next to him. "Take off her handcuffs, Gretchen."

"I can't move, you bastard."

"Sure you can move."

"I can't. You all but flayed the skin of my ass just now."

Beauregard poked her in the ribs with his bare toe. "Get up and take off the cuffs, goddamn it, or I'll show you what flayed really means."

Gretchen groaned and eased herself gingerly off the bed. "You're a bastard, Colonel Johnny. You're a fucking bastard, and I don't know why I go on coming here."

"You're like Odonatta, you come here because you love me."

"I don't love you. I submit strictly for the material benefits. I am a whore. I make no pretense about that."

Instead of going straight to Bridewell and removing the cuffs, Gretchen first went to the table, wrapped a handful of ice cubes in a napkin, and applied them gently to each of her buttocks in turn, gasping each time the napkin touched her livid flesh. "Oh God."

Beauregard's drawl was languid. "Stop pretending you're hurt, my dear. You're much too loaded to feel any pain."

When Gretchen had finished attending to her welts, she picked up a ring of keys from beside the bottles on the from the table and approached Bridewell. "You'd better turn around."

Thyme did as she was told without comment or reaction. Gretchen fumbled at first, confirming for Bridewell that Beauregard had been right. The blonde was totally loaded. Finally, she managed to fit the key into the hole and turn it. One cuff hung loose, and having done it once, the drugged Gretchen managed the second one a great deal faster. As Thyme allowed herself the small luxury of massaging her wrists, Beauregard indicated that he was far from finished with her. "Now strip her, Gretchen."

Thyme was determined to show neither surprise nor shock. She would treat his arrogant order as if it was the most natural thing in the world. She had, after all, been in many far worse situations. "I can do that for myself, Colonel Johnny."

As Bridewell removed her leather jacket, Gretchen poured herself a brandy and retreated to perch on the end of the bed and watch. She continued to hold the ring of keys and the padded manacles that were still warm from Thyme's wrists. Bridewell looked round for somewhere to hang the jacket. Beauregard dismissed the idea with a gesture. "Just drop it on the floor. We have servants to take care of that kind of thing. This room could well be a disaster area before the night is through."

Bridewell dropped her jacket on the floor as instructed, but paused before either unzipping her jeans or pulling off her T-shirt. "Does anyone mind if I have a drink before I continue the striptease."

Beauregard crawled down the length of the vast bed to observe her more closely. "Help yourself, my dear."

Thyme turned to the table and, like Gretchen, poured herself a straight-up scotch. She saw to her surprise that an antique pistol lay on the table, in among the snacks, drugs, and booze. Somehow it seemed in keeping. If it was real, it probably dated back to the Civil War, a long-barreled, double-action Army Colt, but with its chamber converted for modern cartridges. Bridewell sipped her scotch, then pulled off her T-shirt. Beauregard nodded. "You have a nice pair of titties, my dear. Small but shapely."

Bridewell thought of a number of retorts on the subject of diminutive body parts. Instead she picked up the pistol. She inspected it with a professional eye. The ammunition looked real, and the weapon seemed sufficiently well maintained not to blow up in her hand if she fired it. Maybe her best plan would be to shoot Beauregard right there and then, but she thought better of it. A gunshot could bring a mess of guards tumbling down on her. Instead she spun the gun round her index finger, like a gunfighter in a Western movie. "A family heirloom?"

For the first time since she'd met him, Colonel Johnny

looked nervous. "Indeed it is, but why don't you bring it over here like a good girl?"

"Is it the one your great-great-granddaddy carried at Shiloh, Colonel Johnny?"

"Just give me back the gun, my dear. We don't want anyone getting hurt."

Bridewell spun the pistol on her finger again and walked slowly toward Beauregard. Since she was naked to the waist, she decided to go the distance, and she undulated her hips as seductively as any strip-joint lap dancer. "Did you hear how, up on the surface, they sell erotic videocassettes of naked women firing guns?"

"You look capable of shooting me."

"What, and miss all the fun?"

She spun the pistol by its trigger guard for a third and last time, and then offered it to Beauregard butt first. Beauregard stood up, and took the pistol from her. He looked round the room. He seemed to have a need to reassert his masculinity. "Pick a target."

"A target?"

"Any target?"

Bridewell played the airhead. "I can't. You choose."

Beauregard grinned. "The carving on the headboard."

Thyme nodded. "Okay."

"See that third serpent on the right, the one coiled round the woman's leg?"

Thyme signified that she did. Beauregard turned and fired in a single fluid move. The report was deafening in the enclosed stone room. Natasha winced, Gretchen hardly seemed to notice, and Odonatta had really no way of reacting without cutting herself. The head of the carved snake was now a smashed hole in the wood. Thyme looked insincerely sad. "It seems a shame to spoil the carving just to prove a point."

"If I'd fired at anything on the wall, the bullet would have ricocheted all over the room."

"I suppose that's one way of looking at it."

"How is it we don't have Iron Guards beating on the door wanting to know who got shot?"

Beauregard shrugged. "They're used to much worse. What's a gunshot when the colonel's having a party?"

He didn't seem to realize that he'd just made it abundantly clear to Bridewell that a gun could be fired in his private quarters, and no guards would rush to investigate. He walked to the table, put down the gun, and helped himself to a twist of fungus. Natasha raised a penciled-in eyebrow. "Should you be taking that stuff the night before your great mission?"

"They don't give a blood test to a Stormleader. Only the aircrew have to be fungus-free."

Bridewell was openly curious and she let it show. "What is this mission?"

"I have to attend an assassination."

"You don't strike me as the lone gunman type."

"And what would you know about lone gunmen, Miz Bridewell?"

"For my sins, I know rather a lot about lone gunmen."

"For your sins?"

Thyme nodded. "For my sins."

Beauregard laughed. "So why don't you take off those rather provocative jeans, and let us provide some practical absolution for those sins?"

"Who's getting assassinated?"

Beauregard shook his head. "I can't tell you that. It's a state secret."

"I won't tell."

"Take your jeans off."

"And then you'll tell me?"

"Perhaps."

Thyme slid her jeans down over her hips. Beauregard applauded and then turned to Natasha. "Will you do the first honors, Natasha?"

The dark-haired Natasha picked up the leather-and-ivory paddle from the flag stones. "It'll be a pleasure, Colonel. I'm already taking a dislike to Ms. Bridewell. She is altogether too sure of herself."

Thyme eyed the paddle bleakly. "And what do you intend to do with that, Bride Natasha?"

Natasha slapped it against the palm of her own hand as though testing it. "I intend to chastise you into a sufficiently malleable frame of mind to solve the puzzle of Odonatta."

Beauregard laughed. "Nothing is so purifying as the mortification of the flesh. Don't forget that I am not only an officer and a gentleman, but also a priest."

Thyme looked at him coyly. "Could Natasha's pleasure and my mortification be postponed for a moment? I would like to hear more about this assassination."

She knew that Beauregard wouldn't be able to resist talking about himself. He waved off Natasha and smiled smugly. "Tomorrow I will lead a formation of *Flugelrad*s to shoot down the private aircraft of Mervyn Talesian, the Special National Security Advisor to the President of the United States."

"You're joking?"

"Indeed not."

"Isn't that likely to start a war?"

"With whom? As far as the US government is concerned,

Talesian's plane will have been attacked by flying saucers. They'll be too busy trying to explain it to carry out reprisals. The president doesn't know about us."

"Why Talesian?"

"Dr. Wessel considers the man dangerous."

"I'm awed."

"So you should be. But enough of this, my dear. Let's proceed with the punishment. We have much time still to decorate."

"I don't think so."

Beauregard looked at her in surprise. "What?"

"I said I don't think so."

"Show her the error of her thinking, will you, Natasha?"

All the time they were talking, Bridewell had been moving toward the table, now, in a move just as smooth as Beauregard's, she seized the pistol, thumbed back the hammer, and shot Natasha squarely between the eyes. The woman was dead, knocked backward by the heavy-caliber slug. Perhaps 40 percent by volume of her pink brain matter, embedded with a mass of lighter skull fragments, was splattered on the wall behind her. Beauregard didn't know whether to be outraged or terrified, but Thyme didn't give him time to make up his mind. She shot him next, using exactly the same spot on his forehead as a target. She must have been a hair off in her aim, because Beauregard spun and fell onto the bed, facedown, one side of his head effectively missing. He sprawled next to Gretchen, whose only reaction to the twitching corpse was to stare dejectedly at Bridewell. "Are you going to kill me, too?"

"I'd like to let you go, but I can't. You'd give the alarm the moment I was gone."

Gretchen nodded; so drugged that even death was mundane, or maybe welcome. "Yes, I understand."

Natasha's blood was already spreading in a pool across the flagstones. Since there was no gentle way to shoot someone. Thyme did the next best thing and made it fast. "I'm sorry."

Odonatta saved herself by making absolute sense. "You don't have to shoot me. I can't give the alarm. Lets face it, I can't even move. All I can do is scream, and screams coming from in here are extremely common. Standard you might say; a nightly occurrence when the Stormleader was off duty. No one would so much as think to come and investigate."

Bridewell nodded. She was already pulling on her T-shirt. "You are absolutely right. Logic and reasoning have just saved you."

She slipped on her jacket, tucked the pistol in the back of her jeans, even though there was only one shot in it, and started for the door, then, at the last minute, she turned back, hurried to the bed, and snatched up the fur rug. She was convinced it was the one that belonged to Renquist. Fortunately, no one had bled on it.

Renquist was in the grip of violent hallucinations that put all trace of reality to flight.

He rode a rainbow, but, at the same time, his flesh was melting and flowing off his bones.

He was carried on tides of fire, and the very ground on which he stood trembled and was no more.

Memory scattered, and fragmented images roared by him too fast for thought or even recognition.

Marieko Matsunaga appeared with flame behind her.

The pallid and often mourned face of Cynara was briefly in front of him, as though she called to him from the other side of destruction, pleading for him to join her.

Yet he was totally enjoying the sensation. A wild jubi-
lation raced among the flames, leaping high with each curl-
ing wave.

In a moment of horrific reason he tried to cry aloud; if
this was only a partial dose of the fungus, what hell could
the full effect do to those who dared its horror and its
glory?

As his own voice howled in an unrecognizable tongue
to some empty and lost dimension, echoing the scream of
dying wolves, searing flashes, bright as the radiance of the
deadly sun, burst in a formerly midnight sky, all but blind-
ing him, burning his eyes, and he wondered if this was the
capacity for death entering his DNA.

Ragged armies of pure fury surrounded him, slashing
with naked and ethereal knives, and again he found that he
hardly cared.

Albino rats with silver teeth feasted on his eyes.

He should have been in a state of galvanized panic, but
he was tranquil and uncaring. It was little wonder the fungus was so attractive.

A tubular pillar of light appeared in front of him, a vertical spiral, revolving at the full velocity of the black energy
of the universe, mesmerizing and disorienting, and tearing
at the very integrity of cellular structure.

A broken pattern was created like the beating of great
dark wings.

A bat or a bird?

Renquist wasn't sure which, but, then again, Renquist
wasn't too sure about anything.

After what seemed like an eternity the spiral began to
slow and gradually rolled to a stop.

Even before the motion ceased, he realized that the
whirling vortex had been a tall double helix, the double

helix of his own DNA, and the flashing lights were the atoms contained therein.

Almost immediately after the helix ceased to move, the lights began to wink out, one by one, until he remained, little more than a discorporate, a missing casualty drowned in a foam of darkness.

Except that was not absolutely true.

The darkness itself had a kind of substance.

A great leather wing enfolded him, and he was convinced that, after a millennium of walking the Earth, his existence was finally over.

He had partaken of the poison, and doom was upon him.

He was disappointed that he would see nothing of what happened down the time line.

He enjoyed the experience of existence, and was reluctant to see it go, but he was neither afraid nor angry.

His only emotion was one of surprise at how serenely he accepted the totally unacceptable.

He had never attempted to go gently, but now he was doing exactly that.

His resignation spoke volumes for the power the evil fungus might have on a modern nosferatu with no tolerance for it.

Or was he going into the great and infinite darkness?

Was it now his time for great and infinite darkness?

Was he to learn and also teach by example that nothing can ever be truly immortal?

Even the universe itself was fated to collapse.

How in overweening pride could he have believed himself the exception?

But he found himself with an awareness of motion where no motion should have been.

He felt himself being borne up.

Was this another phase in the mechanism of the true death?

He saw the moon, gentle and comforting, somewhere above him.

Not one moon, but two, three, four, an entire collection of moons, each with a rainbow aurora that seemed to stretch to infinity.

And then the motion changed, and he felt himself going down.

Victor Renquist resigned himself to the fact that he was now no more.

Jack Coulson stared at the wall of the cell. The wall, being made of hard living rock, was free of the stains and graffiti that were a usual feature of most of the jails and lockups in which he had found himself over the years. He had been confined in a Guatemalan police station, under arrest and waiting for the secret police. The walls of the cell into which he had been tossed that time had been decorated with an entire silent roll call. Dozens of names had been burned into the filthy and flaking paint that covered the rough cinder block. They had been scratched with smuggled sharp objects or burned with the tips of many flaring matches. Almost a third of the names had a small noose drawn next to them, indicating that Pablo and Cortez, and all of the rest of those so annotated, had left the place to be executed.

This Prison of the Serpent was entirely different. Only a single prisoner had managed to leave his mark, with what had to be such a prolonged and insane dedication, possibly over the course of years, that it mutely spoke volumes about the power of human individualism even in the face of captivity. Somehow, with an implement or series of implements, over a span of time that Coulson found hard to imagine, the incarcerate had managed to grind the single word KLAUS into the surface of the rock. Of course, he realized he was making the obvious, if not wholly guaranteed assumption that it was Klaus who had carved the name. Perhaps it wasn't Klaus who had scraped for so long. Klaus could have been an object of affection, and the one who etched the name was Klaus's lover. Coulson also realized that he had been assuming the dedicated prisoner was a man, but that didn't need to be the case.

He knew he'd been looking at the wall for too long. Unfortunately, the only alternative was to watch the three nosferatu sleep, and wish he could sleep himself. More than that he wished he could smoke. Lupo, who seemed to have taken total charge of the situation since Renquist had taken off, had made the obvious and highly practical suggestion. "If we cannot feed and we cannot fight, the best thing to do is sleep." Coulson had been surprised at how easily the three undead had laid themselves to rest. After all the nonsensical mythology generated by folklore, Hollywood, and Hammer Films about soil, coffins, and all of the rest of the dreary paraphernalia, the sleep of the undead turned out to be about as uncomplicated as it could be. He'd seen tired children sleep with greater difficulty. Philipa, Lupo, and Julia had merely stretched out on the stone benches, folded their arms across their chests, and closed their eyes.

Coulson had obviously wondered how the three would wake. For all he knew they might return to the conscious world ravenously hungry, and immediately fall on him and open his jugular for their version of a Continental breakfast. He supposed that this was the chance you took when you hung out with vampires. On a much more mundane level, he was now alone. Where previously the four of them at least had conversation to pass the time, he now had nothing to listen to except the silence, and nothing to do but loiter in his own thoughts. He had deliberately not looked at his watch, so he had little idea how much time had passed when Lupo sat bolt upright and exclaimed, "Something is wrong with Don Victor."

Lupo spoke before he was even aware of his surroundings, and seemed almost surprised to find himself in the Underland holding cell with the two sleeping females and Coulson staring at him in surprise. "Did Victor contact you in some way?"

"I . . . am not certain. Something came to me in the dreamstate."

Lupo's first reaction was one of extreme discomfort that he should have uttered such an outburst in front of a human, and Coulson found himself in the unique position of attempting to calm a clearly shaken, six-hundred-year-old vampire. "Renquist spoke to you in a dream?"

Lupo shook his head, trying to control both his concern and his embarrassment at allowing the concern to show. "I don't know. It was like nothing I ever encountered before."

"Should we wake the others?"

"No, not yet. Let the females sleep."

Despite his alarm at seeing the normally unshakable Lupo so obviously distraught, Coulson was amused that the veteran nosferatu seemed to consider, in the moment of crisis, the comradeship of a human male to be somehow superior to the attachment to other nosferatu should they happen to be females. No wonder he was always referred to as old-fashioned, or from the traditionalist school. "So what exactly did you see in the dream."

"It was not something I exactly saw. I'm not even certain

that I was actually dreaming. It simply came to me." He hesitated, as though miserably reluctant to say the words. "I sensed that Renquist had met his true death."

"Are you telling me that Victor is dead?"

"That was the feeling, except . . ." Lupo trailed off.

"Except what?"

"Except that I can still sense him."

"You and Renquist are always aware of each other?"

"There has been a bond between us for a very long time. I can feel that he is not as he should be, and that he is now in a very extraordinary and dangerous place. He is hardly thinking, but he is still in this world. If he had suffered the true death, only an emptiness would remain."

"So, Lupo, what do we do about this?"

"So, Jack Coulson, I frankly do not know."

Because she'd had other things on her mind at the time, not least of which was the fate that might await her, Thyme Bridewell had not paid much attention to the direction the two Iron Guards had taken when they'd brought her to Beauregard's quarters. As a result of her preoccupied inattention, she had little idea of how to make good her escape, now that she had freed herself from Beauregard's deviant soiree, and she spent a great deal of time taking wrong turns and generally losing herself in the labyrinth of stone corridors of those parts of the Temple of the Serpent never revealed to the public. Her focus on negotiating the building's mazelike internal geography might also have been a little off. She had, after all, just shot and killed three people. Even with her past experience of wet work, and working agency hit-team assignments, it still took at least a modest emotional toll. She clutched Renquist's fur rug for comfort and thought hard.

One of the few things she did remember was that her escort had taken her up at least two flights of stone stairs and that they had never at any time gone down. Thus, plotting her route by reverse navigation, she descended each stairway that presented itself. On the second flight, this plan was thwarted by the sound of voices and noisy military boots coming up from below, and she had been forced to flee back up the way she'd come. Being in Underland, and away from the sun, somehow made it harder to tell time by instinct, but, after wandering for what seemed like a good half hour, Bridewell felt panic creeping up on her. She leaned against the cold stone wall of the corridor in which she found herself and attempted to manage her agitation by concentrating on the positive. She had shot Johnny Beauregard, and that surely had to be a blessing, if not to the world, at least to the young women who circulated among the Underland elite.

She realized that, by shooting Beauregard, she might well have saved the life of Mervyn Talesian, and she wondered how that might figure in the grand scheme of things. She wasn't totally sure if that qualified as a positive. She suspected that Lupo and Julia had conducted some lengthy telepathic conversation on the subject of Talesian, just before the guards had come to take her away. Unfortunately, being only darklost, she had not been a party to the discussion, so she was in no position to know for sure. Was the Special National Security Advisor one of the good guys or one of the bad guys? And according to whom? She realized that she was happily ready to accept the geopolitical viewpoint of a crew of vampires, and that said a lot about how much Renquist had changed her. She knew that, down the line, she might have to give the subject of Talesian a good deal more consideration; but, for the moment, she

could only take a nasty pleasure in the look on Beauregard's
face as he had spun away with the neat hole just above his
eyes.

With that last-ditch blind luck that can arrive miraculously at the moment when all seems about to fail, she
walked on and, almost immediately, came upon an open
archway that led to the outside. The archway gave access
to the perpetual grimy twilight, and a wide expanse of flat
roof beside the rearing ugliness of the Temple dome. She
moved with caution through the arch, hoping that her luck
held and she would not find that the roof was just a spacious dead end, or came with its own complement of black
or red guards. Bridewell realized that this was the first time
she'd been out of the Temple since that short walk from
the landing pads and across the piazza. The lights of the
city were all round her, and, with what seemed like a
wicked irony, they twinkled like jewels in the haze of pollution. Above them were the mirror-moons, which shed
enough light to reveal that the expanse of roof in front of
her was completely deserted. Her intention was to walk
around the edge to see if there might be stairs, a fire escape,
or even some kind of emergency ladder that she'd be able
to use to get down to the ground. Once there, she had no
clear plan, except to look for Renquist. Although he could
be anywhere in the city, she trusted that her new darklost
instincts would lead her to him.

She had walked halfway along the first side of the roof
when a shadow in the sky caused her to look up. Early in
her operational training, many years ago, when she was
scarcely a teenager, she had taken a combat course at the
training camp in Florida. The sergeant in charge of night
exercises had gone to great pains, both his and hers, to
point out that the fatal weakness of most men and women

was that they rarely looked up. They supposed, sometimes with fatal cost, that danger was always beside or below them. The lesson had stayed with her, and even before she knew what the shadow might be, she let go the fur and dropped into a crouch, scanning the air above her. A dark shape moved swiftly past one of the moons. She assumed, or perhaps she hoped, that it was nothing more than a high-flying *Flugelrad*, hovering up near the roof of the cavern. She had no idea why one of the peculiar aircraft should be doing something like that, but it obviously had nothing to do with her.

She had also been trained never to easily accept the obvious, so she remained crouched and watching for a few moments longer. The shadow passed a second of the mirror-moons, creating a brief but frightening silhouette, and Thyme knew that it was no *Flugelrad*, or any other man-made flying machine. The thing was alive, a great bat-shape against the false sky. For an irrational instant, she wondered if somehow Renquist, or one of the other undead, had taken flight, even though she knew that was impossible. They were no more able to wing through the air like giant bats than she was. The whole idea of shape-shifting and vampire aviation was a combination of popular fiction and fireside mythology.

Once she'd seen the thing against the light, she could easily track its progress, even against the indistinct backdrop of the city. Her first realization was that she wasn't even looking at a single one of whatever it was. Two of them flew side by side, and they didn't flutter and circle like bats. Instead they propelled themselves with steady, even strokes of wide membranous wings, gliding smoothly between each beat, like the animated reconstructions she'd seen on TV of the movements of prehistoric pterodactyls.

The second shock came when Bridewell realized that think-ing of them as being *like* pterodactyls was only protecting herself against the madness of the unacceptable truth. For all practical purposes, they *were* pterodactyls, massive flying reptiles from the Jurassic, displaced by millions of years. She neither knew nor cared if they were clones created from fossil DNA, as hypothesized in the movies, or figments from some incredible lost world. They were there, and that alone was enough to set her mind reeling. Later she would discover that the monsters were know as the Messengers, and that they differed fundamentally from true and wholly extinct pterodactyls, the most important dissimilarity being their almost human intelligence. In that first encounter, though, she only knew she was looking at a pair of incon-ceivable terrors.

As they came closer, she was able to make out a much smaller, third object supported between them in a kind of harness grasped in their hind claws. Closer still, she could see that the thing in the harness was a man, and, using it as a gauge to their relative size, she could estimate that their wingspan was as much as twenty feet, if not more. Thyme was also able to judge their intended direction, and that only served to compound her fear. They were coming di-rectly at her, and the flat roof beside the Temple. In the face of this calculation, she didn't turn and flee as most would have done. It was her first self-protective impulse, but her training held good, and she resisted it. Instead she pulled Beauregard's antique Colt from the waistband of her jeans. The cylinder might now only contain one live round—four shots had been fired and one chamber had been empty under the hammer—but, if worse came to hid-eous, she could always use the bullet on herself.

As the flying lizards approached the roof, Thyme Bridewell went into that place of final composure that lies on the other side of fear. With an agility of wing that enabled them to hover in mid-air, the flying reptiles lowered their living cargo to the roof. When his feet touched, their human burden stumbled forward a few steps, then fell to his knees. The lizards now settled for a landing themselves, closing their wings in complex folds, and shuffling forward a number of paces with a walk that made them resemble Balinese stick puppets. In the moments before the man had fallen, however, she had recognized him beyond any reasonable doubt, and the recognition caused her to scream from the depths of her darklost soul.

"RENQUIST!"

Renquist opened his eyes, and found himself staring straight up at a mass of extremely alien machinery. For a moment he thought he was back in Deerpark, in that very first phase of totally locked-down restraint and confinement, in the red-walled room in Virginia with the laser pointed at his right eye and Agent Bauer standing behind it, asking him pointless questions, trigger poised to cauterize his brain.

"Isn't this where I came in?"

But he knew that could not be the case. The technology that enclosed him was constructed from a totally unique combination of metals, ceramics, and other materials that he didn't even recognize. A considerable quantity of gold seemed to have been utilized in the components of the hardware that all but encased him. A hard volcanic rock that could have been obsidian had also been used, except that he had never seen obsidian so precisely cut and micro-finished. Other modules of the machine had an unearthly organic look to them, as though living tissue had been grafted into the system. That was at least partially confirmed by the transparent tubes that appeared to be feeding fluids to those units. Renquist was left without the slightest doubt that this equipment, or any like it, would never be found at Deerpark, or any other federal facility, no matter how well guarded a secret. It was simply too radically advanced. Indeed, he was hardly able to accept that it was of the twenty-first century, or, for that matter, of the planet Earth. The weirdest part of all was something that, at other times, might have been considered trivial. He was laying on his very own favorite fur rug.

The only real resemblance to the red room at Deerpark, once Renquist had recovered from the initial shock, was that a shadowy figure stood in the dark beyond the massed banks of mysterious devices. He didn't believe it was Agent Bauer, so he tried a tentative first inquiry. "This may sound like a cliché but where am I, and who are you back there?"

Like any human with an alcoholic, blackout hangover, Renquist truly had no idea where he was or how he came to be there; but the moment the figure responded, and he heard her voice, the second part of his question became redundant. "Victor, you're awake."

"I'm either awake, or this is some illusion beyond the true death."

"This is not death."

The voice and the figure behind it both unmistakably belonged to Thyme Bridewell, but it was not Thyme Bridewell as he remembered her. She radiated a power and a cold authority that she had never possessed before. Without hesitation or preamble, he asked the one obvious question. "Who Changed you?"

"You did. Indirectly."

"I don't understand. How could that be?"

"Just rest, Victor. It will all be explained very soon. You need to replenish yourself. You've had all the blood in your body changed."

"Like Keith Richards?"

That would explain why he was naked on the fur and had IV tubes in his immobile arms.

"Very funny, Victor."

"I try, Thyme Bridewell. Even when I don't know where I am, I still try."

"So stop trying and do your best to relax; very soon there will be much to do."

"The last thing I remember is being in the compound of the Gayal, and discovering that I'd accidentally ingested the fungus toxin when I fed from the guard at the landing pads."

"The Messengers brought you here."

"The Messengers?"

"Victor, please, if you keep talking, the Dhrakuh will want to sedate you again."

Renquist hardly understood what Bridewell was saying, and his mind was whirling. "Are you sure this isn't just one more hallucination?"

"I've already told you. All this may be strange, but it's real."

"But the Dhrakuh?"

"Do as you're told Victor and rest."

"Are you ready?"

Julia, Philipa, and Coulson all nodded, and Lupo tensed to lead the attack. The footsteps were at the door of the cell, and a key was being inserted in the lock. A decision had been made. Many hours had passed during which Renquist had neither returned nor sent word, and Lupo reported that his sense of his don was going through wild fluctuations. "I have never experienced anything like this. It's as though he hovers on the edge of some frightening abyss."

Concern over Renquist had finally brought Lupo round to Julia's way of thinking, and although not one of the remaining quartet had any idea of how they might ultimately escape from Underland itself, they knew that they had to get out of the cell. Julia hadn't even needed to exert pressure. He could not sit idly by while something so inexplicable and disturbing happened to Don Victor. The plan was a simple one. The next time any guards came to the door, the three nosferatu would quickly and efficiently immobilize them. Once the guards were helpless, they would feed, then kill the humans. The three nosferatu knew it wouldn't be pleasant for Coulson to watch, but the situation warranted urgent and drastic action. As Julia characteristically put it, "He can always close his fucking eyes."

When feeding was complete, and if the victims weren't already dead, they would be killed to ensure their silence. After that, the four of them would try to locate Renquist, and having found him, attempt to find a way out of the Nazi-blighted supercave.

The key turned in the lock. The time had come. The door swung back, and Lupo sprang, only to be stopped dead in the middle of his lunge and left barely able to keep his balance. Victor Renquist stood in the doorway, in the neat black uniform of an officer of the Iron Order, but mercifully without the usual insignia. Thyme Bridewell stood at his side, except Thyme Bridewell was now undead. Three Companions of the Serpent stood behind them, and they appeared to be there to protect him rather than hold him prisoner. After the buildup of anticipation in the cell as the three hungry nosferatu had readied themselves for their violent breakout, an explosion was inevitable in the face of this inexplicable anticlimax. It was Julia who put the thwarted energy into words. "What the fuck do you think you're doing in that outfit, Victor? Have you changed sides and sold us you, you son of a bitch?"

Just to make matters worse, Renquist actually laughed. "Of course I haven't changed sides. My other clothes were ruined, and this was the best of the selection I was offered. If it's any consolation, I insisted the emblem of the cross-in-the-circle be removed."

Even Lupo seemed to be disturbed by Renquist's attitude. "This is nothing to be taken lightly, Don Victor. We received manifestations that you were dead."

Renquist took a deep breath. "I'm sorry if I startled you, but I came very close."

"What happened?"

Renquist shook his head. "It's too long a story to tell right now. The important thing is that, under no circumstances, must any of us feed on the Underlanders. Their blood is toxic from the fungus. I tried it, and it almost finished me."

The resentment in the cell was still running high, and De Reske's aura was filling with open and angry disbelief. "I thought it was just the local nosferatu who used the fungus."

"All of them use it. Even Beauregard. And, incidentally, Bridewell shot Beauregard, if that's any consolation."

"Is he dead?"

Thyme nodded. "Quite dead. He took a thirty-eight right above the eyes."

De Reske was far from satisfied. She glared at Renquist,

displaying something close to jealousy. "So how did she get Changed?"

"That's part of the long story."

Julia's eyes narrowed, and her aura burned green. "Are you sure you haven't changed sides, Victor? What's the fucking deal here?"

Even the one remaining human was not exempt from serious doubt. Coulson pushed his way to the front of the group. "You owe us an explanation, Renquist."

"There's no time. We have an audience with The Dhrakuh."

"The Dhrakuh? What the hell are the Dhrakuh?"

"They are the ones who really rule here. I'll try and tell you as much as I can on the way."

Julia stood her ground. "Wait just a goddamned minute . . ."

"Accept and adapt, Julia. We're off to see the wizard of this place, and it very definitely isn't Kansas."

"We hear that the frogs are dying on the surface."

Renquist could see that this discussion with The Dhrakuh was going to be a long process. "They are also being born mutated and deformed."

The voice came from the small translator lizard, no larger than a Yorkshire terrier, with penetrating black eyes, and a ruff of multicolored wattles framing its sharp face; but the thoughts expressed were those of the much larger companion—The Dhrakuh itself. At first a degree of confusion had reigned over the difference between the Dhrakuh and The Dhrakuh, then Renquist remembered how Celtic peoples created the same problem for themselves, where the land, the clan, the clan's leader, and even his residence were all called by the same name, and distinctions were a matter of subtle inflection. The Dhrakuh were the species, while *The* Dhrakuh was the genetically selected leader of the Dhrakuh, and possessed of something known as the Central Mind, an almost Jungian concept of a single being who knew all and saw all, and who, in a single hereditary biological package, was the embodiment of the universal consciousness of his entire species. A central and living clearinghouse and database for experiences, thoughts, and memories. Renquist's first reflection was that it probably made for a gargantuan efficiency, but, at the same time, a monstrous soullessness. What else, though, could one really expect from reptiles?

After leaving the cell in which all but Renquist had been confined, the party from the surface had been conducted by their escort along corridors and tunnels. They cast long shadows and the hollow echoes of their footsteps followed them. If they all shared a common sentiment, it was a sense of grim relief. For better or worse, they were finally coming to grips with Underland. They could be striding to their doom, but at least they had fallen into approximate step. The five were no longer waiting for a mission. The deceit, the lies, the deliberate disorientation were all at an end. For as long as it lasted they could at last make the darkness their own. No matter how infernal the twilight, they advanced into it with a sense of purpose.

Along the way, Renquist had done his best to feed their sense of purpose and prepare them for what was to come by recounting all that had happened to him since they had been separated. It was not only a way to bring them level with the unfolding events, but also a method by which to marshal his own thoughts. Much of his mind was still reeling from the shock of the discovery. It was no small feat to find out that fantastic creatures of prehistoric myth still dwelled under the Earth, and were possessed of knowledge and technology that totally outstripped anything he'd ever encountered.

Even while he continued to assume the mantle of leadership and authority, he felt a numbness he could only keep at bay by focusing on the mechanics of the moment. Between fungus and revelation, Renquist had taken a beating. The only one with an experience to rival his was Bridewell. She had, in just a matter of hours, shot Beauregard, confronted the reptiles, and been through an approximation of the Change. She seemed to be handling herself remarkably well under the circumstances, although Renquist could not be a hundred percent sure that it had been a real Changing or that she would emerge as a complete nosferatu.

Although he again took on the mantle of leadership, nosferatu would not be nosferatu if a light sprinkling of pettiness couldn't be added to the otherwise epic mix of high drama, impending doom, and walking legend. Renquist was hard-pressed to resist layering on some modest guilt as payback for the storm of anger and distrust he had walked into when he had arrived to free Julia and the others. Lupo, who was the least guilty, was the only one who showed any contrition. Julia kept up a slow burn that Renquist might have forgiven under more normal circumstances. He knew that she, just like Lupo and Philipa, was hungry, and hungry nosferatu could present a whole shopping list of problems. They became fractious and irrational, and, when the craving for blood became too intense, they could easily be driven to actions that were totally against even the obvious dictates of logic or good sense.

Although Renquist repeatedly tried to impress on Julia that to feed on any Underlander, either soldier or civilian, was courting the true death, he was far from sure she heeded him. Thyme had mentioned that crews who flew the *Flugelrads* took blood tests and might provide a source of benign and digestible blood, but he didn't stress that option. He didn't trust a ravenous Julia to accurately spot an Iron Order airman, and they definitely did not have time to go and seek one out. Thyme had also pointed out that Beauregard used the fungus whenever he wanted and treated the blood tests as a joke.

In the worst-case scenario, there was always Coulson as the feast of last resort, but to even consider him in that context would be an act of the most base betrayal after they had come so far together. Renquist would only throw him to the metaphoric wolves in the most dire emergency. Already he could see that the man was disturbed by the prospect. He'd been in proximity to nosferatu through so much and done his best to understand and adapt, but he still had a horror of the more raw aspects of vampirism, especially if he himself might be the victim of those aspects. Renquist finally had to lighten up on the repetition of the dire and possibly fatal consequences of any rash act, when he saw how, beyond a certain point, he was only making Julia worse and Coulson worried. He was pleased when Bridewell was able to take over the story and fill in the gaps about which he knew nothing.

As the story unfolded even Julia was a trifle mollified by its sheer fantastic extravagance. When Renquist had refused to tell Philipa who had brought Thyme through the Changing, he had been evasive because he himself was far from sure. He knew that a two-way process had taken place. Bridewell's human blood had been pumped into him, while his own blood, tainted with toxins from the fungus, had been sanitized by a process of filtration that he could not even begin to understand, then recycled back into Thyme's veins. Somehow that had transformed her from human to nosferatu, completely bypassing the formal energy rites of the Changing. Simply stated, it sounded absurdly easy, but such crude simplicity would have killed her and finished him if it hadn't been for the Dhrakuh and the lizard scientists or doctors—he had no idea what they called themselves—who operated the weird machinery that had encased him when he'd woken from the death delirium.

As Bridewell told it, the process only worked because the energy levels of the subjects could be monitored and carefully maintained. The reptile beings had seemingly translated the nosferatu's spiritual control of the energy flow into quantified and precisely calibrated hardware. The Dhrakuh appeared to have been fascinated by the undead's immortality since the Nephilim colonial days, and had conducted their first experiments on actual Original Beings who had escaped from the massive atomic annihilation in which the Nephilim had attempted to wipe out their imperfect and unruly creation before abandoning their colony on the Earth. Supposedly, for thousands of years, the Dhrakuh had lurked in their underground strongholds, watching and learning, and, in their own cold-blooded style, studying human and nosferatu alike, and making their own self-serving manipulations in the lives and societies of both. Their ages-long interest in the mechanics of nosferatu immortality had not been entirely altruistic. They hoped it might ultimately yield the secret of how they, too, might become functionally immortal, but, thus far, that had eluded them.

Much of what Thyme was now telling Renquist about the Dhrakuh dovetailed surprisingly neatly with what he had learned from Zarralhapad; but many contradictions, paradoxes, and incongruities still remained. The most glaring of those was that he could not see how, advanced as they were, the Dhrakuh could have studied the question of immortality for almost fourteen thousand years, and so entirely failed to solve the problem that they still needed a live nosferatu like Renquist as a subject for observation and research.

It wasn't that he doubted Bridewell. She was a trained observer, but much of what had happened was way beyond his experience, let alone hers. She had, like him, been unconscious for much of the time while she was being Changed, and a good deal of what she remembered could also have been illusion, or, at the very least, reality distorted by the macabre and arduous process she had undergone. The real problem for Renquist was much of this shot fatal holes in his current theory that he had been brought to Underland to participate in the latest round of Dhrakuh experiments. Unfortunately, they were almost at the Hall of the Dome, and the account of what had happened, and what had been done to Renquist and Bridewell, and why they might be there in the first place had to be put on hold.

In the Hall of the Dome, Wessel had waited for them. As they entered the great circular space a sudden rekindling of suspicion occurred when Julia and the others saw that the Grand Companion was waiting for them. Julia had gone so far as to fire an angry thought at him.

"What the fuck is this, Victor?"

"It's all according to plan. Just keep quiet and follow my lead."

Unlike the previous time they'd been there, the place had been cleared of worshipers, and armed Companions made sure the entrances were barred to intruders. Without the constant procession, and the small noises of the faithful and their sacrifices, an eerie quiet had fallen. The escaped doves, sensing all was not as normal, rustled uneasily in the roof beams. Dr. Wessel had not looked overly pleased to see them, especially Renquist, at whom he glared angrily. "I see you have recovered."

"I believe I have the Dhrakuh to thank for that."

"I wouldn't be too grateful. The lizards are not exactly acclaimed for their philanthropy."

"I thought you honored them as your Gods?"

"It is a wise man who knows his Gods sufficiently well to appreciate their deficiencies and their flaws. But you can judge that for yourself. I understand, after your excursion to the heart of the city, and your disastrous visit with Gayal, you are now finally prepared to cooperate."

Renquist did his best to look humble, but humility had never really suited him. "I will cause you no more problems, Herr Doctor."

"Then we must hurry. The Dhrakuh does not like to be kept waiting."

Renquist treated Wessel to a sidelong and questioning glance. "Such is the dynamic? The Dhrakuh summons, and we hasten?"

Wessel look at him coldly. "Don't judge what you don't understand, nosferatu."

"I learn fast, Herr Doctor."

"Believe me, Renquist, you still have a long way to go."

Without further delay the entire party went to the huge copper trap that protected the entrance to the domain of the Dhrakuh. Wessel gave the signal, the steam vented, the mass of metal swung back on its counter weight, and he led the way down into the scarlet mists. Renquist followed, then Lupo, Bridewell, Julia and De Reske, Coulson, and, last of all, just two of Wessel's red guards. After the cover had closed over them, the mist quickly dissipated, and Renquist knew that it could only be a deliberate special effect to humble and strike terror into the hearts and minds of the lowly worshipers. The tall, upright lizards, on the other hand, were no special effect, and they came as something of a shock, even to Renquist, who had been expecting them. Aside from Wessel and his guards, who had seen it all before, the only one not registering considerable surprise was Bridewell, who had, of course, already encountered such things operating the machines that had Changed her and saved Renquist.

The colors of the lizards ranged from acid yellow, through brown and tan, to a vibrant green. Short by human standards, many less than four feet tall, they were bipedal, and roughly humanoid, each with a vestigial stub of a tail, and hands with three very deft and precise fingers and a spiked thumb. They were all dressed in the same identical garment, a square-cut tunic of a dark green, velveteen material, which hung to what would be midthigh on a man or woman.

Renquist observed a certain disturbance in the auras of the other nosferatu. Lupo, needless to say, was the least put out by the manlike reptiles, but Julia seemed irrationally offended by them. Perhaps it was because they conformed too precisely to the popular concept of an alien from outer space, or one of those Discovery Channel computer simulations of how dinosaurs might have evolved had they survived the asteroid impact all those millions of years ago.

Renquist also observed that each lizard had a pale blue jewel implanted in the center of what passed for the forehead of its flat, ovoid skulls. Renquist knew instinctively that these jewels had to be weapons. He had no idea how he knew this; but he was so sure it was the case, he became a little nervous that, although he felt no different, the process of saving him from the toxins had somehow subtly altered his perceptions. The lizards paid little attention to the party descending from above. They simply went about their business, occasionally communicating with each other with high, piping whistles, but making little effort to acknowledge even Wessel.

Entering the lair of the serpent lord was very like walking down endless curving steps into a very wide and very deep well. The deep cylindrical shaft, another marvel of engineering bored into solid rock, was uncomfortably warm, and the decorative cascade of water that ran down one section of wall ensured that the heat was supplemented by an equally uncomfortable humidity. On top of that, a cloying sweetness filled the air, and Renquist could only assume it was the result of the patches of mold and fungus that had attached themselves to the timeworn walls of the shaft.

They had descended for maybe a hundred feet when they reached a circular ledge with a wrought-iron rail, what appeared to be a viewing area that resembled the minstrels' gallery in a medieval castle. Wessel indicated that they should all stop. "Renquist is the only one permitted to descend to the very bottom of the shaft."

Julia turned and faced him. "What's at the bottom of the shaft?"

"The Dhrakuh of the Central Mind."

Julia turned and walked to the railing and stared down. "You better see where you're being permitted to go, Victor."

Renquist went quickly to where Julia was standing. Bridewell moved to join him, an act that in no way pleased Julia. Renquist could see the suddenly bristling auras around the two females, but decided it was not the time to begin adjudicating nosferatu rivalries. He said nothing and looked down. A further fifty feet down the shaft ended in a circular space. The outside of the area was overgrown with fungus that looked like it hadn't been cut back in decades. In the center was a shallow depression, that was filled with what looked like a heaped-up bed of dried fungus. On the bed reposed something that for all the world looked like a shapeless leather sack.

Julia turned back to Wessel. "That's The Dhrakuh, Herr Doctor? That's your God?"

"This is hardly the place from which to judge The Dhrakuh."

Renquist straightened up. "Whatever it looks like, I have to go down there."

"I'm glad you're taking that attitude, Renquist."

"Enjoy it while it lasts, Dr. Wessel."

Renquist nodded to the others and, without further hesitation, started down the final spiral of steps to where he hoped, and certainly, to a degree feared, that he would find the answers to a great many questions.

When Renquist had first approached The Dhrakuh, the being appeared to be sleeping, or at least lost in some equivalent of slumber. The tiny translator also had its eyes closed. Some ancient ancestor of The Dhrakuh might have been a variety of python, but this was only really suggested by the pattern and texture of its skin. That was the limit of any resemblance to a sinuous constrictor. The Dhrakuh of the Central Mind appeared to have no supporting bone structure at all. The reptile also had no visible limbs and, as far as Renquist could tell, no eyes. It was like a huge and ponderous snakeskin sack, that simply lay on its bed of fungus, making gurgling sounds from within, and sonorous and vibrating exhalations without. Every few seconds a section of its skin would ripple and undulate as though from a subcutaneous movement of liquid. The most striking thing about it was that its hide was encrusted with small precious stones. Where the jewels in the heads of the lizards on the higher levels were a standard and uniform pale blue, the ones embedded in the skin of The Dhrakuh came in all colors, and, once again, Renquist knew with an uncanny certainty that they were control devices. At that point, though, his newfound instincts failed him. He had no idea what they controlled. It was a form of technology so far advanced he would never understand it.

For close to five minutes, neither The Dhrakuh nor its little translator made any noticeable attempt to communicate. Wessel had said The Dhrakuh was waiting impatiently but Renquist saw no sign of this. Quite the reverse. The Dhrakuh was an image of sloth. A low stone wall, eighteen inches high, surrounded The Dhrakuh's nest. There Renquist sat down on the wall and waited. In the end, the body of the shapeless thing twitched spasmodically and gave a cumbersome heave. At the same time the translator's eyes snapped open, and the creature fixed him with a penetrating stare. "We hear that on the surface, the frogs are dying."

It was about the last thing that Renquist had expected to be asked, but he gave a direct and simple reply, and prepared himself to go wherever the dialogue might lead. "They are also being born mutated and deformed."

"We have heard that, too."

"It's because they breathe through their skins. The toxins spread by humanity are gradually destroying them."

At first it had been hard to shake the idea that he was really holding the conversation with the tiny translator lizard, but he quickly accustomed himself to the procedure. The next statement was blunt, so blunt, in fact, Renquist would never have expected it this early in the encounter. "The Dhrakuh are also dying."

Renquist wasn't sure how he should respond. Close up, The Dhrakuh had a faint aura, but he was quite unable to read it. It seemed to shimmer and change color in a way that bore no relationship to any feeling or emotion on the reptile's part. He decided a factual question was preferable to any expression of regret? Indeed, what did Renquist have to regret. He wasn't human, nosferatu did not pollute the planet. "Because of man-made toxins?"

"Perhaps. They are certainly a factor. It may also be that we have simply existed for too long. It may simply be that we have run our course, and are cumulatively worn-out. Very few eggs are laid, and of the few that are, only a tiny percentage are fertile. Most hatchlings live only a few days. Worst of all, no fledgling Dhrakuh, with the potential to assume the burden of the Central Mind, has appeared in more than a hundred years."

"I'm not sure I fully comprehend how exactly this Central Mind works."

"We work well in these enclosed caverns. We provide a single common memory, and the means to make continuous collective decisions. We share collective joys, and we comfort collective sorrows. We dream collective dreams. We also ensure that no item of knowledge is lost, and no experience is dismissed as too trivial. In that it happens to the least of us, it happens to us all. It is hard for humans to visualize how beneficial this can be inside a specialized and close-knit society. We all know, and we all do all that is needed. We function without resort to compulsion or conditioned motivation. We have an empathy that is total, and a collective sense so far beyond the bounds of the limited human imagination that it will never be grasped by them. You nosferatu have your telepathic capabilities, so you do not suffer the absolute isolation of men, but we have also seen that you are fiercely independent. We believe that you can understand us, but we doubt you could ever merge your consciousness in the way of the Dhrakuh."

Renquist didn't feel as though a response was required, and after a short pause, the translating lizard continued.

"At times we wonder if the Central Mind would have worked anywhere but in the confines of these caverns. We occasionally speculate how we might have been had we inhabited a place under the open sky, where we could spread in every direction. Perhaps we, too, would have favored wild individualism."

"How long have the Dhrakuh been in these caverns?"

"Since we took refuge from the coming of the ice."

"Since the last Great Ice Age?" So the various legends of the Dhrakuh were more true than he had expected.

"You are surprised?"

"Not surprised. Just experiencing a little difficulty at hearing supposed fables confirmed as fact."

"We do have one thing in common, Nosferatu Renquist."

"We do?"

"Neither of us might be what we are now if the Nephilim hadn't come to this world."

"The legend is that you went to war with the Nephilim."

"We were not powerful enough to make war on Marduk Ra. We merely sealed ourselves deeper into these caverns that had already become our home. By the same token, Marduk Ra was not powerful enough to break in on us here."

"A stalemate?"

"In the terminology of the chess game. And it was during that stalemate that we began to evolve the Central Mind. It began as a biotechnical weapon system, but as the centuries passed, it became the perfect way of life."

"But now that life wanes, you require yet another nosferatu to teach you how to live forever?"

"That is what the man Wessel believes, but other agendas are at work here, Nosferatu Renquist."

"Are you telling me that you didn't arrange for me to come down here so you could continue your experiments?

"Other agendas are at work here, Nosferatu Renquist."

Thyme Bridewell leaned on the iron railing of the gallery and stared down to where, far below, Renquist sat on a ring of stones. The railing was wet with condensation and the rock surface underfoot slick and slippery. Coulson stood beside her, and with her newfound ability to read auras she could see that he was disturbed and worried. He saw himself as a man who was completely in over his head. She knew that he felt betrayed. He was the only human left in the party. Both Philipa and she had been changed to things that Coulson still must, to some extent, regard as monsters. He irrationally wanted her to regret what she had become, but she wasn't able to feel guilt. A nosferatu cannot feel guilt at the fate of a human. It was one of the lessons she was quickly learning. And, indeed, why should she? Sure, it had been Grael that had given her to Renquist in the first place, and Jack Coulson had, to a degree protested, but let him carry his own burden of culpability and shame. He had not protested either very long or particularly loud. He certainly hadn't pulled a gun and tried to bust her loose, or even so much as threatened to quit. *Yeah, Jack, go fuck yourself.*

Coulson caught her looking at him and gestured to Renquist. "He's a long time down there."

"Some people have all the fun."

"Are you, okay?"

"I'm fine."

"I'm glad."

Coulson was a lying bastard. He wasn't glad at all. He was frightened, isolated, and supremely conscious of being the last human standing of those who had originally left Deerpark and flown out of Andrews Air Force Base. He was bitterly angry at what he saw as having been sold out by just about everyone. He was spooked and resentful that not one, but two ex-lovers were now undead, and, oddly he also feared going back to what he considered his "normal" life, although she was unable to detect the exact reason for that.

So much for Jack Coulson, though. The scene at the bottom of the shaft was much more interesting than the human feeling scared and sorry for himself. She noted that she was already referring to the man she once had slept with as "the human," as though he was a different species. *Go, girl. You're becoming a full-fledged nosferatu.* She was too far away to hear what Renquist and The Dhrakuh were talking about, and she had a long way to go before she dared to read Renquist's aura, let alone his mind. All she could see was Renquist sitting on the wall, relaxed and motionless, except when he nodded or leaned a little closer to the big, shapeless, dappled lump that was The Dhrakuh. A fanciful set of ideas entered her head uninvited. The scene would be a stunning piece of film for CNN, or a front-page story for the *New York Post*. "REPTILE LORD OF UNDERWORLD CONFERS WITH VAMPIRE." *How about them apples, Wolf Blitzer?*

Along with learning to read minds and auras, Bridewell was also learning an undead deviousness. Prompted by some newly acquired instinct, she hadn't told Renquist everything that had happened in the reptile laboratory. Some of what had taken place was so beyond her understanding that she couldn't put it into words, and she had yet to master the technique of transferring nonverbal images as he and Lupo could do with such fluency. Some parts she also wanted to keep to herself. The ecstasy and the visions, the roaring euphoria of the vivid fire, the delirium of pain and rapture, the joy at being loosed from the confines of humanity's limits and freed of the ever-present certainty of death, those were hers and hers alone, and none of his business. He might guess at them, and he must have felt much the same after his Change, but that had been a thousand years ago. Renquist almost certainly had some idea of what she had experienced. He had witnessed countless others come through the Change, but she didn't see why she should voluntarily add to his catalogue of second-hand emotions.

She didn't know by what process she had seen the strange vignettes of Dhrakuh history while she drifted in and out of consciousness, but, since the telepathic information had come to her and not Victor, she had decided that it was her own private property, and should be held back, perhaps as a bargaining chip for future use. It had been as though, while she floated in that distant, three-way limbo where life, death, and immortality intersected, the Central Mind had run a condensed history of the Dhrakuh, for her information and amusement, or maybe to keep her mind focused on something other than what was being done to her. She had seen the first conversion of the caverns as the reptiles' refuge from the snowfields that deepened above. The sequence had been frighteningly vivid as the gales howled without cessation from an iron grey sky, and the snows were compressed down to pack ice, which then streamed forward as full-blown glaciers and relentless, implacable ice sheets that drove all animal life before them. She had watched in drifting awe as the network of tunnels had been created by both the searing blaze of shaped atomics and the quieter, but equally impressive, action of controlled rock-eating bacteria. Bridewell almost felt she was there, when many hundreds of years later, the Dhrakuh fortified the same caverns against the alien invaders who occupied the surface.

When humans began to find their way into the caverns, the Dhrakuh had evolved a policy of only allowing the newcomers to share as much of their advanced technology as their own science was able to handle. The Gayal had arrived long before the humans, but they had no desire to learn, and possibly no concept of scientific advancement. In fact they had done nothing but settle in and wait for others to find solutions to their problems, and, when a combination of indolence, stupidity, and starvation pushed them into a nosferatu version of cannibalism, surface parties of lizards went out and actually brought back victims for them. In their gratitude, the Gayal had worshiped the Dhrakuh as Gods, but, at around the same time, they had discovered a partiality to the addictive fungus. By the time either the Gayal or the Dhrakuh found out about the long-term effects, it was already far too late, and their downward path was firmly mapped out. The story was hardly a great advertisement for what were now Thyme Bridewell's ancestors. But humanity had its own share of the self-destructively ignorant, so she supposed she couldn't complain.

The lizard forays on behalf of the Gayal had opened the way for the Tibetans to discover the complicated path that led down into Underland. The Tibetans had manifested as little interest in Dhrakuh technology as the Gayal, but they had been more than eager to assimilate the reptiles' psychic techniques, and had learned levitation, *Dumo* yoga, telekinesis, consciousness transference, and the concept of the *Bardo*. During the Christian era, the arrival of humans had been spasmodic, and few had stayed. Some Vikings had come in by one entrance, a group of displaced Hopi by another, a strange party of Nepalese, who had come with generations' worth of hashish and settled in to do nearly as little as the Dhrakuh. Incas had found the access route in the Andes, but quickly fled with alarming stories of snake gods and vampires. A seafaring Irish saint with a boat made of leather had drifted in by accident, totally misunderstood everything, but fortunately had drowned off the coast of Limerick on his return journey, before he could spread the word that he had found the location of the gates of Hell.

As the Dhrakuh saga drew nearer the present, the narrative moved into a somber, more melancholy mode. Toward the end of the nineteenth century the human traffic had radically increased, but the numbers of the Dhrakuh were already on the wane. The English eccentric, Professor Challenger, had made it into one of the subsidiary caves, but never discovered a major underground city, unlike the Norwegian, Nielsen, and two years later the Prussian, Erich von Stalhein, who had come with a well-equipped expedition funded by the Krupp family. The reports of the last two, overlaid with excessive flavoring of phony Nordic mysticism, had ultimately come to the attention of Adolf Hitler, who, during his short but hideous reign, had sent no less than five missions of exploration, complete with companies of crack SS ski troops and Luftwaffe air support. The Nazis had not only mapped what would soon be Underland, but cataloged most of the potential of the Dhrakuh technology.

With the arrival of the Nazis in full force in 1945, everything had changed. The refugees from the Third Reich had come with bag and baggage, and loaded for bear. They had commenced a massive program of construction and weapons-motivated scientific development, as well as selling the Central Mind a whole bill of disinformation—the primary item being that they had fled the surface world to escape the exterminating Americans. When the Nazis came they had enough knowledge to see the great caverns as a wonderland of future science, all but abandoned, with only a comparative handful of Dhrakuh remaining. They had extorted all they could from The Dhrakuh until the Central Mind had finally realized just how mad, evil, and dangerous they were, shut off the supply of scientific data, and retreated into their last stronghold in the deep wells like the one in which Bridewell now found herself. They had not, however, been strong enough to exclude humanity totally, and they had allowed the serpent cult to flourish as a final means of protection. At the end of what she thought of as this telepathic history lecture, one image had presented itself that could only be a vision of the future, or a vivid piece of wish fulfillment. It had shown the Temple of the Serpent being vaporized in a monumental explosion. The final insight had seemed like a message of some kind and, for the moment, she didn't feel inclined to relate it to Renquist, at least until she had a chance to consider it more fully.

*   *   *

The Dhrakuh was emitting long, booming sighs, and the translator lizard was starting to show signs of agitation. Renquist frowned. "Are you becoming tired?"

"We can continue for a little while."

"Then I must tell you that one thing has puzzled me since I came here."

"What is that, Nosferatu Renquist?"

"Are the Dhrakuh of this Earth?"

The translator lizard fluffed its wattles and made a fast, birdlike movement with its head. "Of course."

"Stories are told on the surface that the Dhrakuh came from space."

"Before the ice came, the Dhrakuh journeyed into space and to the nearby planets. We even created a colony on the desert planet, the one that is fourth from the sun. But this has always been our home."

After the statement, a long silence ensued, and Renquist was certain that the audience was over. He rose from the wall, but the translator lizard spoke again.

"Nosferatu Renquist."

"Yes."

"When you leave here, the human, Wessel, will want to talk to you."

"He will?"

"He will put a proposition to you."

"Indeed?"

"You will accept that proposition. Even if you don't like it, you will accept that proposition. Do you understand?"

"No, I don't understand, but I will do as you say."

Wessel removed his robe the moment he entered his private quarters, like a judge leaving the bench and going into his chambers, or a priest in his vestry after mass. Aside from all else that was happening to him, Renquist seemed to be on an accidental tour of inner sanctums. Wessel dropped his robe on a bench. He ran a hand over his close-cropped hair and sighed, as though relieved to be casting off the trappings of power. He went to a small wet bar and poured himself a brandy. He really was like a judge in his chambers. "Drink?"

"No thank you."

"I'm sorry. I forgot that you don't."

"Actually I do on occasion, but not right now."

The private quarters of His Eminence Dr. Heinrich Wessel could not have been more diametrically different from the lair of The Dhrakuh if it had been planned that way. Wessel might have been The Dhrakuh's Grand Companion, but his taste was entirely different and not in the least reptilian. As usual, stone was the primary building material, but the large and imposing study in which Renquist found himself, instead of being hewn from the living rock, was built from square-cut blocks, laid without mortar in the style of Aztec or Inca masons. The floor was a pattern of polished flagstones, but covered with what looked like a very old, very rare, and very expensive Persian rug.

Wessel liked to be surrounded by art, and evidently he liked his art big. A massive bust of Frederick the Great, rendered in carved and polished rock, that measured more than eight feet from the Prussian king's Adam's apple to the top of his head dominated one whole side of the room. The life-size gold, silver, and bronze horse from the Chi'in Dynasty that flanked his desk was slightly less overbearing, but must have been truly priceless. Renquist inspected the horse, running his finger tips over its cold polished neck. "You have some very rare and valuable objects here."

Wessel halted in midsniff and looked at Renquist over his brandy glass. "You surely aren't of the school of thought that believes religious leaders should live in abject poverty?"

Renquist smiled. "I have encountered a number of religious leaders in my time."

"I don't doubt it. What was your impression?"

"That a public display of too much excess was probably ill-advised, but that an all-too-encompassing embrace of poverty and chastity was usually one of the more tedious affectations, and could be a step on the road to madness. The only exception would seem to have been Mahatma Gandhi."

"I am not Gandhi."

"So I observe."

Wessel also liked his technology, and demanded it be state-of-the-art. Two ultramodern computers were built into the marble top of the desk. A section of wall was taken up by a bank of twelve monitor screens that could be programmed to function independently or, as they were at that moment, be the compound tiles of one large image. As Wessel had ushered Renquist inside, the screens had come to glowing life, showing a skyscape of white clouds scudding across a blue sky. "That doesn't bother you, does it? You don't shun *images* of daylight, do you?"

Renquist shook his head. "I'd only turn from it if it was real. A picture can't hurt me."

"But it's worth a thousand words."

"I've never been too sure about that axiom."

Wessel dropped into the high-backed chair, behind the desk. The surface was completely empty except for a multifunction computer mouse, and an exquisite Fabergé egg. He picked up the egg and stared at it as though the contemplation afforded him some kind of comfort or inspiration.

"So now you have seen the Dhrakuh, do you understand?"

Renquist kept his expression neutral. "The word *understand* is something of an overstatement. The Dhrakuh could require a lifetime of study."

"Your lifetime or mine?"

"I don't know, maybe theirs."

Wessel put down the egg. "If all goes according to plan, the lifetime of the Dhrakuh will prove to be extremely short."

"Why should that be?"

"Because after you have performed the task that you were brought here for, their days will be severely numbered."

After so long, Wessel was finally coming to the point. Renquist looked at him curiously, still reluctant to enter the man's mind. "And what is this task?"

"You are going to kill The Dhrakuh for me."

This must be the proposition of which The Dhrakuh had spoken. The neutral demeanor became hard to maintain. "Kill The Dhrakuh? Why should I want to do that?"

"Do I take it that you intend to refuse?"

"I've hardly had time to consider the idea. Might I know why?"

"The Dhrakuh explained the principle of the Central Mind to you?"

"It did."

"And how a new one hasn't appeared in over a century?"

"That's right."

Wessel used the mouse to change the image on the composite screens. The blue sky was replaced by a livid, orange, magenta, and purple California sunset. "The Dhrakuh are approaching the end of their time."

Renquist gestured to the screens. "I live in California. Sunsets like that are caused by high levels of atmospheric pollution. You might say the beauty is in the poison."

Wessel ignored him. "The Dhrakuh are finished."

"So it would seem, but I thought your whole power base was built on the foundation of your venerating them as Gods?"

"So why kill them? Is that your next question?"

"It's the obvious one."

"The Dhrakuh have outlived their usefulness. The Serpent Cult was a means to an end when we first assumed power in this place, but now it merely hampers our wider ambitions. These reptiles limit our access to their advanced technology. They have become suspicious of our motives and restrict our exploitation of the many military applications their science has to offer."

"They constitute a brake on your political ambitions?"

"Exactly."

Renquist frowned. "I thought you just told me that their time was at an end?"

"At an end, but not ended. Their longevity is impossible, and I don't intend to spend the rest of my days in this polluted hole in the ground. I crave the sky and the air, Renquist, and I will not have a collection of snakes and lizards keep me from my rightful place in the sun."

"And you intend to have me release this brake on your ambition by killing the Central Mind?"

"The Dhrakuh are not the only obstacle being removed from the path."

Renquist had encountered his share of advanced megalomania, but Wessel's will to power seemed to be moving at a quite alarming rate. "I'm not sure I understand."

"There is something I would like you to watch."

As Wessel entered a command on one of the keyboards sunk in the desk, Renquist turned and looked at the bank of screens. All of them dimmed to black except one, and that showed a video sequence of an aircraft in flight. What Renquist recognized as a commercial Boeing 747, with blue-and-silver livery, cruised in level flight in a clear, cloudless, daytime sky. At first the airplane was too far away for Renquist to make out any markings, but the camera, presumably mounted on another plane, was closing fast. Very soon Renquist was able to make out a circular symbol on the side of the jet's fuselage. It was the presidential seal of the United States. "That's Air Force One, isn't it?"

"Air Force Two to be precise."

"The vice president is on board?"

"Mervyn Talesian."

"I don't understand."

"Just continue to watch."

"Where is this taking place?"

"Over the Atlantic, about two hours out of Washington, heading east. Talesian is on his way to Europe."

"And when?"

"About three and a half hours ago."

"So why are you showing me this?"

"Just watch. All your questions will be answered in due course."

The camera continued to close on Air Force Two, and then another object appeared in the frame. It was a *Flugelrad*, identical to the one that had brought Renquist, Bridewell, and Coulson from Ice Station Zebra. It appeared to be running on a parallel course to the jet. An uneasy feeling came over Renquist, but he said nothing for the moment.

After perhaps a half minute, a second *Flugelrad* entered the picture. Now Renquist turned to Wessel. "Am I to assume this tape is being shot from a third *Flugelrad*?"

Wessel nodded. "A precise deduction."

A sudden and violent electrical discharge flashed from the first *Flugelrad* and struck the wing of Air Force Two. "They're firing?"

"Indeed they are."

"But . . . ?"

"Just watch."

The second *Flugelrad* also opened fire. Its first salvo from the strange weapon, mounted just under the leading edge of the machine's disc-shaped body, struck the 747 just to the rear of the cockpit. Suddenly the image bucked and jiggled, and the previously perfect picture quality started to resemble CNN war coverage. Twin electric discharges flashed from either side of the camera. The otherwise unseen third *Flugelrad*, the one that carried the camera, had opened fire. The three flying machines from Underland continued to fire at Air Force Two, establishing a deadly triangulation. Even in the now-less-than-distinct picture, Renquist could see that smoke had begun to stream from two of the 747's four engines. A lick of orange flame ran down the length of the fuselage, and then the screen was suddenly and totally filled with smoke and flame.

Renquist's face was an expressionless mask, and he protected his thoughts from any rudimentary reading by Wessel. "I take it that Air Force Two is no more."

Wessel nodded. "It was shot down over the Atlantic a few hours ago by three *Flugelrad*s acting on my orders."

"Are you insane?"

"Insane, Renquist?"

"Insane, Dr. Wessel. The US government will turn rabid.

America will literally go ballistic. This act could spark a nuclear war."

"With whom, may I ask?"

Renquist shrugged. "I imagine they will find a scapegoat nation."

"Right now the United States government is having the greatest difficulty explaining how Talesian's plane was brought down. They have the final radio transmissions, but no one in the White House or the Pentagon wants to be the first to go public with the fact that Air Force Two was destroyed by a formation of UFOs. The citizens might balk at a war with aliens."

Renquist let out a deep breath. "I can imagine. I think I'll take that cognac now."

He didn't need alcohol, just something to do with his hands. Wessel rose from his chair and returned to the bar. "They are currently avoiding telling the nation and the world."

"I can all too clearly imagine."

Wessel uncorked the brandy bottle. "The flight was going to be commanded by young Beauregard, but after Ms. Bridewell shot him, he obviously had to be replaced."

"Do you intend to exact reprisals for the shooting?"

Wessel handed Renquist his brandy and resumed his seat. "No. It's likely she did us all a favor. Beauregard was a fool. Oversexed, overdressed, and far too impressed with himself."

Renquist now asked the obvious question. "What does the killing of Talesian have to do with The Dhrakuh, or any of this, for that matter?"

"We have begun to clean out the monsters."

"Talesian was a monster?"

"Do not be overly disingenuous, Renquist. It doesn't

suit you. We both know that Talesian was an Urshu, that he was one of the Watchers. Indeed, my undead friend, down here in Underland we know our ancient history far better than they do on the surface. We are well aware of the entire genetic engineering program that took place during the Nephilim colonization."

Renquist swirled his cognac. "Then you will know enough to check very carefully that he's really dead. The Urshu were effectively immortal. They have few weaknesses and are extremely hard to kill from what I've seen. You are talking to one who's tried."

"If he isn't dead, it will still take him a very long time to swim up from the bottom of the Atlantic. Reports credit the ocean with being three miles deep at the point where the aircraft went down."

Renquist nodded. "That should effectively keep him out of circulation for a while."

"That was why we mounted the attack where we did."

"First you kill Talesian, and now you want me to slay The Dhrakuh. Would you care to elaborate on this grand plan to destroy all monsters?"

Wessel looked sideways at Renquist. "*Destroy All Monsters* is the title of a Japanese movie. Part of the Godzilla saga."

"Nonetheless apt."

"The oligarchy which I lead has made all the use it can of this place. Our next move has to be to earn the gratitude of a grateful planet by eradicating all the things not of this Earth that have power over human lives."

Renquist's expression became hard and watchful. "Does that include the nosferatu?"

"Not if you successfully carry out your task."

"And what about the Gayal?"

"Do you really care about the degenerate Gayal, Renquist?"

"I suppose not. They might be an interesting study, but they do feed on each other."

Wessel stood up. "So can we discuss the task at hand?"

"Killing The Dhrakuh?"

"Killing The Dhrakuh."

"I suppose after I carry out this task, and The Dhrakuh is no more, you intend to reveal yourselves and return to the surface?"

"That has to be our next move. We have nuclear weapons, and we have antigravity. It has only been the Dhrakuh preventing us from emerging into the world to take our rightful place. The time is obviously now. The wreckage of the former Bolshevik states is in full collapse. Christianity and Islam are all but at war. America is a corrupt and degenerate quasi democracy, and China is little more than a rampant disease. With a correctly orchestrated public relations campaign, we would be hailed as saviors. The great majority of the world's population would flock eagerly to our banners."

The innate megalomania of Underland had been evident from the moment that Renquist had first set eyes on Beauregard and the *Flugelrad*. Now he was learning its full extent. "To be hailed as saviors, you must surely be perceived as saving the world from something."

"That part is easy. We do battle with the alien infiltrators. The aliens that have now forced our hand by bringing down Talesian's aircraft. You said yourself the action could start a war, and indeed it will." Wessel's voice began to take on a rhetorical stridency. "It will be the spark that will kindle the conflagration from which my New Order will emerge. It will set the fire and drive the alien infiltrators from our society and our world."

Renquist spoke very quietly. "But there are no alien infiltrators."

Wessel actually laughed. "Then we can't lose, can we?"

Wessel was plainly quite mad, but, as Renquist grimly reflected, that had never stopped any human gaining power in the past. In practical terms, his grand design could scarcely be faulted. In reality he was doing little more than updating the political tactics of his direct forebear, Adolf Hitler. Instead of demonizing a human minority as the lurking threat, Wessel intended to galvanize conditioned and easily managed blind hate on a global scale against a menace from another world. He knew there was no point in arguing with this infinitely alarming lunatic, so he made a simple gesture of surrender. "Very well. You think you've killed Talesian, and you want me to kill The Dhrakuh. Just tell me one thing."

"What's that?"

"Why me? Why couldn't you just send a squad of your Iron Guards or scarlet Companions to do the job? Why me, Herr Doctor?"

"Why you, Renquist? Because you are the one who could achieve it. All of us down here have grown up with the Dhrakuh. They know us too well. They would observe our intentions and stop us. You have the power of a venerable nosferatu mind. The Dhrakuh will not be able to read your intentions."

"Are you sure of that?"

"It's a calculated risk."

Renquist's expression turned bleak. "Your calculation, but my risk."

"That's why I bought you from Grael."

"Grael?"

"Herbert Walker Grael. The dark lord of Deerpark. We have had an arrangement for many years. He wanted to keep you for his longevity experiments, but I persuaded him that my need of you was greater."

Renquist decided he would think about the ramifications of Grael's part in all this at some later time. It was a course of speculation that would do nothing to alter his current situation. "And suppose I refuse to go along with your plan. Do you intend to destroy me?"

Wessel laughed. "I don't need to destroy you. How long do you think you will survive down here? How long will it take for the fungus to contaminate your blood and make you and your companions just like the Gayal?"

Renquist knew that Wessel had him. He also knew that Wessel realized it. It had been a long time since a human had outwitted him. "So, do you want to explain your plan?"

Wessel sprang the catch on a concealed door in his desk, and took out a set of keys. "I can do better than that. I can show you the weapon you will use."

Renquist could see that there was a pistol in the same drawer, an antique Luger. Renquist quickly shook his head. "No, I'm sorry, I never resort to firearms."

Annoyance colored Wessel's aura. "I know that. You think I haven't done my homework? I have something much more dignified for you."

He moved to a large brass-bound chest near the monumental bust of Frederick the Great and unlocked it. Bending over, he moved some objects in the chest to one side and produced a long narrow bundle, wrapped in black sheepskin with the fleece on the inside. He brought it to the desk and set it down. Renquist observed the reverence with which Wessel treated the object and the care with which he unwrapped it.

"See, Renquist, the Sword of Siegfried."

The sword that lay on the black fur was old, a long and beautifully forged broadsword, probably from the thirteenth or fourteenth century. The noticeable Moorish influence on the crafting of the hilt, and the pinpoint damascening at the top of the blade, demonstrated it was certainly from a period after the Crusades. That it was the Sword of Siegfried, however, was total bullshit. Siegfried was a figment out of the Dark Ages whose authenticity was doubtful before even Renquist had walked the Earth, but Renquist didn't feel that any purpose would be served by pointing out to Wessel that the name was almost certainly nineteenth-century Wagnerian nonsense.

"It's a very fine blade."

"Pick it up."

Renquist touched the blade, but felt no tingle of vibration. Every so often he would encounter a sword with a need to hint at its own history, of how a strange faux-life had been forged into it, but this one told him nothing. It was just a serviceable weapon, or maybe its history had yet to start. He picked it up and tested the balance. The hilt was long enough for a two-handed swing, but, of course, Renquist didn't need that. He had more than sufficient strength to wield it with just his right arm.

"You like it."

Renquist nodded. "It will serve."

He placed the sword back on the sheepskin, and Wessel rewrapped it. "Then let us go down to confront The Dhrakuh. It has already sent word that it wishes the audience to resume. Once you have killed the thing, we can commence the extermination of the lower lizards."

chapter Nine

N osferatu Renquist."

"Dhrakuh."

Renquist didn't need to read the tiny translator lizard to see it was afraid, or how it needed to gather its courage to speak. "Do we have further matters to discuss?"

Renquist shook his head. He carried Wessel's sword, hidden in its sheepskin cover, across the crook of his left arm. "No, I don't think so."

"He made the proposition to you?"

"He did."

"And, as we asked you, you will do what he proposed?"

"That is why I have the sword. But is that what you really want?"

"That is what we want, Nosferatu Renquist. The time is right."

"Are you sure?"

"We are absolutely certain. Please don't hesitate. This isn't easy."

"I don't see why it has to be done this way."

"You will see very soon."

Renquist shook the sheepskin wrapper from the sword. "You are certain about this?"

"Before you do our bidding, there is one thing that must come first."

"What's that?"

Again Renquist had descended the final curve of stairs to the lair of the Dhrakuh on his own. As before, Lupo, Julia, De Reske, Bridewell, and Coulson, plus Wessel and a squad of his Companions and a half dozen of the biped lizards, waited in what Renquist now thought of as the minstrel gallery. Wessel had instructed him to cloak his mind, to concentrate on the trickling of the water down the sides of the well, the damp air, the cloying smell, to hide his true intentions with a concentration on his senses; but, of course, Renquist did no such thing. Unknown to Wessel, he had made his bargain with The Dhrakuh, even though he hadn't been aware of its content at the time. From the start of the exchange, the translator lizard was terrified, and at the sight of the naked sword it backed away and pressed itself against The Dhrakuh's side, barely able to speak.

"There is . . . one thing . . . that must . . . come first."

"Just ask."

"Kill us, Nosferatu Renquist, but avenge us first."

Before Renquist could say anything, The Dhrakuh opened the Central Mind to him and showed him a single vision. It was of Wessel, impaled by the so-called Sword of

Siegfried, against the background of an apocalyptic explosion. Renquist knew what he had to do. He turned from The Dhrakuh's nest and looked up at the minstrel gallery. "Please come down here, Dr. Wessel."

Wessel came to the railing and stared angrily down. "What the hell do you think you're doing?"

"Come down here, Wessel."

"You know I can't do that."

"I will make you."

"Not from that distance you can't."

"You underestimate me, Wessel. Also you underestimate my associates. Lupo, Julia, Philip, Thyme, would you all please help me bring Dr. Wessel down here, and to make sure none of his people interfere."

The four undead advanced on Wessel, and the air above the minstrel gallery was suddenly alive with nosferatu compulsion. One of the Companions fainted, dropped his machine pistol, and crashed to the flagstones. Wessel put up a fight, but had no chance. He could only start down the spiral of steps, walking like a man going to his execution, which, indeed he was. If Renquist had been blessed with the time and capacity for pity, he might have felt sorry for the human. To see one's vaunted power crumble so easily must have been painful. One moment Wessel was setting world conquest in motion, and now, as a result of a single oversight, he couldn't even control the direction of his limbs. As the Grand Companion emerged from the stairwell he was pale and sweating. "You have betrayed me, Renquist."

"You betrayed yourself, human. Did you really think you were too clever for a thousand-year-old vampire? Did you really think it was that easy?"

The translator lizard retreated, seeking shelter behind the bulk of its master as Wessel spoke in a painful rasp. "Damn you, Renquist."

"I have been damned for centuries."

Wessel had put up an exceptional fight, but exhausted himself in the process. He faltered, staggered, and dropped to his knees. "Finish me, Renquist, if that's your intention."

Renquist's voice was soft, almost gentle. "Get on your feet, Wessel. I don't want to kill you like that."

With what must have been his final strength, Wessel lurched to his feet. Renquist didn't delay. He thrust hard and clean, plunging the sword clear through the chest of the Grand Companion. Wessel's entire body cringed around the painful foreign metal. He seemed to want to speak, but blood suddenly gushed from his mouth, choking off the words. Renquist dragged the sword from the human's flesh and he fell forward. An evil dream was over.

The same could not be said for Renquist's own problems. A burst of machine gun fire reverberated from the minstrel gallery, and bullets struck chips from the flagstones beside him, but neither he nor The Dhrakuh was touched. Lupo instantly seized the Companion who had pulled the trigger and hurled him over the rail, so he fell screaming to the stone below and landed with a sickening sound a few yards from The Dhrakuh's nest. A sudden burst of sporadic rippling light erupted from the gallery, like the popping of photographic flashbulbs, only a hundred times brighter. Renquist's first thought was that the Companions had somehow acquired a new weapon, the deathray he had always expected, but then he saw that the flashes came from the jewels in the heads of lizards. They had silently burned down the Companions. Only Coulson and the nosferatu remained, looking both shocked and relieved. At the same time words came from the Dhrakuh. "Just wait and trust."

Renquist stepped away from Wessel's body and toward the nest with the bloody sword in his hand, but faltered when he was facing The Dhrakuh. "I'm still not sure I can do this. You are a unique being. Perhaps the last."

"Don't be absurd. We are near death anyway."

Renquist replied, "It is such a pointless waste. This planet is too good for the humans to have it all."

"When I die, my people will also die. They have lived so long with their every action directed by the Central Mind that they will become dysfunctional without it. At least this way it will be fast. They won't have to wander in a twilight of confusion as we fade and decline. This way, the Dhrakuh, and all of this, will be gone within an hour if you strike now."

"An hour? I don't understand."

"Nuclear changes have been placed in all the caverns. When the sensors in our skin confirm that we have died, a sixty-minute timer will cut in. Wessel's Underland and his plans for a world tyranny are finished."

Renquist was shocked, and shock was not a common emotion for him. "What?"

The translator lizard began to repeat falteringly what it had just said, but Renquist cut it off. "This is madness."

"It's not madness, my friend. Our bombs will cauterize all of the malignancy that is left. It will kill his slaves and destroy everything from his flying machines to the spawn of Cthulhu he so treasures. The head that contains the thing will burn up in the atomic conflagration. That portal will be closed to the old ones. The surface will be saved from him, and no more humans will come here to exploit us. It will also give you just one hour to get out of here."

"There must be another way."

"There is no other way. We are already destroyed. You have the chance to make it clean and final."

With a terrible reluctance, Renquist turned the sword, reversing his grip, so both hands were on the hilt and the blade was pointed down. He stood over The Dhrakuh and raised his arms. He paused for a moment that seemed eternal, closed his eyes, and stabbed downwards with all his strength. The Dhrakuh made no sound, it just slowly seemed to deflate. As he let go of the sword and stepped back, the translator lizard buried its face on The Dhrakuh's rapidly sagging skin and let out a doglike keening. This was too much for Renquist. He lifted his head and screamed. His voice reverberated up the shaft, and Coulson clasped his mortal ears.

The gems that encrusted The Dhrakuh's hide had grown dim with its death, except for a solitary yellow stone that glowed with a brilliant light. Renquist knew it was the death sensor sending its signal. The clock had started. For Underland, just a single hour remained. Just as predicted, all would die with The Dhrakuh. His state of mind was such that, at that precise moment, he would have waited and shared the end.

From his vantage point in the gallery, Lupo looked down into the deep shaft. The red-robed guards lay dead all round him. De Reske and Bridewell appeared dazed, and Coulson had yet to recover from Renquist's anguished undead scream. Lupo had seen the vision from The Dhrakuh, and he knew all this would be vaporized in a single hour. Only one course of escape was open to them. They had to commandeer a *Flugelrad* and its crew by force, and fly out. Speed was of the essence. Even the climb back up to the

Temple would consume precious minutes. Yet Don Victor
was not moving. He simply stood and stared down at the
dead reptile. Lupo knew that his don had admired the organization of the Dhrakuh, and his enforced role as their
destroyer was a crushing weight. Lupo didn't share his feelings, but he could understand them. He knew, however,
that this was not the moment to allow oneself to be immobilized by regret or guilt. It was time for flight, and
Renquist had to be reminded of that.

*"Don Victor, we cannot linger. We have less than an hour
to get clear of this accursed place."*

He received no reply, and, had Lupo been inclined to
curse, his reaction would have been foully profane. Instead,
he tried again. *"Don Victor, we have to go."*

This time there was a response, but Lupo could scarcely
recognize the tone of the thought. It had the flat resignation of one who had been pushed too far. *"No more, Lupo.
No more."*

"We have to get ourselves out of here."

"Go, Lupo, take the others. I have no strength left."

*"You have to find the strength, Don Victor. I do not intend
to leave you."*

Renquist was silent again. All that was left for Lupo was
to play the final card, the one that he was completely loath
to use, even as a last resort. *"If you will not do it for yourself,
you must do it for me. Honor dictates that, if you stay, I must
stay with you, and I sincerely do not wish to be destroyed."*

Again Renquist did not respond, but he did move. He
turned from the dead Dhrakuh of the Central Mind and
the body of Heinrich Wessel, and walked slowly away. As
he approached the foot of the stairs, his pace quickened,
and Lupo knew the fugue was over.

*   *   *

Julia saw that their luck had held. A single *Flugelrad* was parked on the Templeside landing pad, but its three-man crew loitered beside it. They had no idea that their leader was dead, or that their whole world would be destroyed in precisely forty-three minutes. For them, all was a picture of normality. While the others hung back, concealed by the pillars of the Temple, Julia and Thyme sashayed up to the airmen like two young women looking to flirt and maybe more.

"Hey, guys, want to take us for a ride?"

Though nominally on duty, an alert having been called for later in the day, when some unspecified action was supposed to go down, the crew had nothing to do but wait for their orders, and the brace of young women represented a pleasant relief from the boredom. Alerts were always being called, but without exception, nothing ever came of them. The only recent excitement was the still-hot scandal of the whore who had put a bullet through the head of Stormleader Beauregard. "Hey, girls, what are you two doing here? You don't look like the kind to be feeding rats to snakes."

Julia and Thyme both giggled, as though drunk on the local gin, and muttered double entendres about snakes, giving themselves enough time to come face-to-face with the airmen. When suitably close they sprang the trap, taking over the three humans' minds and locking them down so they'd be unable to move, but still understand every word that was said to them. It had been agreed that a saucer crew could not function safely under full nosferatu mind control, but that didn't preclude its use to get the crew's attention and convince them that doing exactly what they were told was the only way they would save their wretched skins. To reinforce this idea, Julia ran a short preview through their minds of the physical horrors that would be the penalty for anything less than total cooperation. It culminated with their slowly being burned alive, and with Julia's unique imagination, that was quite enough to impress Bridewell, let alone the humans.

"We're going to relax our hold on you enough for you to nod or shake your heads in response to a short list of questions. Do you understand?"

Not one of the aircrew moved.

"That was the first question."

Now all three nodded in unison.

Bridewell glanced at Julia. *"Have we overdone it?"*

"No, they'll be okay."

"If they're too fucked up to fly . . ."

Julia was curt and impatient. *"They'll be okay."*

She turned her attention back to the aircrew. "Are you ready to get on that thing and fly it out of here, under the instructions of someone we will designate?"

The crew nodded.

"Of your own free will?"

Again they nodded.

"And fully aware that you will die horribly if you attempt to double-cross us?"

Another synchronized nod. Julia waved the others to come to her. Coulson, Lupo, De Reske, and Renquist came out from the shelter of the pillars and hurried to the *Flugelrad*. Julia smiled at the crew. "Okay, boys, let's get on board."

Coulson had started to think that he'd been forgotten, and was more than a little surprised when Julia suggested, as they climbed the spiral of steps that led up to the bridge, that he should take the command chair on the raised dais. "What makes you think I know what to do?"

"You saw the crew in operation on the way out here, didn't you?"

"As much as anyone else, I guess."

"And how much of it do you remember?"

"Some."

"So now you're the captain. We have thirty-nine minutes, so start the process."

The steersman was at the wheel, the engineer was at his bank of monitors, and the navigator stood beside the plot table. They seemed willing to allow themselves and their craft to be hijacked.

"For ease of communication, just call me 'sir.' That way you don't need to know my name, and I don't even want to know yours. You have seen the power of those women, and you should be convinced that if you fuck with them, you will be in a world of pain far beyond any man's tolerance. Do you understand?"

"Yes, sir."

"Good."

Coulson tried to remember the routine that Beauregard had used to get his craft into the air. "Engineer?"

"Yes, sir?"

"Are we powered up to lift?"

"Yes, sir."

"Navigator?"

"Yes, sir?"

"Can you get us to Ice Station Zebra?"

"Yes, sir."

"Then set a direct course."

"Yes, sir."

"So take us up."

It turned out to be as easy as that. Again the sound of the propulsion unit was little more than a faint hum that rose in pitch as the saucer lifted from the apron.

As the machine rose, everyone on the bridge could see the batwing shapes beyond the clear dome. The Messengers flew alongside them, as though the big flying reptiles were offering a last, doomed salute. Then the *Flugelrad* was into the access tunnel, and picking up speed. It was the flight from Ice Station Zebra in reverse. For a short time, the red glow of Underland stayed with them, then they were in darkness. They emerged into the thick dark clouds of the Fissure although, this time, there was no vortex effect. Finally, they were over the surface, again in cloud, but now a swirling blue-grey.

Bridewell voiced what everyone was thinking. "I can't tell you all how very pleased I am to be out of that underground nightmare."

Julia called a time check. "Twenty seven minutes."

Coulson checked on the crew. "Navigator?"

"Yes, sir?"

"Are we holding course?"

"Yes, sir?"

"ETA?"

"Thirty-six minutes."

He looked round at the others. "We'll still be in the air when she blows."

At the twelve-minute mark, Julia may have saved the lives of all the nosferatu on board the *Flugelrad*. "I've just thought of something extremely unpleasant."

Renquist, who seemed to have recovered himself, looked round. "What?"

"Depending on how the Dhrakuh placed the charges, could there be a nuclear up-blast into the atmosphere?"

"Easily."

"And the light from an atomic fireball is not unlike the light from the sun, am I correct?"

"I never thought about it, but it is certainly a possibility."

"So if were sitting under this nice transparent dome, we could all fry anyway."

"Damn."

"Do I take that as indicating agreement?"

"Yes."

"So what do we do?"

Renquist didn't waste any time. "We seal ourselves in the lower compartment. We should be safe from the light down there."

Lupo looked up at Coulson. "Can you stay there and watch the crew?"

Coulson hesitated. "My eyes? I don't want my retina burned out by the flash."

Lupo looked swiftly round. "Engineer, are there any spare pairs of those goggles you people wear on the surface?"

Quickly the engineer leaned down and opened a small locker beneath the bank of monitors. He produced a pair of goggles and handed them to Coulson. Lupo watched as Coulson pulled them over his head and adjusted them. "Will they suffice?"

Coulson grimaced. "They're going to have to, aren't they?"

Five nosferatu in the lower compartment was a tight squeeze, but Renquist had been right. Although they felt the shock, no light entered. The impact, however, was more than enough with which to contend. The zero moment came and, a second or so later, the *Flugelrad* bucked as though it had been violently kicked by a giant. The antigrav immediately malfunctioned, and, for about fifteen seconds, the nosferatu in the sealed compartment floated in free fall, but then crashed painfully to the deck. The saucer shuddered and vibrated, and the airframe groaned as though it was being stressed, twisted, and tortured beyond all endurance. They heard the sound of tearing metal, as if parts of the fuselage were ripping loose.

"We're going down. Brace yourselves."

The *Flugelrad* was spinning out of control; yawing and wobbling, but all the time descending. Renquist received an image from the steersman, and wished he hadn't. The human was mortally terrified, and only a threadbare hope kept him at his post, fighting the wildly spinning wheel, trying to stabilize the craft sufficiently so it would skip across the snow and ice, like a pebble on a pond, dumping more and more of its destructive forward momentum with each bounce. The man actually did a magnificent job. They hit once, twice, three times, then, on the fourth, slewed to a stop. The stillness after the impact was eerie, and that they were no longer moving, and more or less in one piece, almost unbelievable. All that remained was the hiss of escaping fluids, the creak of cooling metal, and the clamor of the polar wind. They were down.

Lupo was the first to speak. "Can anyone hear me?"

He immediately received an affirmative response, so he ran a fast individual check. "Don Victor?"

"I'm battered but fine."

"Julia."

"The same?"

"Thyme?

"In one piece."

"Philipa?"

"I'm okay."

"Then let's check topside and see how the humans have fared."

The framework of the saucer was so bent out of shape that both Lupo and Renquist had to use all of their inhuman strength to force open the hatch. When that had been accomplished, they found the machine so canted over on its side that they had to traverse the spiral stairs hand over hand. The bridge was a twisted and broken mess, little short of carnage. Pieces of equipment had been thrown around like items of clothing in a spin drier. A considerable part of the dome was missing, and snow was already blowing in, forming a small drift of white beside the plot table. Coulson was the only human still conscious. As the nosferatu gathered around him, he smiled wanly. "I think both my legs are broken. The only consolation is that I can't feel the pain yet."

Philipa checked on the crew. The news on them was even more grim. "One dead and two busted up and barely alive. Humans are just too fragile."

Renquist faced the others. "It's midwinter in the Arctic, so, with the advantage of round-the-clock night, the five of us could, in theory, walk out of here without too much difficulty. Coulson is a different matter. He can't walk at all, and, in as little as fifteen or twenty minutes, he'll be dead of hypothermia."

Maybe because Bridewell was so newly Changed, she was the first to come up with the idea. "We could make him one of us."

"What?"

"We could Change him. Then we'd only have to wait a couple of hours while his legs mended at nosferatu recovery speed, and we could all walk out of here."

Renquist thought about the idea and nodded. "It is a solution. I certainly feel something of a bond with the man. We've been through so much that I don't feel like leaving him here."

De Reske immediately agreed, but Lupo looked doubtful, and Julia actually objected. "Lupo is too polite to say anything, but we're going to need Coulson."

"What do you mean?"

Julia lowered her voice so Coulson couldn't hear. "Neither Lupo nor I, or Philipa for that matter, has fed in days. We're going to have to feed on Coulson if we want to survive this walk in the snow."

Bridewell immediately protested. "You can't do that."

Julia snarled. "Shut up, you fucking ignorant neophyte. You don't get sentimental over a human when it's a matter of survival. He's going to die anyway."

For a moment, it seemed like the two females were going to attack each other. Then Bridewell was struck by a thought that came like a bolt of lightning. "Wait a damned minute. You don't have to feed on Jack. There's the crew. Two are still just about alive. You can feed on them."

Julia's voice was acid. "Did you forget about the fungus, darling?"

Bridewell glared. "No, I didn't. And don't call me darling."

Renquist stepped between them and faced Bridewell. "What are you saying?"

"I'm saying that Julia, Philipa, and Lupo can feed on the

dying crew because they're clean. The aircrews don't use the fungus, they have to take blood tests."

"How do you know that?"

"Beauregard was boasting about it. How he could get high, and his crew couldn't. There was no reason for him to make it up. Don't you see we can Change Jack *and* feed, and we all get to live."

Coulson interrupted them. His voice was weak but grim. "I'm sorry to disappoint you Thyme, but I want to stay exactly as I am. I've lived as a human, and I'll die as a human. I don't want to be one of you. I don't want to be a fucking . . . vampire."

Renquist quickly stepped into the shocked silence. "Shall we all stop talking and do something? Lupo, take the females and feed."

Lupo nodded. "Yes, Don Victor. And you?"

"I want to talk to Coulson."

Renquist climbed over and through the wreckage, to kneel beside Coulson, who weakly waved him away. "Don't bother, Victor. You won't persuade me to change my mind."

"I wasn't going to try. I just came to give you something."

"What's that?"

"I've been carrying these for you since I ducked out of that damned reception. I even took them with me when I switched clothes."

Renquist fished in his pocket and brought out a pack of battered Underland cigarettes with the cross-in-the-circle logo, plus a cheap brass lighter made from a nine-millimeter shell casing. "Here. I understand they're a nasty smoke, but if they'll help . . ."

"My God. A butt."

"It's no exchange for immortality, but the fatally injured with a cigarette is a classic of both war movies and the air crash genre. Richard Burton in *The Longest Day*, for instance."

Coulson made a superhuman effort to laugh. "Since the *Flugelrad* doesn't run on gasoline, can you light one for me?"

"Of course."

Coulson took the lit cigarette and inhaled deeply. "You know something? This could be an exchange for immortality, right now."

Renquist remained with Coulson until he died, and then, a few minutes later, five nosferatu set out across the frozen windswept waste, walking easily on the top of the snow, giving thanks for the sunless Arctic night and homing by undead instinct on the closest human habitation, leaving the wreck of the flying saucer to be buried by the ice, and maybe puzzled over by archaeologists in the distant future. After a while, Renquist stopped and looked back. A white, mushroom column of smoke, marking the Arctic Fissure, and the location of Underland's remains was rapidly unraveling in the wind. Lupo halted beside him. "The great majority of humans will never know what was here, Don Victor, or what has passed."

Renquist smiled and shook his head. The last Urshu was at the bottom of the sea, the Dhrakuh was gone, and, except maybe among the undead, the story would be a dark secret. Renquist was reminded of a very old but still popular nosferatu text. "The darkness enfolded the light, but the light comprehended it not."

"They are an ignorant species, Don Victor."

"And blissful in their ignorance, damn them."

Lupo laughed. "And thus they are punished in their ignorance by beings like us."

After all that had transpired, Renquist could only join Lupo in his laughter. The three females looked back to see what was so funny.